R. McGregor was born in Uganda, lives on a narrowboat and teaches at the National Film and Television School.

0749 930527 1521 40

W.M.
RESERVE STOCK

Schrödinger's Baby

2 2 JUL 1998

H.R. McGregor

WOLVERHAMPTON LIBRARIES		
JFR		

0749 930527 1521 40

A 4 2 2 2 FA   CA

PIATKUS

Copyright © 1998 by H.R. McGregor

First published in Great Britain in 1998 by
Judy Piatkus (Publishers) Ltd of
5 Windmill Street, London W1

This edition published 1998

The moral right of the author has been asserted

A catalogue record for this book is available from the British Library

ISBN 0 7499 3052 7

Set by Action Typesetting, Gloucester

Printed and bound in Great Britain by
Mackays of Chatham PLC.

I would like to thank
my parents and Maureen Thomas

For
Dominic Power
and
Stephen Devereux

Prologue

Live quantum cat is one possible outcome of Schrödinger's famous thought experiment, in which a radioactive substance, on emitting a particle, would trigger the release of lethal poison. The problem posed by the experiment is to reconcile the two following facts. The first is that, empirically, cats invariably appear to us either alive or dead. The second is that the linear quantum-mechanical equations of motion seem to predict that cats can be in an almost unimaginably bizarre state in which they are neither alive nor dead. In the standard formulation, sometimes called the Copenhagen interpretation, the approach to this problem involves assigning a unique and indispensable role to observers or measuring devices in bringing about a determinate outcome.

David Z. Albert, *Scientific American*, May 1994

WOLVERHAMPTON PUBLIC LIBRARIES

The missing agents have been found. A little over a year after their disappearance. I am besieged in my parents' house in Highgate, the press are at the door. Photographers waiting for us to succumb to their siege. They are an ugly sight, holding their cameras ready like guns, waiting to fire at the smallest sign of movement. We have drawn all the curtains and changed our telephone number.

Edgar has just come in: I watched him from a peek in the curtains as he ran up the drive, with his hands over his ears. I heard him slamming the inner doors of the porch, and locking them as fast as he could. Desperate to get away from the cries outside, the questions:

'Mr Porteus, can you tell us about your wife's relationship with the agents?'

'How do you feel about your wife's connection with the Glasgow sauna network?'

'Can you tell us anything about your sister's involvement in all this...?'

'Is there any link between your sister and your wife, and the latest police discovery?'

'Mr Porteus, what about the mystery baby?'

I haven't read any of the newspaper articles. It doesn't really matter what they are saying. There will be lies, and half-lies, truths and half-truths and no one will know the difference.

I only know that the police have issued a statement, and that Kerry and Petruchio's names were in it.

I don't need to read their wild presumptions. I, more than anyone else, have the facts. The facts that they want. They think Edgar knows, but he doesn't. It is I, who am only a side-interest to them, who knows. I have this particular knowledge. I was, shall we say, the observer, the measuring device. It is only because of me that it all exists now. In a manner of speaking, it exists only in my head, in my memory bank, in my dreams, appalling dreams which bear a horrifying verisimilitude to events which took place.

The baby is crying. I do not need to go. My mother, father and Edgar are all there, ready to jump up, to feed, change, or comfort and hold.

I don't mind about anything else, but I mind about the baby. I don't care that they all know, that speculations about Kerry's life are splattered across the gutter press; I only cared that the baby shouldn't know, and now that seems impossible. After all, *they* are out there. Those dirty, lying, prurient low-lifes out there. Kerry hated prurience. It was one of her words, like cadaver and concupiscence.

I am lying. I do mind about, well, almost everything else. I care about my parents and Edgar, and I feel that this is all my fault, that I have brought all this about, not actively, but passively, not by what I did, but by what I didn't do, what I didn't know.

My cat has just come into the room. Or rather, Kerry's cat. Kerry's kitten as I still think of it. I remember a word-association game I played once with Kerry. I was the respondent.

Life	Death
Drama	Art
Science	Schrödinger
Cat	Depression

I linked cats to depression. But I love cats. Perhaps I link everything to depression somewhere along the line. At the moment I feel I could be classified with ease as a paranoid schizophrenic. Well, I will allow the quantum to offer me the consolation that at the most primary level, being itself is schizophrenic, coexisting chaotically with non-being.

My mother worries about the cats, she thinks they might

suffocate the baby. I have other things to worry about.

It is only a matter of time before Inspector Godfrey will come to see me. He will want to talk, not to Edgar, but to me, he will want my story. My story. The greatest irony for me is that all Kerry's stories have become mine. I am the guardian of her chaotic narratives.

If no one hears the stories, then do they really exist? Does the event die with its witnesses? And if I turn the experience into language will it be any more real? Is it possible indeed? Kerry thought that you could represent experience away. I wonder? But I think perhaps that is what I am trying to do as I sit here with memories, both my own and others. I am not sure I can make any sense of them for I do not know them cognitively, but emotionally. It is not a story to me, but an atmosphere, a pain, an unwilling suspension of disbelief.

Where would I start? What was it Kerry said about how pointless it was trying to find antecedent cause after antecedent cause, searching in vain for an absolute, final one?

But things have changed now.

The wave function has collapsed – *remember they are neither dead nor alive until somebody opens the box* – and all the infinite possibilities of Kerry have been ousted into one sordid ending. Or beginning: I am forgetting the baby. The new life crying in the room next door.

Part One

Felis Catus

The unfortunate animal in question is incarcerated in a closed box which also contains a radioactive atom with a 50-50 chance of decaying in the next hour, emitting a y-ray in the process. If this emission takes place it triggers the breaking of a vial of poison gas which instantaneously kills the cat. At the end of the hour, before I lift off the lid of the box, the orthodox principles of quantum theory bid me consider the cat to be in a state which is an even-handed superposition of the states 'alive' and 'dead'. On opening the box the wavepacket collapses and I find either a cooling corpse or a frisking feline. It is scarcely necessary to emphasise the absurdity of the proposition that this state of affairs, whichever it is, has been brought about by my action in lifting off the lid. It must surely be the case that the cat is competent to act as observer of its own survival or demise and does not need me to settle the issue for it. Along the chain of consequence, from atomic decay to my act of observation, things must have got fixed at least by the time that the cat's experience entered into it.

J.C. Polkinghorne, *The Quantum World*

7

My name is Juliet Porteus and I was born in London. My mother runs a dancing school, having once been a ballet dancer. My father is a professor of literature at London University. I am one of four children, two girls and two boys. When I was two we moved to this big house in Highgate, where we are now incarcerated.

It has often been said that we are a very 'un-English' family: certainly we are very loud and there is not much of the stiff upper lip about us. With the exception, that is, of myself. I am the quiet, phlegmatic and pragmatic one alone in a noisy, sanguine and romantic family. All my siblings 'went into the arts'. Helena, the youngest, is a dancer. My brothers are ten years older than me and they are twins. Edgar has been making a name for himself as a movie director – his first feature after leaving film school won an award – and Benedick is an actor.

I astonished the family by my scientific and mathematic abilities at school. They all rather prided themselves on their innumeracy. It is part of the family mythology now that when I was about seven I asked to be excused from the bedtime story (*David Copperfield*) because there was a programme on the radio about particle detectors. I was the only 'square eyes' in the family too, and was constantly nagged at or teased about the hours spent in front of the TV. It fascinated me. Books were easy, there was nothing mysterious about them, they were made of paper, and quite straightforward, but *television*, that was impenetrable. I remember the frustration I felt because neither of my parents, nor my elder siblings could explain to me how the television worked; 'It's a sort of magic tube,' was my father's contribution to my technical education. Undeterred by his ignorance, I took a screwdriver and opened up the TV to have a look. My father said this was probably a lot better for me than watching it. I also bought myself a chemistry set and, when I wasn't watching television, began experimenting. Nevertheless, in spite of my triumphs in and around the house – from unblocking sinks to mending stereos and, of course, the television, my family marvelled and patronised me, treating me as if I were from another, and decidedly inferior, planet.

I was a happy, if a little serious, child. I loved lessons, particularly science, maths and geography. At home, I spent hours reading the *National Geographic*. I thought that literature was a waste of time, not even a real subject. 'It's just invented,' I argued endlessly with my father, 'I want to know about real things.'

I was close to my brothers and sister, especially and naturally enough, Helena. Edgar was the most demanding of family members; he was, I suppose, the problem child. He was a Buddhist for a short while recently, the last in a long line of absolute commitments to a faith or philosophy. His life has been a series of fads, of crazes. When I was a child he was in the Workers Revolutionary Party and he gave me *The Communist Manifesto* for my eighth birthday. I was only nine when the Falklands war happened, but I remember him spending long hours lecturing me about imperialism and insisting that I call the islands the Malvinas. Edgar was excited by the war, which he was convinced would trigger the international socialist revolution and reshape the entire world in the image of Gerry Healy and the Redgraves.

One of my childhood memories is of Edgar's devastation when the party folded after its leader seduced some of the comrades' daughters, and of the trouble that ensued afterwards. Edgar took the shattering of his revolutionary dream very hard. He responded by becoming a complete debauchee, running up huge debts from cocaine and long summers in Italy. But even the craze of decadence ran its course, and he emerged from it, had a brief spell directing

10

wacky physical theatre pieces on the fringe, then went to film school.

Ours was very much an 'open house' and, because of my parents' radical attitudes, it was regarded by our friends as the cool place to be. So for all four of us, the home was also the centre of our social lives and we were afforded status from our peers on account of our parent's tolerance of underage drinking and dope smoking.

When I was about twelve years old I got depression. It was diagnosed as such by the educational psychologist. My parents rejected the diagnosis, or rather, rejected the term because of its seeming dislocation, in its medical use, from the world of cause and effect. My father's diagnosis was that I was suffering from nothing more nor less than adolescence; but his prognosis was bleak for me. As I did not read, I would never know the comfort to be found in it: the alleviation of alienation to be gained from sharing the expressed alienation of others. Alas for me, the sequence of events that had caused my migraine of the soul was also to seal the lid on my contempt for the arts.

It happened just after I was twelve. During the Christmas holiday, my mother read aloud from the local paper that four cats had been found crucified on road signs in our area. At first, I think, my 'depression' was merely preoccupation. I wondered whether the cats had died quickly or slowly bled to death, the nails ripping through their bones. I became consumed with hatred for the perpetrators of this act, I fantasised about torturing them, crucifying them.

Back at school there was talk of the cats, and gruesome cat jokes made the rounds, none of which, thankfully, I can remember. Then, one of the swots in my class wrote a short story about the incident in which he described having very much the same kind of feelings as I had been having, particularly the ceaseless speculation about their last moments.

11

He won a prize in the school for the story, and it was published in the local paper. All my anger and hatred transferred on to him. He was so smug, quite the star of the school because of that horrible little story. How could he? How could he use such a thing, such a thing that really happened in order to further his literary career? Pretentious creep.

I was very low and disinterested for about six months but eventually I thought less and less about the crucified cats and I began to show an interest once again, firstly in whales and sharks (after a BBC wildlife programme), and then, and more powerfully, in a girl in the year below me at school whom I used to follow home. She had slight pigeon toes and I thought she looked like Ingrid Bergman. She also had a boyfriend and at morning break and lunchtime, I would watch them walking across the playing field hand in hand and kissing each other sweetly when the bell rang and they had to part. I remember mentioning how hard this was to Helena, and this led to one of the very typical arguments I so often ended up having with members of my family. She thought it was wonderfully romantic.

'How sublime! It's just like Sappho,' and she quoted some piece of poetry to me.

'No, it's not,' I grumbled, 'it's nothing of the sort. It's only me having a crush on another schoolgirl, it's mine and it isn't at all inflated and it certainly has nothing to do with Sappho or anyone else.'

'All right, all right, keep your hair on. You just want to hold on to your belief that you are utterly unique. Well, so you're "in lurve" and you can't bear to see her with her boyfriend. So was Sappho, take it or leave it.'

'I'll leave it.'

I don't think that I wanted to believe I was unique; after all, I regarded myself primarily as a collection of particles, and the mind and its phenomenal consciousness as a peculiar and as yet unknowable activity at the sub-quantum level. I was just irritated that everything in our house had to be referred to something else, usually a work of literature or a film.

My crush lasted only a few weeks before another rather cruel incident brought this girl, Melissa, and me together in a friendship that ended my gloom and despair. This incident also involved a cat.

I was following her home in my usual way one afternoon when she stopped suddenly in the middle of the pavement and looked down at something in the gutter. She then looked around and beckoned me, urgently. When I got to her she was crying and I looked into the gutter and saw a cat: black, white and red. Its face was squashed into the Tarmac and it was lying in a pool of blood. Its back was twisted and broken and flies were settling around its one eye that was not squashed into the pavement but was alive and full of pain.

'Oh God,' said Melissa, 'what are we going to do?'

'It can't survive, we should put it out of its misery.'

'Oh God, how?' Melissa was really sobbing, her eyes wide with panic. I took off my school tie and tied it round the cat's neck. I pulled. The eye went out. Melissa wailed and wailed.

I picked the cat up and put it by some bushes on the grass verge. There was blood on the arm of my blazer. I comforted Melissa, putting my arms around her. She sobbed into my neck and I felt her tears trickle under my collar. I told her that it was for the best and we walked on together.

After the cat incident, we walked to and from school together every day. She regarded me as a sort of hero. Melissa was into clothes and pop music and she was as sentimental as she was pretty. She split up with her

13

boyfriend, saying that he was too demanding and she preferred to spend her time with me.

Melissa and I did do things with the others – Edgar, Benedick, Helena and their friends – but for the most part we isolated ourselves, and very soon we were teased for being lesbians. At school, this was the worst insult that could be thrown at a girl, but for some reason, some peversity in my nature perhaps, I took the taunts as compliments, and I nurtured a secret pride that I passed on to the younger Melissa as a useful weapon. We became rather superior, and scornful of our peers, tolerating only the company of my older brothers and their friends.

In the summer term of my fourth year, Melissa and I spent one Sunday at Camden Market. She bought lots of clothes and we walked home along the canal. She looked exquisite, chattering away about her new things – buying clothes always gave her a high. Suddenly I pulled her in towards the wall and kissed her on the lips. To my surprise she kissed me back. When I leaned back against the wall, she said:

'Mmm, much nicer than boys, they're all sort of rough and out of control.'

My mother came into my room on our first morning together.

'Come on, Juliet, you'll be late for school. Oh!' she exclaimed, on seeing Melissa's sleepy head peeking over the duvet, 'I didn't realise you were here, Melissa. Oh, well, up you both get, it's twenty to nine.'

Later on that evening my mother came into my room while I was doing my biology homework and asked me whether I was all right.

'Yes, of course I am. Why?'

'I just wondered whether there was anything you wanted to talk about?'

I knew that she had a scene all worked out in her head. Where I would cry and tell her I was gay and she would hug me and tell me that that was OK and I must never let anyone convince me otherwise.

'No,' I said, and then rather ungraciously, 'I'm busy.'

'Yes, well, I'm glad to see you are having some healthy underage lesbian sex as well as all that counting and alchemy,' she said, and left the room.

It was Melissa who first suggested that I should be a vet. It had never occurred to me before but when I thought about my love for science and animals, I realised it was probably by far the most sensible thing to do. I accepted a place at the University of Glasgow's School of Veterinary Science; I enjoyed my studies and had no doubts about my chosen profession.

I liked the city enormously. I have an interest in architecture, which, in stubborn arguments with my father, I claimed as a scientific endeavour: engineering, not art. I liked the city's red brick, its parks, its municipal pride. I liked the Glaswegians too – even the taxi drivers are nice there – and I came to love the city's extremes, its roughness and exuberance.

My parting with Melissa was painful. I assumed that I would love her forever; that is what love was supposed to be, and I was pragmatic about these matters as with everything else. I remember not being able to conceive of doing what I did with Melissa with anyone else, of being that intimate with any other body, or of my body responding to any other's touch. I was horrified therefore when, in my very first week in Glasgow, I was seduced at a party by a student from the art school. It was my first sexual experience with a man and it was pleasurable and exciting but afterwards I felt treacherous and very sad.

Melissa came up to stay a few weeks later. I was dreading telling her. Remembering the feeling that it would not be possible to be with anyone else, I could well imagine how she would feel on finding how easy it was. Fortunately, she had already discovered that for herself. She burst into tears as soon as she got off the train, hurled herself in my arms, saying:

'Oh God, I do love you, I'm sorry, I'm sorry.'

I was delighted and hugged her. 'You've been unfaithful? It's OK, so have I!'

'Yes, but you haven't gone and got married, have you?'

Indeed I had not. Melissa and I had a good weekend together but she decided she couldn't face going back to a divorce so she would give the marriage a go. And off she went. I was relieved, any grieving I had to do for the relationship had been done when I had been unfaithful. That, I knew, was the end.

The rest of my first term passed quietly by.

I met Petruchio on the train on the way back to Glasgow after the Christmas holiday. He sat opposite me, we got chatting, and when he told me his name I laughed, and then had to explain that I was also from a family who had insisted on giving their children names from Shakespeare. He had never heard of *The Taming of the Shrew*, even when I mentioned Liz Taylor and Richard Burton.

I was never very good at describing people. I don't seem to notice things. When I got back to the halls of residence and told the girl in the room next to mine that I had met a pharmacologist called Petruchio on the train and was going to go to the Burrell Collection with him at the weekend, the first thing she asked was, 'What did he look like?' and I couldn't remember. To her amazement I couldn't even remember whether he wore glasses or had a beard.

16

He did have a beard, and he was dark and, as the girl next door immediately pointed out when she eventually met him, he was Jewish-looking. He wasn't Jewish, but a Catholic from Italy. Petruchio was twenty-nine when I met him. He had trained as a doctor in Milan, then completed a year of psychiatric training before having a nervous breakdown. He was now working at Glasgow University, doing research for a pharmaceutical multinational. He was a pleasant companion on that long journey to Glasgow. He didn't talk too much, allowing me to get on with my crosswords and an assignment I was working on about the stomachs of the cow, but every now and then we would pass the time in conversation. He was interested in my lack of interest in the arts, given my family circumstances, and when he asked me to go with him to the Burrell Collection, which he said was the only good thing about Glasgow (later he said Scotland, and later still, Britain), I agreed, because I liked the sound of the architecture.

We met the following Saturday and got a bus out to the Burrell. Petruchio was quite hard-going. At the time, I put his lack of humour down to the language barrier. He looked very intently at all the things in the collection, squinting his eyes and moving his head around to get different angles. Then he would look at me and ask whether I liked it or not. I shrugged my shoulders each time but I was aware that day that it was all becoming a bit of a pose, this aesthetic anaesthesia of mine. I did like some things. Some things were pleasing. And I *really* liked the building. But most of the time I was hoping that Petruchio wasn't going to get the wrong idea and think that there was even the remotest chance of us going to bed together.

On the bus on the way back, he said:

'If you like, we can go and have some supper some place. I can pay because you are a student and I am sold-out

17

bastard experimenting on animals for unspeakable compa-
nies.'

I asked him if he really did experiment on animals.

'No. Mostly I just cut up the dead cat.'

'Why cats?'

'They are more useful to us because they have brains
nearer to the human's brain than other animals.'

I remember thinking that that was probably true because
cats were independent, they had independent brains, unlike
dogs. Then I looked out of the window and saw crowds of
people going in and out of shops festooned with sales signs,
rushing through the streets, loaded with carrier bags and no,
I thought, it isn't true. We are slavish, pack animals, much
more like dogs, or even sheep, than cats.

The cats Petruchio cut up were bred for experimentation,
living all their lives in the artificial environment of a laboratory pound. They were given drugs, monitored, and
eventually killed for extensive post-mortem examination.

'What kind of drugs?'

'Mood drugs, of course. I am working in neurological
field, in psychopharmacology. We experiment with little
neurotransmitters in the brain and wooof ... the little kitty
gets depressed. We reverse the experiment and wooof ...
the little kitty has a party in the head.'

We ended up at a tasteless but very popular restaurant
near George Square. It was all done up like a trench, sandbags and helmets everywhere, while the Battle of Britain
was captured up ahead in the form of squadrons of model
aeroplanes. Vera Lynn and Bing Crosby sang out from the
stereo behind the bar and the waiters and waitresses wore
what looked like costumes from an amateur production of
Happy as a Sandbag. The restaurant was called War and
Pizza. The sandbags piled up around each table meant
privacy, which was possibly the secret of its success.

18

Petruchio ordered some wine and, when it arrived, he virtually snatched it from the waiter, who was preparing to offer him a taste.

'Yes, yes it will do.' He poured us each a glass and toasted me.

'Well, Juliet, I have found you a very nice person and think we two can spend some time together but I must tell you now and here that I detest sexual intercourse as well as any touch of the smallest kind. I cannot bear even to shake hands. Here it is better because of the cold, no one wants to open their arms up, but in Italy, you know, you have to kiss more people.'

I wanted to hug him.

'Good,' I said. 'I'm off sex too so I promise never to touch you and here's to friendship!'

So Petruchio and I became friends, which meant that we saw each other at weekends and usually about one night during the week. We went to the cinema, we watched television together, we played cards, we talked about drugs and differences in the medical and veterinary sciences. Petruchio was odd, but I preferred him to my fellow students, most of whom were seventeen and let loose for the first time. Their innocence shocked me. I felt quite jaded in relation to most of my peers. Student life was not new to me. When I was thirteen, I had gone to stay with Edgar in Oxford, and then I had drunk vast amounts, smoked some grass, vomited on the quad and, or so Edgar tells me, asked him to make love to me. I don't believe him, of course; Edgar is a pathological liar. He was writing a thesis on Byron at the time and he was extremely impressed by the man.

I went home to London for the summer holidays after my first year. I earned some money working for my mother. There were summer schools and weekend workshops held at

19

her dancing school during the vacation and I worked in the office, co-ordinating and administrating these courses.

Towards the end of August, Petruchio phoned me. He said he had found a flat, a big flat in the west end of Glasgow. It had four bedrooms, so we would have to find two others to share, but should he go ahead and rent it? I said yes. We had talked about getting a flat together for a while. Petruchio's digs were very unsatisfactory and I was keen to get out of the halls of residence. Petruchio had to find the two others fairly quickly because the rent was high. I sent him up my share and told him to go ahead and choose anyone he thought suitable.

I hadn't told Petruchio exactly when I would be returning to Glasgow and I arrived at the flat hoping he, or somebody, would be there to let me in as I didn't have a key. The flat was close to the University of Glasgow, in a road lined with Indian restaurants. The smell of hot spices greeted me as I got out of the taxi at a Victorian corner tenement. There was no door in the entrance to the building and I walked through into what seemed like a grim dark tunnel, a prison-like corridor with a concrete floor. This was an open close. Posher tenements tend to have closed closes, with doors and buzzers, they may be nicely tiled and attractive, but this one was dank and I still found them rather forbidding. The passage ran through the building, bending slightly around the stairs and continuing through to the courtyard at the back.

I could hear loud music – the Velvet Underground – coming from a door to the right of the stairs. I knocked. A boy – he looked about sixteen – opened the door. He glanced down at my bags and cases and beamed at me.

'Oh, how ye doing, you must be Juliet. I'm Billy, your new flatmate – here, do you want a hand with those?' I still hadn't got entirely used to some Scottish accents, and his was particularly broad.

20

We went through a large hall. Billy dumped my bags and ushered me through an open door on the left. It was a big room, divided into a kitchen area, separated by a breakfast bar, and a living room. Petruchio was slouched on a large sofa in his dressing gown and a girl wearing sunglasses with a short crop of peroxide hair was sitting on the floor, rolling a joint on the coffee table.

'Hi.' She grinned up at me, her voice surprisingly deep for her diminutive form, deep, husky and Irish. Petruchio sat up.

'Hello, you are back then. Well, this is Billy, our flat-mate, and his friend, Kerry. And Chris has gone out for some more beer – he is our other flat-person.'

'Oh, are you students?'

'Yes,' Billy grinned. 'We're at the SNAMD.'

'The what?'

'The Scottish National Academy of Music and Drama,' Billy explained, sitting himself down cross-legged on the floor beside the girl.

'Oh,' I said hopefully (the last thing I wanted was to share a flat with a pair of theatricals), 'are you music students?'

'No,' said Kerry. 'We're all drama.'

By the end of my first week in the flat, I was beginning to wish I was back in the halls of residence. There was a constant stream of people coming in and out and loud music at all hours. Chris's girlfriend, Christine, stayed most nights, so there were, in effect, five of us living there. Chris was amiable enough; he was older than all of us, being thirty-five. He had once had his own business, a shop in Edinburgh that sold Indian clothes, jewellery, statues, pipes, all that sort of stuff, and Chris had travelled extensively through India, gathering his 'hippy junk' as Kerry called it. He was tall and thin with a great bush of hair and an open,

21

mischievous face, laughter lines like whiskers around his eyes. He wore loose clothing, Turkish trousers and caftans and he smoked Beedi cigarettes which he got sent over from India – their pungent aroma pervaded the flat.

Chris's girlfriend Christine was a self-consciously pretty girl who always seemed to be ill. She suffered from migraines and her period would take her to bed for a few days each month. Chris would nurse her with immense tenderness. He was interested in photography and photographed Christine endlessly. Kerry once pointed out to me that by being ill so often, Christine made herself ugly and that her illness was, in a sense, rebellion. Having always been healthy I have little tolerance for sniffly psycho-somatics and was inclined to agree with her.

Petruchio enjoyed our new lifestyle. He was enormously popular with the drama school crowd, not only because of his general wackiness and funny intonations, but because he supplied them with Valium, of which he received an endless supply from the company he worked for. He told me he had chosen Chris and Billy because he thought they would liven us up a bit, and it was what we needed. Billy was nineteen but still got asked for ID in pubs. He was from a notorious slum in Edinburgh, his father was in prison, his mother was a cleaner. He had joined the Scottish Youth Theatre when he was about thirteen. His hero was Jimmy Boyle and he looked a real artful dodger, black hair framing a cheeky, boyish face. He had a slack easiness about him, enormous energy, charm and a good measure of depravity. He boasted constantly about the size of his penis. He was eager to please me, to make a good impression, and I liked him well enough.

As my family had done before them, Billy and Chris treated both Petruchio and myself as curiosities and, to some extent, as an audience. We were teased mercilessly too. With me, the fact that I was logical and calm and knew something about the physical world in which we live was freaky enough; with Petruchio they had any number of things, including the above, that they could tease him for. He spent a great deal of time in his dressing gown and slippers, padding around the flat making endless mugs of tea, every now and then saying with absolutely no irony whatsoever:

'I suppose I must take a Valium.'

His toilet habits were also a source of mirth. It was a ritual that lasted at least half an hour twice a day. He would disappear into the bathroom with a book, and sit, sometimes suffering loud and painful wind. Then he would shower, always, regardless of whether he had managed to shit. If he hadn't managed he would take a Valium immediately on leaving the bathroom. Kerry once told him that she was sure the Valium caused constipation and that too many showers would dry out his skin. On another occasion, for a joke, she bought him a parcel of high-fibre products, cereals, fibre-gels and pills that looked like guinea-pig pellets. Petruchio never laughed, and rarely smiled. He would only raise his eyebrows and say in his glum voice:

'Yes, yes, I think this is very funny.'

Billy had a stream of girlfriends that he brought back to the flat, but Kerry, who was 'just a friend', was his most frequent visitor. Kerry was from Omagh. She was just the kind of girl that I most disliked: a sort of hysterical wild-child, the kind which always irritates me when it is, as it so often is, represented in films (and I imagine in literature too, but I haven't read it), but which piss me off even more in real life. I never believe it. Kerry was loud, sometimes funny, but often she just showed off. She was attractive, sometimes pretty, sometimes rather beautiful, and sometimes ugly; her face was quicksilver, full of deceptions. The perfect face for an actress. She dressed in a wide assortment of styles, sometimes punk, sometimes exotic 1920s, sometimes totally Marks and Spencer. At times Kerry would look like Julie Andrews and at others like Johnny Rotten. She prided herself on being one of the boys. She would talk dirty, and when they were watching something on TV, Kerry would ogle at any attractive women before the men had a chance to. I though she was one of these girls who pretended to be gay to titillate men. She and Billy would often try to outdo each other in filthy talk, the boys screaming with laughter each time Kerry's unutterably revolting imagination left even Billy speechless. She seemed to have an ability to make anything seem funny – to turn everything into humour. Having come from a family with old-fashioned and desperately sincere socialist values, this attitude was rather novel to me, and, I suppose, rather attractive.

Kerry looked very young, she was small and thin and waif-like. Once someone commented on her diminutive form and she stuck her hands on her hips and said, in drawling tones which became more lascivious as her sentence ended:

'Yes, she's only thirteen but she's the body of a nine year old!'

We all laughed a lot. We all thought that she was an absolute scream.

Kerry insisted that not only was she not gay, but that gayness didn't really exist. I am bisexual, she said, as is everyone really, and whenever she talked about it she would immediately refer to Freud.

'I am in what is really an infantile state, I never grew out of polymorphous perversity,' she would say with a cackle of laughter. One of the surprising things to me about Kerry was that she seemed to have read a great deal and to have spent at least some time considering and thinking about things. Surprising because she was almost always drunk or on drugs – her life was like one long party.

'Oh, I'm a complete dipso,' she would laugh, 'and for me, as the old graffiti goes: "Reality is for people who can't cope with drugs".'

Kerry was also promiscuous.

'I am cursed with concupiscence,' she would say, and it was a word she was to use over and over again with great enjoyment, exaggerating her lip movements as if savouring each syllable.

I think I am probably too fastidious to ever be promiscuous, and maybe when I am older, I will be full of regrets about my well-spent youth.

Kerry was fascinated by Petruchio and myself, not least because of our chosen professions. At first we thought that Kerry merely had an exaggerated squeamishness, but when she got bronchitis we came to realise that it was a severe phobia about doctors and hospitals. She refused to go and get treatment for what was obviously a serious infection and, to my horror, she confessed she had not registered with a doctor in Glasgow.

'But you need to have smear tests and things, Kerry, you must get yourself registered.'

She looked at me with genuine horror.

'You've got to be fucking kidding.'

Christine lectured her too, telling Kerry that if she really felt this way about it, then she must seek help, she must get some therapy. We tried to get to the bottom of Kerry's phobia, but rationality cannot be applied to the completely irrational. They cancel each other out.

'I would just honestly rather die than go to hospital or have doctors ordering me about, I've been like this since I was a child, and no, there wasn't a "bad experience" or anything.'

25

In every other way, Kerry was utterly contemporary: a Nineties babe, a 'laddette', a thoroughly modern Ms. But here was also this atavistic fear. This potentially lifethreatening fear. Petruchio was very interested in this aspect of Kerry. He seemed amused by it.

'I think perhaps this fear is not so primitive, we must remember such things as thalidomide – is this medical science of ours infallible, Juliet? Should we not fear it just a little?'

Petruchio shocked us by relating stories about the pharmaceutical industry, about risible drug trials and tests.

'The doctor Kerry refuses to see will only give her an antibiotic, Kerry can fight this herself, if she stops smoking,' was his remark when we tried to enlist his support in persuading Kerry to get treatment.

I got on with my studies, although the higher achiever in me was beginning to slacken off a bit. I began to be late for classes, and go out every night till late. We went to the cinema, to the Citizens' Theatre, to the shows at MacRADA, as the drama school was known, but mostly we just went to the pub.

We talked, like I suppose all students do, a great deal about sex. We learned then that Petruchio was not without his own phobias. He would rant on about the hideousness of all physical contact. He explained that it was base and animalistic and that what separated human beings from all the other animals was that they knew this, they had consciousness, and therefore control over what to other animals was biological necessity.

'In fact,' Petruchio concluded, 'the most truly *human* thing one can do is not be driven by these things, not to do it, not to do these revolting things like have sex, have babies.'

This particular conversation happened, of all places, in

26

War and Pizza. Kerry had a part-time job there as a wait-ress. The rest of us had been to some dreadful thing at the Drama School. The restaurant had long closed but the staff often stayed around drinking and eating until the early hours. There were about eight of us round the table, I think. Petruchio, Chris and Christine, the chef, another waiter, who was also a drama student, Billy and his latest girl-friend, or as Kerry had put it, 'his latest victim from the first-year music students' and Kerry herself, still wearing her khaki uniform and peaked hat.

'You're absolutely right there,' she said, taking a swig from a beer bottle, 'but, Petruchio, that means that the right to choose, to choose abortion is absolutely the most impor-tant issue, since it is to do with our most humanness aspect of us.'

Kerry often spoke like this. Her sentences, particularly when she was talking about something serious, or some-thing which she cared about, would tail off into cute-speak, ungrammatical, childish. It irritated me because so often I agreed with what she was saying.

'Oh, no, Kerry, abortion is not the same,' Petruchio said. 'We must choose before, before the human life and poten-tial is there.' He was agitated and leaned forward aggressively over the table. 'Definitely not abortion. I don't think so.'

This kind of argument was not unusual whenever Petruchio and Kerry were together. They fought almost all the time, and yet nobody sensed any real animosity between them. It was as if they both enjoyed the challenge. Kerry coined the word 'discument' to describe their ideological skirmishes. Petruchio, in spite of, or maybe *because* of his cynicism, was deeply conservative, and I realised when we moved to the flat and our lives became engulfed by the 'Kids from Fame' how little I had known of him previously, how totally incurious I had been.

'Oh, Petruchio,' said Kerry, 'you are so full of shit. You hate human beings, you say that life is hell, a torment through and through – well, if we are all so base and animalistic, why the fuck is it so necessary to make more of us, more and more and more miserable human beings forced into existence in order to be miserable all their lives? I shall never have children, the whole idea revolts me, it is completely hideous, besides you have to go to hospital and have doctors peering up inside you with their diabolical instruments – I might have guessed you were going to suddenly turn Catholic on me, just when I was going to ask you to abort the stupid, slimy monstrous worm of human potential in here.' She thumped her lower abdomen. 'Oh, well, I suppose you can do it, can't you, Juliet? Vets, doctors ... we're all the same after all, aren't we, Petruchio, we're all animals.'

'What dew mean?' Billy said. 'You're no pregnant, are ye, Kerry?'

Kerry paused long enough to look around the table at us all. 'No, of course I'm not sodding pregnant – just winding Petruchio up. Got you all going though, didn't I? You should see your faces.'

Kerry loved to lie. Her lies were often quick; almost as soon as she had been believed she would relinquish the truth with great glee. She said it was fun. She told us how she would often completely invent things, a whole life, a whole new self.

'You know, like if I meet someone for the first time, I'll just invent stuff, a name, a character, and you'd never believe what people will listen to without so much as blinking an eyelid. People are very gullible.'

Petruchio told her that she was suffering from a psychological pathology, but Kerry only laughed. I laughed too, amused by Kerry's deceitful games. Little did I know then how much her particular psychological pathology was to affect me.

'So why do people lie?' I asked Petruchio.

'Bouff, it is a sad attempt to manipulate this reality which oppresses us all. It is because of the pleasure the powerless can have in the illusion of power.'

'Yeah, nice one, Petruchio,' Kerry said.

One evening I arrived back in the flat to find Kerry and Billy watching an old episode of *Star Trek*. I had been a big fan when I was a child and I had seen the episode before. It was the one where the crew of the *Enterprise* encounter two alien lifeforms who can materialise themselves in any shape or form. One chooses mostly to be embodied either as a sex kitten of the *Homo sapiens* species – white, North-American variety circa AD 1970, or as a slinky black cat. She is, of course, the evil alien. In the end Captain Kirk forms an alliance with the decent male, the female (in cat form) kills her mate, Kirk destroys their power to shape change, reduces her to the pathetic insect that she really was, and leaves her twitching miserably on the rocky and otherwise lifeless planet.

'Neat device,' Kerry said of the little crystal globe that was the source of their ability to make such groovy quantum leaps.

'Yes,' I demurred. 'Look – her wave function is collapsing.'

'Her what?' Kerry hissed, but then motioned me to be silent and we watched while the woman left the room as a cat and returned as a woman. We laughed at the device, but we were nonetheless entranced by the story.

'Her wave function collapsed – from cat to woman. It's a bit like Schrödinger's Cat.'

I thought they had not heard me, and anyway, I didn't

expect them to be interested but when the programme was over, Kerry turned to me immediately. 'What's a wave function and what did you say about somebody's cat?'

I did my best to explain the Nobel-prize-winning physicist's intriguing theory and Petruchio came in halfway through and aided me in my explanation. Kerry insisted that we were winding her up and, when we persisted, she became quite incensed. There was no way she was going to swallow that, she told us, even science, for which she had no respect, wasn't stupid enough to come up with anything so ludicrous as that.

Eventually Petruchio rooted round in his bookshelves until he found some kind of scientific tome where Schrödinger's Cat was mentioned. Kerry read it and quietly asked us to explain it again. We did and she had a tantrum, stamping her feet like a child, her face tight and turning purple.

'I don't fucking believe it, I just don't fucking believe it, what is this ... this makes me sick, I mean, of course the fucking cat dies, if the poison is released the cat dies, regardless of whether Schrö-arsehole-dinger knows about it or not. There's a word for that kind of up-arse philosophy, oh shit, what is it?'

'Solipsism,' said Petruchio, highly amused by the whole thing.

'You fucking scientists, you don't care what you do, do you? And you said yourself that cats were closer to humans than other creatures, how could anyone do that? Well, how about if it was a baby, your fucking baby, Schrödinger's baby? How does that sound, yeah, let's put Schrödinger's baby in a box and play Russian roulette with quarks, see how he likes his theory then, whether you'll all be quite so scien-fucking-tific about that.' She was shaking with anger and her voice was breaking. I thought she was going to cry. She hated us because we had told her something about the world she didn't like.

Petruchio said, 'Yes, yes, this is very funny I think.'

Billy put his arms round Kerry, saying, 'Take it easy, wee man, it's only a fucking conversation.'

'There isn't a cat at all, Kerry,' I explained. 'It's all hypothetical, a theory.'

'Science shouldn't tell stories,' she said sullenly, but calm again, 'that isn't its role at all.'

I am trying to recall those days. Probably there are thousands of significant acts, clues, prefigurations which went unnoticed by me, that I cannot now remember. I panic when I think of all the things that I do not remember. Of course, everything that I *do* remember is significant, every word, each every-day occurrence seems to be part of it all, to be important, to have led eventually to the final catastrophe. It seems now like it was in the very air all the time.

Catastrophe? I remember once when Kerry came flouncing into the flat, in a panic because she had lost her script. Throwing things around the room, she searched, while I watched her with, what she called, one of my patronising smiles. Eventually she had said:

'Don't just fucking sit there, Juliet, this is a complete catastrophe.'

I had replied, 'No, Kerry, there are some things in life that one could call complete catastrophes, but you losing your script is completely minor.'

She threw an ashtray at me, missing my head by picometers.

Kerry had an energy about her that was exhausting. She sought attention and people scorned her for it while nonetheless giving it to her in abundance. Any attention – even negative – was welcome in a way, and she enjoyed her notoriety. She was, however, surprisingly easy to hurt and a particularly catty remark could send her into a very non-attention seeking shell lasting days or even weeks. She once told me that she had been bullied at school. I wasn't surprised. I noticed that behind her tough, street-wise persona she was terribly eager to please people, to be liked, and that of course made it very easy for her to be bullied.

The most perceptive thing I think I ever heard Petruchio say was one evening when Kerry was upset, crying over an incident at college that day.

'Oh, but you are far too sensitive, Kerry, you must get a skin, look at you, you have no skin. It is almost that you have an emotional immune deficiency.'

Kerry had looked at Petruchio with wide, admiring eyes. 'Yes. Yes, that's exactly how it feels. I have. An emotional immune deficiency. What am I going to do?'

'Bouff,' said Petruchio. 'You probably just spend the rest of your life being a pain in the arse.'

Kerry would sometimes be round at the flat for days on end; at other times we wouldn't see her for a week or so. When she was around, she was either extremely hyperactive, spending money like water, treating us all to bottles of champagne and lines of cocaine, or she was very quiet and subdued, 'moody', as I remarked to Billy at the time.

I was puzzled by Kerry's spontaneity and, I realise now, jealous of it, which is why I needed to put her down, to dismiss her responses as histrionic, to diminish her to 'the actress'. I wondered what it must be like to be so unguarded, so explosively sincere.

Kerry would have 'complete waves of happiness' coming over her, or she was 'engulfed in despair', or she was 'in a state of absolute terror'. She seemed sometimes like some fearful conduit through which these awesome emotions flowed.

'Oh, Kerry, man, she's completely mental, you know, she's just mental,' Billy explained. Kerry had more or less moved into Billy's room with him by then, but it was clear that they were not involved sexually. Kerry had a mattress in the corner of Billy's room, and on evenings when Billy had 'a bird in' Kerry slept on the sofa in the living room.

We all got on so well we would often comment on how remarkable it was, how pleasant a flat-share. Petruchio made the most complaints. He loathed the fact that we all smoked and in one of his tirades against the habit he informed us that he used nicotine to put animals down with. I was able to corroborate this, having just done a term of Anaesthesia and Euthanasia but Petruchio and I were not believed.

There were disagreements sometimes but these were mostly amicable, if spirited. Things did get a bit tense, however, when Chris and Christine became obsessed with what Kerry always called their 'hocus pocus'.

It started when Christine had read some book or other, the latest bestseller on the theme of the power of positive thinking. This had led her and Chris to whole piles of such books, each one getting more and more mystical, and they evangelically blessed us with regurgitations of the stuff each evening. Kerry once picked up one of these tomes and threw it aside, saying:

'Jesus, this makes Shirley MacLaine's methodology look like Einstein's!'

One day Chris and Christine asked the rest of us for details of our birth so they could draw up star charts for us. Kerry lost her temper, just like she had done over Schrödinger's Cat. Christine looked at her with her big brown eyes, and said, 'It is a science, you know, Kerry, I mean I'm only just learning about it myself, but it is a proper science.' Kerry was like a volcano, spluttering out her inarticulate anger.

'Fuckwits – you are complete and utter fuckwits.' She appealed to Petruchio and myself for help.

I remembered Edgar's insistence that socialism was a science and I felt a harrowing sinking feeling that the world was an impossible place where people went around making up the meanings of words as they went along.

For a few months Chris and Christine immersed themselves in an alternative spiritual world. They would never do anything without first consulting their many totems and talismans. They went to have their fortunes read and Christine was told that she was going to get a part in a BBC serial; the fortune teller saw Regency costumes. Christine decided that it was likely to be Jane Austen, and she started reading the novels.

Petruchio and I, and eventually Billy, felt that we had to put up with a lot from our flatmates those few months; with their tarot cards that no one was allowed to touch, their endless horoscope charts, their wretched books, not to mention the almost constant playing of Neil Diamond's *Jonathan Livingstone Seagull*.

One evening they left their precious tarot cards out and Petruchio, Billy and I came back from the pub before them. Billy picked up the cards and shuffled them, then he took out his prick and rubbed the cards over it in mock masturbation.

'This'll gie 'em some magic powers,' he giggled.

Christmas came and Kerry went back to Ireland, Chris and Billy to Edinburgh and I to London. Petruchio was to remain in Glasgow alone and we all planned to meet back up in the flat for Hogmanay.

I arrived the day before at Central Station in thick fog and got a taxi back to the flat. Billy was there on his own. Kerry, he told me, was in hospital. She had taken an overdose of pills.

34

'I found her and she was unconscious, so I fetched an ambulance and I went with her and it was fine until she woke up and found herself in hospital – she went ballistic, man, fucking wild, I'm telling you ... she refused to see me, started trying to smash things up until they removed me from the ward. Well, she's under sedation now, but she's in a real bad way, I dunno wit te do.'

Billy was very upset. For some reason he thought that Kerry might talk to me 'lassie to lassie' and so I went to the hospital.

Kerry was sitting up in bed, a drip in her arm. She looked very pale and small, like a sick child.

'I had to see that stupid fucking shrink of a bastard for an hour this morning.'

Sedated or not, Kerry's words had energy.

'God, get me out of here, Juliet, they want me to go into a fucking mental hospital for a rest.'

'Well, say no. They can't make you.'

'No, I know. But I don't know what else to do.'

'Why, Kerry, tell me why?'

'There's nothing to tell, except that I am going mad in here, if I don't get out in the next fucking nano-second, I'm going to die of madness, and listen, I know I have always been slightly barking, but I'm talking Tom O'Bedlam here. And don't tell me to calm down because I can't.'

'When do they let you out of here?'

'They're kicking me out tonight, they're going to take the drip off in a minute. I'm all right now apparently, just weak. Either I can go to the loony bin or I have to go home and not be alone, because they want someone to be responsible for my pills.'

'What pills?'

'Pills that they are giving me.'

I had a week before I had to go back to college. Some friends of my parents had a cottage in Argyll, very remote, and they had given me a set of keys that Christmas, saying that I could phone them any time and, if there was no one there, use it as a bolthole. I had had an idea that after Hogmanay I might go up there for a few days and have a quiet time.

'Please help me, Juliet,' Kerry said. 'Even if you just lend me some money, I can pay you back when I get my top-up loan, just enough for me to go somewhere, where I can be alone.'

'You shouldn't be alone.'

'Well, I hardly feel I should inflict these horrocious heebie jeebies on anyone else.'

I laughed.

'Why are you laughing?' she snapped.

'You just said horrocious,' I said. 'Look, what do you need from home?'

'Why?'

'Because I'll go back and fetch whatever you need, and what I need. I'll go and hire a car and we'll go up to a friend's cottage for a few days. I was going to go anyway, after Hogmanay; we'll just go now. But, Kerry, you must get a grip, in one sense at least, you must get a grip.'

She looked at me for a second with absolute hatred, then it left her face and she nodded. 'You didn't need to say that,' she said.

Kerry gave me the key to her bedsit. I had never been there before. There were other students in the building, and they all shared a bathroom but apart from that each bedsit was self-contained. Kerry's was a large room, with the wall partly knocked through into another smaller room. This was curtained off. There was a small kitchenette at one end of the living room.

The place was a disgusting mess, with books, scripts and papers spilling out all over the room, piled up in corners, covering half of the bed, the desk, the floor. Clothes were scattered everywhere, and shoes, cups, dirty plates, cigarette papers and overspilling ashtrays. The bedroom behind the curtain was even worse, I scrambled around trying to find the items Kerry had listed. Under the bed I found a pile of pornographic magazines. I flicked through them and they were, even to my by-no-means naïve mind, hard core. I shoved them back underneath the bed and went on with my search. There was a carrier bag full of clothes: a rubber bodysuit, a rubber mask with zips for eyes and mouth (this made me feel sick – it was something a rapist might wear) leather manacles, whips and cords. These things disgusted and alarmed me.

I left, and began rushing around getting organised and hiring a car. I left a note for the others. If I try to picture myself then, I see a self-important busy body, flapping around like a hen, feeling important because I had taken charge of sweet little, mad little Kerry.

Kerry was dressed and waiting for me in the ward. As soon as we were in the car she asked whether I had remembered to bring the dope.

I had. It had not been hard to find. There were pieces of it all over her coffee table, along with remains of other drugs and paraphernalia. I had decided I would take it to her, as she had been so adamant and I didn't want her brewing up some fearful withdrawal symptoms on top of everything else. I told her where she could find it, and she started skinning up straight away, with fervent anticipation.

We decided we would just head north-west and see how far we got. The fog was still bad and got worse as we headed north up Loch Lomond. I realised that it was stupid to continue but I didn't want to stop. When we did stop it was too foggy to know where we were; we vaguely saw lights and we stumbled around until we found a hotel that thankfully had a room due to cancellations because of the fog. We had missed any chance of dinner but they managed a plate of sandwiches and cake, and the bar was still open so we both had several double whiskies. Though centrally heated, the bedroom was freezing. We climbed into icy sheets but in spite of the cold were soon asleep.

The fog had cleared by the morning and fortified by a large breakfast we headed north again. Kerry was quiet in the car, reading the paper and rolling endless joints. She didn't take any of the pills the hospital had given her. I didn't ask any questions and when we did talk it was very easygoing chit-chat.

The radio was on and the song *I'm Nobody's Baby* played. For some reason I had been thinking of Kerry's outrage about Schrödinger and in my head the plaintive lament became 'I'm Schrödinger's Baby'. I mused to myself on how Kerry's reaction to that conversation had been a case of extreme identification. She identified with the cat, she couldn't bear the callousness of the thought experiment. I remembered my reaction to the crucifixion of those cats all those years ago at school and I felt suddenly very fond of Kerry. I tried to understand where she was coming from: she sees Schrödinger taking a large black box. She imagines with horror him setting up his experiment, placing his radioactive material in the corner, where it might, depending on the whim of the decay particle, on whether it is a wave or particle at that exact moment in time, go up to release the poison or down to release the Whiskas Supermeat. He places the cat in the box, but not *the* cat to Kerry, no, probably *a* very particular cat, one that she has loved. Schrödinger shuts and locks the box and waits with a villainous smile. He believes that the cat is in a state of perpetual and perverse duality. It is both alive and dead, quantum dead, quantum alive, wave/particle. Until he opens the box, of course, and when he does that – he causes a happening. What joy! What power! He has a cageful of cats beside him. He can go on and on with his game. Like heads or tails. Each time it will be only his observation that will determine whether or not the wave function of the cat has collapsed into dead matter or whether it is enjoying a snack in the dark. The life of a cat is in the eye of the beholder.

Sure, if you have to be so literal about everything, I can see it's an upsetting little hypothesis.

I smiled. Kerry asked me what I was smiling at and I told her how the words of the song had changed in my head. We laughed and sang, 'I'm Schrödinger's Baby'.

I then asked her what she found so terrible about the thought experiment: did she, like the pessimist seeing the glass half-empty, always see the particle going upwards to release the poison? No, she replied, she saw the cat in the terrible, because unimaginable, state of suspension between life and death.

'That eternal moment of death or not death, that's what I can't bear, Juliet, that absolute uncertainty.'

We stopped in Inveraray to buy provisions and we arrived at the cottage at about two pm. It was basic and unheated, so we were busy for a while making the fire, sticking electric ones in the bedroom and bathroom and unpacking our food. Then we walked up the hill a short way to sort the water out.

The water came from a tank which was fed from a pipe that lay in the burn. We had to break the surface ice and re-lay the pipe, then we had to clear the leaves and mud from the inlet inside the water tank. We had just managed to do all this, as well as humping a large supply of wood from the woodshed, before it was dark and we settled down in the two armchairs by the fire. We ate, we read, we found a backgammon set and played for hours. We drank large amounts of whiskey and at midnight we went out into the garden to see if we could hear any bells and to greet the new year.

'Why did you take the overdose, Kerry? I mean, you're so frightened of hospitals,' I asked, when we were inside again having lingered in the garden looking at the stars until the cold forced us in.

'I had no intention of going to hospital, I intended to die.'

I looked at her, I suppose intently; she became embarrassed after a few seconds and got up and fetched more whiskey.

'You know, I sometimes think you are from another planet, you and Petruchio.'

'Oh yes, I know you do,' I said. 'My family does too. It's amazing how unimaginative you artistic types can be.'

I sat looking at Kerry and I was trying to imagine her in that rubber bodysuit and horrible mask that I had seen in her room. I wanted to confront her, but I was afraid she would think I had been snooping. After several more whiskies, I felt bolder, or no longer cared, and smiling casually, I said, 'That's some pretty horrendous gear you've got under your bed, Kerry, I couldn't help noticing it, when I looked for your case.'

Her face was blank, then startled, then she blushed, and it was the only time I ever saw Kerry blush.

'Oh, that,' she said, composing herself, and then, transforming herself into a repentant child, 'Oh, Father Juliet, I have sinned most heinously – will ye take confession, Father, from one so base and vile as me?'

I nodded gravely and rubbed my hands together, taking my part rather well I thought, but Kerry changed again, and was businesslike.

'Well, shall I tell you a story then, a true one, I mean?'

I put more wood on the fire and stayed sitting on the rug, poking and tending it while Kerry began.

'A few months ago, I started going for saunas at that place by the park. There's a sort of bar there, where people sit around in their robes reading magazines, and one day this guy chatted me up. He said he was the owner of the place and after a while he went over to the bar and came back with a bottle of champagne. I drank a couple of glasses with him but then I said I had to go. I went back into the changing room and got dressed. He was lurking in the foyer when I went out. He asked when I would be back and I said probably next week sometime. I did go back the following week, on a Tuesday afternoon. I had a sauna, a shower and then I was just getting dressed to go straight home, when he just barged into the changing room. I was dressed by that time, you know, so that was all right, but all the same I was a bit spooked. Anyway, he wooed me into going for a drink with him and I found myself getting into his car, you know a real prick of a car. There was this kind of third person saying to me all the time, you're mad, what are you doing getting into this car with this man?'

'What was he like?' I asked.

'He was a medallion-man type, lots of flashy jewellery, tanned, bearded, a kind of obvious sort of no-no really, and I go getting into his car! We drove to a bar round the corner, but it was closed, so he said why don't we go to this place in the south side where we could have a jacuzzi, and we could stop and get something to drink on the way. I agreed, but as we headed out south, I became nervous. He stopped the car and went into an off-licence. I sat in the car thinking – now is my chance to escape, for God's sake, woman, go now. But I didn't, I sat there until it was too late and he was back in the car, and we were driving out of the city again. I was frightened now. We seemed to be leaving

41

Glasgow far behind and then we did suddenly stop and it was at a health club and it was fucking closed too. So, at this point, I said I would just like to go home and, would you believe, of all things, he just comes out with – "Why don't we go to the Holiday Inn and get a room for the afternoon, they have a jacuzzi there, we can order some food, and seriously relax ourselves." I said I don't think so, just take me home. And he did, he took me as far as Byers Road anyway, I told him to drop me there and, d'you know, he gave me the carrier bag, he insisted on it, and when I got back to my room, it was champagne, two bottles. Well, the next week or sometime I went back and he was there again. He asked me to go for a drink with him again, but first he offered me some coke, which of course I took. Anyway, he was on and on at me to go to bed with him, to go to the Holiday Inn and get a room and suddenly I thought, why the hell not? I mean, he wasn't repulsive, I mean, yes of course he *was* repulsive, but, you know, he was clean, he was quite good looking in a tacky sort of way and he did have a good body, a well-cared-for body. Anyway, I agreed. Yes, I know, I agreed. He had this huge sort of case thing in the car which he took into the hotel. He winked at me and said "toys". We took some more coke, ordered champagne and then he opened the case and took out this rubber gear and whips and all sorts and told me to put it on, including the mask. Well, I didn't really mind, you know me, I like dressing up. Anyway, all he wanted me to do was to whip him with this sort of horse-whip thing. He didn't want to fuck me at all, which was a huge relief really.'

Kerry looked at me, and I shifted suddenly, aware that I had been gawping, open-mouthed at her. She paused to fill up her glass and relight a joint. There was a camp naughtiness in the way she was relating her story, and this made me suppress the laughter that was welling inside me. I would not give her the satisfaction. She suddenly closed her eyes and rested her head on a cushion.

'Oh, God, are you not totally bored out of your mind, Juliet, and wanting to get to your bed?'

'No, I want to hear the rest.'

Kerry smiled. 'Well,' she continued, 'he was terribly grateful to me and he told me that I must keep the gear because it suited me so well, and anyway he couldn't take it home in case his wife found it and he hoped that we might do this again sometime.

'I vowed to myself that I wouldn't go to the sauna ever again. One day I was walking up the road, coming up to where I live, and he suddenly loomed up behind me in his car and asked me to hop in, so I did and he said come for a drink, you know, usual stuff. I said no and that I had enjoyed it the once but that was enough and I didn't want to do it anymore. After some protestations, he got the message and dropped me at the back of Byers Road. We said goodbye and that was that.'

Kerry burst out laughing. I laughed too, that sort of drunken, completely helpless laughter.

We slept together in the big double bed, piled up and heavy with blankets and quilts. We woke at lunchtime and took trays of food back to bed as it was too cold to get up. We eventually dressed and lit the fire and then went for a walk along the loch. The next day we decided to drive along the loch until we came to the sea. We parked the car and walked down to the beach. Kerry insisted on running through the waves, the water up to her shoulders. She then shouted, crying out for a merman to come and whisk her away – she would swap her legs for a fishy tail and live happily ever after in the kingdom under the sea. She shivered histrionically in the car on the way back and took a hot toddy up to the bath with her when we got home. I went for a walk in the woods beyond the burn. I sat for about an hour

43

on a tree trunk. It was so quiet and I sat trying to be as still as I could be, to ease myself into the silence and disappear into it. A couple of deer walked across the clearing; I hardly dared to breathe as they passed. The woods were bathed in a luminous green light. I had a sudden, strong desire to take my clothes off. For my body to be green and bare, I wanted to dance wildly in the woods. I also wished that Kerry were with me. I imagined her lying in the bath, whiskey in hand and wished I could transport her here, *Star Trek* fashion.

When I got back Kerry was on the sofa, reading a Dostoevksy novel.

'No wonder you're depressed, reading that stuff,' I said.

'Have you read it then?' she asked hopefully.

'No, but my family has.'

We laughed and I sat by the grate to warm myself and told her about the wonderful green light in the woods.

'I wish you had been with me ... it was beautiful ...'

Kerry's eyes filled with tears, and she looked at me in a mawkish manner.

'*You're* beautiful, Juliet,' she said, and I was embarrassed.

Apart from her wild-child-of-nature sea-bathe, Kerry was actually the sanest I had ever known her those few days in Argyll, which, I suppose, means the calmest and quietest. As soon as we got back to Glasgow, however, she changed. Her colour literally changed as we neared Dumbarton. Then she vomited. I pulled in and we cleaned up a bit, and she sat with a carrier bag under her chin.

'What do you want to do?' I asked.

'Go to bed ... but I can't go back to my place, I can't, and I don't want to sleep with Billy, I just don't!' Her voice rose to a wail.

'All right,' I said, already starting the engine, 'you can sleep with me.'

Kerry went straight to my room and climbed into my bed. I fetched buckets and bowls and a cup of tea. She drank it eagerly and threw it straight back up again. I went through to the living room. Petruchio was asleep on the sofa in his dressing gown. Billy was rolling a joint on the coffee table, an empty bottle of Scotch by his side.

'Whoahowye deng,' he spluttered, 'howze wee man?'

'She's OK, she's staying in my room, but she's ill, stomach ulcers or something.'

Kerry slept soundly for the rest of the day whilst I did laundry and shopping and other chores. I also phoned the hospital and spoke to a nurse who assured me that Kerry's stomach would be very sensitive for some time; the cocktail she had taken had damaged the lining.

The following morning we got up early and I walked with Kerry to the hospital. She had an appointment to see a psychiatrist, and she wouldn't go unless I went with her. She was petrified. Anyone would think she was going to have major surgery, without an anaesthetic.

I waited while she was in seeing the doctor. She came out as white as a sheet and went straight to bed on our return.

Later, she told me that nothing she had said to the psychiatrist was true.

'What do you mean?' I repeated dumbly. Kerry looked exasperated.

'I mean I told lies and quoted at him, played roles, deliberately misled him, it's hopeless, isn't it?' I shook my head. I didn't know what to say.

I was worried and so I talked to Petruchio. He had, after all, trained as a psychiatrist. He almost laughed when I told him of Kerry's deviousness in misleading the shrink.

'Yes, yes,' he said delightedly, 'they are so stupid, of course one such as Kerry can run the ring round them.

Kerry is right, they will not be able to help her so she may as well take the piss.'

Petruchio didn't believe in psychiatry, but he did believe in drugs.

'The drugs alleviate the more horrible symptoms of the human condition, they do not cure neurological illness, hah – they make them worse, if anything.' He took from his pocket a small packet of pills. 'My little nullifiers,' he said, kissing the packet. 'Some people prefer to be clever but me, I like to be a chemical lobotomy.'

'How can you work in something that you don't believe in? Petruchio, you experiment on small animals and kill them and then you say you don't believe in it. . .'

Petruchio did not reply, he took a Valium and shuffled out of the room, his back hunched.

Kerry was ill in bed, my bed, for about two weeks. During this time I came back every lunchtime to check on her. One day as I walked into the hall I heard voices coming from my room.

'All right, yes, all right,' I heard Kerry saying tiredly, and Petruchio replying, 'Well, you understand something now, I hope, because I am not taking things personally at all, it really was just a stupid joke, I hope not to make you mad but to surprise you, divert you. I am sorry, Kerry, you are special person and I am very glad you do not die.'

I darted quickly into the living room as I heard Petruchio move towards the door. I dumped my bags on the sofa and opened the fridge. Petruchio came in and looked startled.

'Oh, Juliet, you are back,' he said.

'Yes, but only for a while.' I put the kettle on and went through to my room. Kerry was in bed.

'Kerry, I want to know what is going on with Petruchio and you. I heard him in here and I just want to know what's going on.'

46

'Why do you want to know?' Kerry asked. I had no answer to that.

'Just because you're being so nice to me, it doesn't mean you have a right to know anything about my life,' Kerry continued.

'You didn't need to say that,' I said.

The following day I came home and Billy and Kerry were sitting in the living room together. Kerry was still not smoking but she did have a can of beer in her hand. She was dressed and had put some make-up on. She still looked very pale and painfully thin, but she looked better.

She was also playing with a kitten, a little black and white thing. She said that she and Billy had been given it, and begged me to allow it to stay in the flat. She was convinced she could get round Petruchio, if I would agree.

'Juliet, Billy says I can have his room for a while, he's going to stay mostly with his girlfriend. That means I can move out of your room and give up my bedsit – that is, if that's all right with everyone else in the flat, I mean, if everyone agrees.'

'Sure,' I said, 'it's fine by me, but which girlfriend is this, Billy? And how long do you expect this one to last?'

'Exactly, man, that's why I'm no gonna gie up the room, just sorta lend it to Kerry and we'll see how it goes, you know what I mean, man?' Billy started to giggle.

That evening when Petruchio and Chris were back, and the kitten hidden away in Billy/Kerry's room, Billy made the suggestion again and no one had any objections.

Kerry still didn't want to set foot in her bedsit and so arranged for Billy to go over there the next day and pack everything up in boxes and bring it over here. She would pay for the taxi and reward him with alcohol.

I was in the laboratory that morning, doing a supervised post-mortem on a Labrador and I was finding it hard to

47

concentrate. I was thinking of Kerry's bedsit. I decided to take the afternoon off and go and give Billy a hand.

There he was, sitting in the middle of the room, snorting any likely looking bits of white stuff left around on the various trays, tables, books and mirrors scattered around the room. He had packed a few boxes of books and stacked up all her clothes in one corner of the room, ready for punching into bin-bags.

'I thought I'd pop in and lend you a hand.'

'Oh, cheers, yeah great, man, I'll buy you a drink, we'll get pissed later, hey?'

'Yeah,' I said, 'look, I'll do the bedroom, OK?'

'Yeah, OK, man, on you go, I'll just finish up the hoovering here.' He laughed heartily at his joke, stuck the five-pound-note tube up his nostril and jigged around the room, sniffing.

I went to the bed and pulled out all the junk that was lying around and started stuffing it into a suitcase I found in the wardrobe. It was with particular speed and distaste that I packed the porn and rubber gear, desperate that Billy should not see it. It felt to me very private.

It took us a good few hours to get everything done and there was far too much for one taxi journey. We just about made it in two, Billy with one lot of stuff and me another. My car arrived first and Kerry came out to help us unload. When all her stuff was in Billy's room, it was impossible to move in there, since Billy had not taken his away.

I offered to help Kerry unpack but she insisted that she wanted to party, to celebrate the fact that she never had to go back to that disgusting bedsit again. I thought to myself that it was a rather nice bedsit, as they went, and that the only disgusting thing I'd found was the gear under her bed, and that was now here, in the suitcase.

Billy agreed that we should have a party and so he rang

round spreading the word. We allocated a role for each room, Chris's for dancing, mine and Petruchio's for smoking, and the living room for eating. Kerry's room was obviously out of use, which relieved Kerry, who believed she could keep the kitten in there and spare Petruchio any knowledge of its existence for a while longer. But during the hectic preparations the kitten escaped and, with great enthusiasm, hurled itself at Petruchio's groin as he was on his way to the bathroom, and started to abseil down his legs. He screamed, thrashed the kitten off him and then curled his lip in disgust.

'An animal!' he gasped. 'So, now we have an animal in the flat with us?' He couldn't believe it, he couldn't believe that such a thing could come to pass. Chris, however, was in love with the kitten at first sight and within five minutes had been persuaded by Kerry that they couldn't part with it now. Petruchio fumed, ranted about filth and fleas and then looked at the kitten, sniffing around gallantly on the sofa, tail high, nose twitching.

'I will give you a hundred pounds for this thing, so I can experiment with it tomorrow morning,' he said and left the room. Kerry followed him, shouting.

'Fuck you, Petruchio, you bastard, you pig, you'd better be sweet to this kitten or I'll kill you.'

Petruchio came out of his room, clutching a packet of Valium and marched back into the living room. He sat at the table, his head in his hands. 'Yes, Kerry, I will be sweet to your animal, but you are insane having such a thing in your bedroom, it is a dirty thing.'

'Oh, for God's sake, Petruchio – Juliet, tell him that it's not dirty.'

'No, it isn't, but it's not going to like this party.'

Kerry said she could lock her door and keep the kitten away from it.

'What's its name?' I asked.

'But it is obvious,' said Petruchio, with a horrid sneer, 'it has to be Schrödinger.'

'No!' shrieked Kerry, 'that's obscene, don't you dare call it Schrödinger. Besides I think it's a girl.' I verified this, and we all started to throw in names, until Kerry decided upon Freyja.

'It's what I would have liked to have been called myself,' she explained, 'after the Norse goddess, mistress of magic and goddess of sensual pleasure.'

When we had cleared the flat of breakables and dispatched Billy and Christine to the shops to buy booze and party food, Kerry disappeared into her room to change. Chris and I fiddled with lights in the living room while Petruchio complained about the party, insisting that he needed particularly to sleep on such a night as this, as tomorrow happened to be a very important day.

'What?' said Chris. 'You're having a leopard flown in from Zimbabwe for you to cut up, nice and fresh?' Petruchio went to his room and slammed the door, but he came out after about half an hour, once the music was going, with a pile of tapes he insisted we play at some point. Kerry didn't appear until the party was well in swing. She was wearing a long black T-shirt, with black lacy cami knickers and a suspender belt, badly laddered stockings and high heels. She greeted people as she wandered into the kitchen, until suddenly someone shrieked:

'My God, your earrings, Kerry. Oh, for fuck's sake, that's disgusting, here, look here at Kerry's ears.' I turned to look, with everyone else who was near, and Kerry winked at me.

Her earrings were constructed of tampons dangling off safety pins, tampons dipped in what I later learned was nail varnish, but what we all for one minute thought was blood. Kerry laughed at us all.

'Don't you just love them,' she said, dangling one in some guy's face. He winced and looked glum. 'Oh, I know,' sighed Kerry, 'I'm just the pits, aren't I? Hey, Billy, come on, let's dance!'

'You know, Kerry,' said a guy called Martin, whom I had met a few times before, 'sometimes you really go too far. I think this is really bad taste actually.'

'Well, I'm hardly going in for the *Country Life* Award for Etiquette, am I?' she said, and waltzed Billy out of the room.

At a certain point in the evening I couldn't take it anymore, and I left the flat and went for a walk. As I walked along the road I met Petruchio. He stopped.

'Let me walk with you, I don't want to go back, I have been out for two, three walks but still I don't like the party, they won't play good music, there are ugly people making sex and drunkenness. The world, I think, is nicer by the park.' We walked together in an amicable silence.

'Juliet,' Petruchio said suddenly, 'I wish to now tell you what troubles I have with Kerry. She comes to see me after Christmas and tells me she is crazy. So, I gave her some anti-depressant. She come back and ask to stay in Billy's room. I play a trick on her, I admit, a little cruel. She is hysterical anyway, and so I go out. Next thing, Billy has come home and found Kerry nearly unconscious and taken her to the hospital. She has stolen my drugs of course for this suicide. A punishment for me.'

'I see.' I was feeling a little drunk, and barely taking any of this in.

'So, I think Kerry has told you what a wicked evil bastard I am and you don't like me no more and I don't want this, Juliet, I don't want it.'

'OK. Did you see Kerry's earrings?'

'Yeees,' drawled Petruchio, 'very amusing, I think.'

There was a lot of clearing up to do the following morning, and various comatose people lying around on sofas, cushions and bits of floor, who were soon woken and enlisted to help. Kerry could not be roused. She didn't wake until about seven that night. When she did, she made herself a tray of food and took it back into her room with her.

I watched the television with Petruchio and Billy but after a couple of hours I went and knocked on Kerry's door. She was sitting in the middle of the room with the suitcase I had packed to one side.

'I'm just sorting all this lot out,' she said, 'and then I'm going to have a bonfire in the courtyard.'

'With this?' I picked out one of the porno mags.

'Uh-ha. But not the rubber, the neighbours might complain of the smell, I'll just put that in the rubbish.'

'Petruchio told me last night that he played a trick on you and you stole his pills and took the overdose to punish him.'

'Petruchio is full of shit.'

We sat in silence then for some time, as I looked through her collection of photographs and she sorted things from the suitcase into piles. She sniffed. I looked up and tears were streaming down her face, which was otherwise calm and businesslike. She brushed them aside brusquely and I spontaneously reached out to hug her. She tensed up slightly at my touch and I, hurt by this, left her to her sorting.

About an hour later, I was in my room reading a book on the reproductive organs of small rodents, when Kerry came in. She asked me what I was doing and I told her.

'Well, how would you fancy stopping doing that and making mad passionate love to me instead?'

After we had made love, slept, woken in the early hours and were talking softly in the dark, I asked Kerry again about

Petruchio's trick. I wanted to know what was going on between them.

She said that she had been feeling really down and had spent a terrible Christmas with her parents, so she had returned to Glasgow a few days earlier than planned and, feeling sick and frightened and knowing that everyone else would still be away, she had gone to see Petruchio.

'I thought he could help, you see, and there was no way I was going back to any doctor or anything like that.'

She had told him that she thought she might be going mad and told him some of her symptoms. These were: most noticeably, something wild and poisonous running through her veins, like a squillion angry ants trapped in her bloodstream; uncontrollable rages against the world; bitter self-hatred; paranoia; a throbbing, welling pain in the solar plexus; olfactory hallucinations – she could smell sweat and stinking genitals, bits of rotting food in people's mouths – all of which amounted to what felt like cancer of the soul.

Petruchio went to his desk and opened up a drawer with a key. Inside he had a large white medicine box full of drugs. He had taken out some small white packages and told Kerry that these contained the purest, finest cocaine in the world, and if he ever wanted to be illegal he could make millions of pounds. He then gave her a handful of pills. Kerry noticed that the box also contained syringes and some phials containing liquid.

Petruchio told Kerry that the drugs he had given her were anti-depressants and they would help her sleep and be less anxious.

'You are clearly an hysterical person, Kerry,' he had said.

She asked him if she could stay in Billy's room and went straight to bed. Petruchio went to work the following morning and Kerry had gone shopping and to the pub. She returned to Billy's room, slightly drunk and very tired and woozy from the anti-depressants.

There was a large box in the middle of the room. It was a black, anodised flight case, about two feet deep and two and a half feet square. It had a combination lock on it and a note placed on the top reading:

THE NUMBER OF THE BEAST

Kerry clicked the numbers 666 together, and then began at zero for the final digit. It was also 6. Kerry opened the box, and stared in, long enough to read the message, long enough for the sight to make her retch. She then screamed.

Inside the box there was a dead tabby cat, and a makeshift contraption in the corner; a plastic box with a little skull and crossbones sticker on it which was linked by wires to a set of scales on which were balanced two dishes of cat food. In one dish there was a note reading:

HELLO, AT LAST SOMEONE LETS ME OUT OF HERE

On the other dish, the weighted one, the note read:

CURIOSITY KILLED THE CAT

Kerry did not stop screaming, until Petruchio came in and when he did she began throwing things and kicking furniture. He caught her arms and held them behind her back.

'You must calm down, Kerry, I am sorry, this is silly joke, of course, I think you laugh, for fuck's sake now, please be calm.'

Kerry began to cry and told Petruchio to take his hands off her and get rid of the box. He did as he was bid, grace-

54

lessly muttering, 'So much for this little joke, I don't understand you peoples.'

Kerry heard Petruchio leave the flat, and she went into his bedroom. She was frightened that the box and the cat might still be in there, but Petruchio had obviously taken them with him. Kerry rummaged around his desk looking for the key to the top drawer. She found it eventually in his jacket pocket. She took two packets of the anti-depressants and a bottle of Valium. She then took a package of the so-called premium cocaine, licked her thumb and dipped it in. She tossed the medicine box on to the bed and left the drawer open. She went back to Billy's room, swallowed all the pills, and stuck her powdered thumb into her mouth.

'And you know, Juliet, this wasn't out of any horrifying existential despair, or a wave of anger or desolation, it wasn't particularly grim at all. I was just terribly tired. So tired. That's all. I had decided that there was no point to life, everyone dies anyway so why not now?'

I said nothing. I was thinking about the cat; where had Petruchio got it from? I later learned that he had taken it from his laboratory. It was young, barely six months, an unneutered female. It had not yet been experimented on. An epidemic of FeLV (Feline Leukaemia Virus) had broken out in the pound. The infected animals were put down and there was a pile of dead cats in the dustbins by the incinerator in the Clinical Waste Unit. Petruchio had been thinking about Kerry and the dead cats gave him an idea. When he took it back to the laboratory, after carrying out his joke, he tossed it into the incinerator, along with dozens of mutilated white mice.

Kerry knew nothing of this. She merely experienced the box. Kerry, the actor, was used to experiencing things which were not real. She had found the thought experiment horrible. She did not experience the box in Billy's bedroom as a joke. She had enough problems with the theory without

Petruchio so graphically illustrating it for her. Personally I like the whole idea but then I have always been more than a little in love with scientific mystery. I do not try to reconcile the unreconcilable. There is a war of realities here: the real quantum world versus the real biological world of cause and effect, life and death.

What happens in the box? On what level does it happen? It's a real Pandora's box that one, surely one of the most unsettling of recent hypotheses, a real mind irritant.

Pandora's box. A little like Schrödinger's maybe? Perhaps all Pandora did in opening that box of hers, was to collapse the first wave function. Where things were once solid, real, *either one thing or another*, safe and comfortable, Newtonian, a world with mathematical syntax, they now become slippery, duplicitous, uncertain, ungraspable, the quantum playing tireless status games with reality, *now you see it now you don't*, a world of t-quarks and b-quarks, anti-quarks, gluons and such stuff as dreams are made on. An architecturally incoherent world.

It was Pandora who dunnit, bringing contradiction and curiosity into the birth-free, oestrogenless, homosociety. What made her open the box? The same goddam feminine perfidy that made Eve eat the apple. Two things we learn about women from these two paragons:

1. They are disobedient, rebellious and inclined to disobey the orders given by gods.

2. They are curious, they are seekers after knowledge at whatever cost.

It makes me feel quite good to be a woman. Good on you, girls, fuck him, what does he know? He's only God.

How amusing that I am identifying myself with Pandora and Eve! Well, I, too, had to know. Kerry warned me, but I had to see the cat come out of the bag.

*

Petruchio had changed for me. I still found him amusing, I was fond of him, but whenever I thought of him going through all the many actions of setting up his trick, I shivered and felt nauseous. There is something macabre about someone who can go to all those lengths for a jest, I thought to myself. When I asked him about it, he shrugged and said that he had done it to cheer Kerry up. Of course he was aware now that he showed no understanding of Kerry in his belief that she would laugh. To him, this cat was a dead cat, that was all. He worked with them all day so it was no big deal. He forgot that to Kerry this cat was a sentimental thing. Well, I work with dead animals too, they are part of everyday life for me, but anyone with half a brain cell can recognise that to plant something like that somewhere as a joke is sick and liable to offend and upset. I began to think that Petruchio had planted that gruesome box to punish her.

Part of my distaste was merely infatuation and over-protectiveness. Now Kerry was mine, I was in her corner and so Petruchio was a villain. Whatever, the fact is that my discovery of Petruchio's misdemeanour coincided with the beginning of my love affair with Kerry, to which everything took second place, and around which everything revolved.

I thought long and hard about Petruchio's horrible joke and I came to the conclusion that it had been a flirtation. I have always associated teasing with lust, and so I saw the flight case and its elaborate contents as merely a grown-up version of worms down the jumper. Little boys in the playground are always beastliest to the little girls they fancy.

It must have been two or maybe three weeks since Kerry and I had first made love when we had a flat dinner party. Christine cooked again, a vast curry, and she had invited some other people over, including Billy and his girlfriend. There were about ten of us squeezed round the table.

In my first year of veterinary training I had taken a course in veterinary ethics. In a flurry of spite against Petruchio, I invoked that learning that night and challenged him about his experimentation.

'Yes, yes, Juliet, there are many regulations which we follow. We cannot cause undue pains to the creatures.'

'Oh, what a shame!' I said.

Christine was getting upset at the topic of conversation, and Petruchio closed it with:

'I am not interested anyway in your veterinary ethics, I am not a fucking vet, I am a pharmacologist and I do not like animals.'

Kerry became very drunk later on. There are three sorts of people in the world: non-drinkers, that is either total teetotallers or people who do not regularly consume alcohol to a point of intoxication; benign drinkers, those who do drink a great deal, but on whom alcohol has the effect of making them mellow, sentimental and affectionate, and so no one minds; and lastly malignant drunks, those whom alcohol turns into depressive, aggressive, loud-mouths, full of self-pity who are loathed, when in this state, by everyone. I am one of the first. That is to say, I drink, but never very much. I do not like being drunk, being out of control, and I am blessed with a constitution that rejects what it knows harms. I am always sick before I get too inebriated. Kerry, on the other hand, was a nasty drunk; aggression was always followed by self-pity and on this occasion when we went to bed she started to cry and talk a whole load of maudlin, self-hating nonsense. Knowing she was drunk, and could barely be said to be herself anymore, I was unsympathetic. Besides, I was tired and needed to sleep.

'Why don't you just hug me?' she cried out, rolling herself into a little ball at the end of the bed.

'Why don't you just save your acting for the fucking stage?'

58

'You're doing it,' shrieked Kerry, unfolding herself with a snap like a party whistle, 'you're doing what everyone always does. I hate you, I can't believe it, you insist on turning me into an actress at the very points when I am most sincere. Why? I can't fucking believe it.' She burst into tears again.

'Because your sincerity is just too much. It's ... over-acted.'

'I hate you,' she said, and rushed at me, fists flying. I caught hold of them and pinioned them behind her back.

I hugged her then and she became calm again. I coaxed her into bed, and stroked her head. I was sure she had dropped off to sleep and I had just kissed her temple and turned over to sleep myself when she spoke.

'Juliet, do you ever see yourself in the third person? I mean, when you think about yourself, is it ever in the third person? Do you visualise yourself in future situations, like it were a film?'

'No,' I said.

'No. I didn't think so. I do, you see, and so does Billy, I asked him, and Petruchio does sometimes and Chris does and Christine does – it was my grandfather who first told me about it. He said that when my grandmother was ill once, terribly ill, and we all thought she was going to die, for all those weeks she was in hospital he constantly saw himself, was aware of himself, as if he were outside. So he experienced making a cup of tea, as "he walked over to the kettle and filled it with water, he switched it on", etcetera, etcetera. Always there was this commentary, until the moment came when the commentary went – "he falls down on to the floor/sofa/bed and weeps bitterly." Then he would weep bitterly and the commentary would go away and usually he would weep himself to sleep and when he woke up the commentary would be there again. You're lucky if you don't,

59

Juliet, I think it makes us all mad.'

Of course, the next day a commentary appeared in my brain. I experienced the entire day, almost, in the third person, and, as the day at college drew to an end, I began to create images of myself going home to Kerry and of our evening together. I saw it like a movie, with us going down to the new bar on Great Western Road and having a drink, us walking home later arm and arm, us making love in bed, our bodies intertwined balletically in an impossibly becoming light.

'Well, it's horrible,' I told Kerry when I got home. 'I want to stop. Come on, let's go to that new bar on Great Western Road.'

'What, now? Must we?' said Kerry. She was sitting comfortably with the kitten curled up on her lap, reading. 'I was hoping we could just get a bottle of wine in and watch TV. I've also got some lines I have to learn, you could help me.'

'All right, but let's go to that bar first, and then get wine on the way home, come on just one drink.'

We went to the bar, but I was not to have Kerry to myself, for we met up straight away with some people she knew, who introduced us to some more people – you know the way it goes. We meet so many people. How many people do we all meet, all the time? There was nothing significant about that evening at the time, and I am inwardly rebelling against the fact that subsequent events suddenly give it such import. It was the night that I met the agent Geoffrey Daniels, but there is no real consequence there, I am nothing in his story.

Were it not for subsequent events, I might not remember that night at all. It was a very usual night, except, perhaps, for the fact that I was newly in love with Kerry, and so everything was more exposed.

At first I was a bit sulky. I was polite but I didn't pay much attention to anyone, certainly not to their names, when we were introduced. Someone offered us another drink and Kerry seemed happy to stay, so we did, though by now I was wanting to go home with a bottle of wine. I listened to Kerry.

'Yes, well, we really are trying hard to get that Spanish passion and repressed sexuality into it, but the trouble is we keep corpsing, all of us. It's very hard, we're doing it in sort of Hollywood Mexican accents and camping it up something wicked. The director wants me to wear nothing but a corset and a sort of petticoat and I've refused – I tried it on, but I would spend the entire production worrying if my tits were falling out. No way!'

What was she talking about? My mind filled with images of Kerry acting in some horrible pornographic film, Kerry dressed in kinky underwear, my sweet, child-like Kerry dressed up like some thrupenny tart.

'Anyway,' she continued, 'who wants another drink? Juliet, will you come and help me carry them?' We went to the bar.

'Oh God, am I all right?' Kerry said anxiously. 'I mean I keep hearing myself spouting rubbish and feeling like I want to die, but I can't seem to stop, am I really awful?'

'Yes, what *are* you talking about, Kerry, what are you doing with your tits falling out in Hollywood Mexico?' I had spoken savagely but Kerry just burst out laughing.

'The Lorca play, you idiot, I told you we were doing a workshop on it, God, what is the matter with you Juliet?' I sulkily said that I wanted to go home.

'But I want to speak with those people. That man, the one that Jonny introduced us to, is a big London agent, one of the biggest. His name is Geoffrey Daniels and he and his wife are partners and they're thinking of opening a branch in Glasgow. Oh my God, I do wish I didn't know who he was, then I could just be normal.' We carried drinks back and sat down.

I eventually relaxed enough to enjoy the evening moderately, and we were there until closing time. We were joined at some point by Petruchio and Chris and then later Billy turned up too, having had a row with his girlfriend and asking Kerry if he could have his room back for the night. Kerry was engaged in deep conversation with this man Geoffrey, and my eyes kept straying over to where they sat. I was certain that he was falling in love with her and I felt nervous.

He was an urbane, and to my mind, slimy individual; greying hair, piercing, cold, blue eyes and an air of superiority and sexual confidence that I imagine many women found attractive. I wanted Kerry to look over at me, to reassure me, but she was passionately gesticulating and totally absorbed in whatever she was saying. I remember that I rather spitefully hoped that she was talking a load of shit. And then I felt disgusted with myself for such a thought. I was supposed to be in love with Kerry, that meant love didn't it? L.O.V.E. – when you want the very best for someone. What was the matter with me? When we left I noticed the agent warmly kissing Kerry goodbye. I walked on ahead with Petruchio.

'You are jealous, I can see this, Juliet,' he said. 'Kerry is going to make you mad, you know, it is not the sensible idea to have relationship with her.'

'I know.'

'Still, I think it is understandable in ways I think I know. If perhaps my sexuality were not a corpse I might find myself attracted to such a one as Kerry, in spite of her perversities and stupidities.'

'You mean you fancy her?' I asked, incredulous.

'Yes, yes, this is very funny, I think. You see what I mean, Juliet, you better watch out or you turn into green monster completely very soon.'

The following evening Kerry was out until very late. I was lying in bed, unable to sleep, when I heard her come in and go into Billy's room. I fretted for hours, turning into a green monster, completely.

I was appalled at my feelings, and shame made me keep a check on myself. Also Kerry would laugh at me when I showed signs of jealous sulking. I even became jealous of Freyja, the kitten, whom Kerry would insist sleep with us in my bed. Freyja would choose to lie between us, and Kerry would not allow her to be moved. I knew my feelings were completely irrational and this bothered me. Kerry laughed, saying I was mad to put so much faith in rationality; it was really so frail a thing. The kitten would climb around Kerry's body, looking for an acceptable wallow, pawing away at her, nudging her with her little face, pushing into Kerry's flesh with her velvet feet. It was as though she couldn't ever get close enough to Kerry and looking at her doing this one night, while Kerry tried to sleep, I felt complete empathy for the kitten; that was exactly what I felt about Kerry. I could never get close enough to her.

For months we were completely immersed in one another and I believe that for a while at least, Kerry believed that she was going to be faithful, regarding our love as some sort of safety blanket, or a cradle that would keep us safe for ever.

She would dress me up, put make-up on my face, and we would go out, believing ourselves to be the bee's knees. There was a period of about two months when we went dancing every weekend, to a night club, to one of the gay clubs perhaps, or to Glasgow's only reggae joint. Kerry loved to dance. She had no inhibition and would often clear a space around her on the dance floor and have a gaggle of admirers watching her, clapping and cheering. Sometimes she and Billy would dance together, raunchy dancing, simulating sex acts and turning their hips into gyrating drills.

Due to these late nights we would spend whole days in bed. We talked about the sciences a lot, particularly physics and astronomy. Kerry was entirely ignorant but she began reading popular science books and asking endless questions. She greeted my explanations with gasps and cries of 'No!' or 'Oh my God, it's all too beautiful to be true – say that again about the event horizon.'

Prior to this Kerry had divided people into Canine or Feline. 'I got it from a Scott Fitzgerald book,' she explained. Sometimes the categories would become Shark or Dolphin, and everyone Kerry met would be placed in one of these camps. Now her categories changed entirely.

'Canine and Feline is too gendered somehow,' she complained, 'and Shark or Dolphin is a bit extreme, no, people are either Waves or Particles, that's it absolutely. I'm a wave and you, Juliet, you are a particle.'

'I thought that the whole point is that we're all Wavicles,' I said.

One night she asked me how much I loved her. I thought for a while.

'I love you all the way to the red-shift.'

'How far is that?'

'It's as far as it goes and getting further every second, it's the end of the universe and it's growing all the time.'

'Wow. I hope you mean that.'

During those long hours in bed, we told each other about our lives before we met and hearing Kerry humorously enumerate her many sexual encounters caused me jealous feelings; the most absurd jealousy in the world, that of the past. Kerry did not share these feelings, but then my past paled into innocent insignificance in comparison with hers. Nevertheless she loved to hear about Melissa, and the games Edgar, Benedick, Helena and I had played with our friends when children. Games that Kerry called Proto-sexual.

My jealousy of her past fuelled a possessiveness towards her present. She's always been promiscuous, I thought, she does what she wants when she wants, she isn't going to change for me. I waited for her to be unfaithful.

The first time, I caught her red-handed. I went back to the flat earlier than usual one afternoon because my classes had been cancelled. I heard low voices from Kerry/Billy's room, one of them Kerry's and for some reason I didn't knock, as we all usually did, I just walked in.

Kerry was lying on her bed, naked, and her legs open. Billy was sitting on the chair, wanking furiously. He groaned when I entered and pulled a cushion over his head. Kerry sat up and crossed her legs.

'Now, this is exactly what it seems, Juliet. Billy is having a wank and I, generously, was giving him some visual stim-ulation. It isn't being unfaithful ... he hasn't touched me, I swear.'

I laughed. Kerry was very drunk and she had this habit, when she was very drunk of talking in a terribly precise way, clipped vowel sounds like a sort of Irish Celia Johnson. It was very funny. You could tell how drunk she was by how she talked. She looked utterly ridiculous, terribly pert, holding her mouth very carefully in a face that seemed to be gathering itself together by some incredible act of will. She looked like an awful sprite of some sort, some naked and utterly malignant sprite. I hated her.

'I don't give a shit if he fucks you from here to kingdom come.' I snatched the kitten from where it was peacefully sleeping on the radiator and walked out.

'Oh, don't be such a stern-faced cow. Billy, put your clothes on, and let's go into the living room and all get drunk,' Kerry said, hastily putting on her dressing gown and following me out of the room and into my bedroom. I put the kitten on to my bed, and she instantly scampered off and away back into Billy's room, that den of iniquity.

'Don't be like this, please don't be like this. I'm sorry,' Kerry wailed.

'Have you been doing that all along?'

'No, this is the first time I swear, I'm totally and utterly out of my head.'

'I know, and don't think that makes it any better, I hate your drunkenness.'

Billy poked his head round the door. 'Er, I juss wanna say I never touched her, yer honour.'

When I woke up the following morning I went into the kitchen and did not make Kerry a cup of coffee as I usually did but stayed drinking on my own, until she surfaced, looking contrite.

Then we talked more calmly, but I was shocked by the nature, not just the fact, of her infidelity. Kerry laughed and indignantly told me that if I thought for a minute about what I had done with my brothers it wouldn't seem so odd that she could 'show Billy hers, while he did his own'.

'Yes, but we were children, Kerry.'

'Oh,' snarled Kerry, 'I don't believe in this separation between childhood and adulthood, it was all just invented, you know. We're all people, only there are smaller and more vulnerable people, with less empirical experience.'

The summer came and Kerry stayed in Glasgow working at War and Pizza. We wrote to each other and talked regularly on the phone. She also came to London briefly and met my family for the first time. Everyone really took to her and Edgar, of course, flirted with her. I wasn't jealous, perhaps because Kerry did not flirt back, instead she seemed rather shy of him. I questioned her about this and she shrugged and said that he was a bit manic. Coming from her, this could only make me laugh.

I interrogated her a lot about possible infidelities whilst I had been away. She protested innocence in a bored, resigned way.

Kerry's final year at drama school began. She was cast as Juliet in the big Shakespeare production that the third-year acting students did each year. We all went to the first night. When she walked on to the stage for her first scene she looked like a child. I fought against my emotions during the whole play. I was distressed by seeing her loving Romeo on the stage. I wanted her to come down and over to me, to where I was sitting and to say, in language as beautiful as that she was speaking on stage, that she loved me, that she would die for me. She lay still on the stage for a long time, dead. I wondered what she was thinking. Whether she was thinking of me. There was a huge round of applause at the end. Kerry looked humble and very sweet as she took her bows, holding Romeo's hand, and gazing adoringly out into the audience.

Waiting for her afterwards in the bar, I felt immensely proud of her, everyone was saying how good she had been. I wanted to be on my own with her, but of course Kerry had other ideas. We went in a crowd to War and Pizza. We sat at the largest table, with another pulled in to join it.

Kerry ordered a vast amount of food, drank a couple of glasses of wine before it arrived, took one mouthful when it did, and then leant her head on a pile of sandbags and fell asleep. Billy laughed and went to wake her.

No, leave her, I thought.

'No, leave her,' said Petruchio.

Kerry went to Ireland to visit her grandmother, who was ill, when the play's run was over. She was worried about leaving the kitten behind and begged me to make sure that Freyja was looked after and 'loved to tiny little pieces'. She said she was afraid Petruchio would do something terrible.

'Don't be silly, he would never do anything like that. He's only teasing you, winding you up, he's really quite fond of Freyja now.' But just as Kerry was leaving the flat to go to the airport, Petruchio gave Kerry a frightening grimace.

'Now at last is my chance to introduce the kitten to the decay particle.' Kerry threw a cushion at him.

Petruchio insisted on calling Freyja Schrödinger whenever Kerry was in earshot, but once I heard him in the living room, late one night, padding about making tea.

'Do you want some milk, Freyja?' I heard him ask politely. I went through in time to see him bending down with a saucer of milk, Freyja looking up at him in wonder.

The cat was never quite so fixated on Kerry again, after that first desertion. And shortly after it Kerry compounded her treachery by taking her to the vet to be neutered. I had won my argument against Kerry's sentimental desire for more kittens. After a few days of demonstrable misery and pain, Freyja cheered up again but was now promiscuous with her attentions and, in that peevish way cats have, seemed to become more devoted to the one person who was not in the slightest bit interest: Petruchio. This seemed to please him in some way, although Freyja was never permitted to sit on his lap and Petruchio's was the only room that was barred to Freyja. She would spend hours sitting outside his door, every now and then giving a plaintive cry. Petruchio would not relent. He would sometimes address the cat in a civil manner but he never, to my knowledge, touched her, let alone picked her up or petted her in any way.

When Kerry returned, she announced that she was going to give up smoking.

'I bet you canna,' said Billy.

'I bet you I can,' retorted Kerry, 'what d'you wanna bet?'

We were sitting round the living room, on a bored Saturday afternoon. Billy, Kerry, Chris and myself.

'If you smoke you have to do a strip tease, how about that for a bet?' said Chris.

'Yeah, man,' said Billy, 'aye, spot on, we'll bet you a strip tease that you'll no stop smoking.'

'OK,' said Kerry. 'Fine. I know I'm not going to smoke, so that's OK, isn't it?'

Kerry lasted only three days. Billy and Chris constantly nagged her about the strip, teasing her about welshing on her bet. Kerry would insist that no time had been specified and that when she was 106 she would strip for them. I also made several teasing comments about welshing on bets.

I was with Chris in the living room one evening watching TV, when Kerry and Billy burst into the flat with carrier bags of booze including two bottles of champagne.

'We've been kicked out of the next production,' Billy announced. 'Fuck's sake, man, it's serious news.' He burst out laughing. Kerry opened the champagne.

'It's true,' she said delightedly, 'we're not going to be cast in the musical, we're in serious disgrace and,' she mimicked, '"we're jolly lucky not to have been asked to leave".'

'What happened?' Chris asked. 'What have you done?'

'We got caught smoking dope in the dressing room, that's all. I don't give a shit about the fucking musical. Rumour has it it's *Salad Days* anyway.'

Kerry poured us each a glass of champagne, ordered Billy

to 'put the Pistols on', and the two started pogoing glee-fully.

'Oh, well,' said Chris, 'I guess it's a party.' And Petruchio came in at that point and helped himself to a pint glass of champagne.

It became a story, that party. A story that we all told each other every now and then, all except Kerry. It was one story I never heard her tell about herself and she never discussed it with us again. Not after her immediate explanation of why it had happened, when, like a Brechtian actor, she stood outside herself, commenting on the action – 'Look, it's like this, you see, like this, I'm doing this, because of this, that and the other'. It was extraordinary, watching her calmly dissect with great perspicacity what had, moments ago, been her own wild, bizarre behaviour. She became so possessed by ideas, by the idea of a thing, that she could act out almost anything in her extreme explorations.

This is what happened: Kerry got very drunk very quickly. We all danced a bit as I remember, and then Billy started making little lines of speed for us all. We tossed a coin and Petruchio lost and had to go out and buy more champagne. Kerry and Billy were high as kites and infested us with their manic jollity. Kerry leapt up and took hold of a champagne bottle.

'I know,' she said, 'I'll do that strip I owe you. I'm in the mood.'

'Ow, wow, man, far out ...' Billy said, while Chris started to beat his hand on the coffee table and leer and shout, 'Yeah, yeah, a strip, a strip.'

'Well, hold on then, I must prepare,' and she disappeared with the bottle of champagne and a glass into the bathroom. Billy and Chris faffed around with lights, Chris fetching spots and filters from his room, and together they constructed a stage for Kerry out of the table. Petruchio arrived back with more champagne. He said he did not believe Kerry would do a strip, she was having us on.

Billy banged on the bathroom door: 'Come on, wee man, we're all waiting on ye.'

'Won't be long.'

Kerry appeared. She seemed to have done nothing to herself to warrant all that time in the bathroom. She was still wearing the same clothes and a very drunken and secretive smile on her face.

She stood up on the table, which was strategically positioned underneath the large mirror that almost covered one wall. Chris put on some music, I forgot what now, and Kerry started to dance. She had her back to us, making gentle swaying movements with her hips as she slipped her leggings off; she turned round wearing only her socks and long T-shirt and started thrusting her pelvis around quite convincingly. She sat down and stretched her legs along the table. The boys were cat-calling and jeering, except Petruchio who watched silently with a sardonic expression. Kerry took her socks off and threw them into her audience. Chris and Billy screamed for more. She stood up and took her pants off, spun them round her finger and sent them whizzing across the room. Billy made a leap for them and I was watching him rubbing them over his face, making incredibly silly faces, when all of a sudden he froze. I turned and saw Kerry kneeling down on the table with her back to us. I stared at her reflection in the mirror.

She had slipped her top off and her breasts and stomach were covered in blood. She stood up, turned round and came towards us, then she lay down on the table, like a sacrifice. I noticed that she was shaking from head to foot.

Christ laughed nervously and went towards her and put his finger out and scooped up some blood.

71

'It's make-up,' he said, but he looked at his finger and shrunk away from Kerry.

Billy started to scream, 'For fuck's sake, man, what's happening, who the fuck did that te ye, what's going on?'

. Freyja, who had been sleeping in the corner, jumped up and scarpered out of the room when Billy shouted, slinking back in only a few moments later.

Kerry, meanwhile, suddenly ran from the room and to the bathroom, locking it behind her.

'Oh, what's she playing at now?' Chris snapped.

He addressed this question to me, as if I should have any insight into Kerry's unbelievable behaviour. Billy went to the bathroom door and tried to coax Kerry out. Chris, Petruchio and I joined him in a long petition outside the bathroom.

Eventually she told us she would come out if we absolutely promised that we wouldn't do anything, and she meant *anything*, about it.

'You have to swear that you won't call a doctor to take me to the hospital.'

We promised on our lives, on our mother's lives, and Billy cheerfully offered up his anatomy. 'For fuck's sake, man, if I break my promise, I'll cut my dick off and gie it to youz on a plate served up wi' neeps and tatties, cross my heart and hope to die.'

Kerry came out sheepishly, wrapped in her dressing gown. 'You promised, guys, no fucking hospitals. I'll kill you if you break your promise.'

Billy was staring at the blood seeping through Kerry's gown.

'It doesn't hurt,' she said, and Billy started to cry.

'Why, Kerry? What the fuck did you do that for?' Chris was muttering. 'Fucking hell, it was all a joke, wasn't it?'

'Yes,' said Kerry, 'exactly, what's the big deal, it was all a joke, my little wheeze.' She looked at her chest and laughed. 'This is nothing, really. Most girls do this, according to Simone de Beauvoir. It's internalised oppression. Strangely, it always feels incredibly liberating.'

I wanted to slap her so badly my hand hurt. I took hold of her arm and led her into my bedroom. Petruchio followed us with a bowl of hot water, cotton wool and Dettol which he placed on my dressing table and silently left. Kerry took off her dressing gown and I started to clean her up. There were hundreds and hundreds of tiny little cuts criss-crossing across her torso. They were, I noticed, particularly savage around her belly button and breasts but none of them were very deep, although they had produced a spectacular amount of blood.

Kerry's face remained expressionless throughout my none-too-gentle clean-up operation. I wondered to myself what I would have done had Kerry needed stitches. Would I have broken my promise? There was no way I would have stitched her up myself, but maybe Petruchio ... he had been a doctor, after all.

'That was a terrible thing to do,' I said at last.

'Why?' she snapped. 'They deserved it.'

'Why did they deserve it?'

'I will not be the object of their disgusting prurience, if there's one thing in the world that I loathe and detest, it's prurience.'

The others were making tea and putting the living room in order when we returned. When Kerry sat down, she began to cry.

We asked her what the matter was, over and over again. Eventually she stopped crying and her face, which had been shrivelled and shrunken with angry pain, became smooth and peaceful again.

'I'm sorry, I don't know what came over me.'

No one spoke. I was staring at her in wonder and disbelief. She had changed so totally from one moment to the next. She was suddenly fine again, chatty, inconsequential. She continued in the same mild, warm voice. 'Hey, I'm sorry, guys, I didn't mean to scare you.'

I was angry, but when I spoke my voice was sweet and ingratiating. 'Kerry, you need help, you can't do things like that. Petruchio, do you think that Kerry might be mentally ill?'

'Hah, mentally ill! What is this mental illness? It is the human species, that's what it is. Consciousness itself is a mental fucking illness.'

'What do you mean mentally ill, you bitch.' Kerry was all fired up again. 'You think you're so smart and cool, don't you, stuck-up English cow, you treat me as though I were some kind of dirty joke. You, piss me off, all of you.' She turned her spiteful face on to the others. 'You are all such complete shits with your stupid hypocrisy because you've got no respect, no respect whatsoever, you all detest me. Nothing I can do will ever change that, you hate me, hate hate hate me, hate and disrespect.'

'That's not true, wee man.' Billy was vehement. 'Fuck, I respect you, man, you're fucking wild, man, you're my best mate.'

'It's not true,' Chris repeated tiredly, 'you're paranoid, Kerry, we are your friends.'

'It's true for me,' said Petruchio, 'of course, because I am a Catholic but I think absolutely it is on the symbolic level only that I detest you, Kerry, because personally, as an actual human being, I not in the least detest you, you are very amusing.'

'Do you promise that you don't hate me?'

'I do not hate you. *Gurio su Dio.*' Petruchio placed his index finger on his mouth diagonally and kissed it.

'Kerry, nobody hates you but I really need to chill out on

my own for a while – I'm going to my room.' Chris left, shaking his head sadly as he went.

Billy hugged Kerry. 'I love you, wee man, mad as you are but ...' and he and Petruchio left and I was alone with her. She grinned at me.

'In Japan they cut their fingers off for honour, self mutilation is an honourable thing. It's only cultural – this condemnation and misunderstanding.'

I didn't say anything, but I was thinking that what with Kerry and her slashing hysteria, Petruchio and his Valium, Chris and Christine and their hocus pocus, I was living with a bunch of nutters. Only Billy, with his somehow benign, testosterone-governed responses, seemed remotely normal.

'I'm sorry about what I said earlier,' Kerry continued, 'I don't think you're stuck up, and you can't help being English, can you?'

I smiled at her but I felt anxious and worried. Kerry's 'wild-child' behaviour had always slightly revolted me, and I found it just didn't match up to the other Kerry that I had known; the earnest, insightful Kerry wittering on about Joan Miro or Language Poetry, the Wooster Group or Fassbinder films with enough enthusiasm and delight to interest even me at times.

'Kerry,' I asked, 'if you have read about these things in Simone de Beauvoir, why do you have to do them?'

'I'm just playing, I suppose,' she replied.

Playing. Sometimes I think I hate Kerry but, deeper down, I know that if only emotions were so black and white, things might be easier. I see her again as she was when I first saw her, imp-like, seated at the coffee table. How could I possibly have known then what she was to become, what, perhaps, it was her destiny to be? Destiny. How comforting that concept is, when you are faced with the emptiness of the utterly random. It is easier to believe that things could not have been otherwise. That our choices are predetermined. That way there is order. What a pity that I can't believe it. What a pity that it is bollocks. Kerry was not destined for anything. Shit happens.

Kerry's striptease shook me enough to make me question my involvement with her, the shock great enough for my sexual passion for her to cool – how could I fancy her when her body was a Jackson Pollock of scratches and cuts?

The weeks following were uncommonly quiet. Having been banned from the musical production, Kerry had a lot of time to herself and she told me that she was spending her days in the Mitchell Library. I didn't believe her. In my mind she was far more likely to be out drinking or having sex with someone than sitting quietly in a library reading. She said that she wanted to get to the bottom of this quantum stuff and she would come home with a great many questions for me, about wave-particle duality, about possible-worlds theory, about Schrödinger.

'He, the little minx, was quite a womaniser, Juliet, I read that today – they've got so many books there, I wish I could live there, I wish I could live in the Mitchell Library, there is so much out there to be learned. Now, tell me about spinning particles again.'

'I don't know, I'm not a bloody physicist.'

She went on to tell me more about Schrödinger's private life; it seems she spent more time in the biographical section of the library than the scientific.

The Easter holiday came and went. I stayed in Glasgow and I managed to catch up on almost a term's work, a term in which I had been asked by my supervisor to 'reconsider my commitment to veterinary science'. Kerry laughed when I told her and told me to 'reconsider indeed' and to work hard to make sure that I got a job afterwards. She was going to have to live off my earnings when she was a struggling actress. I entertained ideas about Kerry and me living in some idyllic Yorkshire cottage, surrounded by hills and animals and kind villagers.

The summer term began and there was a frantic atmosphere among Kerry's year at the drama school; everyone was writing letters and sending photos out.

Petruchio surprised us all one day by buying a car, a clapped-out old Saab. He said he wanted to see some of the so-called beauty Scotland had to offer and for a few weekends we all piled into the car and went off to Loch Lomond, Fort William, or Glen Coe for days. Petruchio seemed to enjoy having the car and the Big Daddy status it conferred on him, but though the rest of us would absorb these days in the country with relish, like ponies coming out of the pit and on to the mountain side, Petruchio sneered at our Romanticism and said he found the landscape sentimental, savage and oppressive.

He said this at Glen Coe, where we climbed around on the rocks and had a picnic. Billy had been telling us about the massacre.

Kerry stood up and looked around her sadly.

Christine said, 'There *is* an atmosphere here. It's in the very rocks and stones. It's a palpable atmosphere, can you feel it?'

'Yes,' said Chris and Billy.

'Bouff,' said Petruchio. 'Ridiculous. This place is gloomy, yes, it is Scotland of course, but this absurd subjectivity of yours. There is nothing in the rocks and stones but in your silly heads alone.'

'The American Indians don't think so,' I said. Edgar had often lectured me about the superiority of the Native Americans' consciousness, likewise the Aboriginal. This was in his one world/ethnic-clothing phase, in between the

77

decadence stage and becoming a Buddhist.

'They believe that events leave a trace, that places have essences and things.' Christine and Chris made approving noises while Petruchio gave me a disgusted sneer.

Auditions started. Several local directors came to the school to audition the final year for productions and Kerry came home after each one, very depressed, saying she had 'fucked up'. She also told me at that time that she wasn't sure she could bear being an actress, it was too humiliating.

'I'll turn into a monster if I stay in this profession, a horrible, fawning, frightened little monster.'

Then Kerry and Billy went together to audition for a production of Anouilh's *Antigone*. The day before the audition Kerry had found an old porcelain lavatory bowl on a skip outside the flat. She insisted on bringing it into the house.

'We can put it in the hall,' she said, 'for a laugh.'

Kerry had been looking for speeches to do at the audition but finding the lavatory bowl inspired her and she decided to write her own. She wrote a scene set in a bathroom where an actress is stuffing her face with chocolate while insisting that if she was thin she would get work.

Kerry took the lavatory to the audition, making Billy help her carry it. She ate three chocolate bars and drank a pint of water during the speech and she finished by sticking her fingers down her throat and throwing up into the bowl, which was propped up by layers of newspaper.

She got the job. Her first professional role with an Equity card. She would start rehearsing at the beginning of July and the play would open in Cumbernauld, then go to the Edinburgh Festival and then a small, fairly local tour.

Kerry started rehearsals a week before the end of term. She changed almost as soon as her wild celebrations at getting the part had run their course from ecstasy to headache after a binge lasting several days and nights. She became serious, consistently serious. There was no hysteria, no playfulness, no pranks, no story-telling, none of her exuberant explosions of anger, misery, or ecstasy. She was intense and 'frighteningly cognitive' as Petruchio put it, and it was at this time that Petruchio and Kerry started to become close.

I came home one evening to find what I thought was an empty flat and then I heard voices, very low, concentrated voices coming from Petruchio's room. About half an hour later Kerry came out.

'I've been talking to Petruchio about the play and philosophy and things.'

'How nice,' I snapped, hating the play and philosophy and all those things which took Kerry away from me.

Antigone opened. Kerry was so still, so sure of everything. I felt overpowered by her performance and watched with awe while she demonically possessed the stage with her anger.

When I saw her again in the bar, she was back to her own animated, ignoble Kerry. She accepted praise graciously, and I noticed her eyes darting around the bar, clocking who was there. The agent we had spoken to in the bar on Great Western Road, looking even more superior than when I had first met him, was sitting in a corner of the bar talking to a minor Scottish celebrity. Everyone was talking about how this agent and his wife were setting up a branch of their agency in Glasgow; not only that but that the wife, Sophie, was also co-producing a film that would be made in Scotland, and that she would soon be casting.

When we left the bar, Geoffrey Daniels smiled at Kerry and gave her the thumbs up. I noticed that she did not smile, but she stared back at him looking again exactly as she had done on stage.

'You should have gone over, wee man, said hello.' Billy nudged her.

'Why? I'm not going to creep around poxy agents, if he's got something to say he can say it.'

We drove back to Glasgow and went to War and Pizza: Billy, Chris and Christine, Petruchio and other members of the cast and their mates. About twenty-five of us in all, we soon took over the restaurant. Kerry, the man who had played Creon, the director, Petruchio, and myself were seated at the end of one table.

'Well, Kerry,' said Petruchio, 'you are, of course, very good as the martyr. You, as Creon says, will not be satisfied until you have cosy tea party with death and destruction.'

'Destiny,' said Kerry, 'and yes, you're absolutely right there.' She laughed rather wildly and punched Petruchio on the back. 'You thought I was good though, didn't you? Admit it.'

'Of course I may admit it, but it's easy for you, I think.'

Kerry was on top form that night; she was radiant, drunk with her own ability and the beauty of it having been recognised. She didn't put a foot wrong, gliding through the evening as Kerry at her very best, most charming, most funny, everyone loved her and she gave everyone the same attentive energy. The same smiles, the same radiant eyes gazed into everyone's eyes equally and I sat miserable throughout the meal because I was not special, because for me at that table, no one else really existed but Kerry, and because she did not feel the same about me.

I smoked about twenty cigarettes during the meal and by the time we left I had a splitting headache. In the taxi on the way home I decided that I was going to give up smoking.

I hardly saw Kerry for the next few weeks. She was in Edinburgh doing the show and, after her first night, I went to London and then to France for a week, where my parents had rented a house for the summer. Edgar and Helena were both there too and it was a good week, marred only slightly by some of Edgar's more erratic behaviour. He was trying to raise money for his film at the time and was constantly on his mobile phone, hustling with producers and financiers. Though he was thirty-one, he still had tantrums and sometimes after these phone calls he would fly into a rage, or go into a deep sulk, which affected us all. He reminded me sometimes of Kerry and this made me slightly uneasy.

When I got back to Glasgow, Petruchio was slouching around in his dressing gown, clutching a bottle of Valium and popping them like Smarties. He stayed like that for about a week, not going to work, spending most of the time in his room with the lights off, shuffling into the kitchen every now and then to make a cup of tea and glare disgustedly at anyone who happened to be about.

Chris was on a high, having just got a job at the Lyceum in Edinburgh, playing Jimmy Porter in *Look Back in Anger*. The idea of 'hippie Chris' playing 'the angry young wanker' made Kerry shriek with laughter, though not when Chris was in earshot.

I was managing not to smoke, but had resorted several times to a Valium from Petruchio and I was also rather compulsively reading anti-smoking literature.

During Kerry's last week in Edinburgh I went across to see the show again. We went for a walk in the afternoon and passed the Caledonian Hotel.

'I've always wanted to spend the night there, why don't we, Juliet? Why don't we book a room for tonight – oh go on, let's, I know it's crazy and extravagant but let's.'

It was a sunny day, my mood was good and I didn't need much persuasion. We booked a room and continued our walk, feeling very grand and rather naughty. I did have one nasty fleeting thought about Kerry's escapade at the Holiday Inn in Glasgow, but I banished this from my mind. Kerry's past had a capacity to ruin my present but, as she and I walked arm in arm through the festival crowds, my jealousy waned as the security of having her all to myself pervaded. I was, after all, special to Kerry, I wasn't one of her one-night stands, one of her messing arounds.

Kerry's performance that night was exactly the same as it had been on the first night. How do they do that? I wondered, how do actors repeat stuff like that night after night? Don't they get bored?

We went to the hotel and had drinks in the bar. Kerry made up stories about the other customers. Whole stories about who they were and why they were here at the Caledonian Hotel. It was a great night. Sometimes I look on that night as my last night of serenity.

We made love and then watched Sky TV and fell asleep with it still on. When I woke at about ten thirty, Kerry was sitting up reading *Asimov's New Guide to Science*. The phone rang. It was Billy with an urgent message for Kerry to phone the agent Sophie Daniels who had been to see *Antigone*.

'This isn't a joke, is it, Billy, you're not taking the piss?'

This was the sort of joke the drama students were wont to play on each other, toying with each other's vanity and insecurity at once, but satisfied that Billy was for real, Kerry hung up on him and phoned the agent. There were two phones, one either side of the bed and Kerry motioned to me to pick up the other receiver so that I could listen.

'Hello, could I speak to Sophie Daniels, please?'

'Yes, who's calling?'

'Um, Kerry Riordan.'

'Hold the line.'

Kerry squealed, 'Oh fuck, oh, Juliet, what am I going to do?'

'Hello, Kerry, darling, thanks for getting back to me.' A smooth-as-honey voice purred down the phone. I felt jealous.

'Look, I saw you in *Antigone* last week and I have to tell you I thought you were absolutely brilliant, I mean really, one of the most moving performances I've seen for I don't know how long. Now look, darling, have you got an agent?'

'No.'

Sophie's voice was so utterly 'actressy' that I wondered whether this was a joke after all. I tried to think whether I had heard that voice before, whether it was possible Billy had given Kerry a fake number and some drama student was giving her their 'agent' over the phone. The voice purred on.

'I would really like to represent you, Kerry, and there's a film that I want you to be seen for straight away. Is there any chance that you could come down to London this week? We are seeing people in Scotland too, but not for a few weeks and I would really like the director to meet you ASAP.'

Kerry explained that she had another three performances in Edinburgh and then a week off before they went on tour. They arranged to meet in London the following Wednesday.

'That's wonderful, darling, and, listen, I have a really good feeling about you, your performance was out-standing the other night ... you have this quality, it's almost spooky ...'

When Kerry put the phone down she laughed.

'God, talk about over the top, did you hear what she said to me?'

'Yes,' I said, 'she was truly and utterly vile. Who is she, for God's sake, some toady little beast from Roedean who slipped into a job in an agency after leaving her finishing school in Switzerland?'

'No,' said Kerry, suddenly earnest, 'she's really clever, Juliet, they both are, they met at Oxford and ...'

'Fell in love, married, became agents, became richer ever after.'

'Oh, you're so fucking cynical. OK, she was over the top but it was nice things she was saying and I think you are really hateful laughing like that.'

'It was you who laughed, not me,' I protested. Kerry's face was about to crumple into tears, so I took hold of her. Come on, let's celebrate, not fight, you've got an agent, that's the important thing.'

'Yes, and they are like the very tops, you know.' Her voice was excited, but she looked terribly uncertain and I thought how ridiculously fragile she was.

Kerry took a train to London the following Tuesday. She was going to stay with my parents for one, possibly two nights, depending on what Sophie had arranged for her. We had toyed with the idea of me going down too, but decided against it. I could ill-afford the fare, especially since our night of luxury in Edinburgh, and Kerry was going to be busy anyway. She phoned me that night from my parents'. She sounded as high as a kite.

'I've been talking to your mother about soufflés and pirouettes and to your father about John Donne – your parents are so cool, Juliet, this house, everything, it's sort of 'brown' – do you know what I mean? Warm, leathery, pipe-tobaccoey brown.'

Kerry often coloured people and places, she had to make a metaphor of everything. But I did know what she meant. When I tried to see my family and home as she might, it was a liberal 'brown' paradise with a touch of glamour thrown in.

I thought about her almost all the time she was away. On the Wednesday I wondered how she was getting on at the agents, and worried when it got later and later and she didn't phone. By lunchtime on the Thursday, when I still hadn't heard from her, I phoned my parents. They said that Kerry had left that morning, her train should be in Glasgow by the evening.

But Kerry did not turn up or phone and by the Saturday afternoon I was frantic and ready to phone the police. Chris and Petruchio restrained me from doing so.

'Fuck's sake, Juliet, we all know how unreliable Kerry is, she'll turn up right as rain on Sunday night – she has to, she's a show to do on Monday.'

Chris was right. At about ten-thirty on Sunday night she arrived back, pale and feverishly excited. We went into my room and she sat cross-legged on the bed.

'Don't be cross with me, *please* don't be cross with me. I've had the most amazing time.'

She had gone to the agents' smart Soho office. There, Sophie had gushed over her for several minutes before becoming business-like.

'I think you are absolutely perfect for a part in this film I'm co-producing in Scotland and I want you to meet the director. Thing is, he's not around until Friday – can you stay till then?'

Kerry shrugged and nodded and Sophie continued, advising Kerry on how best to spend her time in London, namely by getting some flash photographs taken and buying a suitable outfit to wear for her meeting with the director.

'Something floaty and childish. You have a frail and vulnerable quality that we must exploit to the max.'

Geoffrey appeared at that point, greeted her like a long-lost friend and invited her round to their house for dinner that night.

Kerry went shopping and then back to my parents'. She dressed and took a cab to Sophie and Geoffrey's house in Kensington. Dinner was fine, she said, and her voice seemed to drop an octave as she continued with her tale.

'When I left your parent's house the next morning I fully intended to go to the station and get the train to Glasgow. I had decided that I didn't want to meet the director after all – I'm sort of reconsidering my choice of career – but I just wandered around without being really aware of what I was doing or where I was going, until I realised that I'd missed the train and then I got really drunk and I ended up – you won't believe it, Juliet – I ended up sleeping rough and *surviving* the next two nights. I just slept rough, I did it, I really did it.'

'You're completely nuts,' I said, 'so ... you didn't go and meet the director?'

'Ah well, yes I did, actually. It was something to do, but I fucked it up badly, I don't know why, I just did. I wasn't myself, I felt awful, as if I wasn't really there and ... well anyway, it didn't go very well, shall we say. I don't think I can be an actor – I can't bear auditions, they make me ill, truly and utterly ill.'

'And how did Sophie respond to this – was she there? And I want to know more about the dinner at their place,' I interrupted.

'She was OK. Juliet, have you been listening to me, don't you realise I slept rough for all this time ... nobody could find me, nobody knew where I was – it was like I didn't exist or, no, I know what it was like, it was like I was a particle, an electron or photon or whatever and nobody could trace my movement – I was neither here nor there and now here I am and I survived!'

'You want a fucking medal? You want locking up in my opinion, certified, sectioned – what about me, didn't you think I might be worried?'

'No. You shouldn't have been anyway, you're not my sodding mother, Juliet.'

'Where did you sleep?'

Kerry continued rapturously, telling me that she had slept in quiet places, frightened of intruding on another's patch. She was scared, she said, almost all the time, but that was part of the fun – seeing what she could survive.

'I feel much stronger now, now I know how far down I can go. I can cope with anything now and I'll be all right.'

Kerry could be very convincing.

'So you're telling me that you dossed out in London, and then went to the audition ...'

'Casting,' Kerry corrected.

'And then you dossed out again.'

'True.'

Later, Kerry related her story to the others in the flat. I noticed that she was very dismissive whenever the agents were mentioned.

Kerry's tour started and she was away a lot; when she did get back to Glasgow for the night, it was late and I was asleep. I had a job doing some indexing for the veterinary school library, Chris had started rehearsals for what sounded like a particularly hideous production of *Look Back in Anger*, and Petruchio was still mooching around, not going into work and staying in bed most of the time. Chris, Billy and I had a flat conference on whether we should do something. Petruchio came in on this conference and padded over to the fridge.

'Petruchio,' said Chris, 'we're all really worried about you.'

'Yes, yes, well, worry about yourselves is better way to waste your time.'

'But you haven't been to work for about two weeks,' Chris persisted.

'I have sick leave.' He shuffled back to his room in his tartan slippers.

One morning I answered the phone to hear a familiar, silky smooth voice.

'I wonder, could I speak to Kerry Riordan, please?'

'She's not here.'

'Oh well, might I leave a message for her, it's Sophie Daniels from Dream Management, could you ask her to ring me as soon as she can?'

'Sure.'

'Thanks darling, by then.'

The first thing I said to Kerry when I saw her was, 'You never told me the agency was called Dream Management, that's truly awful.'

'It's not,' said Kerry, 'it's called Daniels and Daniels.'

'Well, Sophie phoned today and said Sophie Daniels from Dream Management.'

Kerry paused and then without expression said that she must have been joking. She didn't go near the phone that day but the following morning, early, I answered its persistent ring and it was Sophie again. I took the phone into my room where Kerry was slumbering.

'Hello,' she said sleepily and she took the phone and listened silently. I pretended to be looking for a vest. She grabbed a pen and notepad at one point and seemed to be taking details of something down. At last she just said, 'OK, goodbye then,' and put the phone down.

'What was that all about?' I demanded, all pretence of indifference gone.

'Just some bollocks about an audition in London on Monday.'

'Great, what for this time?'

'I'm not going so it doesn't matter.'

'But why?'

'It was *pornography*,' Kerry snarled viciously, and she pulled the covers over her head and turned her face to the wall.

The agent phoned again on Tuesday morning. Chris answered the call and when he gave Kerry the message that evening, he casually wagged his finger at her.

'You'll get yourself into trouble, Kerry. Sophie wants to know why you weren't at the auditions for the Lloyd's Bank commercial.'

'I thought you said it was pornography,' I said. Kerry looked at me witheringly, and raised her eyebrows.

'I did, yes.'

I wasn't aware of any other phone calls between Kerry and the agent but there must have been because we had one of our flat dinner parties around this time, with Christine doing the cooking as usual. I remember there were constant battles over the cat jumping up on the table while we ate. Petruchio had once refused to eat at the table because Freyja had been up on it and he had taken his food into his bedroom. This evening Petruchio won the day and the cat was locked in my room until after the meal. Kerry's sulk over this lasted longer than usual.

'It's not fair,' she said, 'Freyja is every bit as much a part of the flat as any of us, it's not fair to do this to her just because she can't speak and reason with you.'

'Oh, shut up, Kerry,' said Petruchio.

The conversation turned to agents and someone said how an actor they knew had been complaining that most of the work he got, he got for himself but the agent still took their ten percent.

'So why doesn't he do without an agent then, if he's getting all that work anyway?' demanded Kerry, and Billy replied, 'Well, you've got to hae an agent if you're an actor, man, huvn't ye?'

'No,' said Kerry vehemently, 'they're fucking bastard middle people, the most contemptible aspect of capitalism, they suck away the artist's blood, they live off artists like parasites. I haven't got an agent, not anymore, and I shan't ever have one either. We've had the death of the author and the death of the critic, well I'm waiting for the death of the fucking agent!'

Billy and Chris gasped.

'How come you're not with Sophie Daniels anymore – Kerry, what have you done?'

'I told them I wouldn't do adverts and they told me to go fuck myself, basically, so that's that. Do you know, Sophie actually said that I couldn't call myself an actress unless I did adverts – yuck, I'd rather give any ten percent I earn to the National Front than to those two,' she finished grumpily, and with a conviction that tapered off towards the end of the sentence.

'Why will ye no do adverts, wee man?' Billy asked.

'Because it's not the job I want to do, it's not acting, it's something else; listen, when young girls get stage struck and decide they want to be actresses, they are dreaming about playing Hedda Gabler, or Joan of Arc – and me, I was going to star in Margarethe von Trotta movies – but they are not dreaming of doing fucking bank commercials are they? To my mind nothing would be more boring and humiliating, I'd rather earn less money waitressing until some real acting came up, you know: drama, catharsis, art.'

The conversation put Kerry in a foul mood. When we had finished eating she went to release Freyja, who followed Kerry into the living room.

'Cats,' she announced, 'are a much finer species than ours. I think it would be much sadder if cats became extinct than humans.'

'But who would appreciate the cats?' drawled Petruchio.

'Oh, you probably *were* a cat in your last life,' said Christine, which was sure to make Kerry angry.

'Well, I must have done something really bad as a cat to have ended up as me,' she snarled and then went on another rant about how cats were superior to human beings because they didn't suffer from guilt – they fuck fifteen different toms in one night or they kill a mouse, so what? That's fine, they don't have to spend hours talking to their therapists about it, or boring their friends to tears about how they feel, or be treated like a slapper or a psychopath. She finished by saying that nothing she could have done as a cat could have been evil, since cats don't operate within a world where evil has any meaning.

'Evil is a concept, and cats don't have concepts. So fuck you and your stupid karmic recycling theory.'

Term started for me, now the only student in the flat. Sophie and Geoffrey Daniels arrived in Glasgow and were the big news of the day among the acting community in Scotland, who talked endlessly about the film Sophie was co-producing and casting. Everyone was writing to the new branch of their agency in Hope Street (appropriately enough), asking to be taken on by the dynamic duo.

The film was a contemporary vampire movie, set in Glasgow and the Highlands. Billy, Chris and, it seemed, the rest of Scotland, with the exception of Petruchio and myself, were going to audition. One night in the pub someone asked Kerry whether she was auditioning.

'I've already been seen for it. My tits were too small apparently.'

'What?' I demanded.

'That's what Sophie said, she said the director thought I was "divine" but my tits were too small.'

'I don't believe you,' I said.

'I swear that's what she said, she might have just been being bitchy, but that *is* what she told me and anyway, as you can all see, I haven't got the part.'

The lead roles in the film had been cast and had already caused a controversy. The male lead was warmly approved; one of Scotland's most famous actors returning from Hollywood; but the young girl, who was supposed to be from the Isle of Skye, was to be played by an English girl fresh out of RADA. Several other major roles had gone to English actors and this had outraged the nationalist wing of Scottish Equity. Actors of both sexes complained and bitched about this iniquitous casting. I don't know how many times someone whined on at me about how perfect they were for a role that had been given to some toffee-nosed Sassenach who couldn't do a Glasgow accent to save their lives.

Billy and Chris both got minor roles. Then the famous lead actor announced that he was to have an enormous party to celebrate his fiftieth birthday. It was to be a grand affair and a castle, one of the locations for the film, was to be used for the occasion. Everyone connected to the film was invited, which constituted a large proportion of the acting crowd I was now so associated with, and those not in the film were organising to go with those who were. It was to be a fancy dress party and the conversations mercifully changed from derision and self-pity to endless debates about what to go as, or how to get a ticket and what to go as.

Kerry was conspicuous in her lack of interest in the party, and she responded with such a stony 'drop dead' expression when anyone mentioned it to her that people grew wary and tried not to talk about it when she was around.

The change in her persisted. She was more consistent

than ever. Consistently quiet, consistently tense and irritable, consistently aloof. I got home from college one evening to find her lying on my bed, crying her heart out.

'What's the matter?' My concern made her cry even harder and she tried and failed to speak over her tears.

'I'm pregnant,' she wailed at last.

'What?'

She shook her head as if she couldn't bring herself to say the words again.

'Who is the father?'

She gave me a look of great exasperation and sighed. 'There isn't a father. There won't be a baby. I have to get it out of there.'

I was so angry. In spite of all my suspicions and accusations, I couldn't believe that Kerry could have deceived me, and was now telling me about it quite calmly, talking to me as if I was her sister or friend and not her lover, her spouse.

'Why did you deceive me, Kerry? You're a lying bitch. You're always going on about "truth" and "principles" but you're a liar ... a spineless, cowardly profligate, living beyond your emotional means. You're incapable of loyalty, you Judas.'

'I know,' she said, 'I hate myself,' and she started sobbing again.

'You really are a baleful opportunist, you react to the surface of events for instant gratification, grabbing like a little child, and when you later find yourself betrayed by your own lack of principle you weep and say you hate yourself.'

'Christ, Juliet,' she said, her voice suddenly normal and strong, 'that's bloody true as well.'

I sat down, exhausted. She cried softly and began to beat her lower abdomen with her fists. 'You've got to help me, Juliet – can't you get it out for me? I can't bear it, I can't bear it in there, I really am going mad, I won't survive this, and I can't go to hospital, I can't, please don't be angry with me, please just help me?'

'Oh, pull yourself together, you put it up there without any complaints so now you have to face the consequences. If you'd been faithful to me as you were supposed to be, this wouldn't have happened. You think of nothing but yourself, you're so selfish ... what about me?'

'What about you? You have no idea what I'm going through, how every moment is like hell, how I can't get out of myself, how I can't escape this fucking fish monster inside, this fucking parasite, I hate myself, don't you see I fucking hate this body, I fucking hate its stupid fucking cunt and womb and fucking fucking fucking little monster of a bastard fish monster inside ... it's going to kill me, I won't survive, I won't be a woman, I won't.' She was beating herself now all over, her head, her belly, her legs, whipping herself up into an hysterical state and hyperventilating. I waited until her thrashing subsided and then held on to her and made her take deep breaths.

'You hate me,' she muttered, 'you absolutely hate me – to the red-shift and back again.'

'Oh, don't be so stupid,' I said angrily and went to leave. She sat upright, suddenly completely energised.

'I'm sorry, Juliet, Juliet, please don't go, please please please please please don't go.'

The exact number of pleases stayed with me as I put on my coat and went to the door. I went first to the park and then to visit a friend from the veterinary school. We went for a drink and talked about our course, gossiped about the lecturers and discussed what kind of vets we wanted to be. I felt cool relief at the normality of it and I never once mentioned my tumultuous private life. This was my real life. I am clever, practical Juliet Porteus, I am going to be a vet.

I didn't return to the flat until after midnight. When I got back from college the next day, Kerry was watching TV. I asked her if she was OK and did she want a cup of tea? She said no thank you, and left the room. She barely spoke to me for the rest of that week, she stayed in bed all day and was out late every night. I heard her coming in while lying in bed seething with anger and pain. Was it all over between us?

On the Friday evening I wrote her a letter. It just read: I'm sorry. I love you.

Later that evening I went into my room and found the letter propped up on my pillow. Beneath my words she had written:

> Love is impatient; love is cruel and
> envious. Love is boastful, conceited
> and rude. It is selfish and quick to
> take offence. Love keeps a score of
> wrongs. It gloats over other men's
> sins and has contempt for the truth.
> Love retreats. Its faith, hope and
> endurance are easily exhausted.

Kerry wouldn't eat and didn't sleep. The only thing she would tell me was that she had arranged to have an abortion the following week at a clinic – not a proper hospital – the day after the big fancy dress party.

'That is, if I don't miscarry first, and believe me I am doing everything in my power to make that happen – can't you steal me some quinine from the university labs, Juliet?'

'Who is the father?' I demanded, time and time over.

'There isn't a father, don't be stupid, a father isn't a fuck, Juliet. There's no fucking baby, no fucking father.'

'It was Billy, wasn't it?'

'No.'

'It was Petruchio, wasn't it? You saw him as a challenge and you seduced him and that's why he's been so ill.'

'No.'

'It was that smarmy agent, wasn't it, and that's why you fell out with Sophie?'

'No.'

'You let that slime-ball agent fuck you.'

'Juliet, I don't *let* anyone fuck me. If I want a fuck then I *get* one. It isn't something I *let* people do to me. You sound just like my nana ... my nana always went on as though sex was something men did to women, and now you. It's so naff, Juliet ... like she always told me I shouldn't *give* myself to men. I never experienced myself as something I could give away, in fact, it always seemed like taking to me, especially with men – you give more to women maybe, with men you just take them inside you.'

I was not going to let Kerry divert me in this way.

'Give or take, I don't give a shit. You betrayed me – you don't have an ounce of loyalty or integrity in you.'

I tried questioning her again and became more and more frustrated by her lack of response or interest in my accusations. I became spiteful, like a cruel child poking a hedgehog with a stick, more and more aggressively the tighter it curls into its spiky ball. I was desperate to get through to her and, more and more, I resorted to sheer nastiness in my attempts, which failed anyway. This nastiness consisted of snide, mistrustful remarks, slurs about her promiscuity and infidelity. The more she refused me, the crueler I became, hating the methods she was forcing me to resort to, and so hating her the more. Why can't she just tell me and then things can be nice again? I thought, why must she make a big secret of it, who gives a toss who it is!

Petruchio, probably because he was the least likely, came to be my prime suspect. They had been spending a lot of time together, supposedly having conversations about physics and philosophy.

I tried blackmail, saying that I would tell everyone unless she told me. I was sure that the reason she didn't want anyone to know was that Petruchio would know he was the father and make a huge fuss about the abortion. Kerry told me that I was mad, everyone knew Petruchio hated sex.

'Ah yes, me thinks the pharmacologist doth protest too much,' I snarled at Kerry, 'he's probably lying like a Catholic priest, he's fucking more than the rest of us put together ... what's he like in bed, Kerry, what kind of a fuck is our Prince of Valium?'

Later that evening, we were all of us together eating an Indian carry-out, and I was wondering whether to tell everyone, to announce a new addition to our happy family. Kerry was nibbling a piece of nan bread, as if every crumb were an effort to swallow, and Petruchio, in his dressing gown and slippers, was eating twice as fast and as much as everyone else. I was just about to say something, to let the cat out of the bag, when there was a loud knock at the door. Kerry got up to answer it.

It was Mrs McNicol. Ours was a three-storey building with three flats; the top flat had been empty for the past couple of months and Mrs McNicol, who lived on the second floor, was the only other occupant. Her voice was one of those piercing Kelvinside drawls and we heard it tell Kerry that she was going to be away for a fortnight, staying with her sister in Stirling. Kerry was polite and sweet, and agreed to water her plants and feed her cat, though we all bore grudges against Mrs McNicol for the many complaints she made about the noise we made with our 'wild orgies' and against her cat because it was Freyja's public enemy number one.

97

That was on a Saturday night and Kerry's abortion was the following Thursday. Billy was still trying to persuade Kerry and me to go to the party with him, he was sure he could get us both in. Kerry said that she had better things to do than gatecrash starry parties.

'Likewise,' I said.

In spite of barely eating, Kerry continued drinking and the following day she spent in bed, groaning, while I nursed her hangover with vitamin C drinks and Lucozade. She got up only to go to the loo, and I took everything she needed into her. In between this fetching and carrying, I watched TV, had a bath and tidied up the living room. There were newspapers scattered over the living-room floor and, tidying them away, I saw that someone had been cutting out letters. I never enquired – there might be any number of reasons why any one of my crazy flatmates might be cutting up newspapers.

Another sleepless night with Kerry, who tossed and turned all night, and another Monday morning and a particularly important class I had to attend at 9 am.

Just as I was about to leave and was grabbing my books and papers and stuffing them into my bag, Kerry announced that she had changed her mind and might go to the party after all. It would take her mind off the abortion. I told her she was mad and I would talk to her later. When I got home that night, though, I was tired and nothing was mentioned. On Tuesday night Kerry said again that she was going to go to the party.

'What do you mean? You can't go, you're not well, you haven't eaten for days, you'll only get drunk and psychotic, and you've got to go under a general anaesthetic the next day. You can't go, I won't allow it.'

'Yeah, yeah, and who are you to allow or disallow anything?'

'Please, Kerry, it's because I care for you, you mustn't go.'

When I got up that Wednesday morning, Chris and Petruchio were in the living room. Petruchio was dressed and about to leave to go into the lab.

'Yes, yes,' he muttered when we expressed our surprise, 'I am better now and ready to commence my experiment on the dead cat. I shall work today and then perhaps go to this party with you tonight.'

'Oh yeah, nice one, man,' said Billy. He didn't seem at all surprised, while I was astonished that Petruchio, having been so ill, would suddenly want to go to a party. He hated parties.

When I got back to the flat that evening there was no one in. I went into Kerry's room and looked through the mass of books, papers, and scripts on her desk. I suppose I was looking for signs of further treachery and was disappointed in some perverse way to find nothing of interest. I sat on her bed and picked up one of her cuddly toys, a teddy she claimed she had been given at birth. Kerry's teddy, I thought bitterly, the Whore of Babylon has a teddy bear! On her bedside table there was a pile of books and a notepad. Its pages were all blank, but I turned it over and the back cover was splattered with words and doodles. She had drawn a box, about three by three inches, and inside this box in microscopic handwriting she had written: why why not why why not why why not why why not why why not why why not . . . until the box was full and only after the final why not was there a question mark.

The door opened so softly I did not hear it, neither did I hear Petruchio pad across the room. I did not notice him until he was right beside me. I looked up but made no sound of surprise and he sat down on the bed.

'You are, of course, obsessed with Kerry,' he said.

'Well you seem to be quite interested yourself.'

'Bouff, yes, of course, she is a most interesting person. But you, Juliet, you are above such silly stuff of sneaking through your lover's things, looking for betrayal. I think you should conquer this crush of yours, it is not dignified.'

The phone rang and I, glad to escape, went to answer it. It was my mother and we chatted for a while. When I put the phone down I glanced at the pad on which I had been scribbling. I had written: why why not why why not why why not why why not why why not why why not why why not?

Petruchio was in the kitchen making tea. He was tired, he said, and didn't want to go to the party after all. I felt relieved, and slightly smug, as if I had proved myself right on something. Then he suggested that we go to the cinema and I was happy to be out of the way of Kerry getting ready for the party.

She arrived home shortly after we had decided which film to see. She had been round at Christine's flat, borrowing some beads for her costume. She was going as a flapper and she had bought a beautiful beaded black dress from the antique market behind Byers Road. I watched her try the dress on and she charlestoned for me, with impressive speed.

Kerry seemed disappointed that I wasn't going to be around to help her dress and offer advice; she didn't know what shoes to wear or what exactly to do with her hair. She was so excited and bouncy that I almost wanted to stay, but then thoughts of how she had betrayed me hardened me against her. Petruchio was impatiently holding the door open and insisting we would be late so I kissed Kerry goodbye and, in a whisper, told her not to drink too much – she could die under the anaesthetic if she wasn't fit.

The film was OK and it was like old times being with

100

Petruchio. We stopped off in a bar on the way home for a drink but we were both tired so we left after one pint and came home. There was a pile of vomit in the entrance to the close. Petruchio stepped over it, holding his nose. There was no one in the flat. We went to bed and I slept immediately.

It must have been the deepest sleep of my life.

I woke at about eight with a heavy, dark feeling, a bleakness I had never felt so extremely before. Petruchio was suddenly by my bed with a cup of tea.

'Nobody is here,' he said.

'Where's Kerry?'

'She is not back from the party yet.'

'But . . .'

Petruchio shuffled out and I worried for a while before determining that Kerry would either be home soon and, no doubt, in a state, or she had gone to the abortion already. I heard Petruchio leave the flat and I dozed off again for about half an hour. When I woke the dark, bleak feeling was still there. I got up, poured the cold mug of tea down the sink, had a quick shower and washed my hair, hoping it would make me feel better. There was no milk in the fridge so I put my boots on and decided not to worry about Kerry. I took my purse from my bag and opened the front door of the flat. A noise, or something, made me turn toward the cupboard under the stairs. I took a step forwards, then stopped, seeing not believing.

A woman in a long white robe lying on the floor of the close. She was lying on her back, her head was turned towards one shoulder and her face was half-covered by her thick and long black hair. Sandalled, bloodstained feet peeped out from under the white robe. I stepped towards her, saying a tentative hello. There was no response. I

101

moved closer and lifted the hair from her face. She looked like an appallingly made-up actress in a 1970s Hammer vampire movie. Diaphanous skin, lips a scarlet red and heavy eye make up which was smudged. She was rigid. This was a body in rigor mortis. The woman was dead.

I didn't know what to do. I looked into the cupboard under the stairs and then out into the courtyard. There was no sign of anyone. I called up the stairs, but then I remembered that Mrs McNicol was away. I retreated back into the flat and closed the door.

Of course I realised that I would have to phone the police but I was overwhelmed with a need for a cigarette first. I had done pretty well with giving up but finding that tacky looking cadaver on my doorstep seemed a good enough reason to start again. I searched the flat for any cigarettes Kerry or Chris might have left lying around but there were none. By now I was shaking with my need and so I grabbed my bag and left the flat. As I opened the door, I looked again at the strange body lying in the dark of the close and then ran out into the street and down two doors to the shop. Walking back, I almost forgot about the dead woman in anticipation of my first draw on a much-pined-for Silk Cut but, as I turned into the close, I felt frightened again. Don't be silly, I thought, this is quite straightforward, a strange-looking woman is dead and you must phone the police. And then I saw that she was gone.

I felt an incredible anger. I rushed forward and ran into the courtyard. I shouted. There was no one around. A cat crept towards me, I turned back into the close. I opened the cupboard again. The mop, bucket and disinfectant were in their places. I called out again, I was frustrated and flustered and I had broken out into a sweat. Shit, I thought, I'm going mad, I must be going mad.

'What the hell is going on?' I shouted angrily. I walked

102

to the front of the close and looked up and down the street. Nothing. I walked back up the close and shouted again. A broad Glaswegian voice startled me.

'What's the problem then?'

It was the woman from the shop, standing in the entrance to the close. I looked down at the floor where the body had been. Then I looked at her.

'Nothing,' I said.

'You gave me a fright, shouting like that, I guess I'm a wee bit jumpy the day, what with that murder going on.'

'What murder?'

'Oh, some poor old soul from over the road there, woman in her eighties, they found her battered over the head in her front room, they took her TV and stuff. They say it happened about two this morning. I heard nothing myself.'

'No.'

'Och well, hearing you shouting made me think ... you know.'

'Oh no, it's nothing. I was just ...'

'Well, that's fine then. Cheerio, dear.'

I went back into the flat and poured myself a large whiskey. I tore open the packet of cigarettes, lit one and manically drew on it, but after only a few puffs I put it out, feeling sick and exhausted. Within moments though, I lit another one, which mercifully relieved me of the nausea that the first had caused.

My thoughts were all over the place, panicking around my brain but suddenly they collected themselves and became stuck like a record, the question they formed going round and round and round: did I or did I not see what I just saw?

I saw it. Seeing is a function of the human eye. My eye saw. But was what I saw really there? I smiled and relaxing a bit, took a sip of whiskey. I stubbed my cigarette out in the ashtray, noticing a long white stub, a menthol cigarette, rimmed with red lipstick. I looked at my watch. It was twenty-five to eleven.

I poured some more whiskey. Spots of red began to dance before my eyes. I threw the glass as hard as I could across the room. It hit the wall and smashed, liquid and glass flying out in all directions. The shock of the noise instantly calmed me. Now I know why people do that kind of thing, I thought, and I rested my head against the back of the sofa and closed my eyes. I began to laugh. I saw in my mind the woman in the long robe, her feet smeared with blood.

I heard the clink of keys, then the front door opening. Someone entered the room. I knew it was Petruchio, by the lugubrious way he closed the door and padded across the hall. We had all commented before on how his heaviness pervaded the entire flat as soon as he entered. It was something you could almost smell, something you believed you did smell. Maybe you did. Perhaps depression has its own pungent secretions, as does desire.

'You are ill,' he said, 'this is the laughter of an anarchist.'

'Hello, Petruchio, you're back early. Are you doing your experiments at home these days?'

'No,' he replied, in his usual deadpan manner, 'I am feeling not well again.'

He didn't look well. His always pallid complexion was now a darkish grey. There were huge shadows under his eyes and, when he leaned across the coffee table to pick up my mug, his breath had a bitter, metallic smell. He made us both a cup of coffee.

'Today I shall sleep. You, by the way, are looking very silly this morning. Why do you have whiskey and cigarettes?'

He looked very kind all of a sudden, in fact his expression not only signified deep sympathy but also, I detected to my horror, pity. Petruchio had never looked as though he felt sorry for me before and, even though I had been feeling sorry for myself all morning, the softness of his manner infuriated me and I felt more certain than ever that something had been going on with Petruchio and Kerry and that he was the father of the baby.

'Petruchio, where is Kerry?'

'How am I supposed to know such a thing?'

'I don't believe you. She should be back by now, she's –'

'She'll be home soon, you'll see,' he interrupted me.

I felt cold all over and paranoia took hold of me entirely. Petruchio had drugged me, and possibly Kerry too, in order to prevent her from having an abortion. The tea, the tea he brought me this morning ... yes, but I didn't drink it, it must have been last night, in my pint after the movies, in the coffee before I went to bed.

'Petruchio,' I demanded coldly, 'did you drug me last night, have you drugged Kerry ... *where is she*?'

Petruchio looked affronted, then resigned. 'What crazy, paranoid question is this? You have become as stupid as the rest. Of course, I am wicked scientist turning you all into monsters, beware, Juliet, you wake up one morning with webbed hooves for feet and hairs on the bottom of your hands.' He rose and began to unpack his bags of shopping.

'I'm serious, Petruchio. I just had a hallucination and I want to know what is going on.'

'You have had an hallucination, you say, well, that is what is going on. Do you want I give you some Valium?'

The keys turned in the front door again. Chris entered the room.

'Why aren't you in rehearsal?' I snarled.

'Because they are working on Alison's scenes today, I'm not needed and I'm going to bed. Petruchio, have you got a couple of sleeping pills I could have? I feel awful.'

'No, no, that's enough now. I give no more drugs. Juliet, she accuse me of poisoning her, I am had it with you lot. As soon as I find some place I shall move completely.'

'What's all this in aid of then?' Chris asked, picking up the bottle of whisky and glancing at the cigarettes.

'Juliet is going mad, that is what this aid is for, and she blames me for it, like everyone always blames me for every fucking thing that happens in this stupid place.'

Chris helped himself to a cigarette, took a piece of dope and some Rizlas out of his coat pocket and began to roll a joint.

'Tell Uncle Chris all about it – put the kettle on, Petruchio.'

'She has had hallucinations,' Petruchio said, doing as he was bid.

'Yes well,' Chris said, 'you have been acting strangely recently.'

There was a knock at the front door. I went and found two men, one in a brown suit, who was proffering me some kind of ID card, and another uniformed policeman just behind him.

'Good morning, I am Inspector Godfrey and this is Sergeant Morris. Do you live here?'

I nodded. My heart missed several beats. Kerry has killed herself, I thought.

'Well, we'd like to come in if you don't mind and ask you, and anyone else who lives here, a few questions. You may have heard that there was a murder across the road here last night.'

I nodded again and let them in. As we walked across the hall I called out as casually, but definitely as I could:

'Chris, it's the police.'

'Oh yeah, yeah,' said Chris.

As we entered the living room, Chris, joint in hand, turned jeeringly to look at me. He froze. Petruchio began to laugh. Chris put the joint down in the ashtray and said in his best received pronunciation, 'Oh, hello' and made to stand up.

'No, no, don't get up,' the inspector said. 'If you don't mind, we'd like to ask you all a few questions. Do you mind if we sit down?'

The joint festered away to itself in the ashtray and was totally ignored during the entire investigation. They were there for, I suppose, about half an hour. Petruchio made them coffee. I wanted a cigarette but daren't reach for one in case I drew attention to the Rizla and piece of dope which were on the coffee table.

They were investigating the murder of an eighty-year-old woman, who had been battered to death the night before in her flat. We all had to give details of ourselves, and details of Billy, Kerry and Mrs McNicol. Petruchio and I said we had seen or heard nothing on returning late from the cinema.

The policeman rose and thanked us for our time and the coffees. Suddenly the younger man pointed underneath the dresser.

'What's that?'

We all looked down and I bent over and picked up a toy gun. I handed it to the policeman with a smile. 'There was a fancy dress party Billy and Kerry went to last night, I expect it was for a costume.'

He laughed and put the gun on the coffee table, next to the Rizla, dope tin and joint in the ashtray.

I saw them out and when I came back into the living room, Chris had collapsed on the sofa and Petruchio was leaning over the breakfast bar in exaggerated relief.

'For fuck's sake, they never even noticed,' Chris said.

'You wanna bet?' I replied. 'They're not interested, that's all.'

There was yet another turning of keys in the door and Kerry walked in.

'Where the fuck have you been?' I shouted and would have continued were it not for the expression on Kerry's face, one of almost sublime serenity, tinged with quizzical disbelief. She was not in her party clothes, which meant she must have come back and gone out again. She couldn't have had the abortion already, she had told me they were going to keep her in overnight.

'What?' said Kerry. She seemed befuddled. 'I'm knack-ered, anyway, why are you all here looking so sheepish?'

'Ooh, you've missed all the excitement,' Chris said. 'The police were here and there was a fucking joint in the ashtray and dope and papers all over the table. They never even noticed, we were all shitting ourselves ...' Kerry had gone as white as a sheet.

'The police,' she said, her husky voice breaking even more than usual, 'what were they here for?' Her voice faded. Petruchio chuckled. It was an odd, rather ugly, sound, and I looked at him in surprise. He looked old.

'Oh, an old dear next door was murdered last night,' said Chris dismissively. Getting away with half an ounce of hash was much more interesting than the murder over the road.

Petruchio was sitting in the rocking chair, his eyes closed.

'Another strange morning in Scotland,' he said, his eyes remaining closed. 'First, I feel too ill to work, well, that is not one bit unusual here, but then I get accused by the flat-mate of poisoning her, then the police come and suspect my other flatmates of bashing some old woman over the head for a television, not only that but these policemen do not seem to notice the drugs for which I could be deported. This Scotland is a totally surreal place which I hate with all my heart.'

'Why do you think Petruchio is poisoning you?' said Kerry, putting the kettle on and smiling gleefully.

'Oh, nothing,' I said, 'just that I had what I think must have been a hallucination this morning.'

'A hallucination? What bliss. What did you see?'

I decided not to tell any of them what I saw. Perhaps because, if it was a hallucination, I was ashamed of the image; I felt it showed a lack of taste on the part of my unconscious to produce such a chimera.

'Never you mind,' I said, with a naughty smile.

Petruchio opened his eyes. 'I have a suggestion to make. From my experience as a failure of a shrink. It is possible that you have suffered from a small psychotic episode due to the sudden inhalation of nicotine after an absence of such a drug from your system.' He picked up the toy gun and began playing with it.

'Bollocks,' said Chris.

Kerry was staring intently at Petruchio. 'Well, that explains it, then,' she said. Everyone was quiet for a few moments, and then Petruchio rose and broke the silence.

'Bouff,' he said, 'that explains it ... this drug-crazed household ... and the police go away. Ha! I'm going to bed now. I am tired and sick of it all.'

'Yup,' said Chris, 'me too, I'm gonna get some kip.' The sound of Fleetwood Mac soon blasted from Chris's room.

'Where have you been? Have you missed the abortion? What's going on, Kerry?' I implored, as soon as we were alone.

'Oh, I, er.' Kerry gave a deep sigh. 'Well I went there, but, you know, like you said about the anaesthetic ... I was reeking of alcohol and also very nervous, you know me, and so the bastards wouldn't do it, they're going to make me wait another fucking week. I won't survive.'

'Well, it's your own stupid fault, I told you not to go to

the party. Shit, Kerry, I've been really worried about you.'

I told her about my paranoid suspicion of Petruchio.

'I thought he'd kidnapped and drugged you to stop you from going.'

Kerry smiled, her head falling back against the sofa.

'How was the party?'

'I don't know. I was drunk.'

Kerry went to her room to sleep and I went for a short walk round the park to clear my head. When I turned back into the close on my return I stared into the corner by the cupboard. I shook my head and smiled and moved towards the door. Then, for no reason I can think of, I went to the cupboard and opened it. I moved the bucket. There was a slight smell of vomit coming from the cloth inside. I lifted the bottle of disinfectant. Then something caught my eye. Something white and gleaming. I picked it up and moved back out into the light. It was a tooth. A long tooth. A fang. My hallucination had left a souvenir.

Part Two

Wigner's Friend

Wigner's Friend serves to make a similar point. He is observing the electron being deflected by the magnetic field in the Stern-Gerlach experiment and listening to the Geiger counters to see whether it is the one at A or the one at B which clicks. Wigner knows *a priori* that the probabilities of these two events are equal. The electron beam is unpolarised (as we say), so that there is an even-handed superposition of 'up' and 'down'. On a particular occasion Wigner asks his friend which counter clicked. The friend replies that it was A. For Wigner the electron's wavepacket then collapses into the state in which the spin is definitely 'up'. Yet this state of affairs has surely not been brought about by Wigner's intervention. If he asks his friend, 'What did you hear before I asked you?' his friend will reply with some impatience, 'I told you before, the counter at A clicked'. Wigner has to take his friend's claim to experience as seriously as we take Wigner's. At least by the time that the friend heard the click it must have been settled on that occasion that the electron's spin was up.

J.C. Polkinghorne, The Quantum World

I stood for I don't know how long, clutching on to that fang. I couldn't think, bewilderment and confusion was all I felt. The whole thing was preposterous but there had to be a perfectly rational explanation. I tried to re-live in my mind what had happened, the exact moments of finding the corpse, and then finding it gone. Already, the scene had grown in intensity and, although what I had seen in the close *was* more than a little chilling, now, embellished by a mixture of memory, of knowledge and imagination, not to mention recollections of Hammer Horror movies, it acquired the abhorrence of the symbolically evil.

Now you see it, now you don't. I stared at the floor of the close. She *was* there, I whispered, and Petruchio has something to do with it. He woke me up deliberately. This is some kind of joke. I remembered his Schrödinger's cat prank. The man is sick.

Perfectly rational explanation one: the woman (who probably had something to do with the vampire film and was at the party last night) was not dead, and the whole thing had been staged to scare me, to unsettle me, to shake me up or, better still, to divert me from something else, something sinister – probably to do with Kerry and the abortion. If Petruchio's plan had been to prevent Kerry from going he had, it seemed, succeeded. Kerry was still 'with child'.

I saw the vampire woman again in my mind. Rigor. You can't fake rigor. Could I have been mistaken? Why hadn't I taken her pulse? Could she have been, not dead, but in some kind of drug-induced coma? I had assumed that the woman was dead as soon as I saw her; perhaps my preconception and accompanying fear had clouded my medical judgement?

Perfectly rational explanation two: ... I was stymied. I gave up.

I went into the living room. Kerry was sitting on the sofa

in the gloom. The Thompson Twins' 'We are Detective' was playing on the radio. I switched on the light.

'Kerry, if you saw a corpse in the close what would you do?' I couldn't see her face. She was rubbing her eyes with her hands. When she spoke her voice was quiet.

'Is that what your hallucination was? A cadaver? What fun!'

'If it *was* a hallucination, it was. If not, it was a real fucking cadaver, now what would you do if you saw one?'

'I would scream and run and phone for the police.'

Why hadn't I done that? That is what I was supposed to do, by not doing so I had foiled their plan.

Their plan? It was a conspiracy now, it had to be. Am I paranoid or am I paranoid enough? Was it possible for Petruchio to have had access to human corpses for his experimentation? Everything I knew told me no, it was not possible. It was surely not possible for him to have transported such a thing across Glasgow.

Thoughts, slippery as mercury, transformed themselves into their opposite as soon as they entered my consciousness: *I saw it. I saw it not.* I put my hand in my pocket and felt the sharp, smooth, tooth. But still, perhaps I didn't see it, I *was* drugged and hallucinating and the fang was a coincidence or ...

Kerry was looking at me in a peculiar fashion. 'Are you all right? You look funny,' she said.

'Yes, I'm fine.'

I wasn't fine, I felt truly that I was losing my mind. Petruchio was fucking with my head. Why? And he couldn't have done it alone. Kerry was in on it too. No, she couldn't possibly be involved in some stupid, or even malicious joke, not the night before the abortion – she was surely too preoccupied. Then why hadn't she had the abortion?

Kerry had set this up to teach me a lesson. She was

playing on what she knew I had within me: a ghoulish delight and fascination, which she had aroused in me by leaving the corpse in the hall, only to cheat me immediately of my murder, to make it all vanish, just when my pulse was going and adrenalin racing and a gruesome, captivating horror suddenly making life more vigorous. More real. It was a plot to expose, even if only to myself, the 'drama queen' in me.

Perhaps she wasn't even pregnant.

'Fuck, I'm exhausted. I'm going to go to bed,' I said.

'You never used to swear, Juliet. I've been a bad influence on you.'

Kerry went into her room, saying she was going to do a big tidy-up.

'I've got so much junk still, I'm going to get rid of some stuff, give it to Oxfam or something.'

I sat for a while and tried out a relaxation exercise Kerry had once shown me. Deep breathing, gentle neck rolls and then a deliberate emptying of all thought. You were supposed to picture some sort of syringe going into your head and drawing out all its mucky consciousness. I pictured thick, black gunge, crawling with tiny maggots, filling syringe after syringe.

I heard music from Kerry's room. I went to my room and lay down on the bed and dosed for a while. The sheets hadn't been changed for weeks and, when I woke, I noticed a strong smell of bodies coming from the duvet as I pulled it up over me. It was not a dirty smell, but sweet and pungent and I told myself to change the sheets that afternoon and go to the launderette. I obeyed immediately.

As I left, Petruchio was by the car loading a huge bin bag of stuff into the car and Kerry appeared in the mouth of the close with another bag.

'Petruchio's giving me a lift to the Oxfam shop, see

how much I'm chucking out.' She grinned at me lopsidedly. I wanted her to help me. I suddenly desperately wanted Kerry to help me. I felt afraid and I was going to the launderette.

The launderette was safe, but when I returned I had to check out the cupboard under the stairs again. I found nothing. I unpacked the laundry, made the bed, and went through to the living room to watch TV. That was around five o'clock and Petruchio, Kerry, Chris and Christine didn't return until just after the news at ten. They had been in the pub. Kerry was in particularly manic spirits. She had this sudden idea of us all going up to the cottage in Argyll for a long weekend. It was a bank holiday.

'Oh, come on let's, please, Juliet, we need to have some fun, fresh air and, oh, go on, it's a great idea, isn't it?'

Petruchio seemed keen and Chris, Christine and Billy weren't immune to the idea. Kerry won the day with her relentless begging. I agreed.

It was a beautiful autumn morning when we set off the next day, Kerry, Billy, Chris, Christine, Petruchio and myself. Petruchio was revealing a hitherto unknown side to his character, that of the born organiser. As soon as I agreed to the trip, he organised us all into packing and the following morning he loaded up the car, snatching my bag from me as I walked down the close, and hurried us all into leaving on the dot of his desired time of ten-fifteen.

This was virtually dawn as far as Billy was concerned and, squeezed into the back seat with Kerry (Freyja on her lap in a basket), Christine and myself, he fell asleep on my right shoulder. Petruchio drove too fast and Christine begged him to slow down; what was the big hurry? When we neared Inveraray, I suggested that we stop off for provisions. Earlier, when Christine had suggested she go shopping before we left, Petruchio had said that there was no room in the car. Now he insisted that we would have a lot to do when we got there and that a party must go out again to fetch provisions later.

When we arrived at the cottage, Petruchio, still in sergeant-major mode, told everyone that he would unpack the car, the rest of us should start chopping wood and making the fire.

'Yes, Sir,' said Kerry. 'Juliet, you go with Christine and sort out the water and I'll take Billy and Chris to the wood-shed.'

Christine and I walked to the back of the garden and through the gate on to the hill. When we reached the water tank, Christine stopped to admire the view. We dealt with the water and as we walked back down the hill, my gaze fixed for a moment on Petruchio appearing from around the front of the house and going to the boot of the car. He looked up and gave us a clumsy wave. As we approached the car I asked whether he wanted a hand and he shrugged.

'Not really, I have finished. The bedclothes are in that bag there, why don't you make the beds?'

'Great,' grumbled Christine, but she picked up the bag and I followed her into the house.

'Fuck the beds,' I said, sitting on the sofa, 'everyone can make their own sodding beds.'

The others came back with a pile of wood and Chris lit the fire while Kerry let Freyja out of her basket and made a fuss of her. Petruchio came in with the last of the bags.

'Right,' said Billy, 'let's go back into Inveraray now and get something to eat, I'm starving.'

'Good, yes, you must all go, but I have a headache and so will sleep.' Petruchio looked grey and the shadows under his eyes were larger than ever. Kerry announced that she would also stay.

'I can't leave Freyja until she has settled.'

117

'In that case, I'll stay too.' My suspicions were aroused. Petruchio organised me into changing my mind. He said he needed me to drive the car as he couldn't trust Billy or Chris not to get drunk and Christine didn't drive. I agreed; I didn't really want to leave Kerry, but the idea of a pub lunch was attractive. There was nothing to eat in the cottage and there was no knowing when the party would return from Inveraray with food. I had packed some apples in my bag and I gave them to Petruchio, saying, 'This should keep the wolf from the door.'

In the car I indulged my paranoia, conjuring up images of Kerry and Petruchio fucking on the floor in the cottage. Petruchio hypnotising Kerry into believing that she wanted his baby. Petruchio and Kerry laughing at me.

'Cheer up, Juliet.' Billy slapped me on the back as I got out of the car. I glared at him, and he laughed and hugged me.

We went to a pub. Billy was at his most endearing that afternoon, by which I suppose I mean most flattering, like an adoring puppy dog. Being in a four with Chris and Christine made him behave as if he and I were a couple too; he held my hand or slung his arm over mine. It was comforting and I began playing a game with myself, pretending that Billy was my boyfriend and we were madly in love. Kerry didn't exist, with her infidelities and pregnancy.

I was so relaxed that I began to think again that there was nothing going on at all. Perfectly rational explanation number two came to me at last: someone from the party had come back to the flat, collapsed in a drunken stupor, woken when I was at the shops and sloped off. The fact that my sordid imagination had instantly seen death, even to the detail of rigor, was an indication of my deteriorating state. I really must stop smoking dope and taking Petruchio's pills. Maybe they weren't really Valium at all.

When we had finished our lunch, we wandered around the town, looking in every souvenir shop, and picking up delicacies from the various little food stores. We ended in the off-licence and left with a box of assorted wines, spirits and beer. We put all we had bought in the car and walked along the quay. Christine took some photos. She gave me one of them later. I look very healthy in it, my hair, copper in the sun and blown by the wind, and my face smiling and relaxed.

When we got back, Kerry was sitting in the rocking chair, wrapped in a rug with Freyja on her lap purring contentedly. Petruchio was putting more logs on the fire. We dug the alcohol out of our shopping and settled down.

Kerry was manic, drinking two to everyone else's one drink and chainsmoking joints; as soon as she had lit one, her fingers would set to work on the next, or she would demand that Billy or Chris take their turn. Later, we cooked, or rather Christine did, allocating the rest of us chopping and preparing tasks. Kerry didn't help. She felt her contribution lay in rolling the joints, which she did with great speed. I noticed that her fingers were nicotine stained, and I felt momentarily disgusted by her frantic habit.

The truth is, I was even jealous of Kerry's damned joints. Kerry wanted, loved, needed them far more than she ever did me. She once told me that she associated it so much with happiness that she could never really believe she was happy unless she had a joint in her hand. On another occasion, she told me about a theory she had that the reason she smoked so much was that it killed all other needs, all she *really* needed most of the time was a joint.

She chainsmoked them all evening. I stared at her and then looked at Petruchio. If he knew that she was pregnant and had prevented her from having an abortion, surely he would stop her from smoking, I reasoned with myself.

'So, you're having the abortion next week now, are you?' I asked when we were getting into bed that night. Kerry winced and nodded.

'Please don't talk about it, Juliet, I can't bear it, I really can't. If I think about it for so much as a second I feel sick and I want to kill myself. Please, just *shut up* about it.' Her voice gained strength during the sentence and ended shrill and hard.

She got up at one point in the night and I heard the sound of vomiting coming from the bathroom. Serves her right, I thought, and then I heard Petruchio on the landing asking whether she was all right. She whispered something to him and then returned. I pretended to be asleep.

In the morning I woke early and dressed quickly. I made tea and took it out into the garden, noticing the mess of mud and wellingtons in the passage by the back door and making a mental note to make sure the cottage was cleaned up properly before we went back. I climbed over the fence at the bottom of the garden and walked up the hill a bit, clutching my mug of hot tea. I looked down on the cottage, the road and the loch beyond. Suddenly, something caught my eye and I turned and looked to my right, where the burn ran down the hillside and across which was woodland. A man was clambering out of the woods and crossing the burn. At first I didn't recognise him but then he straightened up and I saw that it was Petruchio. Something made me hesitate in calling out to him and instead I crouched down, concealing myself behind a clump of weed. He was carrying a large spade. I began to laugh, as I imagined Petruchio digging for truffles, or some obscure woodland drug. He is deeply weird, I thought, and seeing him going into the cottage, I got up and walked across the hill to the burn. I drank some water from the water tank and then went back to the cottage.

I entered silently and startled Petruchio, who was making tea. 'Juliet.'

'Hi, you're up early.'

'I say the same for you.'

'Yes, I went out for an early morning walk.'

Petruchio turned his back to me and poured boiling water into the teapot.

'Where did you go?' His always strange intonation was even stranger.

'Oh, across the burn and into the woods.'

I noticed his back tense up, momentarily. Then he turned, smiled and asked me if I wanted tea. I nodded and sat down in the rocking chair. He handed me a mug of tea and sat in the chair opposite. He took a small packet of pills from his cardigan pocket, swallowed two Valium, and offered me the packet. I declined. He stared at me intently, as if waiting for me to say something. I sipped my tea, pretending not to notice his gaze. Then he said, 'Did you see anything interesting in the woods?'

'No, but I did think of maybe digging for truffles.'

He smiled but said nothing.

'Or maybe some magic mushrooms.'

Petruchio was inscrutable.

Chris and Christine came downstairs at that point, and Christine cooked breakfast and started planning the day. Kerry joined us just in time to eat. Christine finally ordained a restful morning, exploring the immediate environs and in the afternoon a longer walk along the loch. We all agreed and then, because several people announced they wanted baths, we organised a bath rota. Kerry had first bath and I went into our room and lay on the bed.

Pictures of Kerry and Petruchio having sex again invaded my mind. When Kerry returned, wrapped in a towel and shivering, I told her that I hated her.

'Yes, I know. Well, it doesn't really matter anymore.'

'What do you mean? What the hell is going on, Kerry? You owe me the truth.'

'Why are you going on like this? There isn't any truth.'

'Is it Petruchio?'

'No, God no. It is obviously all over between you and me, so why can't you just leave me alone.'

'Why is it obvious? You bitch, it isn't obvious to me.'

She walked over to the window and stood with her back to me. My eyes focused on the distant hill.

'I can't have relationships, Juliet, I can't, I don't believe in love.'

'No, but you need it, don't you? You need everyone to love you.'

She was shivering.

'You're just a faithless little whore really, aren't you, Kerry? Don't worry, get dressed, for God's sake. I'll get over it,' I said.

I felt very removed from her. I watched her get dressed and, as she became aware of me watching her, crumple into tears.

I wanted to go to her, to hug her, but I couldn't. *Love is selfish*. My desire to comfort, to reach out for her and make it all better was not so strong as my need to punish her for rejecting me. I walked out of the room. I took my coat from the kitchen, where Billy was sprawled on the lumpy sofa, drinking a can of beer and smoking a joint. I went out the back door and climbed over the fence and headed for the burn. I crossed just about where Petruchio had that morning, and I went into the woods. I wasn't really looking for anything, signs of digging maybe, but soon I was through to the other side of the wood, seeing nothing to catch my attention, and I crossed the field and got down to the road. As I turned the corner and saw the car outside the cottage, Petruchio climbed over the fence on the other side of the road and called out to me. 'Been for a walk?' he asked.

'Just round the block,' I said.

Petruchio looked nervous and edgy, and I derived pleasure from the fact that I had the power to make him so uncomfortable. We walked the rest of the way to the cottage together. I rather skittishly asked Petruchio if he believed in vampires.

'Don't be stupid,' he said curtly and dismissively.

'Petruchio, did you know that Kerry was pregnant?'

Not a muscle on his face moved. 'No.'

I stared at him.

'You should not have told me this, Juliet, it is Kerry's business.'

I don't think I have ever hated anyone as much as I hated Petruchio at that moment.

'It's you, isn't it? You're the father?'

Petruchio sucked in his breath hard and then let it out with a snarl at the back of his throat.

'You are crazy, I think perhaps you better see your doctor, it is this falling in love with Kerry, I told you there would be trouble.'

'Yes,' I said, 'you did.' Suddenly I didn't know how I could have hated him so fervently but moments ago.

Kerry and Billy were lounging by the fire, drinking and smoking, and Christine and Chris were preparing lunch. We all poured ourselves drinks and helped ourselves to piles of bread and cheeses, pickles and patés. I took the joint from Kerry when she offered it, giving her a warm smile. She had cheered up, and with that first-flush-of alcohol energy was telling some story about her escapades in Ireland as a girl. Will I ever not love her? I thought, and what the hell was that fang doing in the cupboard?

After lunch Petruchio, Chris and Christine and Kerry went for a walk by the loch. Billy complained of a hangover and, still bloated from lunch, I just wanted to sit in the garden and get on with yet another late assignment. As I sat on the bench, I became distinctly conscious of someone looking at me. I glanced around me, and suddenly Billy wolf-whistled. He was sitting in the bedroom window.

'You're fucking beautiful, you know that, Juliet. I'm dying because I want to fuck ye so much.'

I laughed, and Billy suddenly jumped out of the window. It wasn't far, the cottage being on a slope and the garden quite high, but he rolled over in mock agony as he hit the ground with a thud. 'Oh, help, help,' he groaned, 'come and gie me the kiss of life.' I stiffened immediately, as he came over, sat down on the bench and began to stroke the back of my neck.

'Come on, Juliet, fuck me please, before they get home, Kerry will no mind, ye know.' I was dismally aware of my heart thudding and of the temptation to stretch my neck forward and arch like a cat at his touch. Billy put his hand on my thigh and stroked gently. I got up, held out my hand, and we went upstairs to the little bedroom Billy was sharing with Petruchio. Billy took off my dress.

'Have you ever fucked Kerry?' I asked.

'No, man, she would never let me, and I'd have frigged and licked her so dry the wee man in the boat would hae had to get oot and walk, but she would never even let me do that te her.' I lay down on the bed and waited for him; he undressed, whilst not taking his eyes off me.

Billy was the amphetamine fuck to end all fucks. I didn't have time to breathe let alone come, but then suddenly he slowed down and grunted, 'Shall we take it a wee bit slower the noo' and I realised from his panting and sweat that he had been taking the pace from me, that it was my manic energy that had driven us so frantically. He came, crying out that I was 'fucking beautiful' as he did and then lay slumped, whimpering gleefully on my chest. We heard the gate click and Petruchio's dark voice as he and the others walked up the path. Billy and I dressed silently and I slipped into my and Kerry's room and lay down on the bed. I heard Billy go downstairs to greet them.

Kerry came straight upstairs to our room.

'I fucked Billy this afternoon.'

'Oh, nice one, where, in here?'

'No, his room. Did you ever fuck him?'

'Christ, no, I wouldn't let him come near me with that thing. No, we just messed around.'

'And you're not jealous, you're really not jealous?'

Kerry looked exasperated, then she laughed. 'And the look on your face, Juliet ... anyone would think jealousy was a virtue.'

Later that evening, we all went to Inveraray and to the pub. When we got back, tired and drunk, we went straight to bed. Kerry snuggled into me, smelling of nutmeg and apples. I stroked her forehead. Soon she was asleep. It'll be all right, I thought. She'll have to tell me eventually. When I finally slept, I dreamed: I opened the front door of the flat and the vampire woman appears and disappears before my eyes.

'Her wave function is collapsing, Captain.' The voice of Mr Spock echoes around me, and I look up and down the close for him. Then I go back into the flat and search for cigarettes. Petruchio appears, reeling in an imaginary fishing line. Then Kerry, Chris, and Billy danced wildly around me in the living room. I grab hold of Petruchio and as he turns to face me he crumbles into dust. Kerry, with an enormous broom, sweeps him up. The police come in at that point, with the body of a very old woman. They say

125

that she has been murdered and they want to check our television set. They switch it on and *Star Trek* is on the air and Spock says again, 'Her wave function is collapsing, Captain.'

When I woke up I had to try hard to stop myself from crying. I found myself asking questions about the old lady over the road. Who was she? Who battered her over the head for a TV and stereo? How did she die? Quickly, or slowly, whimpering, shouting or pleading? Who mourned her? Who cared? Not us. Not us over the road in Number 68. I felt foolish. Jealousy had driven me to lose all sense of proportion.

Petruchio suddenly decided at breakfast the next morning, the Sunday, that we should drive up to Oban. So we did. I remember we sang most of the way, our repertoire ranging from First World War songs to the Sex Pistols. At Oban Billy asked Kerry if she would swap rooms with him that night. She agreed and I was furious and depressed for the rest of the day.

'I was only joking,' Kerry insisted, but jealousy reared its ugly head again and I wondered whether she had deliberately set Billy up to seduce me so that she could get me off her case. The idea that Billy might only have been obeying Kerry's instructions wounded my vanity too much for me to pay heed to it for very long.

We had tea in a café and I was fishing around in my pockets for my cigarettes when I felt the fang. I placed it on the table. Chris and Christine carried on talking, paying no attention, but Kerry and Petruchio froze and stared at the fang. I noticed that they did not look at one another.

'What's that? asked Billy.

'I don't know, I found it,' I said, 'but I have a theory that it's Petruchio's.'

'No,' he said. Deadpan. Billy picked it up and bit it.

126

'It's no plastic,' he said, 'what's the theory, Juliet, do'ye reckon Petruchio here's a vampire?'

'I don't know. He could well be. Perhaps Petruchio can collapse his own wave function and be whatever he wants to be.'

'I wish,' mumbled Petruchio.

Kerry snatched the fang from Billy and ran out of the café, across the road, and threw it over the railings and into the sea. She turned and waved at us. I looked at Petruchio. He had gone pale and was biting his lip so hard, it had turned quite white.

Something was definitely going on between them.

'Why did Kerry do that?' I demanded of Petruchio.

'Bouff, how can any of us know why she does anything whatsoever? And you know as well as I do she is a queen of drama of the first order. Can we now leave this place please? I feel sick.'

'Why did you do that?' I demanded of Kerry when she returned to the café.

'A joke, of course'. She glanced at Petruchio and her voice got stronger. 'Well, it's all a joke, isn't it, Juliet and her stupid fang.'

Another night in the pub in Inveraray. And then back at the cottage we played poker until the early hours. As soon as I was alone again with Kerry I questioned her again about the fang.

'Why did you do that? What do you know about that fang?'

'Nothing, only that you put it on the table ... I was only playing along with your little joke, whatever that may be.'

'You're lying, I know you're lying. Look, if I quietly acquiesce to your actions, it would imply the arrogant assumption that you are not responsible for them, that you are, in fact, mad. Now surely you don't want that? So you have to give me an explanation. You owe it to me.'

'I don't owe you anything and it seems to me that you are the one who is mad.' She refused to say another word on the matter.

We slept late the following morning. After breakfast, we packed up, tidied and cleaned the cottage and drove back to Glasgow. Billy made an attempt to start off the singing again, but Kerry was withdrawn and Petruchio was morose.

A few days after we had returned from the cottage, we were visited by the police again. Inspector Godfrey and his sidekick. Kerry and I were alone in the flat. Mrs McNicol had returned and found her flat had been burgled.

'She tells me that she had given you a key' – the policeman looked at Kerry as he spoke – 'and that you were to go up and water the plants and feed the cat. Did you do this?'

'Yes,' said Kerry, 'why?'

Inspector Godfrey smiled and said that someone living opposite had said that there had been suspicious 'goings on' in our tenement the night the old woman had been murdered. Kerry laughed.

'There are always suspicious goings on going on here, Inspector, we're drug-crazed students, and I'm Irish.'

The inspector laughed and looked at Kerry warmly, affectionately almost. Then he explained that they were taking prints of Mrs McNicol's flat and they needed to know who else might have been there. Kerry nodded and said 'Oh' then she quickly added, 'Well, there'll be Petruchio's too, maybe, you see, I asked him to do the plants a few times, you know, when I was busy.'

The inspector then looked through the file he carried and then said, 'Ms Porteus told us when we were here last that you and Billy were at a party on the night in question. Is this correct?'

Kerry hesitated for just a fraction of a second. 'No, I wasn't at a party.' She looked at me. 'I'm sorry, Juliet, I lied to you, I didn't go to the party.'

Inspector Godfrey looked at me and then back at Kerry. 'Where were you then?' he said.

Kerry suddenly looked very angry. 'Well, I don't have to tell you, do I? What's it to you, you pigs snorting around in other people's private lives. I didn't kill that old woman for a fucking TV and stereo, so I don't see why I should tell you anything more.'

Before the inspector and his silent partner could respond to this outburst, I took hold of Kerry's hand and turned to Inspector Godfrey, who was completely inscrutable.

'Kerry and I are lovers, Inspector, you know, lesbians, and Kerry fucks around a lot on me. That's why she tells lies, that's why she doesn't want to tell you anything.'

The other policeman cleared his throat but Godfrey just implacably repeated his question, 'Where were you then?'

'I was here all the time, I had a headache and I suddenly couldn't face going to the party. I was in Petruchio's room, and I was there when Juliet and he came back from the cinema.'

'Then where were you the next morning?' I snarled.

'Well, like I said, I got up early ... I met Billy and asked him not to say anything about not going to the party. Juliet?' she pleaded.

The two policemen rose as one, with no apparent communication between them. When they had gone, Kerry burst into tears, and I, unable to do anything else, hurled abuse at her, calling her a treacherous monster, a snake, a compulsive liar. I then flounced out of the house.

I made a few frantic circles, pacing around, unable to decide where to go. I went to the park and then decided to confront Petruchio. I walked to the university and found the department where Petruchio worked. I asked at the reception where I might find him, and was directed down several long corridors to a laboratory. I saw Petruchio through the glass of the door, he was on the telephone. I walked in and he saw me and looked surprised but hailed me with his hand. He finished his conversation and came over to me, and I walked back out of the door.

He followed me outside where I confronted him. 'Remember when those policemen came and we had to say where we had been the night that old woman was killed?' Petruchio nodded.

'Well, where were you?'

He looked down, sighed, and muttered, 'Even in my laboratory, the Inquisition finds me.' Then he looked up.

'I was where I said I was, I was in my room. What I did not say to you or the policemen, was that I was not alone, that Kerry was there when I returned and that she and I spent the night together.'

'Christ, Petruchio,' I said, 'Kerry's mendacity is really catching, you know, but why you had to lie to me I don't know ...'

Petruchio interrupted me and said with a look of sneering contempt on his face, 'You are a fool, Juliet, it is Kerry who has made you a fool rather than me a liar. Your mind is full of sex. Kerry wanted to talk to me about philosophy and physics, she has gone to my room to read a book and has fallen asleep. When I wake her we talk until she fall asleep again. Rather than wake her up I decide not to go to bed and to study all night. This is what happens, I swear.' He went back into his lab and closed the door.

I walked home feeling wretched and frightened and a fool. What could I expect? I angrily told myself – of course you are becoming a paranoid hysteric of a person, look at

130

the company you keep, look at the drugs you take with them.

I apologised to Kerry, admitting that my jealousy had taken over my reason. I realised that it was far more likely, knowing all I knew about Petruchio, that he and Kerry were talking about physics rather than having sex, but the fact that they had been together the night before I saw that *thing* in the close convinced me that they had been plotting. They were guilty, or Kerry was. I knew, because of the fang.

I decided to bide my time. Something would happen. It would all be revealed to me. Kerry was ill, morning sickness all day and a lot of the night. She tried, pathetically, to smoke, but she would retch and cough.

Two days before she was due to have the abortion, we went to the video shop to get a film out. I was looking in the comedy section and she was wandering aimlessly around. Suddenly, I heard one of her retches and I turned and saw her staring at a carousel of videos. Her hand flew to her mouth and she ran out of the shop. I looked at where her gaze had been fixed. It was the porn display and the covers of the boxes facing out were of heavily pregnant women, scantily clad or naked and in provocative poses. Kerry was still crouching on the pavement, a pile of vomit by her side and more still to come. I supported her home.

Kerry insisted that she didn't want me to go with her to the clinic, and that she didn't know when she would be finished, so I would see her when I saw her. She was very matter of fact as she prepared to go, and when she said goodbye she said she was sorry.

She came back at about nine the next morning, asked for a hot water bottle and went straight to bed. I decided I wouldn't mention it again. I was hoping that we could still be reconciled. In spite of everything, I didn't want to lose Kerry.

131

Billy had pleaded with me every day to repeat our sexual encounter. He found it impossible to understand why I didn't want to. I didn't understand it myself really, since it had been a wholly pleasurable way of passing the time. He then split up with his girlfriend and the pestering got worse. I told him I loved him like a brother and, though it was OK for it to happen once, it didn't feel right to continue. He groaned and said, 'Well, will ye no just let me gie you a wank? Orgasms are good for you – you're a scientist, Juliet, you should know that.' The idea appalled me. I hugged him and begged him to give up, it was a lost cause, I was probably completely lesbian or something.

Three weeks after we had returned from the cottage, Billy came bursting on Petruchio, Kerry and me while we were watching TV. He flapped a copy of the *Daily Record* in front of us saying, 'Fuck's sake, read this.' Kerry glanced at it and passed it over to Petruchio. I glanced over his shoulder.

TOP LONDON AGENTS MISSING read the headline. I skimmed the column, gleaning that Geoffrey and Sophie Daniels were missing, that they had failed to return from a holiday in Barbados and the police now believed they had not in fact taken the holiday and had therefore been missing for three weeks.

'Oh, good,' said Kerry casually, 'I hope they're dead.'

The missing agents were on the news that night. It was reported that Sophie had last been seen in the film company's offices in the west end of Glasgow. They had both been expected at the birthday party of actor Stuart Devlin that night, but neither of them had turned up. As they were due to leave Scotland for a holiday in the West Indies the next morning, people had assumed they had gone to their hotel to pack. Friends and colleagues in London had not been aware of their absence until two days ago when they had alerted the police.

The news item then milked the mystery for all it was worth while at the same time giving a probably dreadful film a free trailer showing the filming of a scene in which the young English actress is seduced by a pin-striped vampire, all the while protesting in an appalling Scottish accent, but nonetheless thrusting her huge breasts further and further into his face. This was followed by interviews with some of the actors and closed with the statement that Scotland Yard were working closely with the police in Glasgow, and that a major search was being launched.

Kerry said that it would no doubt give the film a huge boost at the box office, it being associated with a mysterious disappearance.

'Yes,' said Petruchio, 'better for the distributors I think, if these two are found brutally murdered somewhere.'

'Yeah' said Chris idly, 'it's probably all just a big publicity stunt.'

Kerry laughed and said that every actor in Scotland, or at least all the ones who hadn't been cast in the film, would be under suspicion.

'Or maybe there's a secret armed wing of Scottish Equity, a nationalist faction that has carried out a political assassination.'

The following afternoon, late, we received our third visit from the police. Inspector Godfrey, this time not with his usual silent partner, but with an older, probably senior officer. They were interviewing all the people who had been involved in the film and who had been at the party that night. So they questioned Billy. We were all of us in the flat that evening. Then the older man turned to Kerry, asking her why she had not been at the party. She explained about her headache again.

'You were a client of Sophie Daniels, I believe, and you attended a dinner party at their Kensington house in

November of last year. Is this correct?' Kerry nodded. She looked as though she might cry and Inspector Godfrey looked kindly at her, and told her that they would like to take a statement from her and perhaps she could go to the police station that afternoon.

I showed the two men out; I always seemed to act as usher. When I got back into the living room, Kerry quickly, before I had time to interrogate her, said, 'Shut the fuck up, Juliet, I mean it, I won't talk and it's none of your fucking business.'

Kerry went out that afternoon, and when she came back she retreated into her room. I was studying, trying hard to concentrate when my curiosity was practically killing me. Petruchio knocked on my door and asked me if I wanted to go for a drink. I said that I had to finish what I was doing. I then heard him knock on Kerry's door and ask her the same.

They left together, calling out the pub where they would be if I wanted to join them later. After another hour of hopelessly attempting to focus my mind on my work, I gave up and headed for the pub. Kerry and Petruchio were talking intently and I slunk upon them slowly enough to hear part of Kerry's sentence; the words 'worried' and 'Juliet'.

Her guilty flush as she saw me aroused all my angry suspicions. I sat down and said in my hardest voice, 'Why are you worried about me, Kerry? Worry about yourself. I think something's going on between you two and I want to know about it.'

'You wouldn't believe me if I told you,' Kerry said.

'Try me,' I replied unpleasantly, 'and you can start with what happened at Sophie's dinner party and where you were for the rest of that week.'

'I told you, I was sleeping rough. And I didn't tell you about the dinner party because it's a closed book as far as

I'm concerned and I won't talk about it to you or anyone, OK?'

But she had talked about it to someone, she had told someone in every intimate detail, apparently crying as she did so and receiving comfort and absolution from the last person in the world I ever expected Kerry to even meet, let alone divulge the darkest, most wretched secrets of her heart to.

And then of course, she had told Petruchio. But I was left to surmise what I could, when the shit hit the fan of the popular press.

The next day the newspaper headlines screamed 'AGENTS IN KINKY ORGIES', 'THE AGENTS OF LUST', and 'MISSING AGENTS' HIDDEN SEX DEN'. Billy had a pile of tabloids spread out over the living room. He was hungrily devouring each salacious word. Kerry said nothing, only that it didn't surprise her and anyway the police had hinted as much when she gave her statement. Kerry went out, saying she was going to spend the last of her holiday pay from *Antigone* on some new Doc Martens.

I read each report. It appeared that when the house in Kensington had been searched, police had found the cellar all done out like a medieval dungeon, with a whole array of equipment, including a projector and a quite stupendous amount of pornographic material, some of it of a very 'serious' nature. Certain people questioned by the police had admitted to taking part in wild orgies organised by the couple, those seemingly 'respectable members of the London literary and theatrical scene'.

The following day there were more stories, this time first-hand accounts from both male and female actors claiming they were forced into hideous tortures and degradations by Sophie and Geoffrey, who were now deemed to be depraved monsters by the press.

'Funny how none of these actors said anything before now,' I remarked, not believing a word of the filthy reports.

The search continued, but it was now believed that the disappearance of the agents was connected to their voracious and peculiar sexual practices.

I had no doubt in my mind now as to what Kerry had done in that house in Kensington and why the police had wanted a statement from her.

Images of Kerry and the agents filled my mind and tormented me. Chris and Billy teased her, inventing all sorts of scenarios that Kerry had taken part in. Kerry dismissed this teasing but one evening when we were all in the flat, I took this teasing further and began to suggest that Kerry had a motive for murder, that perhaps she had done away with the agents and that was why she wasn't at the party.

My imagination was then uncharacteristically unleashed and I began to speak in a phoney Belgium accent like Peter Ustinov as Poirot and to sum up the case.

'Kerry,' I said, 'had been held captive in the Kensington sex den, subjected to cruel and unusual abuse for four days before she escaped, but when her brutal tormentors come up to Glasgow for the film, they seek her out, coming for her on the night of the party, just as she is getting ready. But this time they have a darker purpose: before they were just amusing themselves with her, now they need her blood to stay alive. There is a fearful struggle as Kerry discovers that the agents are, in fact, vampires. She bravely wards off the evil blood-suckers' attempts to pierce her soft white neck with their vile teeth – no thrusting of her bosoms for Kerry – no, she escapes into Petruchio's room where she finds his rosary and thrusts the crucifix into the agents' faces. The vampires die in horrible agony and Kerry hides them in the cupboard under the stairs. But the agents had a new strain of vampirism; like viruses which mutate and become immune to their antidotes, so they have become immune to death even by crucifix. Well, in these multi-cultural days that seems quite reasonable – hell, these vamps might be Sufis or Nichirin Shoshi Buddhists!

'They die only for one night, but they cannot enter normal life again, the game is up in one sense, they can only roam the night endlessly looking for victims. So off they go, *but*, in throwing the seeming corpses into the cupboard, Kerry had managed to knock Sophie's tooth out of her wicked mouth and the poor woman, frantic lest she spend the rest of eternity somewhat dentally challenged for a vampire, risks everything to return in daylight and retrieve her lost incisor.' I stopped, only to give dramatic pause, but Billy and Chris burst into loud cheers and applause, and Kerry and Petruchio followed.

'Poor vampires,' laughed Chris, 'I mean, they couldn't help being vampires, could they?'

'They were fucking cunts,' said Kerry venomously, 'why can't we please stop talking about those fucking bastard agents?'

'Maybe we will if you let us into the secrets of the Kensington sex den,' said Billy and Kerry retorted with, 'Agh, fuck off, you prurient little prick.'

Kerry came back one evening to say that she had got her old job back at War and Pizza. She wasn't applying for any acting work, in spite of Chris and Billy's endless tips as to who was casting what, and who she should write to. She had been amazingly sober since the abortion.

We all went to see Chris in *Look Back in Anger*. It was worse than one could ever have expected, but Chris was surprisingly good much to our relief, as we had arranged to go for an Indian afterwards and we would have hated having to lie to him.

In the restaurant, which was just a few doors down from the flat, Chris informed us that he was thinking of moving to London when the play finished its run, and straight away Billy offered to go with him and share a flat.

It's all falling apart, I thought, it's all going to end; and then Kerry compounded my fear by saying that she had been thinking of going abroad for a while.

Eventually the newspapers tired of the missing agents.

'They probably ended up victims in some snuff movie,' said Billy, and Kerry grunted that it would serve 'em right.

Christmas came round. Petruchio was going to his family in Milan, I was going to go to London, and Chris and Christine were going to her parents in the borders. Kerry and Billy said that they would spend Christmas in the flat together, 'and go completely fucking mental', as Billy said. I asked Kerry to come with me to London, but she said no. She told me she wanted to work over Christmas and she would get lots of tips as the restaurant would be busy and everybody pissed.

It was a great relief to get away that Christmas. A relief not to be around Kerry, with endless questions and horrible suspicions in my head. My home and family seemed wonderfully safe and jolly, and it was a particularly exuberant Christmas with all of us there. They asked me about Kerry, of course, and I was a bit stand-offish. Benedick and Helena twigged that something was wrong but they didn't persist with their questions when I, so obviously, didn't want to talk about it. Edgar was totally absorbed. His film was just about to go into production.

The day after Boxing Day, my mother asked me about Melissa, was I going to see her? Melissa lived in a road parallel to my parents' and my mother sometimes bumped into her.

'I haven't seen her for a few months now, because it was when Kerry was staying that time, to see that fearful agent who has disappeared with her husband. Yes, we met her outside her house.'

'Who?' I said absently. I didn't want to think about Kerry.

'Melissa, of course. Kerry and I bumped into Melissa.'

Kerry had met Melissa? She had never told me that. How odd, I thought, the shock subsiding, and then I sighed, remembering how odd Kerry almost always was.

I hadn't planned on going to see Melissa before; the thought rather depressed me. She had two children by now and whenever I had gone to see her we had not been able to have any kind of conversation due to the infants' constant sticky and smelly demands. But this time when I phoned her, she said she would get a childminder so we could go out to lunch.

We met at a nearby Italian restaurant. She was already sitting at the table when I arrived. She had put on weight and, looking very comfortable, was sipping wine and reading the menu. We hugged; she scrutinised my face and told me that I looked awful.

We chatted inconsequentially, mostly about her children and people we had been at school with.

'How's your love life?' she suddenly asked.

'No,' I said. 'Nothing. I was having a thing with Kerry, who you met, with my mother, remember? But it's all over now.'

Melissa's face changed before my eyes, only for a second, but the calm, placidly happy expression was wiped away and replaced by one of fear, discomfort.

'What's the matter?' I asked and she said, 'Nothing,' but she reddened, and her body tensed as she said it.

I laughed. 'Oh Melissa, you are the most transparently

honest person I have ever known. You are lying. There is something the matter. Tell me.'

'I can't,' she whispered, and then looked at me and said, 'I can't not either, can I?'

I said nothing and we sat in silence for a short while.

I returned to Glasgow and to an empty flat. I went to bed, unable to sleep and expecting to get up when the others came back. But the next morning, after only a few hours sleep, I woke and checked all the rooms. There was no one in.

I went into the university and managed to focus my attention on my work, something which gave me an amazed satisfaction. When I got back home that evening, Billy and Chris were in the living room, looking at an A-Z of London, and with an *Evening Standard* open on the table.

'We're going down to the Smoke this weekend,' Billy informed me. 'Gonnee see some places.'

Petruchio apparently was still in Italy and Kerry had been staying with Christine.

'She's really depressed man,' said Billy.

Later that evening Kerry came round; she had forgotten her key so I opened the door for her and she kissed me and said, 'I thought you'd be back.'

'I want to talk to you.'

'Cool.'

We went into my room and Kerry sat cross-legged on the bed. I went to my desk and turned the chair round so I was facing her.

'Melissa.'

Kerry nodded sagely.

This was Melissa's story: she had met Kerry first one morning with my mother, but the following morning, she had been walking back from taking one child to school, and struggling with the pushchair containing her second scream-ing infant, when she saw Kerry walking towards her. Kerry looked extremely distressed and, when Melissa said hello, she had burst into tears. She said she was just walking round trying to pull herself together before going back to my parents' house. Melissa asked her in for a cup of tea and the use of the bathroom to wash her face.

I can understand why Kerry would have unburdened her heart to Melissa. Melissa has this all-embracing quality, this kindness in her face, almost like a mask. I have wondered whether her face, which by chance is composed of parts that make up this warm, benevolent whole, had shaped her personality. If her face has been mean and spiteful, would her character so have developed, or is it the other way round? Do we inhabit our bodies, or do they inhabit us?

I can see Melissa sitting at her kitchen table, looking at Kerry with completely uncondemning, unshockable eyes, while Kerry tells her, in intimate details, all about her time in the house in Kensington.

And now, Kerry told me, at last.

'And none of your stories, Kerry,' I shouted, before she began, 'I don't want to hear another damned story, OK?'

Kerry smiled and softly said, 'Of course it's a story. They're all stories, whether they are true or not ...'

'Kerry,' I pleaded, 'just tell me the truth. You know I won't do anything, you know that, you know I'll help you even, always, but I just need to know, I just want to know, it's driving me mad, all these needless mysteries.'

'OK,' said Kerry seriously. 'OK: the Truth. Part One.

'It started at the sauna, with the medallion man, you remember that story I told you on New Year's Eve at the cottage. Well, it didn't end when I said it did. I was going to tell you the truth that night but when it came down to it, I couldn't. There was something in your face that made me

141

change my story, a look of ... kind of ... salacious horror. I didn't want you to know then, I still don't really, but ...'

I had believed that on the New Year's Eve in the cottage, Kerry was confiding in me for the first time, and that this had been a turning point in our friendship. Now I was learning that it was a pack of lies. What was coming next? I wondered, and tried not to be afraid of whatever it was.

'That day when I got into the sauna man's car off Byers Road and told you that I'd finished it all, I didn't. I went with him to a party, a weirdo's party in South Glasgow. Everyone was in leather and it seemed everybody at the party could have sex with everyone else. When I arrived they were all watching two men inserting various spiky objects up each other's arses. Everyone was shrieking with laughter, there was something really tongue in cheek about it all. Anyway, I sat in a corner and didn't let anyone touch me, but this guy comes up to me and wants me to whip him, with a sort of cat-o'-nine-tails. He lay down on the floor by my feet and begged me. So I gave him what for with his fucking little whip and then I found my man and told him I had to go. He gave me a lift home and in the car he told me that I could make a lot of money if I wanted to just by beating the shit out of guys, and I thought – Hey! – nice work if you can get it. So that's what I did. He was my sort of pimp, I suppose, I don't know what the guys paid him, but I got about a hundred pounds for each session.

'I had to do crazy things like put nipple clamps on them: one guy wanted Deep Heat rubbed into his testicles, another wanted cigar burns on his chest – I couldn't do it – and then there was this one guy who wanted to be wrapped in newspaper; it had to be the *Guardian*, and for me to whip him until the paper was in tatters.

'It was totally bizarre, Juliet, but remember, here I was into Kathy Acker and the Velvet Underground at the time,

142

and so it all seemed like part of an artistic education. None of them touched me, I always kept my clothes on, you know, the gear he set me up with.'

'I remember,' I said bitterly. I felt so miserable. It was like a clamp had fixed itself tightly around my heart, it was like a million ants crawling through my nervous system, eating away at every fibre of my personality and vomiting up outrage, denial, pain. Why?

'Look at you,' I hissed, 'this is the girl who wouldn't do adverts and you're a whore, Kerry, you *are* a whore.'

She looked at me with a look that was part agony and part pride, a most fearsome, majestic pride. 'What's wrong with being a whore, I'd like to know? Marriage is the worst, the real prostitution, I'd rather be a whore than married. If I am going to be a commodity in a market, I'd rather I was in the pleasure market, not the property. Didn't you know that marriage is just all about the transmission of property? A conduit, as Josephine Butler put it – and she, of course, was branded a whore. All women are whores, don't you know? I'm a whore whether I actually get paid for it or not in our society. A woman who grooves on sex and has it on her own terms is a whore. So I figured that if that was the case I might as well do it properly and get some money for it. Now, do you have a problem with that?'

'Yes, you were my fucking girlfriend.'

'Not at the time, Juliet, not at the time.' She continued. 'At first it was fine. I felt that my secret set me apart from the rest of the world, made me special, different. I felt I had one over everyone but really I was wrong to believe I could be artistically detached and *me*, once a fucking Catholic, of course I sort of began to lose it. That's why I tried to top myself really, it wasn't anything to do with Petruchio's stupid box and dead cat. And that's also why I didn't want to go back to my bedsit. That's where it had happened, you see – a few of the guys used to come there. After a while I couldn't bear to go to the flat which is why I ended up sleeping on Billy's floor all the time.'

Kerry was fighting back tears as she spoke now. All her defiance had gone.

'Well, then we got together and I was really happy, I felt purified by you and our love, I got healed and I didn't see the medallion man again, I told him I didn't want to do it anymore and that he must leave me alone. He was OK about it, much to my bloody relief, I can tell you, I was terrified he was going to get nasty, but no, he was fine and paid me off and told me if I ever changed my mind I knew how to get hold of him. Then I met Geoffrey Daniels, you remember, that night in the pub?'

Of course I remembered.

'He asked me out for dinner the following night, and I went.'

I remembered lying in bed, seething with jealousy and listening to Kerry creep back into the flat late and go to sleep in Billy's room. I folded my arms around me, a meagre defence against what I was about to hear.

'We went to the Grosvenor, and who should walk in to the restaurant but my man from the sauna. I was dying of embarrassment and hoping he wouldn't notice me, when to my horror he came striding up to our table with a big smile. To my amazement he greeted *Geoffrey* warmly and was very surprised indeed when Geoffrey introduced us. I have never felt so awful in my life, so embarrassed and shameful. He joined us for coffee and kept making sly winks and innuendos until I said that I had to go to the ladies' and I never went back, I just ran all the way home.

'But then you see, things went well with you and me, I was happy, *Romeo and Juliet* happened and all I cared about in the world was acting. Then I got the part of Antigone,

144

and I have never been so happy. Honestly, I've never wanted anything as much as I wanted that part, and I think it all sort of went to my head, because when Sophie phoned me after the last night in Edinburgh, I honestly believed that it could all be forgotten. That the sauna man hadn't told Geoffrey anything about me and that even if he had, Geoffrey would be easy to handle as he wouldn't want Sophie to know about his dodgy acquaintances in Glasgow, and so I would have some kind of power ...'

Kerry paused and stared down at the duvet. I was finding it hard to breathe properly, and I stood up and paced the room. There was an atmosphere of suspense, of drama, and I felt as though I were wading through it with difficulty. I hated it and myself. All this *angst* Kerry had infected me with, I hate it, I hate her and her disgusting, melodramatic life.

'This is hard for me, Juliet. I've told so many lies and with successful lying, you have to really believe in them. It's hard for me now to distinguish, to *really* remember. Memory doesn't really care about actuality. The very process, the apparatus, if you like, is creative.'

Her voice had become lyrical, philosophical. She was lecturing me suddenly.

'Kerry, I'm not interested, just tell me the facts. What happened?'

'What happened. OK. I went down to London, stayed with your parents and went to the agency the next morning. Sophie was unreal, she was totally obsequious to me, gushing over my performance and treating me like some precious jewel. Then Geoffrey came in, greeted me like a long-lost friend and they asked me over to dinner that evening. I can be cynical about it now, but at the time I was flattered. You see I knew that I had been really good as Antigone, and so I really did think that they were genuinely impressed and that it was all ... professional.

145

'And at first, it was. I went shopping that afternoon and bought some clothes. I was going to play the game, be what Sophie wanted me to be. I got this floaty and elegant suit from Marks and Spencer, and some dainty little shoes and I wore them that evening. Your mum complimented me on how nice I looked when I left.

'I was the only dinner guest and it was quite informal and relaxed, but then after dinner more and more people started to arrive. Well, you can imagine the rest, can't you? It was a really odd assortment of people, and one of the men I recognised from my dominatrix days in Glasgow.

'I asked Sophie what was going on and she said, "Oh we're having one of our evenings. Would you like to join us?"

'Geoffrey led the way downstairs into the basement: I followed out of curiosity and because I realised that I had to stay cool. The dungeon was unreal, like a horror film set, with all this equipment. It was hysterical really, only, of course, I didn't laugh at the time. I didn't join in either. I just watched. People just sort of got right on into it, off with their kit, and into the toys, like a kindergarten; it really was like playtime ... completely wacky playtime. I didn't mind it. It was like harmless fun and sort of subversive, you know. What was weird was that everyone was terribly affectionate with each other. When they weren't torturing each other. These people were just like babies, they were resorting to a pre-toilet-trained heaven where the body and its secretions are not separate from the world and shit and piss are not the taboos they later become. Babies. Little savages. Beyond bourgeois morality.'

'What were they doing?' I asked, and immediately hated myself for doing so. My prurience defeated my disgust, and Kerry described, with great enjoyment, people chaining each other up to pseudo racks, dunking each other in great tubs of water and grease, whipping, pissing …

'Stop,' I cried, 'enough.' I snatched my pack of cigarettes from my desk, lit one, and then as an afterthought offered one to Kerry. She declined and continued.

'Then someone suggested a little entertainment so a projector was switched on and a film screened. Some people carried on with whatever they were doing, I just sat and watched the film, which was in German and very ugly and the supermarket musack in the background made me laugh.

'Then this balding, middle-aged man approaches me and asks if I am OK or did I not want to ride him like a horse? He brandishes this cruel-looking bridle, complete with the kind of bit only a complete equiphobe – if that's the word – would put on a horse. Oh God, Juliet, you should have seen me, sitting primly on the side in my Marks and Spencer suit, saying "no thank you" – very politely this was – "but I want to watch the movie."'

Kerry laughed but her mirth was cut short by some painful thought which crossed over her face in an almost visible cloud.

'Then someone changed the video. A new film started, this time in English. This film featured young children, and I just stared in horror and disbelief as the people around me watched placidly, or continued with their consensual torments as these children, little children, Juliet …'

My face stopped her and she blew her nose on a hanky she fished out from under the pillow that had probably been there for weeks. Tears fell down her cheeks as she continued.

'You know I don't believe in childhood and you know I agree with Freud about a lot of things, but this was the most evil thing I had ever seen in my life. If I'd thought that I'd understood anything about it at all until then, I was wrong. This was my first real sniff of sulphur. I didn't watch for more than, I don't know, seconds ...'

I looked hard at Kerry and had a very clear image of her in a dungeon, surrounded by all this curious sexual activity, watching in horror while what she had once described as 'smaller and more vulnerable people' performed sexual acts on their empirically advantaged elders.

'It was enough to ... to put you off ... sex ... for ever and ever.'

Her words were punctuated by huge sobs, but when she finished she blew her nose again and took some deep breaths before continuing.

'I got up to go. I crept out of the dungeon, but I met Sophie, carefully balancing a mirror decorated with lines of cocaine, on the stairs. I told her I was just going to the loo. She goes, "Ooh, save it, darling, I'm sure there are those here who would die to be pissed on all over by you" and I just smiled and continued up the stairs. Then I grabbed my coat, ran out of the house and kept on running until I couldn't take another step, till I just slumped down in a doorway.

'Anyway, I couldn't face going back to your parents. I couldn't bear the fact that I had been part of it ... part of that ...' Kerry looked as though she might vomit.

She felt all the time that she should go to the police, but she could only walk, completely unafraid, through the London night. She walked through dawn and at about seven am, she headed towards Highgate where she had met Melissa. She had gone home with her and told her the whole story.

Melissa, having small children herself, was horrified and told Kerry to phone the police. When she was calmer, Kerry went back to my home, collected her things, said goodbye to my parents and walked aimlessly again, not knowing what to do.

'So I slept rough, like I told you. It was like a punishment in a way, because I felt so terrible and this is where we come to what you really want to know about – though why I do not know – the precious non-father of my non-baby. Well, for my first night, I wasn't actually alone as I said I was, I teamed up with this guy. I met him near St Paul's and in the early hours of the morning it was so cold that we went into one of those corrugated-iron, coin-operated toilets and we fucked. I didn't even know his name and he never knew mine. It was pretty horrendous really, but it did keep us warm. So there you go, Juliet, satisfied now?'

I was far from satisfied. It was appalling, this ability Kerry had for astounding and repulsing. But after these two feelings had flooded through me, they left only sadness.

'Poor Kerry,' I whispered.

'Why poor? What do you mean?'

'I don't know, I just can't bear the thought of you just ... your body is so precious to me, and you just throw it away, treat it like a piece of shit that has nothing to do with you whatsoever.'

'I suppose I've never really felt that it did, I mean, I don't really *live* in my body. Women can't really, can they? They have to live somewhere else.'

Kerry would come out with sentences like this, which at the time would sound not only convincing but profound. Only afterwards, when I thought about them again, I would realise that they didn't actually mean anything. Nothing at all.

'Now I've started I'd better finish. I feel like the sodding ancient mariner, driven to tell my tale but this albatross is more like a whale in weight, a Jonah's whale which swallows me up. Is this the deliverance perhaps? Confession!'

149

'Oh, please, spare me your metaphors and lectures, Kerry, just get on with it.'

'Yes, well, on the Friday morning, I ditched my dishy young tramp and decided to go and meet the director. I don't know why. I was repulsed by Sophie and Geoffrey and everything, but in a way I was going to go just to see what I would do. I had no idea how I was going to behave. What would happen. Sophie was there and she greeted me as though nothing had happened. The director was a moron. He asked me a few questions, I said that I had trained in Glasgow and still lived there and the fuckwit asked me whether I could get rid of my Scottish accent. I don't have a Scottish accent, I said, I'm from Northern Ireland and I've been told my accent is as thick as Ian fucking Paisley, and I'm not talking about his girth. No one laughed, it was awful. Then he asked me how I felt about nudity, as there were several nude scenes in the film. I said that I didn't have a problem with it, but they would probably want to use a body double since I had two nipples on my left breast. This time Sophie laughed and so everyone knew that I was joking. But the director had really rubbed me up the wrong way with his stupid remark about my accent and for the rest of the interview I was quite uncooperative. Sophie saw me out, but there was a crowd of other actors outside and so we didn't get a chance to talk anymore. She said she would call me later.

'I was really depressed after the interview with the director. I didn't want to be an actress anymore. I was sick and disgusted with everything. I couldn't face doing anything so I didn't. I just wandered the streets again, keeping myself awake at night and sleeping in the parks or somewhere during the day. I thought of just disappearing for ever, I certainly thought about killing myself but then on the Sunday morning I felt OK again. It was like my psyche

150

suddenly woke up and wanted a cup of tea. I felt strong, as if I finally understood something and so it was finished for ever. There was nothing I could do about Sophie and Geoffrey and so I should just live my life. Also, somewhere inside me was that voice that the drama school had instilled into me – The Show Must Go On. It was too strong for me, even when I was being my most rebellious. I couldn't not do the *Antigone* tour. So I came back to Glasgow on the Sunday night.

'Sophie phoned me as she said she would. She was as sweet as sugar, trying to reassure me and trying to find out why I had left the dungeon. She also let me know that she and Geoffrey knew about my whoring days in Glasgow. Well, I knew they must have done really. I didn't say anything, I let her talk and she was just reassuring. Then she phoned about that bank commercial, which I didn't go to, and then she phoned again, angry that I hadn't turned up. This time she was really nasty and told me that I hadn't got the part in the film because my tits were too small, third nipple or not, and when I said snottily that I didn't want to do adverts, she made the same remark you did, something about a whore having principles.

'Anyway, we had a big row over the phone and she threatened me, said she could make sure I never worked again. She wanted me to keep my mouth shut, I suppose, about her stupid dungeon and revolting videos. The thing is, Juliet, the police don't know about this, they know I was at that orgy and also that I didn't really participate, but they don't know about my row with Sophie, or that I had not turned up at an audition and been crossed off their books. They also don't know about my connection with the sauna people, but if they did know all this, they might suspect me and if I am a suspect then who knows what will happen to me – I've got all the motive in the world and no real alibi for that

151

night. For Christ's sake, I'm Irish, there's no justice here for me. I could wind up in jail for ever just because the police need to wrap up the case. Don't you see, Juliet, you've got to stop this suspicious nonsense. Please, can't you just leave it alone now?'

I thought for a moment about Inspector Godfrey's kindly face and the way he had looked at Kerry when she had joked about her Irishness. I couldn't imagine him carrying the kind of prejudice Kerry feared.

'It isn't even a murder case yet, Kerry, they don't know that they're dead, this is complete paranoia, surely? God, and you talk about me!'

I thought back on how she had first told me her sauna story. That first time in the cottage, New Year's Eve. She told the truth up to the point where she was in the car behind Byers Road with the medallion man. Then she became creative. Telling me she had got out of the car and walked away, no whoring, no dominatrix act. Telling it like she now wanted it to be. Repudiating her past decisions, her past selves. Did Kerry always re-write her life in this way? Was she doing it still, with these awesome new stories?

Once I knew the truth, once the story had been told and I possessed its horror, I kept it in my mind for days, like film on a Steenbeck, rewinding and fast-forwarding bits, moments suspended in my imagination, stuck. But at least I knew. It was all there and once I got used to it, not so bad as my imagination had made it.

Much harder to bear than the orgy, which she had after all merely observed, and even harder to bear than her dominatrix act, which seemed camp somehow, a bit of a scream, was her casual coupling with a complete stranger in a public toilet.

As for the paedophile material screened in the dungeon, I was surprised. One heard about these things, the press

152

seemed obsessed by them, but I had always assumed that it was largely right-wing sensationalism, with a darker ultimate purpose. Accusations of paedophile porn on the Internet was the best way of facilitating government clampdown and a state-controlled information highway.

My brother Edgar had probably influenced my thinking here. He was a great one for conspiracy theories. For Edgar, any paedophile material out there was probably being disseminated by the CIA in order to justify making the strong arm of the law even stronger. Likewise serial killers and even terrorist attacks.

This is largely, I think, because basically Edgar has such a trusting faith in his fellow human beings that for him it is inconceivable to think of real, ordinary individuals doing such vile things. Much better imagine some dark meta-conspiracy, machinations on behalf of the faceless military industrial machine. A corporate enemy.

I wondered what Edgar thought about the scandal of Daniels & Daniels Personal Management.

Billy and Chris found a flat in London and prepared to move. Petruchio came back from Italy only to tell us that he too was leaving Glasgow and going back to Milan. He stayed a week, and then left. We had a special farewell dinner party, but it was not a happy occasion. Everyone was trying too hard to recreate the old atmosphere.

We had given our notice in on the flat. My parents had agreed to buy a studio flat in Glasgow, which I could live in while I finished my training. Kerry was going to move her stuff in and stay with me until she decided what to do.

Chris and Billy left the day after Petruchio, and Kerry and I had one night alone in the flat. We went to the pub, got very drunk, and then went on to a nightclub because we couldn't bear to go back to the empty flat. When we got back, we felt terribly guilty for having been out because Freyja, left in a largely empty flat, had been very unsettled. The following morning, I forced myself to go to a lecture. When I got back home, it was to a frantically miaowing Freyja and a note from Kerry.

Juliet, I am doing this because it is the only thing I can do. I can't explain anything. I have nothing to give you or anyone and so I am going away. I don't want anyone to know where. I just have to be on my own. You said so often that I was always acting. Well, maybe I have to be on my own now so that I can't act anymore, there will be no audience. I have always needed so much reassurance all the time, I just need to be alone for a while, to be just me, unobserved, alone. Up to now, my fear of solitude has outweighed my need for it. Do you understand? Having said that I can't explain, I am now trying to. It won't work. How can you explain the inexplicable? It wasn't until I met you that I learned how totally inexplicable things really were, at the very basic level. It's perhaps best to leave it there – blame it on the quantum, on the absolute relativity of everything, on fundamental uncertainty. I said I really loved you and I do and I meant those words. Goodbye, Juliet. You can keep my stuff or get rid of it, it doesn't matter which.

Where would Kerry go? I phoned her parents in Ireland. They said she had phoned them to say she was going travelling and not to worry, she had plenty of money. They sounded cross.

I had not needed to ask Kerry what she had done with all

the money she had earned from her dominatrix act. She always spent money like water, she was incapable of saving or, at least, had been until the last few weeks. How much could she have saved over Christmas, working at War and Pizza?

I alternated between anger, worry and puzzlement. Why did she do that? This foreboding little note roused all my curiosity again. All my need for her, all my fear.

I put the letter in an old wooden jewellery box, where I kept my Kerry memorabilia.

I hired a van to move all my things and Kerry's too. Christine helped me pack and unpack them in my new home in Partick.

The day after I moved there was a brief paragraph in the *Guardian*, saying that police were questioning a man in Glasgow in relation to the disappearance of Geoffrey and Sophie and that a prostitution and porn network had been uncovered operating from a sauna and health club in the west end of the city.

I tried to get on with my studies but I couldn't concentrate on anything for very long before thoughts of Kerry crept in. I began to doubt that I wanted to be a vet. The trouble was, I didn't really want to be anything. I wanted to find Kerry. I wanted her to come back to me, and help me understand. It was as though she held the secret of the universe and was deliberately and spitefully withholding it from me.

A week later I was in the canteen at the university when I received an urgent message to go to the department's reception. Inspector Godfrey was standing reading the notice board. He greeted me, 'I went to the flat and were told that you had all moved out. You forgot to leave any forwarding address – here.' He handed me a handful of mail, mostly junk, and one letter from Italy addressed to Kerry. 'Lucky I knew where to find you.'

'What's happened?' Kerry's dead, I thought.

'Nothing I know of, I just want to ask you a few questions, like where is Kerry?'

'I don't know, she's gone abroad, travelling, she hasn't been in touch yet.'

'Can I talk to you instead then?'

I nodded and we went to a nearby coffee shop.

'Kerry's name has come up again in our investigations. I can tell you that personally I don't think she is involved at all, but I just want to find out a bit more about her. You told us that she tells a lot of lies. Can you tell me a bit more about these lies?'

'Well, I suppose Kerry told you the truth in her statement, about the agents and the orgy, et cetera?'

'Yes, I think she gave us a pretty comprehensive account.'

'Kerry lied to me a lot about her sex life, I was very jealous and she – well, some people would say she is a free spirit, others would say she was a dirty little trollop. I loved her and I know she had nothing to do with the disappearance, but ...' I broke off, uncertain. Inspector Godfrey said nothing, just waited for me to continue.

'Kerry is paranoid about the police, because she is Irish and—'

'The best way you can help Kerry is to tell me the truth,' the inspector said, 'then I can eliminate her from our enquiry.'

I told him about the man from the sauna and Kerry's career as a dominatrix, leaving out all the obscene details. He seemed totally unconcerned, as if I had told him that Kerry belonged to Amnesty International or something. I became more daring.

'Did she tell you about the child pornography?'

He nodded.

156

'Well, that really disgusted her and she didn't want anything to do with Sophie or Geoffrey anymore. She knew she should have gone to the police then, but she just wanted to forget all about it, I think, so she did nothing. She was really frightened when they disappeared because she hated them and wanted them dead. You know the way we all feel in school assembly when the head is on the prowl for a thief and you feel your face going red with shame, even though you didn't do it, yes?'

He nodded again.

'She also felt that there wouldn't be any justice for her in this country, being Irish, I told you she was paranoid.'

'And you don't think for a moment that she had anything to hide?'

I laughed. 'Kerry always had something to hide, but how could she possibly have had anything to do with it?'

'Did you ever meet this man from the sauna?'

'No.'

'Did she ever tell you his name?'

'No.'

Inspector Godfrey thanked me, and said he didn't think he would need to bother me again, but could he have my new address anyway.

When I got home that night, I threw away the junk mail, opened the letter from the bank to me, re-addressed the one letter for Chris, and then I picked up the letter from Italy to Kerry and wondered what to do. As I was wondering, my fingers tore open the envelope and I can remember being somewhat surprised when the letter, in Petruchio's handwriting, was suddenly open before me. I felt a momentary panic. I shouldn't be doing this, I thought, but by then it was too late and so I read the letter.

Kerry, I am saying goodbye, I cannot live anymore but I wish first to explain a few things. I have no regrets with what we did, and you must not feel any guilt, certainly not for this, my death. I involved myself for reasons I think you can guess, a test or experiment partly and an ultimate rebellion on my part, an up-arse to God and the order of things. The most important thing is for you to be free, Kerry, to forget. I believe I would have killed myself in any case, perhaps not now, but some day soon for certain. So it is not for you to make connections between our secret and my suicide. No. It is only one more thing about this world that I cannot accept, one small thing among many. I have had no capacity for happiness. As for you, you have a far greater problem than I. You know my thoughts but I cannot presume to offer them to you now. You must do what you must do but do not do anything out of fear. You must not be afraid, little Kerry, the wave function won't collapse. Do you understand? Remember the cat is neither dead nor alive until somebody opens the box. Do whatever you must do, but again I say, do not be afraid. *Ciao*, have a party with our friends to celebrate my passing into the perfect peace of nothingness. Petruchio.

The first thing I thought was: had Inspector Godfrey read the letter? Then a relaxed irony. No, the letter had not been opened, but how strange that he should have had it in his hand, that he should have given it to me. Then a barrage of questions: what had Petruchio 'involved' himself in? What had he and Kerry done? And was Petruchio dead now? I looked at the postmark; the letter had been posted nearly two weeks ago. Had he done what he said he would?

I didn't believe that Petruchio would kill himself but all the same I felt an overwhelming grief, which was not really for him, but for all the things that I didn't know. I didn't know what to do with myself. I paced the flat, going to the phone, but realised there was no one I could call; I had no alcohol so the usual first recourse was denied to me. I read the letter over and over again, then realised that I would have to destroy it, and I had a sudden, clear image of Kerry rushing out of the cafe in Oban and throwing the fang into the sea.

What the hell had been going on? How on earth had Kerry and Petruchio been involved in the disappearance of Sophie and Geoffrey Daniels? These questions formed themselves over and over in my mind and then they were accompanied by a sort of mantra in my brain of 'I did see it, I *did* see it, it was real'.

Part of me wanted to take the letter to Inspector Godfrey, to cry in his arms, to tell him to find out for me what had happened. My need to know was stronger, for one moment, than my protective feelings for Kerry. But then I committed the letter to my memory, the way Kerry had learned her lines, and burned it.

I went to bed but couldn't sleep. I longed for some of Petruchio's sleeping tablets to knock me out, I even thought of going out and finding a late-night chemist and buying enough drugs to ensure that I never woke up. Perhaps if I died I would know, perhaps Petruchio would be there, waiting for me with a sardonic smile.

By morning I was sick, with a feverish headache and nausea, able to do little but pace around the flat like a caged beast. Eventually, I phoned the laboratory where Petruchio had conducted his experiments on the dead cat. They told me that Petruchio was dead and gave me his parents' address and telephone number.

Petruchio's mother answered the phone, but I spoke no Italian and she no English; when I mentioned his name she burst into loud tears and left the phone hanging, I called several times down the phone until a male voice informed me in broken English that he was Petruchio's brother and what did I want. I explained I was a friend of Petruchio's, that we had shared a flat.

'Yes, yes,' he said, in just the way Petruchio used to, 'he have injected himself with animal anaesthetic, he dies two weeks.'

My voice sounded strange when I spoke and it was painful, as though there were glass shards in my throat. I said that I was sorry, that I was so sorry, over and over again. I wanted to put the phone down, to not have to deal with this.

I asked him if a girl called Kerry had been there at all.

'Who is Kerry, why she being here? Petruchio have girl-friend?'

No, I explained, only a friend. I was sorry I had mentioned it, and I awkwardly closed the conversation with a confused and upset-sounding brother.

I found it hard to breathe. I packed a few things, put Freyja in her basket, and went to the station. I had to get away, to go somewhere. I bought a ticket to London and got on the train, but after only two stops I got off, knowing I couldn't sit still or bear the hours of confinement. Having obtained more money from a cash point I got a taxi to the airport where I took the next shuttle to Heathrow. As the taxi turned into the street where my parents lived I asked the driver to drop me off at the corner, and instead of going home I went to Melissa's.

She wasn't in. Her husband answered the door, welcomed

me in, gave me a drink, and told me that Melissa wouldn't be long, she was at an Open University tutorial. I didn't really know what the Open University was at the time, and I was so absorbed anyway, that I didn't respond. It must have looked very weird, me sitting there with my duffle bag stuffed full, and Freyja miaowing from the cat basket. We made small talk until Melissa walked through the door, looking very happy. She changed when she saw me. Her face moved from gaiety to an expression of compassion and pity tinged with fear.

'Juliet,' she said, and I must have looked so distraught that she came to me and put her arms around me, soothing me with the same words she probably used to put her children to bed.

Melissa's husband tactfully went off to the pub, and I told Melissa that Kerry had disappeared, that Petruchio had committed suicide, and that I suspected that, between them, they had had something to do with the disappearing agents.

Melissa poured us each a glass of brandy. Then she told me that Kerry had been to see her and stayed one night, leaving in a taxi for Heathrow the following morning.

'I don't know why she came to me, but she seemed upset, as though she were running away from something. She freaked me out a bit to be honest, I was glad she went.'

For one vicious moment I didn't believe Melissa, I thought she was hiding things from me and I wanted to grab hold of her throat, to pin her down and hit her until she told me all she knew. We were sitting very close together on the sofa, and she smelled of a mixture of perfume and children, which in that moment of anger, repulsed me. But in an instance, it was all gone and I felt an overwhelming love. I remembered that Melissa didn't lie.

Melissa put me to bed, and I slept well but felt groggy when I woke and incredibly thirsty. I went downstairs, panic making me retch. Melissa was alone in the kitchen; the kids, I presume, long packed off to kindergarten or wherever, and Mr Melissa making big money in the city. I sat down at the table opposite her.

'Do you know where she is?'

'No, but she was looking in the paper and she made a mark at an advert, she said it sounded fun ... hang on, I kept it.'

Melissa went to one of the large dressers in her kitchen and reached up for a pile of newspapers on the top shelf.

'Here.'

I found the cheap-holiday section and, sure enough, Kerry had circled an advertisement for some kind of 'green' commune or other. I asked for a piece of paper and a pen and I took down the address of this place in Spain. A place called Las Cascadas in some obscure village near the coast of Andalusia.

I grabbed a pen and began to make calculations underneath the address. It was the last week in January, but only the third week of term and my grant money, even with my train and air tickets, was not too badly depleted. Half was still there, at least. I certainly had enough to get a plane to either Malaga or Almeria, whichever was the cheapest.

Melissa didn't try to stop me. I asked her to take Freyja to my parents' house the following day and to tell them that I had had to go away and would be in touch. 'Make sure they don't worry,' I said. Once I had made up my mind, I took the tube to Heathrow and bought a ticket there for Alicante, which was the only available flight for twenty-four hours. I still had to wait for four hours and three whiskies, but finally I took off for sunny Spain. I wanted Kerry, I had to see her, I had to have the truth: Part Two.

It was four o'clock in the afternoon when I arrived in Spain.

I was thirsty, so went straight to a stall and bought a can of Pepsi. Then I went to an information desk to ask about transport to Malaga or Almeria, the place I needed to be being about halfway between the two. My Spanish was non-existent and I was just about to give up, when a North American man, who spoke Spanish, came to my rescue. I could get a bus to Murcia and then a train down to Almeria, arriving at two am in the morning.

The bus was crowded and uncomfortable but on the train I finally slept and woke to the sound of my own voice, saying, 'But what about the fang?' The crowd of young people in the group of seats next to mine laughed and I, too tired to feel embarrassed, smiled at them and shrugged and went back to sleep.

Someone gently shook my shoulder. A cleaner. We were in Almeria. It was 2.44 am.

I spent the remaining night on the station concourse, in an all-night bar where I drank coffee and ate tapas before I eventually fell asleep in the corner and was mercifully left in peace.

With an indescribably foul mouth, I woke the next morning and headed for the *servicios* pronto to clean my teeth and freshen up. Then I bought a Spanish phrase book and, armed with it, found my way to the bus station. I took a bus to Castas, the nearest village of any size and on arrival went into a bar and asked for Las Cascadas. I was pointed in the right direction and began to walk. Two and a half hours later, very hot and tired but exhilarated by the walk, I turned a corner on the mountain road and saw a small collection of derelict-looking houses in the valley beneath. I followed the road down until I reached a dirt track going off to the left, with a wooden sign saying 'Las Cascadas'. I was trying in my mind to place the houses I had seen, feeling sure I was going in the opposite direction, when all of a sudden the dusty avenue opened out into a newly swept courtyard, ivy-covered houses to my right and, to my left, a trellised area with bountiful vines covering three large wooden tables and chairs. Behind this attractive terrace, I could see well-attended vegetable gardens sloping down the valley, stopping abruptly at an irrigation channel, beyond which must have been a steep drop further down to the river below. The river, I had been told, was called the Rio Agua, and I later learned that this was a joke because there was rarely any water in it, running as it did through the Almeria desert.

The door to one of the houses was open, the doorway covered only by a gauze fly screen that looked as though it might fall off its hinges at any moment. I called out through it several times but there was no reply, so I walked on to the next house. This house didn't have any kind of door; I walked through into an empty room, the stone floor recently swept. I shouted but again there was no response, so I started idly following the road, past some more ramshackle houses on my left and vegetable gardens to my right. Just as I was reaching the dead end of the road, which stopped at an imposing, though crumbling, house, a young guy with a helmet of cropped white hair came out of the bushes by the house, and wandered barefoot towards me, dressed only in shorts and with a towel over his shoulder.

'Hi,' he said, 'I presume you've come to the right place, no one ever comes here by accident! I'm Andy –' he proffered a hand – 'I'll take you back to the house.'

We walked in a not uncomfortable silence, back to the first house and through into the kitchen. This time, though, a man of about fifty, like Andy wearing only shorts, with that hide of tanned skin that gave him away as being someone who had lived long in the sun, was brewing coffee with mint in it on the stove.

164

'Hi,' he said, when he registered me through the gloom of the kitchen, 'I hope you've booked because we're stretched at the moment; we've reserved a couple of decent hovels, but if you haven't booked, you'll have to not be too picky about where you sleep. Coffee?'

I nodded and was handed a steaming mug of black liquid. 'I'm looking for someone called Kerry actually, I heard she might be here and I came on the spur of the moment – I haven't booked.'

'Kerry? Irish girl?' The man led us through another fly screen into a tatty, low-ceilinged living room. I nodded and sat down.

'Kerry's gone across to Morocco for a few weeks; you can get a boat for about two thousand pesetas from Almeria, so she did that. She left some stuff here and said she would see us later.'

For some reason, this news did not distress me. Maybe the laid-back atmosphere and sheer physical beauty of the place affected me as soon as I set foot there. I drank my coffee, and, in spite of not having booked, was given one of the reserved beds in a long room upstairs, consisting of some iron beds and a lot more mattresses laid out in lines, each surrounded by territorial boundaries in the form of possessions, clothes, pictures, suitcases, plants and teddy bears. I recognised some of Kerry's possessions around my allocated bed. So she had slept here. I lay down and buried my head in the pillow, trying to smell her, to find her smokey scent in fabric that stank only of mothballs. I sat up and stared down at a pair of her sandals by the bed. Andy popped his head around the corner.

'Everyone else is sleeping or gone to Mojácar for a trip. If you've walked from Castas, I expect you'll want to wash. You know where you met me coming out of the bushes? Well, follow that path and you'll reach the black hole.

165

That's where we wash.'

I followed his instructions and found the place, named, I presume, because of the large caves in the cliffs above, unreachable from the pool. There was water in the river that year clearly, and a dam had been constructed to make two large pools. I tore my clothes off and dived in to the first and largest. As I came up for air, I screamed on being confronted with a creature rising from behind a rock in the other pool, a savage creature of mud and markings that laughed apologetically as he came towards me.

He was a man with a South London accent, covered from head to foot in clay and on his chest and face he had finger-painted in the clay, producing tribal-like markings. The clay itself was only half dry and so gave him a mottled, snake-like look. His head, too, was covered in clay and he held out a slimy hand for me to shake.

'I'm Rob, hi, come on over here and get some clay. It's what we use to wash with. No one is supposed to use soap or stuff here. Of course people do. What's your name?'

'Juliet, I'm a friend of Kerry's,' I said, following him through to the other pool. He stretched out on a rock while I dug down into the river bed, coming up with handfuls of grey clay and plastering it over my body.

'Kerry, oh yeah. She said she would be back soon – I miss her, man, she's a lot of fun. How long are you staying?'

'Until she comes back at least, I guess.'

I lay down in the sun on the rock and allowed the clay to dry whilst my companion bathed. Then I staggered back into the pool in my taut clay-skin and felt the water slowly dissolve this strange armour. I have never before felt so clean. We dressed and walked back up the winding path and up to the sandy road.

'I'm the chef,' Rob told me, 'but every week I get a day

off and there's a rota for the meals. I hope it's good, I'm starving.'

We went back into the kitchen, where several women all wearing leggings and T-shirts, but of varying ages, were scurrying around, mixing ingredients, putting vast dishes in ovens and organising cutlery. I asked about the place and was told that the hamlet had been deserted during the Spanish Civil War, after some massacre had taken place.

I went to the 'dorm' and did what little unpacking I had to do, then went back downstairs and outside to the terrace, where groups of people were sitting with boxes of wine. I was introduced as 'Juliet, a friend of Kerry's', and I sat down. Dinner was announced almost immediately and we all queued up outside the kitchen. On the counter inside there were vast bowls of salad and a bin full of bread. On the stove there was a huge pan of vegetable curry and another of rice. We helped ourselves and then went back to the terrace and ate hungrily. The food tasted wonderful and I remember thinking for a moment – how could Kerry have left this place?

There was a huge bowl of fruit salad afterwards, and more boxes of wine opened. Some people were planning to go into Castas for a game of pool and were organising cars or hitching parties. I declined, needing to get some sleep. There was a brief meeting after dinner in which duties were discussed. Rotas were drawn up at the beginning of each week and so I had to be fitted in, beginning the following day. The irrigation ditch was apparently a priority so that was where I was allocated. The people going to Castas left and the people on kitchen duty went to wash up. Those remaining began to roll joints and someone fetched a backgammon set from the house. I took a joint offered to me and, with the wine, the travelling and the intoxicating environment, it finished me off, I went to bed, where I dreamed again of opening the front door of the flat and going towards the body, the body moving and the vampire woman rising, laughing and rushing out of the door.

Nonetheless, I woke feeling incredibly rested and excited on remembering where I was. Not because of Kerry, nor because of the desperate quest I was on to find her and the truth. It was because of the place. The hot, safe feeling of waking in that whitewashed and windowless room in southern Spain.

I was at Las Cascadas twelve days before Kerry returned. Twelve days in which I lived in what was a kind of sybaritic slumber which then became an erotic trance.

By the end of the first day, I felt I knew everyone there; we had already shared adventures and so bonded. Breakfast was at six am and at six-thirty everyone began their allocated chores. On the first day I went with five others down to part of the irrigation ditch which had collapsed and we set to work, building it back up and creating a channel. The channel ran along the edge of an escarpment, over a drop of about five feet. There was some subsidence, where people had used a shortcut to the river and we built this up, piling branches to block the way. At about ten we stopped and went back to the kitchen for coffee; again, the same mint-flavoured, thick, black liquid which we drank along with mugfuls of water. We then went down to the river, where I had bathed the night before. One of the others, a girl with peroxide blond hair who had, on first glance, reminded me of Kerry, was standing in the river washing sheets and curtains with a scrubbing brush and microscopic amounts of an environmentally sound washing powder. While she carried on with her washing, we checked out the two dams and collected small rocks and stones to build up their vulnerable parts. I started to make a pile near where the girl was washing and we chatted. She was an actress, she said, who was escaping her profession, probably never to go back. I asked whether she had met Kerry; she had briefly, but obviously not long enough to know that Kerry had been an actor. She asked me a few questions about what I did, and I asked her again about her acting. She hauled a pile of wet and heavy sheets from the riverbed, where they had been weighted down with stones. She looked as though she were concentrating hard as she hung the sheets on a makeshift line between trees. I thought she had not heard or was ignoring my question, but as soon as the sheets were all up and drying, she sat down in the shallows.

'I didn't do that much, I was just beginning really: one medium-sized part at Farnham, panto chorus at Croydon and a microscopic part in *Brookside,* that's all. I had these agents, you see, you may have heard of them, the ones that disappeared in Glasgow. Remember those weirdos with their dungeon in Kensington?'

I laughed rather meanly, 'Yes, I've heard of them.'

'Well, I was pissed off enough with the business before then, but that really did it, I mean, they seemed so *sweet*, you know, and to find out all that about people you were trusting with your career ... well!'

'I can believe it.'

At about eleven-thirty we stopped working and went back to the house, where folk dispersed back to their beds or sat in the sun or under the vine until twelve-thirty when lunch was served in the kitchen – a spicy soup consisting largely of rice, served with home-made bread and Marmite or peanut butter, and a selection of fruit including several watermelons.

After lunch people had siestas, played backgammon or cards, or went to the river to lounge in the sun and swim. I went for a walk, following the river downstream and going through narrow ravines where the rocks overlapped, forming caves and tunnels. After a couple of miles there was a fairly obvious path up through the rocks and up the mountain. I followed this path back towards the hamlet until I came to the road.

A couple of hundred yards along the road I noticed a driveway to my right, leading up to a house, almost completely obscured by trees. I heard voices coming from somewhere in the secluded garden, a man with an upper-class English accent.

'Oh, for God's sake, can't we go next week? I don't think it's a good idea to go anywhere right now.'

I wondered who they were and whether they had anything to do with the commune.

Supper was just being announced as I arrived and I fetched a plate of pizza and salad from the kitchen. There were more people than the previous night, and the tables and wooden seats under the vine were full. I sat, with my supper, on the step outside the door to the living room and was introduced to 'our visitors from the village'. They were young boys, about fifteen or sixteen years old, accompanied by an older man, thirty-something, who looked like a pre-Raphaelite Jesus, with long, fair hair and a beard, wearing jeans and a shirt open to reveal a silver crucifix on his chest.

This was the local priest, I was told, who was doing wonders with the disaffected youth of Castas, having formed a hill-walking and pot-holing society. Some of the young boys had Mopeds, which were parked under the trees and, when we had all eaten, they began racing down the road and past the house.

Rob the chef was responsible for inviting them for dinner. He spoke good Spanish and had met the priest several times in one of the bars in Castas. He had even been on one of their pot-holing expeditions. Relations between Las

Cascadas and Castas were not good. The villagers thought the community at Las Cascadas dirty and immoral; there were rumours about naked orgies by the river and of people sleeping in overcrowded rooms with rats and cockroaches. (During my time there I did see a couple of cockroaches in the kitchen, but no rats. There were several mangy-looking cats, no doubt responsible for vermin population control.) Rob was doing his best to improve relations and getting the priest, who was something of a local hero, to visit us with his youth club was regarded as a bit of a coup.

I was tired after my walk so, after supper, I went upstairs and slept for a few hours. When I woke I could hear voices on the terrace below and I went back down to join them. Rob the chef, a few others from the commune and the Spanish boys were smoking and drinking, engaged in a backgammon tournament. I helped myself to a glass of wine and sat down. In one of the other houses, a few doors down from the main house, someone was playing a guitar and others were singing along to mostly Elvis Costello songs.

One of the Spanish lads had a tattoo on his arm, which the others seemed to be teasing him about; Rob occasionally translated their bantering for the non-Spanish speakers. Every now and then, the boy with the tattoo would look at me in a sly sort of way. I stared back at him at one point and he blushed.

I asked Rob about the people in the house up the road.

'What people? That place has been deserted for years.'

'But I heard voices there this afternoon.'

'Perhaps there are squatters, then.'

'No, it didn't sound like squatters.'

'Ghosts, then,' he laughed.

'Where's the priest?' I asked and was told that he had left.

Rob suggested a midnight swim. The blonde girl, the

actress, whose name was Hettie, appeared from the music house just as we were leaving. She whooped with delight at our plan, just as Kerry would have, and rushed off for a towel and torch.

It was very dark and we didn't have a torch. I was anxious; eight or nine drunk and stoned people walking down an extremely dodgy path in the dark – there was bound to be an accident. No one else seemed remotely concerned and when one of the Spaniards fell about ten feet down into the bracken, everyone laughed and cheered as, yelping with pain, he clambered back up. Eventually we got to the river where Rob set about building a fire on the bank and the lads thrust themselves into the pool, fully clothed. Hettie took off her dress – she was wearing nothing underneath – and joined them. I, too, stripped off entirely and waded into the dark water.

The Spanish boys were thrown into exuberant confusion by our nakedness. They spoke excitedly to Rob, who replied seriously to them, explaining something. The boys laughed and then played a game of trying to push each other into either Hettie or myself. Hettie seemed annoyed and I wondered what Kerry would do in this situation. Then I guessed, and I rushed towards them, thrusting my breasts forward and shaking them, my arms outstretched. They ran from me, terrified, and then sat helpless on the rock, roaring with laughter. There was a little round of applause from the bank, where a small fire was smoking excessively. I swam into the next pool where Hettie joined me and asked whether I wanted to see the jacuzzi.

We walked back through the first pool and up-river, clambering over large rocks and wading with difficulty through reeds for a short while until the river widened. Our eyes became accustomed to the dark, the moon was reflected in the water and we followed it. After another hundred yards

172

or so, Hettie led me to the bank and down some rocks to the bottom of a drop, where there was a waterfall cascading, first about five feet and then channelled off by rock formation so it formed three spouts into another pool a few feet lower down. This was the jacuzzi.

'Has Kerry been here?'

''Spect so, she hung around with Rob a lot and he's bound to have brought her here.'

I didn't feel jealous. That's the thing I note now. I felt incredibly happy and wanted Kerry to have been there, so that it was something we shared. I was glad she had been with Rob, since he was gentle and good and cooked wonderful food. She had been looked after.

I can't believe it now, that that was what I felt. What was it with that place? It was incredible: from the moment I had arrived, I had felt this numb kind of peace. It was as if I had forgotten everything else. It was as if I had stepped into another world, in a different skin. I had gone there to confront Kerry with what I suspected might even be murder and I had instantly laid back into the environment, with its irrigation channels, its vegan food, its paradise of hippies, punks, priests, chefs and hooligans.

It was an atmosphere so strong, thick like a soup, into which I walked and then floated there, everything else – all other concerns – suspended, banished from consciousness.

I don't think I have ever lived more in the present than I did during those few weeks in Spain; totally and happily absorbed in each moment. I *was* only what I was doing: eating breakfast, working through the rota of chores of cleaning, kitchen duty, gardening, the construction of a compost toilet, hydroponic gardening, maintenance and admin.

Cleaning duty was the worst, since the sanitary arrangements consisted (until the compost toilet was completed –

173

Mañana!) of two deep, pit latrines some five and seven yards from the main house. For night-time use, there were three or four large 'pee buckets' and those on cleaning duty had to carry them, often slopping over with foamy, warm urine, down to the latrines to empty them. It caused great amusement when, on the day that this was my loathsome duty, I commented on the unhealthy colour of the urine and suggested that people drink more water.

The hardest chore was tree planting, since this involved pick-axing into gypsum, digging small holes for the saplings. By nine am the sun would be blazing down on the mountain. Kerry later told me that when she had done this duty, she had got through it by pretending that she was a political martyr doing hard labour in some unspeakably right-wing state.

Hettie and I finished our jacuzzi and climbed back to the others. Some more people had joined the party, including the guy with the guitar, and they were now singing Beatles' songs. I wrapped myself in my towel, lay down on the ground and looked up at the stars. Hettie started to explain to everyone which star was which. I turned my head and noticed the tattooed Spaniard looking down at me. He was lying beside me, although I had not noticed that when I had settled there. I smiled and he smiled back. I must have then dozed off for a while. When I woke there were fewer people by the fire. Hettie had gone, so had the guitarist and only Rob and the Spaniards were left.

I moved closer to the fire, which was blazing healthily and took the joint Rob passed me.

'I think you've got an admirer,' he said.

I laughed. 'How old are they?'

'Well, Rodrigo is sixteen, the others are fifteen. Rodrigo claims that a whore in Almeria gave him his tattoo, but the others know it is only a transfer.'

174

The following day, after chores, I went for another walk, this time upstream where, beyond the jacuzzi, I came across an even larger waterfall and I spent the afternoon there. When I walked back, Rob and Rodrigo were at the poolside, both naked and covered with mud. I joined them, feeling Rodrigo's eyes on me as I stripped and crouched down by the river to snatch handfuls of clay from the cold, squidgy bed. Rob told me that Rodrigo was going to be a doctor. I said I was training to be a vet and Rob translated that into Spanish. The boy looked at me with new respect and some of the tension seemed to leave his body.

Rob dived into the river, quickly rubbed off his mottled skin of clay and grabbed his towel.

'I have to get back to the kitchen, see you guys later.'

Rodrigo attempted to ask me a question in English. I was unable to help him and we gave up, laughing. I don't remember how we got from sitting on the rocks, awkwardly attempting to talk to each other, to kissing and the rest. Did he make the first move or did I? I think it just happened or was mutually instigated but anyway it was peaceful and affectionate and seemed entirely right. But our sex was unprotected and I had no fears or thoughts of consequences. How easily are the laws of cause and effect banished from our weak minds when our libido takes the wheels of the poor vehicle we call the self!

We saw each other every day after that. Always outside, always within earshot of running water. Walking, swimming, and enjoying each other. We laughed a lot, too, in spite of never really being able to talk to each other.

He arrived every afternoon on his Moped. Everyone at Las Cascadas knew about us and one evening Rob told me that the priest had guessed too; his only comment had been, 'God has created sexual desire and Rodrigo is going to be a doctor, not a priest. I think no harm has been done to the universe by this fucking.'

One evening, I was sitting with a group including Hettie and Rob. Someone had just arrived that evening, fresh from Heathrow, and with an assortment of English newspapers. Hettie was reading one, when she threw it down in disgust.

'Yuck, my agents again. God, I feel sick.'

I picked up the offending article and there was a small item about a definite link between Sophie and Geoffrey, the Glasgow S&M network and a nasty video shop in Finsbury Park. In other words, the police were nowhere with the case. There was a photograph of Geoffrey and Sophie.

There had been other photos in other papers that I had looked at but for the first time now I really studied their polished, smug faces. Sophie was sleek and blond and Nordic-looking, with a vacuous Sloaney face. Absolutely nothing like the dark and sultry Rocky Horror dead person that I saw and then didn't see. Geoffrey's face I knew; he was certainly photogenic; he looked very handsome, his face inclined fondly towards his wife.

What was it that Kerry and Petruchio had done that he urged her to feel no guilt over? Why did I assume that it had something to do with these people, these rich and powerful faces? Coincidence is a dangerous thing, I thought: What the hell was I doing here, chasing Kerry around the continent? I was mad, it was all complete paranoia, I was losing touch with reality. Horrified, I realised that I had been creating scenarios, whole narratives even, that were entirely off the mark when it came to the reality of the actual, external world out there. The external world. The material world.

I blamed the dope; I blamed Kerry; I blamed myself; and then I felt sick. And all this in the few minutes before someone jolted me back into the group by asking me a question. As soon as I could I left the terrace and walked down to the river. I sat for hours feeling rage, self-loathing and, most of all, foolishness.

But later that night, as I lay in bed listening to the sounds of my sleeping companion, I remembered again that Petruchio was dead, that I had his letter memorised in my head, that he and Kerry had done something, they had a secret. *Remember the cat is neither dead nor alive until somebody opens the box*. What the hell is Petruchio's cat?

I had to do that. I had to open the box. Oh, little Kerry, I have to collapse the wave function, whatever that may be. And then I felt furious with myself. I thought of all the lies, the drama, and here I was getting wrapped up in it all. Well, I was going to get to the bottom of this, if it was the last thing I did.

The next day was a Sunday. In the evening, Rodrigo and I were walking back from a day spent downriver, when we passed the drive leading to the mysteriously occupied house. I indicated that I wanted to go in and explore. Rodrigo hesitated and then followed me up the drive. Music was coming from a ground-floor window. We ran to the wall and crept along it to the window. A man and woman were talking.

'Sophie, if we stay here for ever, do you think they'd ever find us? Do you think those hippies will ever come up here?'

'We can't stay here. When it's safe we'll go back.'

'When will it be safe?'

'Never. Sometimes I think it's never going to be safe, never again.' Her voice changed suddenly from panic to mischievous defiance. 'Well, I don't mind if the hippies do come up here, it might be amusing.'

'And you're prepared to break up our safe haven for the amusement value of a bunch of new-age wastrels.'

'All right, you amuse me instead.'

I looked through the glass; the man and woman were embracing, his back was towards me and I could just see a dark head of hair beyond his shoulder. From the back, it could be, it just could have been, Geoffrey. Rodrigo was creeping back along the wall. I followed and we ran down the drive.

Back at Las Cascadas, Rodrigo excitedly told Rob in bullet-speed Spanish about the couple in the house on the hill. Rob questioned me and I said that we had definitely heard people, a man and a woman, but that I hadn't caught any of their exact words. Rob said he would go up there after supper.

During supper the words spoken by the mysterious squatters ran themselves through my mind, a tormenting conveyor belt. *Sophie, if we stay here for ever ...*

I said I would go with Rob, but he insisted that he go alone, so I followed him. I stayed hidden in the road, watching him walk up the drive and knock at the front door. The man opened the door and, after only a few words, let Rob in. I ran up the drive and crept around the wall again. The window was shut and I could hear no voices inside. I peeped in, and the room was empty. I crept round the house, crawling beneath the windows, until I heard voices. I pressed myself hard against the wall and strained to listen.

Rob was obviously explaining the aims and ideals of the community at Las Cascadas. Then the man explained that they were squatting here for a few days. Rob invited them down for dinner the following evening, but they declined. I waited until I heard the front door open and close and Rob's footsteps as he walked down the gravel drive. Then I stole quietly back round the house and slunk away.

I decided to wait until Kerry was back before I took any further action. If they were the agents, then Kerry was certainly involved. Either she was protecting them or they had somehow followed her here and were waiting to do her harm. I had been right in following my instinct and coming to Spain. Kerry might well be in need of me.

The following Tuesday, Rob announced he was going to Almeria for supplies. I was on kitchen duty and he asked me to go with him. Some people were due to arrive that day so, after staggering through the supermarket, loading up several trolleys of essential groceries, mostly boxes of wine, we went to the airport and waited for an hour and a half. Rob was holding up a card reading LAS CASCADAS and two girls from New Zealand and a bloke from Milford Haven headed straight for us. We piled into the van and drove a short way before we stopped at a bar. It was a typical road-side bar, a wooden hut, raised on concrete pillars. Six huge fans were suspended from a low ceiling above a long bar, plastic tables and chairs, a juke-box, a pool table and a pinball-type game.

A very dishevelled-looking boy in a peaked cap stood by the juke-box. He turned when we entered the bar. He was Kerry.

'Oh, wow, man, fucking excellent, I was just about to hitch,' she said, recognising Rob and then she saw me and her expression changed to one of first horror and then aston-ishment. 'Juliet!'

'Hi, there,' I said casually, 'I came to find you, I needed to get away too.'

We had a drink and Kerry told us all about her adventures in Morocco. She had gone to Casablanca and Fez with some South Africans she had met. Kerry noticed my familiarity with Rob and asked how long I had been at Las Cascadas and how I had found out she was there.

'Melissa told me, I've been here nearly two weeks.'

When we arrived back at the commune, I walked with

Kerry and the newcomers down to the black hole but, having introduced the others to the clay and the pools, I asked Kerry to walk with me and I led her in the direction of the waterfall.

She sat down on a rock and said without expression, 'What are you doing here, Juliet?'

I told her that Petruchio was dead, that he had killed himself. Telling her made it real for the first time. To my surprise and relief I cried, I burst into tears and Kerry stared at me while all the life went out of her face and she became smaller. I tried to stop crying but it seemed an age before I was calm. Kerry had moved towards me, she had grown again though her voice was frail and broken.

'When?'

I blew my nose, took a deep breath and explained about Inspector Godfrey and the letters. She looked appalled when I confessed that I had opened Petruchio's letter. Her face contorted suddenly and she began to retch. I reached out for her, holding her and pleading with her to forgive me. She pushed me away.

'What did it say?' she rasped.

I recited the contents of Petruchio's letter. Tears rolled down her face as I spoke and when I finished Kerry stood up and walked into the pool and over to the waterfall. She stood under the white cascade until she disappeared, the water all around her like a tent. She stayed there for ages. I knew she was all right, that she had created a vacuum and could breathe. Perhaps she was shouting or crying; I could hear only the fall of water.

At last she emerged, like a sprite. Her face was hard, cast in misery. I knew that I was going to ask no questions, that I would leave her with her grief. She started to walk back up along the river to the black hole.

'Kerry, I think Sophie and Geoffrey are here. In the house

on the hill. Do you know anything about this or have they tracked you down?'

'What?' Kerry sat down again, completely confounded.

I blurted everything out; all my crazy thought processes since reading Petruchio's letter, how I had convinced myself that he and Kerry had something to do with the vanishing agents, and then how I had spied on the squatters up the hill, one of whom was called Sophie, that I had put two and two together.

'Are you in some sort of danger, Kerry?' I finished.

Kerry's face had visibly relaxed as I gabbled on, then she stood up. 'Come on.'

'Come on where?'

'We're going up there, Juliet, right now. You are completely mad, completely paranoid – dangerously so, but we are going up there right now to sort it out.'

'Wait, shouldn't we be more careful, Kerry if–'

Kerry cut me off angrily. 'Juliet, this is completely crazy, you are out of your mind, you have been for ages – making connections between things, inventing things, playing Sherlock fucking Holmes with my life ...'

'Things were connected,' I shouted, 'and peculiar. You and Petruchio – what were you doing that night of the party? What's the terrible thing that you did? That fang, Kerry – why did you throw the fang in the sea? And that corpse, the corpse by the cupboard that I saw with my own eyes, I can't forget that, I just can't.'

Kerry turned round and looked at me. 'You didn't see it. Petruchio drugged you. He drugged me too that night. You were right, he was trying to prevent me having the abortion, and it wasn't because I was drunk, but because I was drugged that they wouldn't do the operation that day. I also had hallucinations that night, in fact, the reason I didn't go to the party was because I was completely and utterly out

181

of my head, thanks to Petruchio. But afterwards I had to lie to the police to protect him.'

'Do you know how I know you're lying?'

'I'm not lying.'

'Yes, you are, you got more and more relaxed and animated as you told me what you just told me. Easing yourself into the performance – I could see you.'

'I'm not lying.'

'Well, why did you want to protect Petruchio? The bastard drugged you and made you suffer an extra week of being pregnant ...'

'Yes, but you know Petruchio – or knew him. He was different to everyone else in the world – you didn't have the same kind of feelings of anger about anything he did. I loved Petruchio. So did you, so did we all.'

'What was the terrible thing that you did together? What did you "involve" yourself in? And why shouldn't you be afraid?'

'Recite the letter again.'

I did as she bid me, and she nodded sagaciously while I did.

'He was nuts really, totally nuts. The terrible thing he did was drugging you and me and, I suppose, the terrible thing I did was to have the abortion. He thinks I am tearing myself apart with guilt for it and ... oh, I don't know. I don't know what was going in on Petruchio's dark mind, but that letter ... he was experimenting with all sorts of drugs – on himself you know. He said that drugs could collapse the wave function of consciousness – turn it into something different altogether.'

I smiled. She was good, very good, I was almost convinced but I still had a trump card up my sleeve.

'Then what about the fucking fang?'

'We planted the fang there. Petruchio and I. It was a joke.

We were trying to drive you a bit mad, to show you that you weren't immune. You had been behaving hysterically over me anyway, so Petruchio said, and you *were* possessed and obsessed, but you thought you were so cool, so rational –' she broke off, no doubt because of the expression on my face which, I can only suppose, reflected my inner state of pain and unwillingness to believe.

'Juliet, we were fucking with your head, perhaps that's what Petruchio thinks was so terrible. Perhaps that's why Petruchio's dead.'

'So it wasn't that I was paranoid at all; I was absolutely right.'

Kerry nodded. I didn't believe her. 'I'm sorry, I'm so sorry,' she was saying, but I didn't believe her. As though she had read my thoughts, she came over to me. I was surprised to find that I had sat down in the middle of the river in my despair; I had not noticed the water flowing around my legs and stomach.

'Come on, let's go and clear this last madness from your mind.'

I followed her up the hill in silence. I hesitated when we reached the drive but Kerry took my hand and marched towards the front door. There was no response to her first, moderate knock so she banged hard and called out. There was a shuffling sound from inside and then the man opened the door.

'Hello, we're from the commune,' Kerry smiled warmly. 'We wondered if you wanted to come to supper?'

'Come in.' The man ushered us through to the room that I had first spied into. 'We're not going to be left alone by you lot, are we?'

It wasn't Geoffrey. I could see that now. This man had none of the agent's suave superiority. He was rather mouse-like. The woman rose from the sofa when we entered. The couple could have been any age between thirty and forty-five and they both carried an aura of sophistication and calm. Kerry strode over to her and shook her hand.

'Hi, I'm Kerry, this is Juliet, we're from the commune. Why don't you come down and eat with us tonight?'

'Well ...' The woman looked at the man, who shrugged. 'I'm Fiona,' she continued, 'this is Tom, we've just eloped.'

'Fi.' The man's voice held a warning in it.

Fi, So Fi. The man had said: "So, Fi, if we stay here for ever ... " I felt unbelievably foolish. The woman continued.

'Oh, what can it possibly matter? We haven't committed a crime, and everyone's going to know sooner or later. What can it matter now? We've done it.'

'Yes. Oh, I'm sorry, can I get you a drink?' He disappeared for a few minutes and the woman asked us to sit down. Tom returned with some bottles of beer and a bottle of wine. Kerry asked for a glass of water only, while I took a beer.

'I don't care what Tom says,' Fiona looked first at Kerry and then at me, 'I've got to tell someone, I've got to tell you. Tom – it can't matter now and we've got to go back, you know we have.' She had gone over to him and was kneeling at his feet. Tom shrugged his shoulders and gazed at her adoringly.

'Well, you see, Tom and I have been friends for years and years, about fifteen years. Tom and my husband were best friends, and Tom's wife and I were best friends. We all met at college, got married young, and we were all terribly happy.' She looked up at Tom, who nodded his corroboration.

'We've had loads of holidays together and two weeks ago, we all arrived at this villa near Valencia and, well ... Tom and I, we ... we eloped.'

'I think we've loved each other secretly for years,' Tom said, taking her hand and kissing it.

184

'Maybe even from the beginning,' she purred up at him.

Kerry laughed and said oh wow or something, and I asked how they had ended up here.

'We took our car, I mean mine and my husband's car, and just headed south, madly, we didn't know what we were doing. We drove all night and slept in the car when dawn came. Then we decided to head for Seville, but we couldn't stand the main roads, so we took the mountain route, got lost, and we were heading for Castas to find a room for the night, when the car broke down just outside this house. We explored, found the door open and the house deserted, pushed the car up the drive and fell asleep on the sofa there. When we woke up we walked into Castas, bought a whole load of provisions and hitched a lift back. Then we holed ourselves up and forgot about the whole world for a while. It's been wonderful, so wonderful ... I can't tell you ...'

We could see. They were inanely in love.

'But what will you do?' I asked. 'Won't they be frantically worrying about you?'

'Oh, absolutely. Tom phoned his daughter back in England and left a message to the effect that we were all right and no one was to panic or phone the police. Of course, they already had. We don't even know whether they are still at the villa or whether they've gone home.'

'We've done something so terrible and we are both so happy, it's appalling,' said Tom, shaking his head in resignation.

'Oh, believe me,' said Kerry, her voice deep and grave, 'you've done nothing so terrible. Perhaps your respective partners will get it together –' her voice lightened – 'I mean, it's all too *Private Lives* to be true.'

'But you can't stay here for ever, can you?' I said, rather sternly. The whole scene was beginning to irritate me. I didn't want to get involved in someone else's little drama. I wanted to be alone with Kerry.

'Tom, I think we should go down there for supper tonight. It will be like a rehearsal for going back to the real world, which we have to do, any day now.'

'All right then, my love, anything you say.'

We finished our drinks, Kerry and I waited while the runaways got ready, then we walked down to Las Cascadas together, Kerry enthusing about the commune as we went.

When we arrived, folk were gathering around the terrace, opening boxes of wine and getting ready for supper. Kerry announced our visitors and told their story; they were then welcomed like movie stars, and a thousand questions were asked of them, until the food was declared ready and we queued up outside the kitchen.

After supper I asked Kerry to go for a walk with me. We went to the black hole and Kerry tried to climb up to the caves that gave the place its name. She fell and I rushed towards her, crying out in alarm.

'See, you do care for me,' she grinned, then leapt up and began hopping around madly, clutching her limbs and shrieking in pain. Eventually she quietened and sat down.

'Of course I care for you, Kerry, and I admit I have been completely obsessed by you. But you told so many lies – how can I possibly know things unless you tell me?'

She kissed me quite harshly on the mouth and gazed at me with a sad intensity. I told her about my Spanish lover. Perhaps to set up a distance between us, I don't know. The whole idea filled her with glee and she asked endless questions, until I told her to mind her own voyeuristic, or rather audioistic mind.

'What are you going to do now?' I asked her.

'Go back to London with you, I suppose,' she replied.

We hitched a lift into Castas the following afternoon and

telephoned the airport in Almeria to book a flight home. We then had two more days in Spain, days in which I worked with Kerry in the morning, digging a pond in the vegetable garden. Both afternoons, when Rodrigo came, Kerry went off with others into Castas, or down to the black hole with guitars.

Kerry was different. For one thing she wasn't drinking or smoking. She said she really wanted to clear all the shit out of her system.

'And it's easy here, isn't it? This place is so beautiful, you don't need anything else.'

A non-needy Kerry? This was new to me, and I kept expecting her to have a drink or ten, to start manically rolling joints. But she didn't. I wasn't just expecting, I was hoping. I didn't like this wholesome, clean Kerry. The Kerry I had come to need was wild, impulsive, she smoked too much, she drank too much and I could always criticise her, feel superior, dismiss her. But mostly the Kerry I needed, needed.

We had to do cleaning duty the last day we were there.

'Just as well,' I muttered, 'it'll make it easier to leave – our last memory will be of pee buckets.' As we swept and dusted and disinfected the main house, we listened to the radio, and left the arduous task of emptying said buckets till last. There were a lot of houses to sweep and we split them up between us, arranging to meet back under the vine for a coffee break before tackling the washroom. One of the houses, and the carpentry workshop, were at the top of the hill. I walked up the steep and rocky path, the sun hot on my back. I didn't want to leave Las Cascadas. Why couldn't we just stay here for ever, hanging out in the sun and doing chores? Some other members of the commune were working outside the workshop, building more fly screens, simple wooden frames, covered with thick green gauze.

'So you're taking Kerry away with you?' someone remarked to me. 'Shame, man, why can't you stay longer?' I said something about the real world awaiting us and was told that the real world was all over the place, here as much as anywhere else. I pondered over this for a while, reflecting on how I had tended to divide the world into hierarchies of the real. Glasgow was more real than Highgate. My generation was more real than my parents'. The world of veterinary science was more real than the world of the theatre, and everything in Britain was more real than this Shangri-La in Andalusia.

When I returned to the main house, Kerry was already sitting under the vine with a large bowl of coffee. The kitchen was busy with people, either continuing their duties or queuing up for coffee. Those queuing were told that they were in the way and asked to take the coffee pots outside. I wanted to speak to Kerry on my own, but I had to wait until the break was over and we had gone to the washhouse at the back of the main house, bracing ourselves for our grim duty.

There were four pee buckets in all and they were too heavy to carry two at a time. Kerry began to retch as soon as we neared them and I almost told her to get on with cleaning the floor and showers and that I would do the buckets. But my generosity died almost as soon as it was born, and I said nothing. We picked up a bucket each and started our slow and careful trek down the steep path leading to the latrines.

'Why did you come here, Kerry? You said in your letter that you wanted solitude. Well, this is hardly that, and then from the sounds of it, you weren't alone at all in Morocco.'

'Solitude is more a state of mind, isn't it? I suppose I meant being away from anyone who knew me. A chance to start afresh, with no preconceptions. Anyway, I saw this place advertised by accident and thought it was as good a place to start as any. I wanted to come to this part of Spain anyway, because of Lorca – I just love Lorca.'

'I wish I could trust you.'

'So do I.'

We had reached the latrines and we emptied the urine into them, then trundled back up for the other buckets. When we had finished cleaning the areas around the deep pits, and finished off the washroom, we went straight down to the black hole for a thorough wash.

On our last night we went to see Fiona and Tom in their squat. They had had the car fixed, and were planning to leave the next day. They were going back to their real world. Facing the consequences. We wished them good luck.

We were driven to the airport after fond farewells at Las Cascadas, with promises to keep in touch that I knew would not be kept, and we stopped in a bar en route where Kerry drank two double whiskies and announced that she hated flying.

'I thought you weren't drinking.'

'This is medicinal, to calm me down.'

On the plane, she curled up and, as we began to move, she reached for her bag and started rummaging. For a moment I thought she was going to bring out a joint and light it up to calm herself down, but instead she found a pen and, after digging around some more, threw the bag back on the floor and reached across to take a sick bag.

'Are you all right?' I asked nervously; the stench of vomit revolts me. But Kerry merely began writing, scribbling furiously.

'Fine,' she said. 'I'm going to write it all down to distract me from the experience. Don't you think that writing will take my mind of it?' We were just about to take off. I laughed. Kerry grimaced, but carried on writing nonetheless.

'There.' She handed me the bag. 'It's called *Novel on Brown Sick Bag*.'

> im so scared of flying i wish i wish i was dead
> its that im afraid i want retribution of some sort
> so yes why not why not why not why not me it
> should be i deserve it god punish me but don't let
> the devil have the rest not juliet not all these
> other people me on my own with a fucking thun-
> derbolt god don't let this plane crash oh christs
> testicles how can juliet be such a calm plane is
> about to defy all the laws of everything and go up
> into the sky and its pathetic to feel this way relax
> stay cool and yes i think its working i think im
> ok now this is what to do with it represent the
> experience away

I laughed and hugged her. We were in the air. When the hostess arrived she ordered another double whiskey. I had an orange juice.

'It's the worst thing you can possibly do,' I lectured, 'you dehydrate enough as it is flying.' As soon as I said it I thought how pompous and boring I was and that no wonder Kerry had been constantly unfaithful and contrived with Petruchio to humiliate me. Kerry, however, smiled at me affectionately.

It was Friday evening when we arrived in London. Kerry was elated, having survived the flight, and also starving hungry. My mother fed us before she and my father began to lecture me. They had been concerned about me, they had received a phone call from my supervisor enquiring as to my where-abouts and whilst I don't think they had actually been all that worried while I was gone, now I was back they felt quite

190

cross. Especially as I was so deeply tanned.

Kerry was overjoyed at her reunion with Freyja, crying with delight. The next day we went to visit Melissa. She was pleased to see us and keen to hear all about Spain, and whether we had 'sorted it all out'.

Kerry and I said simultaneously, 'I don't know.' We laughed.

Melissa's husband came home, in what seemed to be a bad mood. He grudgingly acknowledged our presence, and asked us if we thought Melissa was looking awful, 'tired and ill?' I said that on the contrary I had been thinking how well she was looking.

'Yes,' he snapped, 'and the secret of that, is that she is having an affair of course, this new bloom in her cheeks, this different and totally *unsuitable* style of dress.'

Kerry and I gaped at him in amazement, while Melissa laughed softly at him and said *sotto voce* to us; 'This Open University course means going to tutorials and meeting people, and I'm really enjoying it and so he thinks I'm having an affair.'

'And are you?' said Kerry, quick as a flash, as if he wasn't in the room.

'No, of course not, but try telling him that.' He scowled at her and left the room, but after a few minutes he returned, kissed her solemnly on the head and said, in a pleasant voice, that he was popping down the road for a pint.

It was strange being with Kerry and Melissa. I saw how much Melissa liked Kerry, how Kerry seemed to make everyone who met her feel protective towards her. There is definitely a form of neoteny at work with human beings; little people, with small features like Billy, like Kerry, they attract people to them, people want to cuddle them, to look after them. I would hate to be small.

On the Sunday we went to see Chris and Billy. They were living in a flat in Crouch End. They had cooked a big Sunday roast in our honour and Kerry and I looked at them in dismay at the thought of breaking the news of Petruchio's death.

They were both shocked, of course. Billy cried and Kerry joined him. Then I reminded them that in his letter he had told Kerry to have a party with his friends, so I insisted that we celebrate his passing into nothingness. We talked about Petruchio all through the meal, remembering his peculiar little habits, his dull intonations. We laughed. We said that, in spite of everything, we had all loved him.

Billy and Chris were doing all right in London. They both had got agents, but so far no auditions. Nonetheless the novelty of the metropolis had not worn off and they were full of optimism. Before the evening ended Kerry said that she didn't know what she was going to do so Billy told her that she was welcome to stay with them for a while.

I took the overnight train back to Glasgow on that Sunday night, and Kerry moved in to the flat in Crouch End.

I was in trouble at the School of Veterinary Science – I had been AWOL for three and a half weeks. I used Petruchio's death to plead compassionate leave and was allowed to continue my studies. Then I discovered I was pregnant. I organised to have an abortion privately and Benedick, who had just landed his first major TV role, gave me the money. It was quick and relatively painless and I forgot all about it very quickly. I assumed that the clinic I went to was the same place that Kerry had been to.

I spoke to Kerry on the phone, but didn't tell her about the abortion. I didn't want to grace it with enough importance to be discussed. She was fine, she said, but she seemed tired and uncommunicative. I asked her what she was doing and she said, 'Oh you know.'

'Why don't you look for work, be an actor again or do something else with your life.'

'Because why? Life isn't something that you necessarily have to *do* something with.'

Kerry had only been in London a month, when one evening she appeared on my doorstep in Glasgow. On first sight, I have to say, I was not pleased to see her. It was a nuisance. I needed to work and here she was back to distract me. She gauged my slight stress, and laughed, dumping her bag in the hall and hugged me. 'It's all right, I'm only staying one night. I'm going back home for a while and then I'm going travelling. I just wanted to get a few things.'

'You've put on weight,' I said.

'I know. It's giving up smoking.'

I cooked supper and sent her out to buy some wine. When she came back she poured me a glass.

'Aren't you having any?'

'No, it only makes me want to smoke.'

We ate in silence until suddenly Kerry started laughing. 'Isn't it funny – the way things are with bodies?'

'What do you mean?' I spluttered, mouth full of spaghetti.

'Well, whenever we were together once, we used to put our bodies together and do nice things and now we don't.'

'We didn't when we were eating, or not usually,' I grinned at her. 'Are you saying that you mind?'

'It isn't really something that you can mind. It just is. Once, we put our bodies together and let them do nice things, now we don't. It just is. Isn't it?'

'Yes.'

Kerry started to giggle. I felt cross momentarily, but then I tried to feel lust for her and failed.

She left the following morning. I thought of renting out

193

my flat and going back to Las Cascadas, but the days went by and I took no such action.

For the next few weeks I lived very quietly. Sometimes I saw Christine but I did not make any new friends. Perhaps the heady intimacy of the bizarre flat-share was enough for me. I had exhausted my need and potential for closeness.

I worked hard at college, trying to make up for my absence and years of under-achievement. Immersing myself in my studies was a merciful diversion from all the angst and drama. I worked hard, not out of any drive, or conviction, but out of a despair which said: if there is absolutely no point in doing this, then there is also no point in not doing it. It passed the time.

Nonetheless, she was still able to penetrate and infect every aspect of my life. During a practical session on euthanasia techniques, in which we had to practise methods of holding and injecting small animals on the carcasses of gerbils, cats and dogs, I was overcome with a most uncharacteristic squeamishness and I had to excuse myself and go to the ladies' to throw up. I suppose I was thinking of Petruchio injecting himself with animal anaesthetic. But I also felt that Kerry had taken me over in some sense, that I threw up because she would have done; she had infected and possessed me.

I had a recurring dream at this time. I am at a public hanging in a town square. There are hordes of people gathering around the scaffold and I am being jostled by the crowd, all waiting for the prisoner to be brought out for execution. The woman in front of me is eating a toffee apple. I am in a sweat. I feel sick. I know who the prisoner is and I cannot bear what is about to happen. I must prevent it.

The dream changed only in size, or if you picture it like a film, in terms of aspect ratio. Sometimes it was like really

194

poor 16mm black and white, and sometimes on an Imax screen in breathtaking Cinemascope, glorious technicolour, stereophonic sound. The dream unsettled me, although I was comforted by Kerry who once informed me that according to Jung all the characters in our dreams are, in fact, different incarnations of ourselves. Petruchio, of course, had said that this was nonsense. I like to hope that it is not. I find it easier to live with the idea that my unconscious wants to kill myself.

One night, about a few weeks after my return to Glasgow, I was curled up on the sofa in my dressing gown, watching a late-night movie. It was a Hammer Horror vampire movie. The bride of Dracula flew across the room at her prey, the innocent blonde threw her hands up in despair and her neck into her assailant's face. The vampire babe drank long and deep and a close-up of her mouth, fangs dripping with blood, filled the screen. An image in my head replaced it: that of Kerry throwing the fang into the sea of Oban. Then I saw her standing in the river at Las Cascadas: '*We planted the fang there* ... it was a joke ... we were fucking with your head.'

And suddenly – and truly like a bolt from the blue – I realised something, something so essential and so obvious that I jumped up from the sofa and shouted out loud, 'How could I have been so stupid?'

Why did they plant a fang? A *fang*? How could they have possibly known what I would see in a hallucination? I *had* told Kerry I had seen a corpse, but a totally non-specific corpse and, in any case, that wasn't until *after* I had found the fang. Her whole story was lies. And what was worse was that as soon as I knew, I felt that somehow I had always really known it.

I tried to find out where she was. I contacted everyone who knew her but no one had heard a thing. I started to dream again of Petruchio, of a rotting Petruchio reaching out of his grave to tell me something, of Petruchio as a vampire planting his fangs into Kerry's neck, of Kerry's wild orgasm as he did so.

I was so angry. I realised now they had well and truly diverted me with the whole vampire thing, the over-kill made me forget entirely that I had never, not once, told anyone exactly what I had seen that morning: the ghostly vampire in her white gown and with blood-stained feet. I had been so paranoid about everything else that I hadn't noticed the one thing that I most needed to be paranoid about.

I went through all her things looking for clues, I picked up all her books and shook them, looking for I don't know what. They were tatty; she had no respect for them as property. I found myself sniffing and looking through these tatty, torn tokens of the works of art she loved. Kerry had the habit of making pencil marks in the margin of books. I remembered how Petruchio had once seen her marking a book. He was horrified.

'I really regard such as an act of vandalism, it is a sacrilege to treat a book so.' The indignation in his voice rose as Kerry glared at him coldly. 'I think it is a kind of rape,' he concluded.

Kerry guffawed with laughter, opened the book and passed it to him, 'Yes, but these wide margins, I mean, they're asking for it, aren't they?'

Over the next few days, I was obsessed with Kerry and, increasingly, obsessed with my obsession for her. I began to loath myself. For the first time I experienced the awful self-loathing she seemed to suffer from so often. A nasty inner voice would accuse me, trash me; what does it say about me if I love her, if I love one so skilled in the art of deceit that her reality is never discovered? The case unsolved. Clever Kerry. The one that got away.

196

I tried to get on with things, but my inner life, or whatever, was totally taken up with questions, blame, fear. It was terrible the way the pain would appear suddenly, out of nowhere, whatever I was doing. I could be working, walking down the road, absorbed in just living, when I would be entirely engulfed by feelings so strong they would wipe me out physically, make me want to keel over, to throw up, to scream. In tiny fractions of a second it would all be there: the love, the constant betrayals, the histrionics, the baffling feeling of having been deserted. I knew I was not going to be happy until I had seen her again and made her tell me the truth, the real truth. Then, I sometimes thought, I might kill her.

One afternoon I decided that I would get rid of all Kerry's things, her clothes and books and paraphernalia. I would, at least, get her out of my space. I sorted her clothes into piles, one for Oxfam, one for the dump. There were two coats, a long white cape-like affair and a black leather jacket. In the breast pocket of the jacket I found a syringe and a little phial containing liquid. Once again, she had the power to horrify and confuse me. I remembered that Kerry had been wearing that jacket when she had turned up on the crazy morning when I saw the corpse, found the fang and the police came round. I put the syringe and phial in her little wooden box and put all her books and clothes away, unable to face the trip to the Oxfam shop and dump.

Then I stopped going into college. I stayed in bed for whole days. I went to the doctor, who prescribed anti-depressants. My parents phoned me and must have gauged the seriousness of my condition, because my mother appeared at my flat one afternoon, finding me watching a movie in a drunken stupor. She took me (and Freyja, with whom I would not be parted) back to London. I had taken Edgar's place as the problem child.

*

For the first week I stayed inside mostly, moping around, watching television. The anti-depressants didn't work and so I was prescribed another kind. These made me feel sick so I gave up. I didn't see anyone except my family and Melissa. Things had been going badly for her. As part of her Open University course she had had to go to various Summer Schools. During one of these, at Bath University, she had met a man whom she had become romantically attached. She had not, however, consummated the affair. She was not thanked for it. Her husband was convinced that she had slept with the entire summer school and taunted her mercilessly with accusations. She came back one evening to find him in the garden making a bonfire of all her course work. He forbade her to continue her studies. She took the children and went to his parents, whom she had always found sympathetic. They agreed to try to persuade their errant son to see a psychotherapist of some sort and organised a reunion on that basis. They struggled on, but Melissa was miserable. The Open University, which she persevered with, had become a great unmentionable in the household. She hid her books away and worked only when he was out, snatching odd moments and longing, most of the time she was with him, to be back buried in some tome or other.

When I visited her sometimes I felt guilty for taking her away from this labour of love and then I remembered my feelings for Kerry, my jealousy of everything – the cigarette in her mouth, the book in her lap. I felt a sickly sort of pity for Melissa's husband and I mused yet again to myself on how the differences within the sexes are so much more vast and various than those between them.

Of course, I told Melissa that she must leave him. Shit, at least I had made some sort of effort with Kerry! Who left me anyway.

On the Sunday afternoon of my second week back home,

I was watching an old movie when Melissa appeared on the doorstep with a black eye. He had hit her.

'You have to leave him,' I said, hugging her and drawing her in to the house. I went to turn the TV off, but she knew the film and begged me to leave it on. It was a Bette Davis movie and I poured us each a whisky and we watched to the weepy end.

'I will leave him,' she began, 'obviously I have to. The only thing that has kept me with him so long is the sex.'

I couldn't have been more astonished. 'The what?'

'Sex. It's always been great, he's a wonderful lover, and it's the one thing that we've held on to. Even when there's anger when we fuck, it's exciting. I suppose we've done it so much we've got good at it – and his smell, Juliet, I love his smell.'

I had begun to laugh during this, and now I couldn't stop, I was helpless.

Melissa joined in and continued, 'I really thought that I could handle everything because of it, if only he had just left me alone and let me study. The OU did change me and took me into areas where he wasn't going to follow, but that wasn't a problem to me; it was OK to have different interests. I never once found him boring – which he was constantly accusing me of – because he didn't understand what I was up to.'

'So dump him,' I said, refilling our glasses.

Melissa went home, packed and took the children once more to her in-laws. This time, she said, there was no going back. Once again they used their powers of persuasion, and whatever grasp on rationality her husband still possessed, and persuaded him to move out, buy a flat, and leave Melissa and the children in the house.

Then Billy and Chris heard from Christine that I was back in London and contacted me. They were devastated to discover that I had jacked in my studies.

'Fuck's sake, Juliet, you cannee throw away all that, you've got the brains, man, what's wrong with you?' Billy said when I went to see them.

'Nothing. I just don't want to be a vet, or anything in particular. Life, as Kerry once said, isn't something you necessarily have to do something with.'

Billy had had a few bits of work here and there but nothing to speak of. He was drinking heavily and Chris was constantly bailing him out of financial ruin. Chris had landed a part in a soap and so far the writers were keeping him in, so he was happy. He had a stream of short-term relationships and spoke sentimentally about Christine.

There was a long article in one of the Sunday papers about the agents, who had now been missing for almost six months. It was written by an ex-client and friend, and was a convincing defence of Sophie and Geoffrey, as well as an academic and well argued plea for tolerance and freedom from sexual taboo. The picture he gave of the Daniels' was that of free spirits, sensualists, people daring enough to experiment, to go to the limits. He ridiculed the accusations of involvement in the production of pornographic films, let alone those catering for the paedophile market. Sophie and Geoffrey rarely watched porn; apparently, the screen in the dungeon was mostly used to video-project Hollywood musicals or films from the avant garde. There was a veiled attempt, too, at a defence of paedophilia, using Freud as verification. Like Kerry, the author didn't believe in childhood but, unlike Kerry, he missed the point about experience and empirical advantage. Kerry hated the word innocence. She said it meant lack of knowledge: 'and knowledge, as we all know, is power.'

The theory expressed in the article was that Geoffrey and Sophie were murdered by a sexual pervert they had picked up. The writer dismissed any speculations that they were still alive. Their money had remained absolutely untouched and there was too much of it left behind for them to have had a secret stash in a Swiss bank.

The article re-kindled tabloid interest in the case, and endless theories were espoused; the most ridiculous being the *Sunday Sport*'s account of how the missing agents had been chosen by randy extra-terrestrials for transportation to their planet and a life of unbridled sexual pleasure.

I cut out all these articles and put them in the wooden box. New additions to my sentimental collection, along with the sick bag Kerry had written on in the plane. I felt sure that whatever had happened to the agents, Kerry knew something about it. I would lie awake at night, in a panic, thinking that I would never see her again.

I went round to see Billy and Chris. Being with people who knew Kerry gave me some sort of comfort. Chris wasn't in but Billy was there, drunk as usual. We drank scotch. I asked him whether he had ever thought there was anything going on between Petruchio and Kerry, anything odd?

'Oh aye, they were shagging, I'm convinced of it.'

I laughed, and asked him why.

'They were often in Petruchio's room for hours and hours, and then I think they used Mrs McNicol's flat one time, when she was away.'

Billy told me how he had seen first Petruchio, then Kerry come down the stairs from Mrs McNicol's flat. He had been coming in when he saw Petruchio, who looked nonchalant, as if he had been watering the plants; but when Billy left the flat almost immediately, he saw Kerry creep sheepishly downstairs. He put two and two together.

I told him I couldn't believe that there was anything sexual going on, but I had thought that they were behaving very strangely.

201

'Oh aye, completely barking, both of them, but then aren't we all? Petruchio was all right, though – I'm sorry he's dead, and as for the wee man, I just fucking loved her to bits, I was jealous as hell of you at first, ye know.'

I hadn't known. 'She loved you, too,' I said, as if I was some kind of authority on Kerry's emotions.

In my third week of being back in London, my father called me to the phone one evening and hearing a gravelly, and at the same time soft, Glaswegian voice made the hairs on the back of my neck prickle. It was Inspector Godfrey. He, too, was very concerned to hear that I had given up my training. He said that he was in London for a few weeks and he thought he would look me up. He had tried to contact me in Glasgow and the university had told him I was back at home.

'Has something happened? What do you want me for?' I asked nervously. He laughed.

'Well, something curious happened a few months ago, and I thought you might like to know about it. I wondered whether you would meet me for a coffee or something.'

We arranged to meet the following day. As I walked down the road towards the allocated wine bar, I prepared myself for the worst, but what worst I daren't imagine. He was already there, looking very relaxed and he greeted me in a friendly, laid-back way. I allowed myself to wonder whether this was just a social call, that he had looked me up because he was attracted to me. I then felt myself tighten with a different kind of nervousness.

'I hope I haven't alarmed you by turning up like this,' he said. We ordered a bottle of wine. He asked me how I was and whether I still saw Kerry. I told him that she had gone back to Ireland about a month ago, saying that she was going to go travelling. I hadn't heard from her. There was quite a long pause; I didn't want to ask him what the curious thing that had happened was in case I appeared too eager, too involved, but then I realised that if I didn't seem interested it might be interpreted as a case of unnatural apathy. However, before I could ask him, he began: 'Your friend Petruchio's brother came to see me.'

I choked ungraciously on my drink. 'I'm sorry –' I hoped that I hadn't gone red.

I looked at Inspector Godfrey. He was inscrutable and, at the same time, unthreatening. I realised, looking at him, that I had always been attracted to him and this thought gave me a momentary panic as if there was something inherently kinky and perverse about fancying a policeman.

He went on: 'You must have all been pretty cut up when he died, you seemed a very close bunch in that flat.' I nodded.

'Have you any idea why he might have killed himself?'

I shook my head. Inspector Godfrey offered me a cigarette which I took and was aware, when he lit it, of how my hand shook.

'Yes, his brother Antonio came to see me in Glasgow. He was trying to find out why Petruchio had killed himself. Apparently Petruchio had become psychotic and before he died he made a rather wild confession.'

I didn't want to know. Now, perhaps, I was going to find out what had happened, and I didn't want to, I didn't want to hear anymore. I felt myself shut tight inside. Inspector Godfrey continued placidly – was he noting my every response, or lack of it?

'He said that he had killed Sophie and Geoffrey Daniels and buried them somewhere between Loch Lomond and Oban.'

I laughed. It was an unnatural laugh, a nervous cackle over which I had no control, but Inspector Godfrey, looking at me carefully, seemed to misread me. 'Yes, I must say that

I didn't believe it at first, but this Antonio was pretty upset. He didn't believe Petruchio's ramblings but feels that there is something in it, and that the agents had somehow driven Petruchio mad. Satanic abuse, agents of the devil, that sort of thing.'

'So you don't believe it, you're not going to do anything about it?' I asked, unable to keep outrage out of my voice.

He smiled. 'Did Petruchio ever meet Geoffrey and Sophie?'

'No. I don't think so, but surely something like this ... you can't just dismiss it?'

'Well, we're not going to dig up the whole of Argyll on the strength of it. We've had over four hundred lurid communications about the missing agents, wild scenarios from corrupt imaginations ...'

'What? I mean, what kind of person makes false confessions?

'Mad people do. Was Petruchio mad?'

I smiled. 'Completely barking.' I longed now to tell Inspector Godfrey everything but I was afraid he would laugh at me, that I would only be making my own absurd confession and that my own corrupt imagination would be exposed.

'There was a lot of publicity about Geoffrey and Sophie. It was in Petruchio's mind as that mind began to deteriorate, and I think it took a hold of his imagination,' said the inspector.

'He took so much Valium,' I said absently.

'Yes, his brother mentioned his drug problem but, strangely, with all the drugs he had access to, he chose one of the drugs he had used to put animals down with, in the laboratory.'

'Which one?' I asked, and my interest was of a vague, by the way, sort.

'Pentobarbitone.'

I knew the drug. It was an anaesthetic that had proved fairly hopeless if you wanted the animal to wake up.

'The strangest thing is,' Inspector Godfrey continued, 'Petruchio injected it into muscle rather than a vein. I believe that causes some pain before death.'

I remembered that class on euthanasia techniques where we practised holding and injecting dead animals and I had rushed to the ladies' to throw up. One of the drugs discussed that day had been pentobarbitone and the necessity of hitting a vein because the drug was an irritant to muscle tissue and intramuscular administration would cause undue pain and distress in the creature's last moments.

'Petruchio would have known that,' I said, 'no one working with pentobarbitone could be unaware of that.'

'Perhaps he just fumbled it.'

'No, he did that on purpose, to make himself suffer. Oh God, poor Petruchio.' I felt very sick and very sad. Inspector Godfrey said, softly, that he was sorry.

'What did Petruchio's brother think about all this – the agents, et cetera?'

'Well, it seems he came to me because he wanted to clear in his mind that this was the rambling of a madman, and also because, if there could possibly be something in it, he thought that Petruchio would want him to take his confession to the police. He was a bright chap, this Antonio, some kind of psychologist. Has a theory that when people feel guilty all the time for no real reason, they eventually invent evil crimes for themselves, in order to validate that guilt. Not that I think that explains the pile of despicable fantasies on my desk in Glasgow. We had a couple of tapes, one from an alleged cannibal who "confesses" to eating the agents.'

'But there *is* a link. I mean, Petruchio lived with Kerry and Kerry was a client of Sophie's.'

'All the more reason for Petruchio to get some crazed idea about it.'

'Then what do you think happened to them? And what if Petruchio did do it?'

'How? You were with him the weekend the agents disappeared, you went to the cinema with him that night, didn't you? Can you tell me how he could have killed two people and got rid of the bodies? And why? Why would he kill two people he didn't know?'

I smiled and went to the bar to buy another round of drinks.

'I'm sorry, I've brought it all back for you,' he said on my return.

I shrugged. 'What kind of people were Geoffrey and Sophie?'

'They were both from wealthy families; they met at Oxford, and they were part of a "drama set" of some kind that took itself very seriously. At one point, apparently, they were all obsessed by Dracula and dressed as vampires. It was a real obsession with Sophie, hence this movie. They were clever, they married while they were still at Oxford, but I gather that the relationship was open and 'experimental' even then. On graduating, Geoffrey got a job with a publisher and Sophie started a Ph.D on the Marquis de Sade. She jacked it in when Geoffrey inherited a lot of money and they established themselves as agents. They were friends with an awful lot of people at Oxford who became successful writers, directors, actors, part of a whole generation, as they say, so they went from strength to strength. Sophie branched out into film and became obsessed with her Dracula project. Their sexual behaviour became more and more extreme the more they experimented. This happens – boredom leads to extremism, and the more you do the more boring you find it, a vicious circle ... is my guess.' Inspector Godfrey looked self-conscious suddenly, and I felt great warmth for him.

'That sounds a bit like the theory that if you smoke dope you'll soon move on to heroin ... if you indulge in kinky or S and M sex, you'll go on to paedophilia?'

'I don't mean that, not at all. No. I don't think it's true of drugs either, for the record.' He smiled. 'I think one could as easily say that if you smoke cigarettes you'll soon move on to cannabis. Actually, in a funny sort of way I think the opposite is true in this case ... if you are playfully indulging in all your fantasies in a self-contained designer dungeon, you are less likely to become a sex criminal. In my experience, it is the most rigid repression that leads to that sort of horror and there was absolutely nothing repressed about Geoffrey and Sophie Daniels.'

'Yes, but what about the paedophilia, when did that start?'

'As far as I know, and as far as I *believe*, they weren't really into that at all. I think that the films screened the evening Kerry was in the dungeon – and others have testified to that evening – were a mistake of some sort, or a one-off at the very least.'

I tried to get a picture of a real Geoffrey and Sophie, but it eluded me.

'Go on, please,' I said, 'can't you tell me your theory?'

'I don't really have one, my mind is open to every possibility. However, I think that, while Sophie and Geoffrey's sexual proclivities were unusual and distasteful to some, they were not illegal.'

'I never believed all those actors suddenly whinging to the press about being abused by the agents. They were grown people; surely grown people don't let themselves get abused like that?'

'I think a lot of actors played the victim for the press,

while the truth is that at the time they were willing debauchees. But, however that may be, Kerry certainly left that dungeon in Kensington a moment too soon. Apparently when Sophie became aware that there were children on the screen, she became extremely angry and broke up the party. It seems a chap from Glasgow was responsible for putting it on, and I believe he planted the other paedophile material in amongst Sophie and Geoffrey's collection. He was connected with the sauna network in Glasgow. We thought Kerry might have recognised him, especially when we knew of her connections in that area.'

'Why would he want to plant the videos?'

'To discredit the agents in some way. Possibly blackmail. An anonymous phone call to the police suggesting an investigation. But who knows why?'

'But you must know some things. Who was last to see them?'

'Sophie left the production company offices and she went back to the Grosvenor hotel. She was seen going in, but no one saw her leave. Geoffrey apparently arrived at the hotel about an hour after Sophie, and left roughly half an hour after that. He was alone and wearing an army great-coat.'

'So where was Sophie?'

'My theory is she left the hotel before Geoffrey, or perhaps even at the same time, but no one saw her because she was in disguise or, rather, fancy dress. I suspect that the great-coat Geoffrey was wearing was hiding his costume and that they were on the way to the party when something happened. The trouble is they had told no one what their fancy dress was to be, so we don't even know what we are looking for.'

'What do you suppose the odds are, that given her earlier obsession, and the nature of the film she was working on, that Sophie would have been dressed up like a vampire?'

'Possible. Probable even. But we don't know.'

'Kerry thought that they were victims in some snuff movie, and serve them right.'

He smiled. 'And you say you haven't seen her and don't know where she is?'

'I've no idea, this was ages ago.' I did not tell him how frantically I had tried to find her. 'I expect she'll turn up one day,' I said cheerfully, wanting to change the subject.

'Are you still holding a torch for her?' He grinned at the quaint expression. 'Or is there a new woman in your life?'

'No, there have been a few men, but no women since Kerry.'

Inspector Godfrey looked down. He cleared his throat.

'Are you married?' I asked. He nodded. There was an awkward silence.

'Look, I confess I had somewhat of an ulterior motive for seeking you out. I find you very attractive, but I thought you were a lesbian, for God's sake, to say nothing about your depressed state, so I wasn't exactly holding out much hope. I was curious, of course, and I thought you would want to know about Petruchio's confession.'

'Why are you so defensive?' I said reassuringly. He smiled. My heart was racing and with a sense of doom I thought, oh no I'm going to go to bed with this man.

'I'm sorry. My marriage is going through a bit of a bad patch and I suppose I am being a bit of a cliché. Please can we change the subject?'

Then I felt a moment's devastation because it wasn't going to happen after all. Followed by a great relief. We parted outside the restaurant and Inspector Godfrey gave me a chaste kiss on each cheek, which I returned with a warm hug.

'Take care of yourself, Juliet.'

As I walked away I remembered our first meeting on that

fateful day in Glasgow. I turned abruptly and called out. He walked back towards me.

'I've got one last question I want to ask.' He nodded seriously. 'When you came to our flat, that very first time, did you notice that there was a whopping great spliff in the ashtray and dope all over the table?'

'Of course,' he said, still serious, 'but we were Homicide and had no interest whatsoever in a bunch of students toking up. I'm not even sure Drug Squad would have been too concerned about you lot.'

'Is it true then that coppers smoke the best spliff?'

'Now, Juliet, you don't really expect me to answer that, do you?'

When I got back to the house I was sick. I felt an overwhelming disgust for that time in the flat and a feeling that we had all been incredibly stupid, that those carefree student days had been unspeakably sordid and we had not even noticed it. Petruchio had been totally mad and we had ignored it, thought him amusing. Even when he had played his revolting Schrödinger's cat joke on Kerry, it had seemed straightforward, comprehensible; I had been so jealous that I had thought only that he had a crush on Kerry, not that he was totally off the rails.

I wanted to contact Inspector Godfrey, to tell him everything that I had left out. Then make him find Kerry, make him find out the truth. I couldn't live with the thought that I was never going to see her again, never going to know, never be allowed to confront her. So I didn't allow that thought to be entertained. I banished the thought, didn't even give it standing space in my head. I *would* see her again. She *would* come back.

In the meantime I decided I wanted to know what the phial that I had found in Kerry's leather jacket contained. I

210

sent it to a fellow student in Glasgow and asked him to get it analysed for me. The result did not surprise me. It was pentobarbitone.

Curiosity made a lunatic of me. I began to suspect that Kerry had killed Petruchio, that she had sneaked over to Italy and cold-bloodedly murdered him. I remembered my phone call to Antonio and my conviction collapsed. But why did she have the syringe and phial? Why why why why why? That word was like a scream taking over my entire being.

How I lived through those next few days, I do not know. Even sleep was no refuge and I had the most unpleasant dreams I have ever had. They came fast and frequent leaving me tired and disgusted the following day. The dreams were obscene, hardcore. They featured Kerry and Geoffrey and Sophie and the dungeon in Kensington and the sauna in Glasgow. One dream even featured Petruchio. He and I were fucking while Kerry, dressed in her rubber bodysuit and mask, whipped us with a cat-o'-nine-tails, and Geoffrey and Sophie applauded from a balcony.

I felt ashamed of these dreams. I would look at my family and friends and wonder whether they had such happenings in their night-heads. When I showered in the morning, I scrubbed my body as if the acts had been physical, as if it had all really happened.

My parents were beginning to nag me into returning to the real world, making plans. They accepted that I wasn't going to be a vet, but insisted that I would have to be something else. They were very worried about me, I suppose. It can't have been easy for them.

It was May, and my parents were going away for a month, leaving me alone in the house with the dogs and cats. The day after their departure was a perfect spring morning, and I went out into the garden, which I had promised my mother

I would look after, and was pruning, weeding and pottering idly with my spade and fork when a voice startled me.

'Oh yes, we must work, work in the garden!'

I turned.

Kerry's head peeped above the garden wall. Of course, was my first thought. Of course she is back. I almost believed that my need for her, my desperation had reached her, wherever she had been. This was no coincidence. She was here because she had to be. I had willed her to me.

She was smiling an enchanted sort of smile. I stood trans-fixed, watching that head move along the wall until it came to the gate and she walked through it and towards me.

'You look truly terrible, Juliet,' she said.

I was then overcome with confusion. This wasn't Kerry. The plump, womanly creature walking towards me was some travesty, some horrible composite, made up of parts of Kerry and parts of someone completely different. I felt unsure. Almost as though I expected her to disappear before my eyes. I am hallucinating, I thought, but then I found myself in a very real embrace. I stared at her and she looked down at her large, protruding belly and smiled. Kerry was pregnant. Very pregnant.

Part Three

Here and There

A daring proposal was made to reconcile the continuity of the Schrödinger equation with the discontinuity of empirical experience. It was supposed that, in every circumstance in which there is a choice of experimental outcome, in fact each possibility is realised. The world at that instant splits up into many worlds, in each of which one of the possible results of the measurements is the one that actually occurs. Thus for Schrödinger's cat there is one world in which it lives and another world in which it dies. These worlds are, so to speak, alongside each other but incapable of communicating with each other in any way. This latter point is supposed to explain our feeling that we experience a continuity of existence for ourselves. The cat who lives is unaware of the cat who dies.

J.C. Polkinghorne, *The Quantum World*

213

'Surprise!' she said.

I wanted to take hold of her and shake her until she broke, hit her, strangle her, punch her. Surprise!

'Where have you been?' I asked absurdly, with my trowel and fork in hand, as if she was merely a couple of hours late.

'Juliet,' she said, her voice small. I relaxed into a shrug and then a half smile. She followed me into the house. I needed a drink.

My parents' cat had recently had kittens again and, while I was pouring the drinks, the little black kitten had crept into the room. Kerry rushed over to pick him up.

'Oh, what a perfect little thing! It's a Bonsai panther.'

The kitten had an exceptionally wide nose, which did make it look like a panther. I laughed and stared at her. Even though she was at least seven or eight months pregnant, Kerry looked smaller somehow, smaller than before. The shock of seeing her was wearing off and was replaced by anger. Her condition had thrown me somewhat and I had forgotten momentarily all that I had been through since I last saw her.

'I hope that now you are going to tell me the whole story, the real story, and nothing but the real story.' My voice was hard.

'I don't know what you're talking about. What story? I've come to you for help. As you can see, I'm about to have a baby and there's no one else I can turn to. I went to Glasgow and heard from Christine that you were back in London. Why, Juliet, why did you chuck in the uni, what's happened?'

'You happened, Kerry, you bloody well happened.'

We sat in silence for a while, she looking at me, with sad eyes. I looked back at her. She's thinner, I thought, her face is thinner and her eyes seem bigger. It wasn't until then that I really took her in. I looked her up and down, from her cropped hair to her muddy DMs, and a look of horror must have crept over my face because Kerry laughed.

'Christ, I don't look that bad, do I?'

She looked Dickensian. She had a long, red and rather worn velvet maternity dress on that was scruffy and grandiose at the same time, with a checked anorak over the top. She looked like a beggar woman.

'Have you been sleeping rough?'

She nodded. 'Only at first; for the past month I've been in a refuge in Dublin. I left because I ... I don't know why ... I'm here, that's why. I suppose I missed you and felt a bit scared and ... needed you.'

'I need the truth, Kerry, the truth – do you know what that means?'

She shrugged. 'Juliet, can I stay with you, can you be there with me? I've no one else.'

'Kerry, I just don't believe this. I don't believe this is happening. You walk in after an absence of several months, without having been in touch, not only that but you are just about to give birth to some fucking baby and you want me to be there for you.'

'Yes. Are you?'

I was. Kerry needed me. And I felt powerful.

'The whole story, Kerry. From the beginning,' I demanded.

'I'll tell you but not now ... I can't explain it without ... well, I can't explain it to you now but I'll tell you when all this – she brushed the back of her hand against her lump, and looked down at it – 'is over. I promise, but, please, can we not just wait till then?'

'When is it due?'

'Any week now.'

'Which week?'

She looked down at her feet, with an expression I knew all too well. The 'you're not going to get it out of me' look that I knew as a perfect representation of her resolve.

I made my calculations aloud, 'May, late May, early June, April, March, February, January, December, November, October, September ... September! The first week of September. That fuck you had in that coin-operated toilet ... but you had the abortion.'

'No, Juliet, no, I didn't have the abortion, as you can see. Now can you please leave it.'

'Why didn't you go to your parents?'

She laughed, a cold nasty laugh. 'You never met my parents, did you?'

Indeed I had not, neither had Kerry ever really talked about them.

'They would have only thrown me out, so I saved them the trouble by not turning up. To them, this baby would be the child of Satan, just because I'm not married, never mind anything else.'

My confusion must have shown on my face.

'You don't really understand about religion, do you?'

'That's why you didn't have the abortion, isn't it? Petruchio won.'

'No, absolutely not. I'm not a Catholic, you know that, I don't believe in anything really, but I believe in abortion. Juliet, I really am not going to talk about this anymore. I've come to you and I've asked you for help. Now, if you don't want me here, then tell me to piss off and I will, but if you do want me here, then, please, no more questions.'

What could I do? Quite apart from the fact that it is not in my nature to turn an old friend in need away, I couldn't let her go for my own selfish reasons: if I let her go now, I might never see her again, and never know what I so needed to know.

217

'Of course you can stay. My parents are away for a month anyway.'

'Thank you, you're a real friend.'

Friend. No, I was not Kerry's friend. I was her ex-lover and that is entirely different and I was now in the most bizarre situation I had ever found myself in. The flat-share and all its brittle mania was nothing in comparison to this. Kerry was going to have a baby. Any day now. How is this possible? Fear took hold of me.

'So, what do you intend ... how? What's going to happen?'

'I'll have the baby, you'll help me.'

'What do you mean, I'll help you – you don't expect me to deliver it for you?'

'Why not? You know how I feel about hospitals, Juliet, and you must have learned how to deliver cows and sheep and things, a little foal must be much harder to get out with all its long legs lolloping about. This is only a baby, and I am fairly sure that it's dead.'

This was total overload time. This was too much, way way too much. I screamed at her.

'For Christ's sake, Kerry, get real! I can't deliver a baby, let alone a dead one! You have to go to hospital – are you registered or anything?'

'No, I don't want to go to hospital, I don't want to register ... please, Juliet?'

No. No Way.

'Kerry, if the baby is dead, there is even more danger and there is no way in a million years that I am going to do what would be tantamount to murder. Women die in childbirth, they used to die all the time, before advances in medical science which you and I have the benefit of. I will be there for you, Kerry, but I don't care anymore about any of your phobias, your secrets, your mysteries, or your lies; that

218

baby, dead or not, will be delivered in a hospital by profes-
sionals and that is my absolute final word on the matter.'

'Medical science,' she said scornfully. 'Petruchio would
have done it.'

'Petruchio was crazy.'

Kerry yawned. 'I need to sleep now.'

Then Freyja crept into the room and stared at Kerry, who
burst into tears, then rushed over to the cat and clutched it
as though it were a lifebuoy in a rough sea. Freyja gave an
endearing trill and thrust her nose into Kerry's face.

I took her to the guest room and told her to have a bath,
and help herself to my clothes. Then I phoned Melissa and
asked her to come round. Kerry did not come back downstairs. I heard her running the bath, and then later leave the
bathroom and go to her room. I presumed that she fell
asleep and Melissa and I spoke quietly and conspiratorially,
though the house is large and Kerry's room at the very top.

Melissa phoned to make an appointment then and there
for Kerry to see her doctor.

'She's brilliant, she's the best doctor in the world, Dr
Bogdanovich – she's just round the corner.'

The receptionist was obviously being protective, but
Melissa persisted and eventually got to speak to the doctor
herself. She briefly explained that a friend had turned up,
in the last stages of pregnancy, having not had any medical
attention at all. Dr Bogdanovich said she would see Kerry
the following morning at nine.

'Do you know what Kerry intends to do when it's born?'
Melissa asked.

'She's convinced it's dead.'

'Oh, poor Kerry.'

Kerry slept right through the night, but when I got up at
about seven, she was downstairs, drinking tea. I told her
that I had seen Melissa and what we had arranged. To my

surprise, she acquiesced without a word.

Melissa and I waited in the waiting room. After about forty minutes Kerry returned with a handsome, middle-aged woman.

'There's an antenatal class that Kerry can go to this afternoon, I've registered her with the local hospital. As far as I can tell at this stage, the baby is not dead, but they'll give her a scan at the hospital.'

When we were back out on the street, Kerry whispered hoarsely, 'I can't go through with this, I can't, Juliet.'

'You can and must,' I snapped haughtily. Some kind of dreadful matron had come to the fore in me. Melissa put her arms round Kerry and softly spoke soothing words to her.

Kerry went to her appointment at the hospital and I waited for her in a busy corridor, hating the smell and feeling glad that I had given up my training. I loathed the atmosphere of illness, pain, death. Most of all I hated the aura of competence, of healing.

Kerry was accompanied out by a nurse, who told me that I was welcome to join the group, as the person who would be going through it with her. I laughed, and couldn't stop.

The nurse looked at me askance, but Kerry laughed too.

'Sure,' I said, 'I'll come along to the next one.' We left, clutching at the spasms of uncontrollable laughter in our stomachs.

I'm the father, I am the father; these words went round and round in my mind. Here I am being the father to Kerry's baby.

At exactly ten o'clock that night, just as Kerry switched off the beginning of the news, the front-door bell rang.

'Don't answer it,' Kerry pleaded, 'I don't want to see anyone.'

'I'll go and see who it is.'

I peered through the spy-hole and saw Edgar waiting

impatiently. Automatically, I opened the door.

'I've lost my key. How are you, sis? Just thought I'd drop by and check that you haven't turned the house upside down.'

Edgar bounced into the living room. Kerry was standing by the French windows, draped with thick, dark-green velvet curtains. The lighting was such that there was a large shadow above her. Edgar jumped.

'Oh, hello, it's Kerry, isn't it?'

'Hi, Edgar,' she said uncertainly.

Edgar went to hug Kerry. 'You still look about twelve years old, even though ...'

Kerry beamed from ear to ear. So the little minx is still vain, I thought, and the matron took over again.

'Yes, as you can see, Kerry's here and she's going to be staying until she's had the baby.'

'Cool.' Edgar shrugged nonchalantly.

'If you don't mind, I'm really tired and think I'll go to bed now.' Kerry started for the door.

'Nice to see you again.'

Edgar only raised his eyebrows at me when she had gone, then he headed for the kitchen to raid the fridge. Edgar was always hungry, he ate more than anyone I know, yet was wiry and tall, as we all are. A family of giants, Kerry once said, and I suppose to her four feet eleven, we must have been. My brothers, father and myself have slight stoops, as if we are apologising for being so tall, trying to be smaller, to be on the same level as everyone else. Only my mother and Helena, being dancers, hold their backs straight and their heads high.

When Kerry had first met my family she had told me that we were tall because we were English – it was centuries of privilege making up those extra inches.

'Honestly, it is a class thing, a political thing. Me, I'm

221

barely an inch high because my lineage is one of oppression and poor nutrition. My ancestors probably all died in some famine or other, while yours had loads of potatoes. Someone once said that I didn't have legs, merely ankles attached to my bottom. Bastard.'

Edgar's first feature film had won an award at some festival and had been sold to America where, to everyone's surprise, it was doing very well. It had been reviewed as being very dark and sexy and un-English. Tarkovsky meets Mike Leigh, wrote one critic. Edgar was being hailed as a great new hope for the British film industry. He regarded this as rubbish and dismissed his film as being totally compromised by its popularity.

Edgar didn't want to be a bourgeois artist. He wanted to starve in a garret and be misunderstood. He lived in a flat in Brixton, and I didn't see that much of him. When I had first come down to London, he had attempted to cheer me up, he invited me out, to music events or the theatre, but he gave up after a fortnight.

I told him that Kerry had just turned up, that she had been sleeping rough and in a refuge in Dublin and that she had come to me because she had nowhere else to go.

'What about her parents?'

'Complete fascists by the sound of it – religious.'

Edgar was excited by this story. He stayed the night in his old room and in the morning he told Kerry that if there was anything he could do, she must ask. He hugged her when he left.

I knew Edgar was a romantic. I knew he had a passion for pathos. But I couldn't possibly have been prepared for the extent to which this now took over, and the speed at which it happened. He came back that same evening, with an enormous bunch of flowers for Kerry and a bottle of expensive red wine for me. He cooked for us both, and then we played Risk. Kerry won, she conquered the whole of Asia and Australasia and had armies in every other continent. She was very quiet, though, and did not gloat gleefully over her triumph as the old Kerry would have. She was almost demure.

I had been with pregnant women before, but there was something different about Kerry, something that made it almost seem as though she wasn't absolutely enormous with child. I realised now what it was. She paid no attention to her condition. She did not touch her lump, or shift around in her seat, changing her position with a happy sigh. She ignored herself, her body, as though it were an irrelevance.

Edgar stayed the night again, and tried to engage Kerry in a conversation about acting and why she had given it up. She refused to be drawn. He then disappeared for a few days, days in which I waited with Kerry. I cooked, I watched TV, I was not depressed. Even my curiosity was subdued. I could wait.

The hospital had confirmed that the baby was alive. Kerry seemed to pay no heed to this information. I went to the antenatal group with her, kept a straight face and found it fascinating, though it confirmed my desire never to have children, a desire that Kerry herself had intensified with her horror of procreation. Before the class, Kerry had great beads of sweat on her forehead, and her hands shook. I felt sorry for her – it must be terrible to be so afraid. During the class, she sat white-faced and did all the exercises as bid. When the class was over, she threw up with relief.

When Edgar returned again, I was out doing shopping, and when I got back there was a note on the kitchen table saying that he and Kerry had gone for a walk on the Heath with the dogs, and to have the kettle on for them when they got back.

Two hours later they arrived, rosy-cheeked and wind-blown. I was unable to mask my jealousy and I was sulky and uncommunicative, busying myself with the over-excited dogs, who regarded the kittens as most excellent new toys, and couldn't understand my problem with that. I knew that my hopes that I was appearing indifferent were in vain. Edgar was muscling in on my role as sole support to Kerry. When he announced that he was going to stay yet another night, I quipped, 'Haven't you got a home to go to?'

Edgar had brought some videos, which we watched. At one point, though, I caught him looking at Kerry, who was sitting neatly, dwarfed by the huge sofa, her feet on a cushion. His face was soft, blurred round the edges, a mixture of pity and lust.

'I don't know, here we are watching videos. Shouldn't we be knitting booties or something, preparing in some way?' The smile on Edgar's face as he said this was sickly sweet. Kerry shuddered quite violently.

'It will die, I know it will.'

Edgar looked shocked. 'Don't be afraid, Kerry, it will be all right, you're just scared.'

She gave him a penetrating look.

'Kerry,' I said harshly, 'you have to prepare for the fact that you are probably going to give birth to a strapping great living baby and you have to start dealing with the question of what you are going to do.'

'Hey, go easy on her, Juliet.'

'Go easy on her! You don't know what she's like Edgar ... she ...'

There was an uneasy silence which Kerry broke with a husky cry. 'But I don't know what to do.'

Edgar went to her and held her, rubbing her back the way I used to, the way our parents had done to us when we were distressed.

'You mustn't upset yourself, Kerry,' he soothed.

'I'm not upsetting myself actually,' she fired, like the old Kerry for one moment but Edgar continued, paying no heed to her sudden anger.

'I promise you that it will be all right, whatever happens. Juliet and I are here for you Kerry and we'll be here whatever you decide, isn't that right, Juliet?'

I grunted.

When I woke at seven the next day, Kerry and Edgar were already up. Kerry was wearing a long T-shirt, and nothing else. Her skinny arms and legs against the protruding stomach made her look bug-like.

'Barefoot, pregnant and in the kitchen,' I said nastily, 'how nice.' My mind was filled suddenly with a horrendous image. I remembered those pregnancy fetish porn videos that had caused Kerry to leave the shop and vomit outside in the gutter. As if she had read my thoughts, Kerry suddenly retched and made it to the kitchen sink in time to vomit.

'Weird,' I said, 'what made you do that?'

'I don't know.' She went off upstairs to wash and clean her teeth.

What had made Kerry change her mind about the abortion? She had always been so adamant about not having children, about how disgusting the whole thing was, agreeing with Petruchio's tirades. She had also seemed to be almost allergic to her pregnancy. And what did she do that day when she was supposed to be at the abortion? I remember her coming back all pale and wan and going to bed with the hot-water bottle I prepared for her. Was there no end to her web of lies?

That Sunday Edgar decided that we were all going to go out into the country for the day to have a walk and a pub lunch. We drove to Sonning and walked by the river, had an expensive lunch in a hotel and explored the village. Edgar kept pointing out 'dream houses' and saying how he wanted to move to the country.

We got back late and Kerry went straight to bed. She woke me at about three am, and I woke Edgar. I drove to the hospital. Edgar had been drinking all day and was over the limit, so he sat in the back, his arms around Kerry, telling her to take deep breaths and all the bullshit that you see people say on the TV in these situations.

The baby was born sixteen hours later, Edgar and I both present, thanks to the gay male midwife, who loved Edgar's film and thought he could bend the rules on this occasion. A little girl. Perfect in every way.

Kerry had been quiet and incredibly dignified during the long hours of her labour. I had expected her to do a huge scene, to demonstrate her experience graphically for us, but she hardly called out at all. She bit into one of Edgar's hankies occasionally, she sweated and her eyes were wild, but her jaw was locked with grim determination. She wouldn't accept any pethadin and she paced the room for hours, doing absolutely the right thing with her breathing, so the nurses and midwife kept saying when they popped in to see her.

When, at last, the baby was born, Kerry, who had been squatting on the bed, froze, her jaw finally relaxed, and she gazed in astonishment as the midwife held out the bloody new being to her. It was choking and trying to scream.

Edgar was crying and hugging Kerry, who held the baby limply, as if in a trance.

'What is her name, Kerry?'

'I should call it Sorrow, like Tess of the D'Urbervilles called her baby.'

'But that's appalling.'

Edgar looked truly shocked, and Kerry laughed bitterly, saying she was just very tired. We left about an hour

226

later, with instructions to collect Kerry the following morning, after she had had a good night's sleep. The nurses treated Edgar as though he were the father, and this infuriated me. He wanted to go and have a meal to celebrate, but I said that I didn't think we had anything to celebrate particularly.

I phoned Melissa when we arrived back at the house, and she came round immediately with several bags full of baby clothes.

'I kept them just in case we had another, but of course Kerry must have them.'

Melissa wanted to hear all about the birth, but I could hardly keep my eyes open and excused myself, leaving Edgar blissfully regaling the whole event in intimate detail.

When I came downstairs in the morning, Edgar and Melissa were carrying a cot in through the front porch, manoeuvring carefully to miss the glass panes either side of the inner doors.

'It's time Sarah went into a proper bed, she mostly sleeps with me at the moment anyway,' Melissa chirped. The telephone rang and it was Kerry demanding woefully for someone to go and pick her up.

'I'll go.' Edgar rubbed his hands together. 'You two get everything ready.'

As he was dressed and I was still dewy with sleep, he had the advantage so I demurred. Melissa and I made the cot up in Kerry's room, and picked out some clothes.

Edgar and Kerry had stopped off on the way back, and Edgar had gone shopping while Kerry stayed in the car with the baby. They arrived back loaded with baby products, nappies, milk, bottles, etc, etc.

Kerry seemed relieved to find Melissa there, as indeed I was. Here was someone who had done this before, who had managed to see two babies through into infancy and childhood. Her competent manner obviously penetrated even the tiny, still foetus-like, thing. Melissa was the only one of us who was able to stop it crying.

The baby was underweight, five pounds only, but there didn't seem to be any other problems.

'Well, what do we do now?' I said, when the baby was at last asleep, and we were sitting round the kitchen table drinking tea.

'I don't think Kerry should even think about anything now, except getting some rest.'

'Oh don't be so pompous, Edgar, we've got to discuss it.'

'Not now, please, Juliet, I do just need to rest,' Kerry looked gratefully at Edgar. Melissa stood up and efficiently began to show Kerry how to mix up the milk bottles. Kerry had not produced any milk and so was unable to breastfeed, even had she wanted to, which I rather assumed she wouldn't. Melissa went home and Kerry went to bed. I launched into Edgar as soon as we were alone.

'Look, Mum and Dad are going to come home the week after next and what are they going to think about a newborn baby in this house? Oh, hi, Mum, a friend of mine has just moved in with her baby! We've got to discuss this.'

'I agree, but there's a time and place. None of us really know what Kerry has been through these past months, and what she's going through now.'

'Edgar, this isn't some romantic scenario for you to indulge in, this is real – there is a bloody baby upstairs in our parents' house.'

'Exactly. So calm down. What exactly do you propose we do, then?'

'I don't know.'

So we did nothing. Edgar stayed on in the house, and our lives revolved around the baby. I was afraid of it. It was so tiny and vulnerable and I was terrified of picking it up lest I break it, drop it, crush it. Like a dog, it sensed my fear, and stiffened up and bawled its head off whenever I held it. They say that the fear of vertigo is based on the feeling of desire to throw oneself off whatever height it happens to be, a strange lemming-like urge. My fear was similar; as soon as I had the baby in my arms, I would imagine myself throwing it across the room, hurling it out of my arms, desperate to be without the horrible responsibility, the fear that I might drop it anyway. I would then look at the little pink thing in my arms and feel a protective tenderness.

Kerry said she couldn't choose a name and we must help her. I was unhelpful, giving only joke names. 'Schrödinger's Baby, it's Schrödinger's Baby, isn't it, Kerry?' I quipped, and sang to the tune of 'I'm Nobody's Baby'.

'Very funny, Juliet. What about an Irish name?' Edgar persisted in the quest.

'God, no.' Kerry was adamant.

'Well, what about Molly? Don't you think she's a little Molly? Seriously, Kerry, you wanted sadness or sorrow in the name – this has the sadness of Molly Malone, sweet Molly Malone, I think it's a lovely name. Molly, Molly, Molly.' Edgar practised different intonations.

'Or Molly Bloom,' whispered Kerry. 'Yes.'

'You like it?'

'Yes, I like it. What about you, Juliet?'

'Who is Molly Bloom?'

An ex-lover, I thought, someone connected to the sauna, to Sophie and Geoffrey. Someone important to Kerry, I could tell by her tone when she said yes; familiar, portentous and full of love.

'She's a character in a book, Juliet. She's the exact opposite of Antigone. She says yes to life, like the baby did.'

Melissa came by several times a day, and was much needed for her advice. Kerry was quiet and peaceful and removed. She was detached from Molly whilst at the same time being tender in her motherly duties. But her duties were only motherly because she was the mother, for they were no different to what Edgar, Melissa and myself were doing. Kerry did no more than her share of the feeding, changing, bathing and soothing. Edgar did most of the worrying, constantly checking room temperatures and barely leaving the baby in its cot for five minutes without taking a concerned peek. That was, until he bought the baby monitoring intercom system, over which we could hear Molly's breathing wherever we were in the house.

Two days before my parents returned, Edgar rather formally opened the discussion we so needed to have. He cleared his throat.

'Kerry, Juliet, the old parentals are coming back the day after tomorrow and we need to talk about things a bit, don't you think? One of the things that I have come to feel over the past week is that you don't have any intention of giving this baby up for adoption. Is this correct?'

'I don't know – that was my original intention, but I don't know what to do, I don't know what my options are ... I'm just living from moment to moment, hoping that everything else will just go away.'

'That's perfectly reasonable in the circumstances.'

'Circumstances,' I blurted out, furious, 'what do any of us know about the circumstances?'

Edgar ignored me. 'We have to think only about what's best for Molly. Now, if, and I think it is very unlikely, my parents object to you being here, there is always my flat. The main thing is, Kerry, you are not alone. You are absolutely not alone in all this. OK?'

Kerry nodded, and smiled first at Edgar and then at me.

My parents, as Edgar had predicted, were startled and then delighted to find a newborn babe in the house. They had missed all the hustle and bustle of having young people around, and told Kerry that she was welcome to stay. They pestered me about returning to my studies, or at least doing something.

Edgar stopped staying at the house after my parents' return, and he also seemed to be busy, working on a new film. Still, he came round at least once a day, even if only for a few minutes of gooing and gaaing over Molly.

My mother adored babies, and Kerry gradually allowed her to take over, she and I doing less and less.

My parents decided to have a party, a barbeque, and all the family came except for Benedick, who was filming in Namibia. Chris and Billy came too. I hadn't been in touch with them at all and they knew nothing about Kerry's baby. When the shock and incomprehension went, it was replaced by a gushing joy. Billy seemed particularly chuffed.

'Fuck sake, I would never have believed it but you know, it suits you, wee man, or wee mother, I should say now. I'll be godfather to this wee lassie here, if you want.'

I laughed and Kerry said sternly, 'The last thing Molly needs is a godfather.'

I was in the kitchen fetching the ladle for the punch, when Edgar came in and slouched across the table.

'Juliet, can I get personal? I'm still not entirely sure about your relationship with Kerry. I'll be blunt. Are you still involved with her, or is it all right if I fall madly, passionately in love with her?'

I dropped the ladle, a large, china thing from Japan, and it broke into three pieces.

Fortunately someone came in at that point and so I was delivered from having to make a response to Edgar. I was thrown into a state of wild panic. It was as though there were some major catastrophe about to happen and I was the only one who could prevent it. Of course I had seen it coming. In fact, I had seen Kerry arrange for it to happen. She had absolutely played up to Edgar's romantic 'saviour' fantasies. Of course, she was out to get him, to get my brother to look after her and the baby.

I had to find Kerry, to confront her, but she was nowhere to be seen. I then got cornered by my mother, who asked me some question about the baby. When I at last edged myself away from her and back through into the living room, Kerry and Edgar were seated together in the window seat, Molly between them, and their heads close together. Oh God, I thought, I must see her, I must talk to her. *This cannot happen*.

I then got into a conversation with Chris and Billy. I went back to the kitchen for more wine and I brushed past Edgar in the corridor. He took hold of my arm and asked if I were OK.

'It isn't a good idea to fall in love with Kerry, Edgar. It has nothing to do with me, but–'

'It's too late, sis, I already am, hopelessly. I thought you knew, which is why you were so pissed off with me. To be honest, I think I fell in love with her ages ago, when I first met her.'

'Yes, you flirted with her.'

'Is it OK then?'

I shrugged and went back out into the garden. But you can't, you can't love her, I thought. You don't know her, you don't know what I know, or rather, you don't know what I *don't* know.

Every fibre of my being, every particle of matter that constituted me seemed to protest, to be rising up, screaming *no*.

But I didn't get a chance to speak to Kerry until the party

was over and all the guests gone. I went up to her room at the top of the house.

'You've planned this from the beginning, haven't you?'

'What do you mean?'

My voice was venomous. 'You planned for Edgar to fall in love with you, you scheming bitch, you made him fall in love with you so he'll take care of you and the baby.'

'You can't *make* people fall in love with you, Juliet.'

'I thought you once said that marriage was the worst, the real prostitution – but you've finally succumbed, going to get a man to look after you.'

'I don't know what you're talking about. Of course I know Edgar's got a crush on me, but what can I do about that? He's infatuated with my situation, he'll get over it.'

'You have to tell me everything now, the whole story.'

'Why?'

'Why, because I have to know. I have to.'

I told her that Inspector Godfrey had been to see me but did not tell her of Petruchio's confession. She stared at me, an expression of disbelief and horror on her face. I said, as lightly as I could, that now, surely, after all this time, she could let me into her secret.

'I know something was going on. Don't worry, I didn't say anything to Inspector Godfrey, but I do know something was going on.'

Kerry smiled warmly, and sat down in the rocking chair. 'You were always so paranoid, Juliet.'

I smiled back. 'I don't think so.'

'No?'

'In fact, I know so. I know I wasn't paranoid. If I know nothing else, I know that one thing I once thought was a kind of paranoia, wasn't. It was real.'

'What are you talking about?'

'I'm talking about your cadaver, Kerry.'

233

She froze. Her expression didn't change, but she shifted in her seat. 'Oh yes, your hallucination.'

'I know that what I saw was really there.'

'How?' She was serious now, leaning towards me earnestly.

'Because you saw it too.'

'Well, I've never been the most stable of people, so I had a hallucination too – besides, I told you Petruchio had drugged us.' Kerry looked directly at me with one of her cheekiest grins. I laughed at her.

'Since when do we share hallucinations? You told me in Spain that you had seen what I had seen. You didn't mean to tell me, but you did. You told me that you and Petruchio had planted the fang, but that means you knew that my so-called hallucination had been of a vampire, a dead vampire, no ordinary cadaver, a rather specific little hallucination. Only, it wasn't, was it?'

There was a silence, then Molly woke up and my mother called me from downstairs. I went. Kerry picked Molly up and followed me downstairs, where Edgar, and my parents were clearing up. My mother wanted me to fix the hoover.

'Can't we do all this tomorrow?' I complained, but I went into the large cupboard under the stairs to find a screwdriver and I heard Kerry in the kitchen, warming a bottle for Molly, who was gurgling happily. I heard Edgar go in, and gushing like a schoolboy, he told her that he loved her. I coughed. Kerry snarled.

'Oh, for God's sake, call a fucking cunt a cunt. You want to get in my knickers, spare me the romantic whitewash.'

'Er, no, actually, Kerry, you're wrong. I really do love you, God knows why, you armoured little wasp.'

I laughed. I knew that Kerry would be furious with him, and she was, I could almost hear her flesh creep with rage.

'Right, fuckwit, I'm going to tell you a bed-time story,

234

and then you can tell me whether you fucking well love me or not, OK? Come up to my room when you're ready.' She snatched the bottle from the pan, picked up the carry-cot and strode out and upstairs.

Edgar followed her immediately and I dumped the hoover and followed him. Kerry glanced at me when I entered her room, where Edgar was already sitting on her bed expectantly.

'Don't you think I've a right to hear this too, Kerry?'

'I don't know about rights but OK.'

Kerry sat down with Molly on her lap and told the story of her time as a dominatrix and about the party at Sophie and Geoffrey's. She told it more or less exactly as she finally told it to me, some details she left out, but others were new.

The first part of the story was funnier somehow the second time round, perhaps because Kerry told it differently, or perhaps I heard it differently. When she got on to Geoffrey and Sophie, it was less dark; they were like evil pantomime baddies.

'These were those kinky agents that disappeared, yeah?' Edgar asked. I nodded. Kerry was silent. My heart was pounding and I was breathing heavily. Was she going to tell us? Tell us the whole story?

She continued up to the point where she ran from Geoffrey and Sophie's basement. Edgar was silent; he looked confused and worried.

'If you think this is going to put me off you, you're wrong,' he said.

The anticipation was almost killing me. I could hardly breathe. How far would Kerry go to disgust my brother, to make him reject her? She continued, about sleeping rough in London but she did not mention the coin-operated-toilet consummation near St Paul's. She went on about going to

235

the casting for the film, coming back and arguing with Sophie on the telephone.

'But that wasn't all. You see, Sophie came to see me on the night of the fancy dress party, and we had a really nasty argument. She threatened me, and hit me and ...'

Kerry paused. I thought my heart was going to push its way out of my chest.

'I pushed her away from me and she fell. I threw her bag and coat at her and told her to get out, to get the fuck out of my flat. She got up, trying to look dignified, picked up her stuff and left, slamming the door behind her. I think that I might have been the last person to see her before they disappeared.'

There was a long silence and then Edgar whistled softly through his teeth.

'Wow. Did you have to tell the police all this?'

Kerry nodded and stood up. 'So don't you go getting any romantic notions about me. You can see now what sort of person I am, a nasty little whore, not at all the person to get involved with.'

'All right,' Edgar said, looking up at Kerry with amused adoration, 'no romance, I promise. Let's get married.'

'Is that it?' I demanded of Kerry, when Edgar had gone. So Sophie had been to the flat, and they had had another row. I remembered the long, lipstick-covered, mentholated cigarette butt in the ash tray the following morning. Sophie's cigarette. But why had she come? What did she want from Kerry?'

'Is that the great secret? I think there's a whole lot more that you're not saying.'

Silence.

'Kerry, you aren't going to fob me off with that. Tell me.'

'There is nothing to tell.'

236

'Nothing to tell, bullshit.' I was unusually aggressive.

'Nothing that you need to know.'

'Who the fuck do you think you are deciding on what I need to know or not? Why didn't you tell Edgar about your fuck with that tramp in the toilet?'

'He's never asked about the father, and he doesn't need to know – you're the one who is obsessed with Molly's paternity. Please, Juliet, you'll wake Molly, please go now.'

Kerry was looking at me with utter disgust written all over her face. Molly stirred in her sleep and I left, feeling loathsome and unloved.

Edgar continued to come round every day. Kerry seemed to enjoy his company and the attention, but she told me that he was wasting his time. She told him so too, endlessly. Edgar was like a man possessed, just as I had been over Kerry. Was it some kind of gene which made us prey to the attractions of mad Irish women? I tried to talk to him.

'You're wasting your time, Juliet. I can't seem to get either you or Kerry to understand that I love her and that I know she is the only woman for me. I will cherish her for ever and she must just get used to the fact.'

'So you're just going to follow her round for the rest of your life, pretending you have a relationship with her? This is ridiculous, Edgar.'

'Both you and Kerry will come to see that marrying me is by far and away the very best thing to do ... for Molly's sake, if nothing else. I love them both and I've got the means to make it all right for them. It may have escaped your attention, but my film is earning me quite a bit of money, and I've already had loads of offers for future projects – not that I shall take any of them. I want to buy a house in the country, not too far from town –'

Kerry was coming downstairs with the baby, and he broke off and went out to meet her.

That evening I was in the bath with Molly, when Kerry came in and perched on the edge of the tub.

'You know, I haven't had sex since you; I've been celibate,' she mused out of the blue.

'I don't believe you.'

'No, but I'm telling you the truth. 'I really don't know what to do – I mean, for Molly, what's best for Molly. Do you care about Molly, Juliet?'

'Yes, of course I do.' Molly had been resting on my chest but I sat up now and held her, swishing her through the water, keeping her head above water.

'I mean, *really*.' Kerry looked me hard in the eyes. I looked away and then back at her again.

'Yes.'

'Then what do you think I should do?'

'Marry Edgar, that's what you should do. He'll become famous and you can buy a nice dream house in the country, and you can play the smug celebrity wife. We'll get *Hello!* magazine round, shall we?' I handed Molly to Kerry and climbed out of the bath.

Kerry's face was expressionless as she gazed at the bathwater, now swirling down the plug. She didn't speak. I waited and waited.

She left her reverie to help me dry and dress Molly, who smiled up at us both, with adoring eyes. Blue eyes. Icy cold blue eyes, like Kerry's.

Two days later, Edgar came round for dinner and over dessert announced that he and Kerry were going to get married and he would adopt the baby.

My parents looked at me in alarm, saw that I was cool about it, and then my dad rushed for a bottle of champagne, while my mother hugged us all.

It was a quiet, registry office wedding, and a small party at our house afterwards. Billy and Chris came and Benedick and Helena. Benedick was very gentle and sweet with me though everyone accepted that Kerry and I were finished and it was all amicable.

I was as sweet as I could be towards Kerry on her wedding day. I felt fine. Sure, she could marry Edgar, good idea. I was able, even on the wedding night, to lie peacefully in my bed in a remarkably un-tormented way. I thought it unlikely that they would be making love anyway. They were sleeping upstairs in the guest room, with its twin beds and with Molly in the cot. Kerry had been affectionate with Edgar, but there was no sign of any real passion for him. I felt sorry for him; I remembered Petruchio's constant advice to me: 'It isn't a good idea to fall in love with Kerry – there will be trouble.'

I do not remember the dreams I had the night of the wedding, but I woke with a strong feeling that I *had* dreamed, and that my dreams were not pleasant. All my ease had vanished. My father was alone in the kitchen, reading the paper over his breakfast. I poured myself some coffee, but couldn't face anything to eat. My mother was still in bed, and Edgar had been down already and taken breakfast in bed up to Kerry. She never eats breakfast, I thought, Edgar will be disappointed. Sure enough, he came down about half an hour later, with a tray of uneaten bagels, smoked salmon and cream cheese.

I took the dogs out for a walk, and my mood became gloomier and gloomier. I got back to find Kerry dressed in a pair of my jeans and a checked shirt, walking around the house watering the plants with a little brass watering can. She was humming contentedly. I looked at her, and lost my temper.

'Look at you,' I shouted. 'Little Miss Normal, watering the plants, pretending she's Doris Day or Felicity fucking Kendal ...'

She looked startled and then confused. 'Isn't this the punishment you chose for me?' she said, and walked away.

Edgar had to go away almost immediately after the wedding, some pre-production aspect of his film that had to be dealt with in the United States. Kerry stayed with us, and was told by Edgar to start looking for a house within a forty-mile radius of the M25. My mother accompanied us on several trips, but one day Kerry and I were alone, driving around the area between Reading and Henley, including Sonning, where we had been the day before Molly's birth. We went into several estate agents and drove out to take a look at some houses.

One Thameside house was backed by acres of woodland and we walked round the back, over a stile and down a leafy path.

'It reminds me a bit of the cottage in Argyll,' I said, 'not the house, but the woods.'

Kerry gave me a rather twisted look. I had a very clear image of those woods in Argyll; I remembered Petruchio coming out of them with a spade; I remembered my walk through them, looking for signs of digging. I also remembered my solitary walk there, before any of the freaky stuff had happened, when I had been mesmerised by the green light, and longed for Kerry to be with me, to share the perfection of the moment. This memory brought with it an almost tangible sense of Kerry as she had been when I first loved her, of her body and how, in our love-making, it would feel so totally merged with mine that I no longer had any sense of being separate.

Whilst I no longer felt this way about Kerry, I felt grief at the loss of this all-consuming passion, so full of vitality and hope. Tears filled my eyes and wiping them away I decided that the time was now. Enough was enough.

'You are going to tell me everything now, Kerry.'

'Oh?'

'Yes. You see, I haven't told you everything I know either. You know I told you that Inspector Godfrey came to see me? He said that Petruchio had confessed to murdering Sophie and Geoffrey and burying their bodies somewhere between Loch Lomond and Oban.'

Kerry did not laugh, as I had done on first hearing this preposterous disclosure. Her face softened with sympathy tinged with pain. She was very still, and she stayed so for minutes, looking sadder than I had ever seen her look.

'Would it make so much difference knowing?' she asked. 'I mean, does Schrödinger open the box, do you think? Surely not, surely he leaves it shut for ever, making sure that nothing happens because it will never be known.'

'I'm not interested in your metaphors – I don't want to know what things are *like*, I want to know what they *are*. It isn't a box, it's a door, something was happening behind the front door when I opened it. If I hadn't opened it at that point, it might never have existed for me. But I did, I opened the door at that exact moment, *that exact* moment. You accused Schrödinger of solipsism, of arrogance. You can't say the same of me. I want to know, and you are going to tell me.'

'Why am I?' Kerry had gone white.

'Because if you don't, I'm going to go to Inspector Godfrey and tell him everything I know, the whole damn lot. Then you'll have to tell him.'

'I shan't. I shall kill myself. Petruchio gave me the means, I have a phial ...'

'No, you don't. You left it in your leather jacket and I sent it to a laboratory for identification.'

Kerry looked disbelieving, 'What was in it then?' she asked uncertainly.

241

'Pentobarbitone.'

'I never knew what it was called,' she whispered.

'I'm waiting.'

'You don't want to know, Juliet, you don't want to have to live with this ... please don't make me tell, just leave it Juliet, trust me ...'

'I quite fancied Inspector Godfrey you know, I've half a mind to call him anyway ...'

'Oh, Juliet,' Kerry said sadly, looking at me with pity, and then, pacing around the log where I now sat, kicking at the leaves and bits of twigs, she told me everything. The truth: Part Three.

At first the familiar old stuff was verified; she *had* gone to the orgy with the sauna man and allowed him to become her pimp. She *had* finished it when she said she had, and felt rescued by me. She *had* gone to dinner with Geoffrey and been joined by this man. She *had* left in horror and shame.

Then Sophie rang, and Kerry went down to London, saw her, went shopping, dressed up in her new suit and went to dinner at the house in Kensington.

But now there was new material, a whole new chapter. This is where it all really began.

The house was one of those large, white, Georgian ones, with steps leading up to the front door. Kerry buzzed at the door, spoke into the intercom and when she heard the click, pushed the door open and entered into a large and spacious hall, with a grand staircase at the far end.

Sophie glided down the staircase in a floaty negligée.

'Oh, darling you look *sweet*. Geoffrey's in the jacuzzi and we're dreadfully behind with dinner. You don't mind, do you? Come on, let's grab some drinks and go and join him in the back.'

Kerry followed Sophie downstairs into an enormous kitchen, where Sophie took champagne from the fridge and loaded up a tray with glasses. They went back upstairs and under an archway to the back of the house, passing stairs leading down on their way.

They went through a gym to a tiled room with a jacuzzi in the middle and comfortable chairs around it. Sophie laid the tray on a glass-topped coffee table by the jacuzzi, slipped off her gown and slid into the bubbling tub.

'Sit yourself down, and don't mind us. Geoffrey, you can open the champagne. You are welcome to join us, Kerry, there's plenty of room in here.'

'Why are you doing this?' said Kerry, backing away from the agents.

'Oh, Kerry, darling, don't be so silly, we're not doing anything. Come on – you're not being an uptight Irish girl, are you?' Geoffrey held out a glass of champagne. She took it from him, took a great slug of champagne and sat down.

'It's divine in here, do join us.' Sophie laughed.

Kerry looked at the handsome couple sitting elegantly in the tub, sipping from their ridiculously long champagne glasses. Why the hell not, she thought. This is bizarre.

She stripped off and got into the jacuzzi. Her hosts behaved as though this were the most normal thing in the world.

'By the way, Kerry, there might be someone you know turning up later, someone from Glasgow – you remember when we had dinner that time and that man joined us.'

Kerry stood up, and then feeling vulnerably naked, sat down immediately.

'Well, not him,' Geoffrey continued, 'but someone who knows him and who you might have bumped into.'

Kerry cut to the chase. 'What do you know about me?'

'Oh, darling, don't worry, we think it's all fine. We know

243

that you were a fantastic act for Sauna Sam, as he is known. That isn't a problem to us, in fact, it's rather cool.'

Sophie leaned over and started massaging Kerry's shoulders. Geoffrey stood up and got out of the jacuzzi.

'I seem to have a hard-on the size of Big Ben for you two,' he said and Kerry giggled, the champagne having gone to her head, and asked them whether they'd met Billy.

'He's got a dick the size of Big Ben, without an erection.'

'Hush, Kerry, you'll put him off, men are sensitive about these things.' Sophie leaned over and stroked Geoffrey who pulled her up out of the jacuzzi and started kissing her all over.

Kerry coughed. 'Excuse me ... excuse me, but I was never into sex as a spectator sport – couldn't we just have dinner now?'

'So join in,' Geoffrey said, and Sophie pulled Kerry towards them.

They all made love, the three of them, on the tiled floor. Geoffrey and she fucked, while Sophie watched and urged Geoffrey to orgasm.

Afterwards Sophie cooked some pasta, which they ate with pesto and salad, and then the guests started to arrive and Kerry went down into the dungeon.

Everything happened exactly like she had said before: when the paedophile porn came on she left and wandered the streets, enjoying her 'adventure'. She met Melissa, told her about the paedophile films, but not about her threesome with Geoffrey and Sophie, and then went back to her wandering.

Kerry paused at this point in her story. She had been pacing around, but now she sat cross-legged on the leafy ground, looking up at me. Shouldn't this be the other way round? I thought, the story-teller in the seat, the children around her feet. But no. The child is telling old Mother

244

Hubbard the tale, I thought, and here we are in the big bad woods.

Kerry's melodious voice, with its broad accent and wide range, was different somehow to how it usually was. Nothing had been taken from it except, perhaps, the rather breathy quality it usually had, but there was something new. An evenness, a moderation.

Now she was locked in thought, what appeared to be dark, morose thoughts.

'I never used to believe in sin. It was one of those things I had shaken off, with the rest of religion, but sin is as good a word as any – and it is real. It is real and one of them, not perhaps the worst, but perhaps one that precipitates the worst, is pride.'

She looked at me for the first time since starting.

'Do you know why, why I felt so bad? My pride, that's at the bottom of it really. I couldn't bear the thought that Geoffrey knew all about me from the sauna man, and that he had told Sophie, and that they weren't really interested at all in my talent – they wanted me for something quite different than ten per cent. I hated myself for going with them in the jacuzzi. That's really why I left the orgy in the dungeon that night, that's the basic reason. The paedophile stuff was just an excuse, and something I could use to make me feel morally superior.'

'According to Inspector Godfrey, so was Sophie – morally superior, I mean.' I hadn't spoken for some time and my voice was gruff.

I told her all Inspector Godfrey had told me, about how Sophie had broken up the orgy minutes after Kerry left, about his belief that the illegal movies had been planted in the agents' house. She was silent and still for a while, staring at the ground, before she spoke.

'This is a long story, I'd better get on.'

245

London. Sleeping rough. The handsome young homeless man was a fabrication to keep me quiet. She had teamed up with no one, but she slept near a coin-operated toilet close to St Paul's on her second night, and a couple did go in for what was obviously a shag.

She used this piece of actuality to create a plausible father for her baby, the baby she knew was Geoffrey Daniels'.

Of all the people Kerry might choose to confide in, when she returned to Glasgow and discovered, after missing two periods, that she was pregnant, Petruchio was the least likely to help. Yet that is who she went to, with astonishing trust, given that the last time she had gone to him for help he had planted a flight case containing a dead cat in her room. But Kerry needed help and she figured that Petruchio could give her what she needed to avoid going to the clinic.

Kerry told him the whole woeful tale. Petruchio did not conceal his disgust.

'You are crazy, Kerry,' he growled, 'you do not have to do this kind of shit – you deliberately sabotage your own life.'

Petruchio told her that the basic contradiction at the root of her condition would probably never leave her. That her life would be plagued by extremes of concupiscence 'as you say' and remorse. He, of course, was disgusted by her sexual life, by what he saw as a needless stream of ugly mistakes. He told Kerry that he was a virgin, having been taken to a whorehouse in Rome by his brother when he was fourteen and failed to get an erection. Learning from his experience, he had for ever after been horrified at the thought of all 'animal' contact.

'Do you think I am totally evil, Petruchio?'

'Bouff, don't be idiotic. You think I think that making money out of arseholes who want to be whipped by girls wearing rubber makes you an evil person?'

'What does make me evil then?' Kerry asked.

'You are not evil. You just have no negative will.'

Kerry was disturbed and her self-hatred, rather than abating, was suddenly fired again. She was repulsed by herself for saying yes to everything passively, for being the lowly object of desire. She said yes to the man at the sauna, she said yes to the orgy in the basement. Even when she watched with horror as the film-show started and abuse filled the screen, she did not say no, she merely ran away, ran, bizarrely, to Melissa, her first confessor. Then, rather than telling the police, as she knew she should, she did nothing.

'Yes, yes,' said Petruchio, 'you are wilfully passive, but why do you do this stuff, this rubber act, with whips, why did you do it?'

'Why not?'

'No. *Why*? Think, Kerry, why?'

'It seemed like a good idea at the time.'

'Ha! Exactly. Why?'

'Because it made me feel quite good inside to beat the shit out of those sad fucks and to know that I was going to get paid shit-hot money for it at the end of the day.'

'Good. So greed and feminist hatred drives you to say yes to vileness. Well, as I say, we do not show our humanity, our will by saying yes, but by saying no. So I say no, I say no! I say no to women and to men, too, and to this disgusting fingerey pokey, touching and indulgence, to this biological imperative driving us all to duplicate our horrid selves. To life as most people lead it, I say no!'

'You say yes to Valium,' Kerry quipped, 'you say yes to having a shit – Jesus, you've made a whole ritual around it.'

Petruchio's face set against Kerry. He turned his back to her, placed a book on his knees and put his hands over his ears.

'You say yes to sulking.'

Petruchio raised his eyebrows. 'Yes, yes, that is very funny, I think.'

Petruchio wanted to hear all about Kerry's sexual life, down to the last detail. Kerry obliged. Petruchio behaved like a psychiatrist, listening, but making no response. Kerry did not lie. She told him what she had done, and how she had felt. When she finished she began to laugh and couldn't stop. Petruchio placidly asked her what she found so funny.

'Me,' she said, 'me playing exhibitionist to your voyeur, that's what's so funny. Sometimes I think everybody, absolutely everybody in the world is a bit of a perv at heart.'

Petruchio was furious apparently, and didn't speak to her again for three days. Then he accosted her one morning and told her that the reason she had come to him for help was that she wanted him to persuade her not to have an abortion.

'Yes, yes, this is clear to me – if you want to have abortion, you tell Juliet, if you want to have baby, you tell me.'

'There's no question of me *not* having an abortion, Petruchio, I just want to know whether you can sort it for me ... there must be a drug you can get hold of, one of those injections they give people to make them abort. Please, Petruchio, I hate doctors and hospitals, you must be able to help me.'

'You expect me to kill this living being ... you expect me to murder?'

'Oh, get real, I might have know you'd be hopeless. I guess I'm on my own then, since I don't want Juliet to know.'

Kerry organised to have an abortion at a private clinic where she could pay in instalments. She was terrified, and her fear convinced her that she would not need to go, that she would miscarry. Petruchio kept his word and told no one about her pregnancy. But then Kerry, in too great a state of stress to conceal it, told me, and I walked out on her, kicked her when she was down, left her when she needed me most. She remembered the lines from 1 Corinthians and copied and inverted them.

She then went into Petruchio's room and he was sitting on his bed with his big medicine box on his knee, looking through the contents.

'How come you say all this shit about negative will and saying no to everything when you don't believe in abortion, which is just saying no to that revolting biological imperative you were talking about?'

'It is too late to say no now. You cannot eat your cake and have it, you cannot make life and then say no.'

Kerry was distracted by the syringes and phials in Petruchio's box. He continued, 'Unless of course it is your own life, which we do not create. It is permissible to take one's own life, it could be said to be the most complete manifestation of will. For example, I find the world sometimes is too horrible, and if one day I find that the torture of existence is too much, I shall, like a prisoner of war, take my cyanide pill.'

He picked out a phial containing transparent liquid.

'What is it?'

Petruchio showed Kerry how to apply a tourniquet in order to locate a vein and how to inject herself.

'And then, very soon, if you are careful to inject properly, you are dead with no pain.'

'Can I have one, Petruchio?'

'No, of course not, if you use it I get blamed.'

'No, I promise I'll leave a note saying that I stole it from you. Please?'

He relented, saying that it was best always to have this escape, somehow it made things better, and he hoped she would never use it.

Kerry put the syringe and phial in her jacket pocket, where they stayed until I discovered them.

Then Sophie had phoned and made the joke about 'Dream Management'. That had incensed Kerry; it was the name that the sauna man jokingly called his own enterprise. Sophie was taunting her. Then there was all the business over the bank commercial and Sophie phoned Kerry to angrily enquire as to why she hadn't turned up. Kerry was furious after their row. Petruchio heard and came out from his room, he was the only person in the flat at the time and he heard the entire argument – from Kerry's side, that is.

'Well Kerry, you can get your revenge on her. It seems to me that in this situation, it is you who holds all the cards.'

'What do you mean?'

'You can blackmail them, of course, and get a great deal of money, over the baby, do you see?'

'There isn't going to be a baby, Petruchio. But you have got something there. I could blackmail them over the dungeon. They wouldn't want the papers getting a hold of that – it's a very discreet little circle of perverts.'

'And the baby, think, you can make them pay for a long time, you and the baby can have a wonderful rich life.'

'Petruchio, you don't half talk crap. How many times do I have to tell you, there isn't a baby at all, only an unwanted pregnancy, but, here, let's do it, let's blackmail them. Come on.'

Together, she and Petruchio cut out letters from old newspapers and stuck them on to a card to form a message:

YOUR MONEY OR YOUR PRIVATE LIFE

The blackmail note was an empowering game. It was like throwing a stone into water in the dark to make a ripple that you were never going to see. Kerry thought it was a wheeze.

Why why not why why not why why not?

They posted the message and Kerry was frightened almost immediately. It suddenly seemed very childish; she was terrified that they would be found out and be humiliated in some way. She was never really going to act on the note, she wasn't interested in their money. It was just a nasty joke to shake them up, to make them nervous.

This was all happening around the time of the fancy dress party. Kerry had shown no interest in going but suddenly changed her mind. She decided she must go and make it up to Sophie, or just be normal and friendly, so that she wouldn't be under any suspicion. Kerry's pride had returned and, in spite of everything, she wanted to hold her head up high in public, show that she was still there, she, the actress who had been so good as Antigone.

Petruchio was horrified that she could do such a thing and, in spite of his being ill, he told her he would go too, he couldn't let her go alone. But later, he changed his mind. He said he was feeling ill again. She would have to go alone, make sure she behaved herself and didn't give the game away.

She survived her unease about the blackmail message by telling herself that it was just a prank and they would get away with it – she always got away with things. She also promised herself that she wouldn't drink too much but the blackmail jape and the party certainly took her mind off her pregnancy. She absorbed herself entirely in preparing her costume, spending hours in the second-hand-clothes shops until she found her perfect dress. Then when she got back to the flat, she gave into anxiety again and cried, wishing that life was like video tape and she could rewind it back to the moment she had got into the jacuzzi with Geoffrey and Sophie. She couldn't believe she could have been so stupid.

She went to visit Christine and was tearful. She wanted

to confess to Christine, everything from the sauna, the orgy, and her dominatrix act to the threesome, the dungeon, and the blackmail, so that Christine would reassure her, tell her it was all right, that it wasn't so bad. She daren't do this, however, for fear that Christine would think it *was* so bad. She walked home to the flat feeling dreadful, not wanting to go out, afraid of the dark and of other people.

But by the time Petruchio and I had left for the cinema she was cheerful again. Kerry loved dressing up. She loved putting make-up on, like a mask. She put a whitish foundation on, ringed her eyes with black kohl, coated her lips with scarlet and censored her face with a beauty spot. She played loud music, Patti Smith and Poly Styrene. She put on suspenders and stockings and little black button-up shoes. She put on her beaded dress and long strings of beads. She wished she had dyed her hair. She rolled joints and drank bottled beer, waiting for Billy. She changed the music to the music from the film *The Great Gatsby*. She charlestoned. The phone rang. It was Billy phoning from a pub to say he could get a lift to the party and could he meet her there.

'I was really pissed off with Billy at the time, but I had no idea then ... not that he can be blamed of course.' Kerry's voice was becoming more faltering and nervous as she continued. 'Damn, damn, damn Billy, I thought, and then I rolled a joint, and was just about to phone for a taxi when there was a knock at the door. I didn't recognise her at first, because of the wig, a long black wig, stark against her pale face. It was Sophie, in a long, fake-fur coat, dark glasses and hat. She swept me aside and entered the flat. I followed her into the living room. Sophie removed her hat and glasses and threw her coat over the back of a chair. "Do you like it?" she said, smoothing out the long white gown, which was like a sort of medieval nightdress, and taking two small gleaming white objects from her handbag. She stuck

252

these into her mouth and fiddled around until she had fangs, perfectly integrated in a mouth that now snarled and came towards me greedily. I backed away and asked her what she was doing here.

'Sophie ignored my question and went on, telling me that she had had the fangs specially made, her dentist had shaped them to fit her teeth. They were so comfortable, you forgot you had them on, she said.

'When she closed her mouth over the fangs, she looked quite normal again. "Aren't you pleased to see me, then?" and she flicked her wig, and snarled, reaching out for me with her arms. I dodged her and offered her a drink.'

Kerry had begun to act out this story, becoming Sophie as she made corresponding gestures, and then playing herself again as she dodged out of Sophie's way. She's a born actress, I thought, but it did have the effect of making the scene very real to me. I had a very clear image of Sophie – but then, I had seen her, hadn't I? Kerry hurried to continue her tale, her performance; she was going to give me the truth now in all its detail.

'"Why, Kerry," Sophie said, "you're not nervous of me, are you? Why on earth would that be?"

'"No, I'm not, do you want a drink?"

'"No thanks," she said, and she eyed me up and down. The thought that I had had sex with her and her vile husband made me feel sick. I hated her eyes, her horrid smug face.

'"Kerry," she said, "you're not going to a fancy dress party, are you? Fancy that! You've got the nerve to try and gatecrash, have you?" I said nothing.

'"Well, what fun, perhaps we could share a taxi. Though I don't suppose you're going to feel much like going after I've finished with you."

'I said nothing still and the bitch went on: "I walked

round here. Only round the corner, really, we're staying at the Grosvenor. No one even seemed to notice that I was in fancy dress. But I'd better get to the point, hadn't I? I came here to discuss a little question of blackmail that has suddenly arisen."'

Kerry shrank visibly before me, as she sat on the ground in the woods near Sonning, a present reality that had faded as much for me as for her. I could see the living room of our old flat. I could smell it. This is what was happening when I was at the pictures with Petruchio, I thought, and wished that I had not gone with him. That I had stayed behind to help Kerry get ready as she had wanted. I couldn't even remember now what film we had been to see.

'Well, I just couldn't believe this, Juliet, how she could possibly have guessed ... I thought there must be some magic at work. Sophie was laughing at me and I was filled with horror as a feeling of utter foolishness reduced and crushed me utterly. Then she sat down and lit a cigarette.

'"So you *did* write this stupid little attempt at blackmail, didn't you?" she said, taking the message from her bag and brandishing it. "I was only bluffing really, we wanted to clear the field – but you were a long shot. I'm surprised, I must say."

'I slowly leaned against the wall – it was just a joke, I said – it wasn't for real, we never thought you'd guess and it was just stupid fun.

'"I am astonished," Sophie smiled, "by your stupidity."

'"It's not so stupid. I wasn't really going to blackmail you – but it wouldn't be such a bad idea for me, would it? I presume you would be prepared to pay."

'"Not you, darling, remember we had you for nothing. Besides, I can guarantee that no one would believe you if you did go to the press. We would go to the police immediately, thus indicating our innocence. Besides, we would have our own story, all about this crazed actress, not very talented, whom we had turned down. The poor sick thing made up an entire fantasy and then went to the press with it. Sounds really sad, doesn't it?"'

Kerry's voice had become a perfect match for the one that I heard over the phone on those two occasions. The Sloaney vowel sounds, the affected breathiness. Then she became herself again and stuck her hands on her hips.

'"Fine, except for one thing. Too many people know me and know that I am not untalented."'

Kerry gave me a sideways glance, to see whether I was impressed with her retort. She got nothing from me but a blank stare. She sighed.

'I moved to the table and lit the joint I had rolled. I'm not going to let her bully me, I thought, I'm going to remember what Petruchio says, I've got the power and I'm going to use it.

'"It suits you," I said, looking Sophie up and down, "the vampire garb. Well, what are you going to do?"

'"Probably just slap your face."

'"No, I mean, are you going to pay up or are you going to read your story in the *News of the World* and expect a visit from the police about your taste in films?"

'"Someone put you up to this, didn't they? Someone is paying you to do this to us."

'"No, don't be stupid."

'"Sweet little naive Kerry."

'Sophie came towards me and stopped, just invading my personal space, and then the bitch looked down at me and slapped me hard across the face. I slapped her straight back, much harder probably, because of the shock of the blow I'd received. I've never been hit like that before. Sophie was screaming at me and calling me a bitch and I laughed at her because of the stupid fangs in her mouth; she looked ridicu-

255

lous, crazy. I poured us some drinks and handed one to Sophie, who took it after a moment's hesitation. All the shock went and I can remember only wishing that she would take those fucking fangs off.

'Sophie stubbed her cigarette out.' Kerry did an exaggerated twist movement with her foot. 'She said suddenly, "Well, I suppose I'd better go to this party. I've changed my mind about sharing a taxi, and, if I were you, I wouldn't bother turning up – I am going to make sure that you won't be admitted. May I use your phone?" I nodded. Sophie moved towards the door and turned to look at me, snarling and baring her fangs.

'"You are going to live to regret what you did, Kerry."'

All the life went out of Kerry's story at this point. All the accurate impersonation, the playful parody of both herself and her agent. Her voice continued in a dull monotone.

'She was as quick as a fox, Juliet, she suddenly reached into her handbag and took out a gun and pointed it at me. Then I heard the trigger go and Sophie was laughing at me. I thought that I was going to die and it seemed to last for ever, that moment, like it was in slow motion. I thought, I'm dead, I'm being killed, Sophie is shooting me, me, Kerry, and every particle of my being seemed to be screaming *no* please, don't, you can't kill me ... those and hundreds of other thoughts, millions even. It's amazing how many fucking thoughts you can have all at the same time. I shat myself too, Juliet, I actually fucking well shat myself, only a bit but I felt it. I thought, I'm dead anyway so it doesn't matter but then Sophie was just laughing at me, laughing and laughing and I realised that I wasn't being killed at all, it was just a joke, the gun was a toy.

'Everything was still like in slow motion, even my anger seemed really slow and strange. I rushed towards her, furious, falling over the coffee table. I kicked it out of the way and fell upon Sophie, who was still laughing at me. The toy gun fell and skimmed across the floor and under the dresser. Sophie tried to push me away. "How dare you," she shrieked, "how dare you, I'm going to get you for assault."

'I twisted her arms around her back, she kicked me, forcing me to let go, she then punched me hard in the stomach. I started crying, and this made me even madder. I stormed towards Sophie and knocked her over. As she fell I pulled at her wig, got behind her and sent her crashing down, crying out in outrage, towards the coffee table. Her head then seemed to bounce up and twist around, and I pushed her again, really hard ... it must have been ...

'Her temple caught the hard corner, and I saw her face falling on to the carpet. It changed suddenly from this really animated, vicious indignation to something like a mask. Then she farted, Juliet, and ... I knew. This is death, I thought and the ordinariness of it made me disbelieve it. No, this can't happen. It can't be like this. I told Sophie to get up, I went down to her and shook her. I took her pulse. There was none. I heard a clatter of noise outside. A cat by the dustbins. Then I felt this laughter welling up inside me, totally hysterical laughter, I felt that if I started laughing I would never be able to stop. I just stood there, staring down at Sophie, and I made myself think that she would wake up in a minute. I shook her again and again. Then I panicked and told myself that I'd better put Sophie in the cupboard under the stairs. As I was dragging her out of the front door I thought, *lug the gut into the neighbour room*, and then I thought, yes I have just killed someone and my thoughts are still quoting.

'The body was heavy but I dragged it down the close and pushed it into the cupboard. Then I threw up violently in the close, whisky and bile that bubbled on the cold tiles. I locked and bolted the front door of the flat and then remem-

257

bered that Petruchio and you would be coming back soon from the cinema, so I unbolted the door and speedily put Sophie's coat, hat and bag in my room.

'Then I put the living room back together and found two pieces of a fang, small and jagged, broken in the fall. I flushed them down the loo, and burned the blackmail note that was lying on the sofa. Then I took my own shoes, coat and bag and went into Petruchio's room. I didn't even turn on the light, I just climbed, fully clothed, into his bed and I lay clutching on to my coat. I heard the key turn in the lock. I heard you make some remark about the pile of vomit outside. Then I heard you say goodnight, and Petruchio came into his room and turned on the light.

'He didn't see me for a few minutes, while he hung his coat up methodically in his wardrobe and took off his shoes and placed them tidily under the bed. Then he noticed that someone was in that bed. He pulled the covers down and asked me what was wrong.

'I couldn't speak at first. Petruchio left me, went to his desk and began to read. I think about half an hour went by. Then I told him, in a voice that didn't seem to be mine anymore, that I had killed the agent Sophie and put her body in the cupboard under the stairs. That's what I said, I said, "I have killed the agent Sophie ..."

'Petruchio went to check the cupboard. He returned, white-faced.

'"What happened, tell me quickly, what happened?"

'I told him. He sat, very still, for several minutes. "Mmm," he pondered. "OK, I will help you. But only on condition that I will help you cover up this crime if you promise to me now that if we get caught, I will be the one to carry the blame. You must agree that I killed Sophie."

'I laughed and asked him why he would want to do such a thing, to take the blame ... He said, "Because it makes

258

no difference to me where I am and of course I prefer to take lots of Valium and not go to work. There will be lots of drugs in prison and it interests me to be there, yes, Kerry, don't shake your head, I think it is true. It is also a wonderful revenge against my family who drove me to this godforsaken Scotland because of their fascist disgust of my failure – so how fitting I should turn out to be the gruesome murderer! It is no problem for me, really. I tell you, I will be amused for life and always by the little joke that I am not a murderer at all, only an accomplice after the deed, and that the murderer is, in fact, free. Yes, yes, this I think will make me laugh. Also, if I am to aid and abet you in this murder ... "

'"Manslaughter," I said, "it *wasn't* murder, I didn't mean to kill her." But Petruchio just snorted.

'"Whatever it is," he continued, "I believe that you should not be punished in any way for this act, that you deserve to get away with it, that your continued appeeness – remember the way Petruchio used to say ap-*pee*-ness? – is an essential thing. This is why I will help you."

'The phone rang. Petruchio answered. It was Geoffrey, he wanted to know what time Sophie had left. Petruchio told him that Sophie was with them and that he had better come round.

'"Leave Geoffrey to me," he told me and I started to cry. He told me to be quiet or I'd wake you.

'I'm amazed you didn't hear the doorbell, Juliet. Petruchio went to answer it and a few moments later he ushered Geoffrey into his room. Geoffrey was wearing an army greatcoat, which he took off and tossed casually on to Petruchio's bed. He was all in leather and rubber underneath. Huge leather boots, rubber trousers and a rubber, capped-sleeved T-shirt, with a studded choker around his neck.

'"Will I do?" he purred. "Why, Kerry, you are looking

rather sedate, my dear, and I've heard you look quite good in rubber."

'I felt sick. Geoffrey seemed highly amused by the whole thing. He stared at me sitting up now in Petruchio's bed, my flapper costume all crumpled, still clutching my coat. It was only then that I became aware of the shit in my pants – I had totally forgotten it till then, it was as though I wasn't really a body anymore. I couldn't *feel* myself. But at this moment I suddenly thought, I hope they can't smell it. Even in moments like that embarrassment can raise its silly head.

'"Well, is Sophie here or not?" he enquired, sitting down at Petruchio's desk.

'Petruchio fetched a bottle of whiskey from the living room and offered Geoffrey a drink. Then Petruchio asked him whether he had told anyone about the blackmail message or about Sophie coming round here.

'"Oh dear, oh dear, what *is* going on here?" he smarmed. Petruchio barked his question out again and Geoffrey said contemptuously, "No, we told no one. Don't tell me it *was* you who sent that darned thing." He looked at me here. "Well, thank God for that."

'"Where have you come from?"

'"The hotel, for fuck's sake. Now, where is Sophie?"

'Quick as a flash Petruchio was behind him, holding his arms. Geoffrey didn't struggle, he just smiled, a horrid smug smile. Petruchio, holding Geoffrey's arms together behind his back with one hand, fumbled to release his belt which he then wound round Geoffrey's hands, binding him. He growled at me; I was staring at Geoffrey's trousers and feeling like I might just honk my entire guts up at any minute.

'"Get up, tie his feet," Petruchio barked, indicating his dressing gown, hanging on the back of the door.

'I took the cord from the hanging gown. Geoffrey

presented his feet to me, with a horrid, knowing wink. "Who's your friend, Kerry? He's a deliciously nasty piece of work, isn't he?"

'I tied his feet to the legs of the chair. I didn't know what we were going to do next. I looked at Petruchio and saw that he didn't know either. I don't know when it came to him. He was standing with his finger on his lower lip, muttering to himself in Italian.

'"Gag him," he suddenly ordered. I went to his chest of drawers, fished out a tie and I wrapped it tightly around Geoffrey's mouth, but not before he had purred sexily, "I do think you should have taken my clothes off first." He wasn't taking any of it seriously, and neither was I.

'Petruchio was behind me, opening up his large medicine box. I stood, staring at Geoffrey, completely at ease with his bondage.

'"I killed your wife," I said, but I didn't really believe it as I said it.

'"Now, Kerry, don't be silly," said Petruchio, quick as a flash beside me again, moving around the chair, concealing something in his hand. He released Geoffrey's arm and held it out. I was looking at Geoffrey's mouth, which was twitching with uncertainty when, in the corner of my eye, I saw Petruchio's other hand swiftly move in on Geoffrey. I shouted, a cross between no and aghh. I think I knew then what Petruchio was going to do – put Geoffrey to sleep, drug him.

'Geoffrey's whole body gave a jump, like one electrocuted, and Petruchio stabbed, missed, and stabbed again. Geoffrey wriggled and squirmed, his cry muffled from his gag, so it sounded like a puppy's yelp. Petruchio's hand fell away and, sure enough, it held a syringe. I looked down at Geoffrey: his body was rigid and his eyes were bulging out of his head. In my mind's eye, I saw them pop out and fall on to the carpet. The noise coming from Geoffrey's gagged mouth was suddenly not like a yelp but a muffled scream, and not a fearful scream, but a scream of pain. The tension left his body, though his eyes still bulged, and he sighed and became perfectly still. He's dead, I thought, recognising what I had seen happen to Sophie.

'I stared at Petruchio, whose eyes were almost a match for Geoffrey's in their glassy terror. Tears were falling down his large, bony face and he was muttering no, no no no.

'"What happened?" I said. "What have you done?"

'Petruchio wiped the tears from his face, and leaned for a moment against his desk. He was whispering in Italian, something that sounded like a prayer. I sat down on the bed and started to cry. At last, Petruchio placed the syringe on the desk and sat next to me on the bed.

'"Why? Why did you do that, Petruchio?"

'"I had to, but I did not mean for it to happen that way, I did not mean it."

'"What? What? I don't understand."

'"The vein, you idiot,' he snarled, resorting to anger to crush the sobs welling up inside him, "you made me miss the vein with your stupid screaming, I put it in his muscle, it was terrible pain that he died in."

'I just started to scream then, but Petruchio grabbed me by the mouth, and held me firm. My eyes pleaded with him, "You promise to be quiet," he hissed, and released me.

'I don't know how you slept through all this, Juliet. I just kept asking Petruchio why he had done that. I just couldn't believe it, I just couldn't understand anymore anything that was going on.

'"It is too late now for whys. We must think carefully," he said. I said nothing. There was nothing I could say. What the fuck is there to say in that situation? I drank straight from the whiskey bottle and, as I was probably in shock, almost immediately I was reeling and Petruchio helped me into bed and I fell asleep. I joined you, Juliet, in the land of nod, of blissful oblivion.'

I couldn't speak. Kerry killed Sophie, I thought, Kerry killed Sophie and Petruchio killed Geoffrey. Petruchio killed Geoffrey the same way he killed himself. The order with which I had come to learn of these events confused me for a moment and I thought how strange it was – to kill someone the same way you had killed yourself. Then I realised the true relationship between the two deaths. I knew now why Petruchio had killed himself and the reason behind his choice of death, but why, why did he kill Geoffrey, why on earth did he suddenly do that?

Kerry waited for me to say something, to make some response to her horrifying revelation, but I couldn't utter a sound. I heard a woodpecker somewhere nearby. Here I am in some woods on the Thames, I thought. I have just found out the truth and it is absolutely unbearable. Kerry's lying, I then thought, need driving my belief. Petruchio wouldn't do that, he couldn't just suddenly cold-bloodedly kill someone. This is one of Kerry's fantasies, one of her games.

I looked at her and she was gazing at me with a look of immense pity and sympathy.

'You see, I told you that it was best not to know.'

I wanted to scream, but my voice-box felt as though it were locked and someone had thrown away the key. Kerry was right. It is possible to have millions of thoughts all at the same time. Memories came flooding back, all cast in a totally different light. I remembered Inspector Godfrey coming to see me in London and I felt angry that he had not known that Petruchio's confession had been the truth. How stupid, how stupid he is, I thought. How can the police be so stupid? Then I wondered whether I was ever going to be able to move again; my legs felt like jelly, I felt that I was going to be here in these woods, suspended for ever, unable to move, trapped in this horrible moment of revelation for ever. But Kerry moved us forward at last, by continuing with her story. What Kerry did and what Kerry did next.

Petruchio had sat up all night, thinking. Kerry believed that he made up his mind to kill himself that night, but only after he had helped Kerry to conceal the crime. When Kerry woke it seemed that he had undergone some terrible liberation. He was calm and had more purpose than he ever had before. He told her he was ready for work. The room stank and Petruchio ordered Kerry to go and clean herself up.

Kerry looked at him, feeling sick 'to the bottom of my boots and back again'. Geoffrey was no longer tied in his chair, but on the floor, curled up in a foetal position. Kerry stared at him.

'Rigor mortis sets in after two hours, give or take, he will be easier to dispose of this way, small as possible.'

Kerry retched. Petruchio suddenly seemed so ridiculous and ugly, she couldn't believe she had ever taken him seriously and listened to him for all those hours. She wanted to kill him. Then, as quickly as it had risen, the rage subsided. He was sad, that was all, sad and sick.

Kerry knew that while Petruchio did revolt her, she needed him, she couldn't get through without him.

'I've got to go for the abortion at eight-thirty,' she said.

'Oh, yes, fine ... you go on with your new murder while I deal with the bodies here. No way, Kerry.'

Kerry knew there was no way. She said she would phone the hospital and cancel.

'No, you must do nothing just yet, until we know what we are doing.'

At six am Petruchio went out into the close and cleaned up the heap of vomit. He and Kerry then waited in silence until it was time to wake me, deciding not to attempt to move the bodies while there was anyone in the building. Kerry went into her room and changed her clothes, while Petruchio went to wake me.

But, as we know, I did not get up. He had stood over me for a few moments, gauging how deep my sleep was, and convincing himself that I had not been disturbed at all in the night.

He did not leave the flat, as I had assumed, but merely slammed the door and then crept back into his room. He and Kerry barely moved and mouthed all communication. I slept on, in my deep and dreamless sleep. Eventually they decided to move the bodies upstairs.

Oh, how ridiculous it all was. How dumb, how clumsy! It was as though they had both gone completely mad, that they acted without thinking, without for one minute taking seriously what had happened. Yet perhaps it was this ability for denial, even while they were doing it, that helped them, that rendered them innocent somehow. It is, nonetheless, a miracle that they didn't get caught.

They had killed two people. They had crossed some boundary. Yet they were still the same. And the survival instinct had come to the fore in both of them, surely their behaviour gives the lie to their depressions? In spite of all their misery and self-disgust, when it came down to it, they felt completely vindicated in their cover-up operation. It was as though they were children, stamping their feet and saying, it's not fair, it's not fair that we murdered two people, why should we be punished?

Petruchio was afraid that Kerry would give in to hysteria. He lectured her. What was done was done. Sophie and Geoffrey had been evil.

'But we didn't kill them because they were evil,' Kerry insisted.

'No.' Petruchio put his head in his hands and rubbed his thick black hair. 'We had better move now,' he whispered, 'while Juliet is still asleep.'

He ordered Kerry to help him carry Geoffrey's corpse up the stairs. Kerry, the squeamish, obeyed, gritting her teeth and trying to imagine that she was acting in a 1940s film noir movie. I can imagine her now, modifying her movements as befitting the imaginary suit she wore, the imagined shadows on the wall. Her gestures at war with her actual image: T-shirt, trousers with zips all over them and DMs.

They took Geoffrey upstairs and dumped him on the living-room floor of Mrs McNicol's flat.

They returned to base; Petruchio's bedroom. That was when I got up. They listened to me going to the bathroom and locking the door. Kerry began to shake, quite dramatically.

Petruchio, loathing physical contact as he did, saw that the only way he could keep Kerry together at that moment was by holding her as tightly as he could. So he did just this. His large hands stroking her spine, easing her into taking deep breaths, into relaxing. After a few moments, she withdrew from him and he nodded gravely.

They went back to the cupboard and hauled Sophie out. Too late they heard the click in the door. Petruchio pushed Kerry into the back of the cupboard and leapt in behind her leaving the corpse on the floor of the close.

If I close my eyes, it will all go away, Kerry thought.

They heard me approach the body, they heard my stupid 'hello'. They were aware of the shadow that my head caused, peering into the cupboard. Nothing happened. They heard me go back into the flat.

They were frozen. They daren't move. We'll stay here for ever now, Kerry thought, it'll be all right.

266

'We're invisible,' she had mouthed.

'Impossible,' I said, interrupting her for the first time. Astonished that my voice did indeed still work.

'I know it's impossible, Juliet, but it is true, I swear it. Petruchio and I were in that cupboard and you looked in and didn't see us – it was dark, or I don't know, I just don't know. I've sometimes thought that there was some quantum confusion and for a second, just for that second, our possible worlds didn't coincide – like we were in a different dimension. Either that or I wanted not to be seen so much, so powerfully, that we became invisible.'

Kerry's capacity to elaborate her story in this way, to continue making theories, metaphors, amazed me. I thought she was truly mad to be able to think in such a way, after such a thing had happened to her. But now I realise that Kerry's story was no big deal to her anymore. She had learned to live with it in order that she could continue with it until the end that she had chosen, until the grand finale. I did not know that then. I did not know then what Kerry had decided. Now I know, I only feel, why not? Why not make crazy speculations, why not elaborate? The fact is that I will never be able to explain why I didn't see them when I looked into that cupboard. It was a sound that made me turn towards the back door, towards the cupboard. The noise must have been them. I have come to believe that the panic and fear, the rush of adrenalin that I felt when I saw the corpse and realised that it was in rigor, must have momentarily blinded me. Or perhaps that what I saw simply did not register on my brain, but was merely a subliminal flicker.

Petruchio moved slightly, then froze again as they heard me once again leave the flat and my footsteps on the pavement outside begin to fade. I had gone for the cigarettes.

'Quick,' said Petruchio. 'Upstairs.' He was out, had

picked up the body and was hurling it up the stairs by the time Kerry emerged from the cupboard and followed him. They stayed in Mrs McNicol's apartment and heard my return from the shops, my conversation with the woman from the shop, my shouts of anger and dismay at having my murder mystery dematerialise before my very eyes.

Then, when I had gone back into the flat, Petruchio told Kerry that he would go down first and that she must stay here.

'What? You can't expect me to stay up here all alone with these two, I'd go mad.'

'Then go for a walk, do whatever you must do.'

Kerry remembered the abortion which she was now over an hour late for.

'I have to go to the hospital, make up some hog-shit about why I've missed it and beg with them to give me another appointment.'

'Be careful, Kerry. Whatever you do or say, be careful.'

Kerry insisted that they shut the kitchen window so that Mrs McNicol's cat couldn't come in and find the bodies. The cat could get out and shimmy along the tenement side until it reached a tree then climb down into the courtyard. Petruchio hissed at her that they must leave all the windows open otherwise the bodies would stink the building out. Petruchio won the argument but Kerry was upset at the thought of the cat being in some way traumatised by the corpses.

They left Mrs McNicol's flat together and Kerry went to the clinic. She lied to the doctor, saying that the father of the child was trying to prevent her from having an abortion and had succeeded, but she was desperate for another appointment. They gave her one and recommended that she go to a refuge.

Meanwhile, Petruchio had done some shopping to calm

himself down, to make things appear normal and entered the flat quietly, not knowing what to expect. He later told Kerry he felt sorry for me and at one point he wanted to explain it all to me, to tell me everything.

I dread to think how Petruchio must have felt when the police came on that first visit. He told Kerry that during that half hour, with Chris and myself nervous about the joint in the ashtray, he had felt a military sort of calm take over his thought processes. He barked internal orders at himself, sealing the secret inside himself so that no one would ever know. It would be all right. He began to even enjoy the visit, looking at Inspector Godfrey with hidden pleasure. *There are bodies upstairs that you will never know about.* He hoped Kerry would not come back because he feared she would give herself away.

He told Kerry how all the sickness and panic he had felt when I had called out my warning, 'Chris, it's the police' had during the course of the interview transformed itself, into a sick and cruel enjoyment.

'Of course,' said Kerry to him afterwards, 'it's the only way to cope. We weren't murderers before we committed murder, but now we have, we must *become* murderers.' Petruchio stared at her grimly and took a Valium.

Kerry described how she had felt when she too had returned to the flat and found all of us there. When Chris said that the police had been round, her heart missed a beat and she broke out into a sweat. Then she saw that Petruchio was calm and she took her cue from him and behaved normally. She was no stranger to deceit, having played the lying game many times before.

The toy gun that the policeman had found under the dresser, Petruchio had picked up and played with, taking it with him when he left.

When I went out for my walk in the park, Petruchio had

woken Kerry. Was she up to it? he asked, since they would have to be as cold and cunning as they could be in order to hide the bodies and get rid of all the evidence, including the gun which the police had already seen.

Petruchio was grim and urgent. 'If anyone has seen Sophie with this toy gun the police just might come snooping back around here.'

'What are we going to do?' said Kerry.

'First, we must be absolutely normal, nothing must be suspicious. We need to get the bodies out of the flat upstairs first. The best thing I think is refuse sacks.'

'They'll need to be big; we'd better get some garden ones.'

'OK,' Petruchio continued, 'then we put them in the boot of the car to start with, then we think again. OK.'

'I don't believe this is happening.' Kerry got out of bed. 'You'd better go and buy the bin bags, and I'll sort some clothes out for Oxfam. I'll tell Juliet that I'm having a clean-out, and you can offer me a lift to the shop. How we get the bodies down the stairs and into the car is another matter.'

'Oh, that will be easy. No one will see.'

Their confidence at this point was part of their madness no doubt. When Kerry said 'I don't believe this is happening', she was actually giving herself a mandate for mendacity; it's OK, I can do this, because it isn't really happening.

Petruchio returned from the shop with the huge garden-refuse bags, and they went upstairs. Meanwhile, I was in my room, lying on my bed in a stupor, thinking about laundry.

Kerry hesitated when she saw the bodies. They were lying on the green carpet in Mrs McNicol's living room. They looked like dolls, broken dolls. Freyja shot out from under a table and Kerry gave a little shriek. Petruchio snarled, 'shut up'; Freyja made a flying leap for the kitchen window, glancing back and giving Kerry an indignant look before she slunk away.

Kerry began to cry and Petruchio shook her. She pushed him away from her, but wiped away her tears and braced herself for folding the bodies into the green plastic bags. Petruchio was standing, frozen, his finger on his lip.

'I will have to break her bones, that won't be very nice.'

'Why, for fuck's sake?'

'How else can she fit in the car?'

Kerry kept having to tell herself that Sophie was dead, that she couldn't feel it, as Petruchio tried to snap the knee joints. He failed. He tried to fold her down at the head, but it was no use. Kerry started to laugh, a high-pitched laugh, and Petruchio ordered her to shut up and get a grip.

He looked around the room, then picked up Sophie's legs and dragged her towards the front door. Kerry followed, asking no questions. Petruchio placed Sophie's corpse so that she was lying with her knees over the top stair.

'Hold her,' Petruchio mouthed, indicating her arms and head. Kerry did as she was bid.

'Tight,' he mouthed again. Kerry shut her eyes and held on to Sophie. She heard Petruchio stamp and stamp again. Then a horrible crack.

'Keep on holding.' More stamps and another, less resonant, crack. 'Shit.'

Kerry opened her eyes. Sophie's legs were dangling slightly over the step.

'Oh, for Christ's sake Petruchio, stop now, she'll have to do, we've got to get her into the car.'

'Well, we have to try anyway,' he sighed, resigned.

Kerry's relief was so great that she almost leapt at the task ahead. They manoeuvred Sophie's body into two refuse

271

sacks, knotting the two sacks together in the middle. Kerry stood back and started to laugh. It looked exactly like a dead body in garden-refuse sacks. Petruchio hissed at her to be quiet again. Kerry kept watch, while Petruchio dragged the obvious-looking package downstairs. He had parked the car so that the boot was right up against the door to the close. When they reached the ground floor Kerry picked up one end of the green plastic shroud and they carried Sophie out and put her into the boot. I shall have a miscarriage, thought Kerry, the shock of all this is bound to make me miscarry, I won't need to go for the abortion.

Sophie was not a tall woman. She fitted, just. Then they went back up for Geoffrey. But they were no longer Sophie and Geoffrey to Kerry, they were no longer even corpses, cadavers. They were part of an experiment. It was a game, that's all. How long could they keep it up? How long could they go on pretending that any of this was real?

Kerry, with a bin bag containing the agents' coats which she was about to put on top of the corpses, saw me with my laundry bag, staring helplessly at her. Juliet needs my help, she thought, and I can't give it to her. I have separated from her in a way that she can never understand. From her, and the rest of the world except Petruchio. Nothing is ever going to be really real again.

They got into the car and drove west out of Glasgow. Kerry asked Petruchio what they were going to do.

'We drive,' he muttered, 'we drive until we find somewhere to put them.'

They drove and drove and drove. They drove to a dump, but although Geoffrey might look reasonably innocuous, being more compact, there were too many people around for them to dump Sophie. Kerry tried not to panic, but she imagined that they were going to be driving around Glasgow and environs for eternity, they would never be able to leave this car with its macabre load.

On and on they drove and still there was nowhere suitable to dump the bodies. They were both getting more and more anxious, and they became afraid of making a mistake.

'I know a great place where we could bury them,' Kerry remarked, 'but it's too far to drive, we'd never get back in time not to be suspicious.'

'Where is this place?'

'That cottage I went to with Juliet, in the woods there. It's so remote, there is never anyone around for miles.'

'How far is it?'

'Too far.'

'Then tomorrow we must persuade Juliet and everyone to go away for a weekend there. Can you do this, Kerry?' Kerry thought she probably could, but wanted to know how they would manage to bury the bodies with everyone else there.

'We find a way,' said Petruchio.

Yes, thought Kerry, we find a way. It's simple. Everything will be all right.

'But what if Geoffrey was lying, Petruchio? What if he did tell someone that he was coming to get Sophie from my flat?'

'Then I am lost, little Kerry, and I will go to prison for being such a bad boy.'

'Won't the bodies start to smell?' she asked.

'It is quite cold enough, I think, but we must act quickly and leave tomorrow as early as we can.'

'Don't expect any miracles,' Kerry grinned, bracing herself for a performance.

She prowled around the living room in a fit of frenzied boredom. She begged us all to do something at the weekend, to go crazy, to make things be like they used to be.

'Couldn't we go to the cottage in Argyll, Juliet? Think what fun it would be, all of us together?'

The next morning at ten we set off. Kerry was in a state of terror on the journey. She was grateful to Petruchio for being so calm, so bossy, for taking control of the situation, but at the same time she hated and resented him for it. She did not dare look at him in the car for fear that she would betray her panic and her hatred. She couldn't believe that the rest of us didn't know, that it wasn't obvious, plain for all to see, that they were murderers.

As we approached the cottage, Kerry's panic worsened: what would happen now? How would they get the bodies out of the car, let alone to the woods for burial, without being seen?

I can see it all so clearly, as if I were there once more, reliving it, but now I know what was really going on and everything is totally different. I know now why Petruchio suddenly became bossy and organisational, snatching our bags from us, making edicts. They had only put mine and Petruchio's bags in the boot, because of the smell, they hoped that none of us would notice, which we didn't. Now I remembered how crushed we all were in the car. Why did none of us complain, berate Petruchio with his lousy job of car packing? I remember too now the tension in the car and, on arrival at the cottage, when Petruchio hovered uncertainly by the car.

But then he took control, and ordered us to our various tasks. I did the water with Christine, and Kerry went with Chris and Billy to chop wood. Off we went, Petruchio winking at Kerry, unseen by any of us. Things were certainly going their way.

Petruchio knew he only had a matter of seconds and that he could be discovered at any moment. He kept a firm eye on Christine and me as we made our progression up the hill. He looked around him and spotted the path on his right, leading to the front door. He poked his head around the hedge and saw a clump of bushes at the bottom of the garden. It would do for the time being, it was only about fifty yards from the car. He unloaded all the stuff packed on top, and then hauled first Geoffrey and then Sophie over to the front garden where he hurled them into the bushes. He looked straight out for us as he turned the corner and gave me a wave. No wonder it looked awkward.

As soon as we had gone into Inveraray, they hauled the bodies into a wheelbarrow. They had to make the journey twice as the corpses were heavy. They heaved the barrow over the fence, across the burn and into the woods, taking Geoffrey first, then Sophie.

There was a deep bed of leaves in the wood, and first they gathered enough leaves to cover the bodies, which they left in their leafy burial mound while they dug a deep pit, working like slaves with tools they found in the cottage. The pit had to be wide as well as long to accommodate Geoffrey's foetal form. The earth was soft and peaty, but it took hours and they realised they should get back so as not to rouse suspicion.

It was Kerry's suggestion that they fill the graves temporarily with leaves and return later to dig some more. This is what they did, placing the bodies into the little pits and then kicking and shovelling leaves in them until they merged with the forest floor. They also hid the spades in a nearby bush. They rushed back to the cottage, and were in time to make the fire and look relaxed by the time we returned from our shopping spree.

They agreed to return to the woods that night, but Kerry slept deeply and Petruchio did not dare wake her, for fear of waking me too. He went alone and, by torchlight, he found the spot and began emptying the graves of leaves. He dug like a maniac, deeper and deeper into the peaty earth until he was satisfied and at last Sophie and Geoffrey were laid in their final resting ground with the bin bag of clothes and the toy gun thrown in on top. Petruchio left the clearing as the dawn broke.

He carried the two spades back to the cottage, unknowingly observed by me as he crossed the burn. He had done a wonderful job, leaving the clearing seemingly untouched, covered by a tranquil blanket of leaves. I noticed nothing when I walked through, looking for evidence of truffle digging. But then, I, preposterously, hadn't even seen Kerry and Petruchio in the cupboard, cowering somewhere behind the mop, bucket and disinfectant.

'It is done,' Petruchio told Kerry at the first opportunity he had. 'But,' he insisted, 'we must be careful of Juliet. She is unhinged from seeing the body disappear so suddenly, but she also suspects us of things and she may have seen me in the woods this morning, I do not know. We may have to divert her by pretending to have an affair, we can even say this baby is mine. It will divert her from all other concerns.'

'That won't be necessary,' Kerry said firmly. 'There are lies enough already, we don't need any more.'

Petruchio shrugged. 'Bouff, have it your way then, but I am frightened that she knows something.'

Kerry was frightened too for a short while, but then, as she spent time with me and observed my behaviour, she knew that I did not know.

When Kerry was in a panic, Petruchio was strong; now Petruchio was the frightened one, it was Kerry's turn to lead.

'No, listen. We have to both understand somehow that this didn't happen, otherwise we'll never live with it. Look, it's like Schrödinger's box. If we forget all about it and no one else ever opens it, then we can say it never really happened, since no one knows about it. That's why we have to understand, believe that it didn't happen. None of it happened.'

'But we are in the box too, Kerry,' Petruchio muttered, so that Kerry only just caught what he said. 'We won't ever be able to get out.'

Kerry saw for a moment, vividly, the inside of a box, containing a cat trapped for ever between life and death. Then she suddenly realised her position in this picture: she was the decay particle, for ever on the brink of choice. She had a radioactive material's eye view and she was watching something that was neither yes or no.

'What are you meaning to do, play a trick on yourself?' Petruchio said.

When, in the cafe in Oban, I put the fang on to the table, Kerry at first didn't make any connection, she just stared at it uncomprehending. Then it dawned on her; it must have fallen somewhere on Sophie's travels to the cupboard or up the stairs. But why did I have it and why was I goading them with it now?

The fang was a terrible sight to Kerry and, without thinking, she grabbed hold of it and ran. It wasn't so much a matter of getting rid of the evidence, but of removing such a hideous reminder from her sight. She threw it into the Firth of Lorn.

Petruchio was furious with her for her rash act. He was sure then that I knew more than they thought. Kerry did try to persuade him to allow her to confide in me, she had enough faith in my infatuation for her to trust me, but Petruchio insisted that I had a moral sternness that could not be relied on in this case.

I wonder?

Later, that night in Argyll, lying in bed with me pretending to sleep at her side, Kerry dreamed of the box, only this

277

time, she, the particle decays and releases a y-ray. The poison is released; the cat dies. Only once. And no one is watching.

Kerry, after describing her dream, said nothing for some time. I looked around me. The leaves were beginning to turn. It is autumn again, I thought, it is a year ago since all this happened.

Then I felt a kind of jubilation. I knew. At least I knew. But almost immediately this feeling disintegrated, and rage and dismay followed. What use was this truth? What could I do with this new-found knowledge? This new story in Kerry's repertoire? And then I felt shame – *how could I have been so blind?* – and a feeling of the utter hopelessness and improbability of everything. The rage I had felt at the time, at being left out of something, returned now and I felt more impotent than ever before in my life.

The next stage was the 'if' stage. My thoughts were full of ifs. If Petruchio and I had not gone to the cinema and if Billy had turned up as planned, then Kerry would not have been alone when Sophie came to call and nothing would have happened. I kept re-shooting scenes in my head. I saw Billy go to the phone booth in the pub and I made him change his mind, *'Och no, I'll go round and get the wee man after all.'* When Kerry pleads with me to stay and help her dress, I decide I really don't want to go to the cinema and tough shit, Petruchio.

What was the point at which things became fixed? I asked myself, the point beyond which things could not have been otherwise? It's not Kerry's fault, we all did this. It needn't have happened.

Moments of peace, following by more anger and fear. The thing that seemed at first to rile me the most was that they got away with it. Somehow this really pissed me off. This makes me think that Petruchio was right, and that if I had known at the time I would have been morally stern, I would have turned them in. But perhaps not. Maybe their confidences would have flattered me into loyalty. Besides I don't think I mind them having had one over the police, only that they had one over me.

'Finish it off then, Kerry, what happened next?' I was remembering vividly the day we returned from the cottage, the miserable car journey back to Glasgow. The days of paranoia to follow. I also knew now why Kerry had finished with me that weekend. I am appalled to say that it helped.

'The smell of death, that's what happened next.' Kerry spoke with even, resigned tones. 'For weeks and weeks, I had this smell in my nose, it was horrible; we had to go up and clear up Mrs McNicol's flat, make sure we left no trace.'

'Billy saw you,' I said, 'he thought you were fucking up there.'

Kerry smiled sadly. I wished that they had been fucking and yet, at the time, I don't know. Maybe at that time it would have been harder for me to accept infidelity from Kerry than murder, and perhaps anything would have been better than all those secrets, all that doubt and mistrust.

Kerry shuddered and then brightening suddenly, continued talking very fast. 'Do you remember the time that you pretended to be Poirot – you were so close – I mean the thing about the Oxfam shop and the fang getting caught on my cardigan. I suppose it must have been something like that that really happened.'

I felt sick, and tried not to feel frightened.

'What about the police?' I asked. 'You must have been shit scared.'

'Yes and no. I was terrified when I had to tell Inspector Godfrey that I wasn't at the party, for a minute I thought all was lost.' She smiled suddenly.

'What?'

'Good job I'm so clever,' she said. 'I *knew* that you would go running straight to Petruchio to confront him ...'

I saw myself frantically spinning in circles in the road before purposefully striding towards the university. How stupid I was!

Kerry continued, telling me that she had phoned Petruchio immediately in his lab and warned him. (Had he been on the phone to Kerry when I peered in through the glass door?) He had been very calm with Kerry, told her not to worry. This time Kerry thought they should admit to an affair, say he was the father of the baby, to divert me, but this time Petruchio said, 'Don't be ridiculous.'

I was outraged yet again by the capacity for deceit in both of them. Kerry went on talking about how nice Inspector Godfrey was to her, and how she almost, the afternoon she went to the station to give her statement, broke down and confessed everything.

'Why didn't you?'

'Because of Petruchio. I wasn't in it alone.'

'Then why don't you now?'

'Why the fuck should I?' she said defiantly and with anger. 'Besides, isn't that obvious?'

I said nothing and got up, yes I can walk, I can move, I can move, I can get the hell out of these woods. To me, our venue for the big revelation scene was too like the final resting place of the agents. I had to get out of the woods. Kerry ran to catch up with me.

'You see, you didn't want to know, did you? Now you know you can see that. I shouldn't have told you.'

'Is that all you care about? That you shouldn't have told me. Kerry, you murdered two people!'

'I didn't mean to kill Sophie, it *was* manslaughter, and

Petruchio killed Geoffrey, not me. Petruchio did that. He did that for me.'

'Why?'

'I don't know. I don't think he knew he was going to right up until he did, and then we had to cover it up and then we got away with it, somehow, we got away with it.'

'How?'

'Because of me, the way I was, the way I knew that we had to pretend that it hadn't happened. I didn't feel guilt, that was the main thing. If I had, we'd have been lost. All my life I've suffered from stupid guilts and suddenly I was cured. You see, never before did guilt seem so useless; it couldn't bring them back. Nothing could bring them back.'

We had reached the car by this point and I started to drive back to London, though I don't know how, my thoughts were not on the road. I had always associated Kerry with guilt, since I had always seen her wild and dissipated behaviour as a desperate kicking against the pricks, a rage against something she knew held her captive. Had she really expended her guilt on trivialities, on sexual peccadilloes, so that by the time she really sinned, she had none left?

But I did not want to get philosophical, I wanted to get the nitty-gritty details, I wanted to know how they had got away with it.

'It must be because of the guy at the sauna,' Kerry avered, 'the one who pitched up at the agents' dungeon do – there were connections there, dark connections I suppose, and the police got diverted by that. Plus the kiddy porn – that was a complete godsend to Petruchio and me, a major diversion.'

I realised how potentially damaging my conversation with Inspector Godfrey had been, when he had come to visit me at the university. I told Kerry that I had told him about her

281

connection with the sauna people.

'Jesus Christ – you shopped me, Juliet, you practically shopped me!'

'Oh, don't be idiotic – how could I have shopped you? I had no idea what you were involved in, I thought you were innocent, so did Inspector Godfrey and, even when I told him, he didn't suspect you. But actually, don't you see now why you should have told me before ... then I could have helped you.'

Kerry nodded.

'I suppose there are a whole load of circumstantial reasons why we didn't get caught. Mostly the fact that they were supposed to be going on holiday and weren't immediately reported missing. Do you remember Petruchio going to get a paper in Oban and looking through every page? Well, he was terrified that there was going to be something about the agents.'

I didn't remember. Kerry's voice fell at least an octave as she continued, almost mechanically, to fill in the details for me.

'We buried everything with them, the toy gun, their coats, Sophie's bag. And then, like I've explained, we pretended that it hadn't happened.'

'And Molly? Where does Molly come into all this? Why didn't you have the abortion?'

'Fear, Juliet. I was so fucking scared so I convinced myself that I would lose the baby anyway. I didn't believe in anything anymore, least of all my pregnancy. I left to go to the clinic that day but I knew I couldn't do it, that I just couldn't do it. It was fear of hospitals and going under – I don't know, I just couldn't hack it and I was absolutely convinced that I couldn't possibly continue to carry this ... thing ... it would abort of its own volition, I knew it would. I cancelled the abortion again, saying that I had lost it

282

anyway and my own doctor was dealing with me. I lost my deposit, but I didn't have to pay the whole amount. One day I had some bleeding and I thought, great, that's it, it's over. But after only a few days, I knew it wasn't. I was still pregnant. I worked at War and Pizza and I didn't think, I didn't allow myself to think. Then Petruchio left and Billy and Chris and you were going to move to your new flat and I just ran away.

'Petruchio and I never spoke, not after it was all over, I mean, once the police had been round and I had given my statement and we thought we were clear. Petruchio knew that I didn't turn up for the abortion the next week. He just knew. I never admitted it, but he just knew. He was right. By this time it was way too late to have a legal and safe abortion. I knew that, but I still didn't believe I would actually give birth. I ran away, I went to stay with Melissa because of her kind face, and because I don't know anyone else in London. She had these green magazines all over the place and in one of them I saw an advert for Las Cascadas and off I went.

'You know what that place is like, don't you? Well, in my first few days I realised what I was doing and what I had to do. Of course the baby must be born. I had taken a life and I must put one back, it is clear, it is absolutely clear, it has nothing to do with redemption or anything like that, but it is what I have to do, what I am doing.'

'So you gave up smoking and drinking and everything?'

'Yes, I had to ... for the baby ... I had to do it properly.'

Kerry's voice had become uncertain as she spoke, she faltered slightly and, although it was subtle, there was a change in her tone. She's lying again, I thought, up to now it has been the truth, but now she is lying.

'Kerry, I think you are lying now, I just sense it.'

'I am not lying, I promise, every word I say now will be true.'

I believed her, and in a sense it *was* true. I only found out later that her lying tone had been, not because of what she was saying, but because of what she was not saying.

'Did you really believe that she was dead ... all that time?'

'No, at first I could feel her, in fact I started feeling her when I was staying with Billy and Chris, when we got back from Spain. That's why I came to say goodbye to you and go home to Ireland. I intended to tell my parents and throw myself at their mercy but when I got there and the grim reality of them was upon me, I realised I couldn't. I didn't have much money so I just got a train down to Dublin and slept rough. I mean, there are a lot of hostels and things where I could stay and I made friends with people and stayed at various squats and the like. I was fine. I made sure I didn't smoke or drink and I tried to eat as well as I could. I didn't feel anything for ages and then only the tiniest thing, that could have been wind. I never got myself checked out, because I just couldn't hack it, people probing me, looking into me, it was none of their business. If it was dead, it was dead, it had chosen. Then I went into this sort of refuge place but they were insisting that I get seen by a doctor and so I used the last of my money to get a passage across and I came to London. I came to you because you were the only person I could come to, and because I was afraid, the time was getting near, I was just really scared and I ... I didn't know, or care, whether it was alive or not, I was just frightened.'

'And now? Molly – she's Geoffrey's child.' The thought that the horribly handsome agent had anything to do with the baby that I had come to love appalled me.

'Geoffrey's dead. Edgar is the father, Juliet.'

'But why did it all happen, Kerry? What *caused* it? How could you and Petruchio behave like that?'

'I don't know, it happened because it happened. That's what was going on at that moment and it happened. I'm talking about killing Sophie, me killing Sophie, that was the first thing after all. We could take it back to antecedent cause after antecedent cause, in search for some grand, final cause, but, really, it just happened. There was nothing exterior to that moment – *that very moment*. She fell, Juliet, I pushed her and she *fell* ...'

Kerry sounded defiant and I realised that part of her remained forever trapped in that moment, that moment when a trinity of consummation occurred between her hand, Sophie's head, and the edge of the coffee table. Forever, Kerry would see the manifold possibilities of that moment, and forever, the better part of her would simmer with rebellion: it's not fair. It wasn't my fault.

'I didn't mean to kill her, but I was angry and vicious, I lost my temper. It was the toy gun, it was that ... imagine what it is like when you think you are going to die?'

I said nothing, but I closed my eyes and tried to imagine.

'That's what I felt, a sort of eternal moment of life and not life, death and not death. It was horrible.'

I didn't know what to say. This was the nearest Kerry had come to a defence of herself. There was no need on my account. It was not the fact that Kerry killed Sophie that bothered me, for that, indisputably, had been manslaughter. It was Petruchio killing Geoffrey as well, and the whole cover-up operation which they got away with that outraged me, that was so hard to live with.

'Does anyone else know?'

Kerry shook her head. 'I was going to tell both you and Edgar that night when I started the story, but I couldn't. I can't. The agents have to stay in the box.'

285

We arrived back at my parents' house. My mother had been looking after Molly. I felt sick as soon as we entered into the bustling, baby-centred atmosphere. How on earth could I carry on as normal? But I took my cue from Kerry, who was used to it, and I got through the evening.

I sat opposite Kerry at dinner and looked from my parents to her and back. She's a murderer, I thought, she killed people and buried them, and your son loves her, he loves a murderer and is going to be the father of her child.

I wondered what would happen if I suddenly said, casually – oh hey, Mum and Dad, it turns out that this baby is Geoffrey Daniels', that agent who disappeared with his wife. Kerry killed his wife, and then Petruchio, you remember, our other flatmate, he killed Geoffrey and they hid them in the cupboard and ...

It was impossible. I snapped myself out of my reverie and behaved as normally as I could, but I'm no actress. My mother put it down to tiredness and suggested that we all have an early night.

I didn't sleep much that night, no relaxation exercise in the world was going to rid me of my racing thoughts. I felt very sick and hoped that I had caught a bug. An honest bug which I could treat with drugs and hot toddies. I remembered those cats, the ones that were crucified on road signs in Highgate when I was twelve. Now I felt much the same way about Geoffrey. I couldn't stop thinking about his last moments.

During my training I had once observed while a cat was 'put down' using pentobarbitone. Within seconds of administration it works on a direct depression of the cerebral cortex, and causes respiratory and cardiovascular failure. Presto: permanent abolition of the central nervous system.

A dead cat.

Animals can smell death and fear. There are veterinary techniques for avoiding the stress caused by euthanasia. Although the animals are all killed in the same place, that place is cleaned and new disposable mats laid down to prevent the scent of previous unquickenings to enter like ghosts into the next victim's nostrils. A distressed animal can be identified from the following:

1. Vocalisation
2. Avoidance or aggressive behaviour
3. Immobility – frozen with fear
4. Urination and defecation

This cat was given a jab of strong sedative five minutes before. The vet was then able to apply a tourniquet and find the target, with the cat barely being aware. Geoffrey's death was so terrible to me that I turned on the light, unable to bear the dark. I watched the second hand ticking on my alarm clock. I wanted to go upstairs, to wake Kerry. I wanted to phone the police, speak to Inspector Godfrey and tell him everything. I wanted to see Kerry hurt and in pain, in prison. She had ruined my life and married my brother.

When, at last, I drifted off to sleep, I dreamed of the cottage. I was flying over the cottage, not in any kind of machine but somehow, through a knowledge carried in my solar plexus, able to propel myself through the air, my arms taking their part by doing breaststroke. I had this bird's eye view of the loch, the road, and then the drive and the little yellow cottage, with its large black door, nestled in a clump of trees. Beyond it the back garden, and the fence and hill beyond, the burn and the woods.

And inside the woods, buried beneath the earth, the bodies of Geoffrey and Sophie. As well as being able to fly, I have X-ray eyes and can see deep into the earth's bowels. The bodies are decomposing but they are larger than they were and they are growing; as I hover above in the air, they stretch and spread, their limbs sprouting out, like saplings; they push through roots, underworlds of ants, moles, all the living creatures of the earth, and go on growing until they are under the foundations of the cottage and their now gargantuan fingers are probing upwards, poking, destroying. A hand comes up through the roof of the cottage, shattering and splintering the wood and stone, their legs stretch out under the country. I am high in the sky and I am not afraid, because I know that even though they can do this thing – grow and creep up and out of the earth – they are still dead.

My mother woke me the next morning, in tears, holding out an envelope.

'She's dead, she's killed herself.'

At first I thought that she meant Molly, but by the time her sentence ended I knew. Babies don't commit suicide. My mother sat down, sobbed and then got up again.

'Oh God, Molly's still up there, I must get her.'

She left, and I opened the envelope, which was sealed with candle wax and addressed to me, Juliet Porteus.

I've done what I had to do. I intended to do this all along, I intended to do it as soon as she was born, but something happened at that moment and I found I cared too much about her to just go without sorting out a future for her. Molly will be OK now, she will grow up in a fine family with good men and women who will love her. She should have the best. The sins of the mother should not be visited upon her. Petruchio is wrong if he thought that his death was honourable, and that through it he extirpated

288

Geoffrey's. It doesn't work like that. Things like this aren't redeemable. I am sure you will work out the rest, Juliet. You were right, I was lying to you at a certain point. I couldn't tell you the whole story because you would only have prevented me from completing it. I have been as good as dead ever since it happened. Imagine an event horizon beyond which is the black hole. I was the black hole, nothing could get beyond the event horizon. No prizes for guessing what the fucking event was. I'm sorry that you know, Juliet. I don't want anyone else to. I want you to burn this and pretend not to understand why I would do such a crazy thing as take my life. You must do what you have to do, Juliet, but don't be afraid ... Remember they are neither dead nor alive until somebody opens the box. I loved you to the red shift and back. Love Molly for me. I hope the wave function never collapses for her.

I ran up the stairs and into the guest room. Kerry was lying peacefully in her bed. I flapped my arms around and wailed. I picked her up and held her and bawled like a baby until my father came in and led me away. The doctor was here to certify the death.

Molly was gurgling happily over her bottle on my mother's lap when I got down to the kitchen. My mother was still crying.

'What a terrible thing to do ... Juliet, why did she?'

'I don't know.'

'What did the note say?'

'Just look after Molly.'

'Oh, poor Edgar. She must have had post-natal depression and none of us knew. Could you see any signs of it?'

289

I shook my head. I felt jealous of the baby in my mother's lap. I wanted to be there, to be held safe in my mother's arms, to cry into her bosom. I sat down at the table and sobbed for a while.

Why didn't I go up and wake her last night? Why did I not stay with her? Why did I not see what she had planned?

'Isn't this the punishment you chose for me?' Kerry had said to me when I found her watering the plants with an aura of wholesome domesticity. Perhaps there was some truth in that but how much more truth now: it was the punishment *she* chose. The whole thing had been her punishment.

Petruchio had chosen to kill himself the way he had Geoffrey; he had forced himself to die in the agony that he had inflicted on the agent. But that wasn't enough for Kerry, that wasn't terrible enough for her.

'I took a life, I must put one back,' she had said, but that wasn't really all. Kerry had decided to face the very worst thing, the thing that she feared the most. She must go through pregnancy and labour. She must go into hospital, she must surrender herself to doctors. I recalled her grim face as she endured her labour, quietly and with dignity, her refusal to take pethadin. Crime and punishment.

I'm not sure that Molly really noticed Kerry going. After all, I could now see how Kerry had engineered for her not to spend any more time with her than she could get away with. The baby had bonded with Edgar and me and my parents, as much as it had with her. She seemed oblivious to the funeral preparations and the gloomy atmosphere in the house. She just did her baby things, which had to be dealt with, regardless.

Edgar returned from the States immediately. He was devastated. We knew that we had both loved Kerry, and so we alone could really understand what the other was going through.

I telephoned Kerry's parents and told them what had happened; that Kerry had had a baby, had suffered from post-natal depression and killed herself.

They didn't exactly say serve her right and good riddance to bad rubbish but that was their general tone. When I suggested that they might want to see their grandchild, they said that it had nothing to do with them.

Their callousness had the effect of making me extra specially nice to Molly, as if I were lavishing on her baby the love Kerry should have had from her parents.

The murders didn't matter anymore. Nothing mattered. Only that Kerry was dead. I missed her. Her anti-presence was stronger perhaps than even her reality had been. The funeral was family only, which included Billy and Chris and Melissa, who all came back to the house. Billy and Melissa wept all the way through, but everyone else was quiet and grim faced.

My sister Helena and Benedick were around a lot, being supportive, albeit in a confused way.

'Whose baby is it?' Helena asked at one point, and Edgar said it didn't matter. Helena looked at me, as if she knew that I knew. I shrugged. Edgar picked up Molly and kissed her.

Kerry was cremated and Edgar was told to pick up the ashes in the morning. He decided he wanted to scatter them over my mother's rose bushes at the bottom of the garden. We did so, and the cat, Freyja, who was there with the little black cat Kerry had called a Bonsai panther, jumped up as the almost substanceless flecks wafted through the air and settled finally.

Freyja knows a thing or two, I thought, remembering that Freyja had been up in Mrs McNicol's flat, and had seen the bodies of Geoffrey and Sophie.

Cat	Depression
Cat	Depression
Cat	Depression

Edgar and I cleared out Kerry's room together and moved Molly's stuff downstairs. Kerry had arrived with no clothes and had not accumulated many. In her underwear drawer there was a large piece of paper which I turned over and saw was Molly's birth certificate. I saw Kerry's parents' names and then I noticed that she had put *my* parents' names as paternal grandparents. I looked in the 'Father' box and saw 'Edgar Porteus'.

'Edgar, look at this, did you know about this?'

He took the certificate and laughed.

'No, I had no idea. It's impossible by the way, if that's what you're thinking. Our marriage was never even consummated, never mind any pre-marital shenanigans.'

I knew this. 'But how did she ...?'

'She had to go and fill it in at some point, after the birth, she just put my name, as if she knew I was going to ask her to marry me. It *does* save me having to adopt the child, that's what I was going to do.'

How thoroughly Kerry had carried out her plan. How well she had chosen her baby's father. I began to cry and Edgar came over to me. I gasped, trying to find words, needing to say something, to tell Edgar. 'There's so much ... I have to tell you ... Kerry ... last year ... she ...'

Edgar came over to me and stroked my head. 'Shush Juliet, hush now, there is no need.'

Though it seemed impossible that it should, time still went by. Sometimes I would have a creepy thought about the murders, but mostly I just got on with being a co-nurturer to Molly and trying to think about my future. My parents were urging me to go back to my studies, but I could not be a vet now. I would never be able to put animals down without thinking of Geoffrey and Petruchio, I would never be able to cope with those thoughts, those memories, which, although not my own, I would carry with me always. No, no way could I ever be a vet. There was nothing in the world that I wanted to be.

When the creepy thoughts came, they were mostly about the graves. I wondered whether I had stepped over or walked by them when I went through the woods that morning, amused by Petruchio's secretive activity. I wondered who else had walked across them, not knowing, or caring, what was rotting below them. Would anyone ever find them? I couldn't see why anyone would ever start digging in that spot, but you never know. I tried not to think of this. Then I thought of Inspector Godfrey – was he still on the case? Again, I tried not to, but Inspector Godfrey often appeared in my dreams. In the most common dream I was with him and I was telling him with great urgency the whole story, and he was looking at me with his absolving, kind eyes while I made my confession.

But mostly, as I say, I was content. The past was irrelevant, I could handle it. For Molly's sake.

Sometimes I would allow myself fanciful thoughts. I speculated about possible worlds theory, surely one of the most consoling of recent scientific hypotheses. Perhaps somewhere there was a Kerry who had been telling the truth when she first told me her 'sauna story' – the one where she got out of the car and told him that she wouldn't see him again, a Kerry who had not been lying when she described Sophie's visit to the flat to Edgar and myself:

'*I pushed her away from me and she fell, and I threw her bag and coat at her and told her to get out, to get the fuck out of my flat. She got up and, trying to look dignified, picked up her stuff and left, slamming the door behind her.'*

I would hear that door slamming in my head. I would see Sophie walking indignantly down the close and into the road. I would smell the hot spices from the Indian restaurants as she strode down the street, her long fake-fur coat floating behind her.

Somewhere there was a Kerry who was not dead, a Kerry who had talked me out of going to the pub, that evening when I had been tormented by third-person images all day and had envisioned Kerry and me having a quiet drink in the pub on Great Western Road, the pub where we had met Geoffrey. This Kerry had not got the part of Antigone, had never met the agent Sophie, had never gone to their house, had never killed anyone and certainly had never had a baby. This Kerry was with me, somewhere in that other world, and I was a vet and we lived in that idyllic village in Yorkshire I had once fantasised about, surrounded by animals and kind neighbours. In this possible world, this other reality, Petruchio would come to visit us and we would spend hours talking and laughing about the good old days, those carefree, halcyon days in Glasgow and at the cottage in Argyll.

But the world we live in is most certainly fixed. The Kerry who killed, the Kerry who died is the Kerry in question now. Now that the bodies have been found, along with the toy gun which the police saw in our flat. They have issued their statement and are piecing a story together from what they have. Which is not much. Causes of death – Sophie: a blow to the head; Geoffrey: a fatal injection of pentobarbitone.

And I am the Juliet who is besieged here in my parents' house. I live in the world where there are murders and massacres and paedophile rings. Cats crucified on road

294

signs. A world of war, pestilence and famine. That ugly, dialectically material world that Edgar used to go on about when he was in the WRP, before he became a Buddhist.

I am the Juliet who is fixed. Here and now. I sit, looking through my old wooden jewellery box where I have kept my souvenirs: reviews of *Antigone*, Kerry's apposite inversion of St Paul, a photograph of her as Juliet leaning over the balcony gazing adoringly into Romeo's eyes, the 'Novel on Brown Sick Bag', and all the previous newspaper articles about the vanishing agents. The only note that is not there is her last. I burned that as I had burned Petruchio's.

Sophie's parents appeared on the television, pleading with anyone with any information to come forward. But what use could knowing do them? It wouldn't bring their daughter back. I looked at their haggard faces on the screen and I recognised their grief as being the same as my own. Mine was for the murderer, theirs was for the murdered. But it was the same grief, only accentuated. They say there is nothing worse than losing a child. Red-raw and total grief I saw on their faces. I could bear their pain even less than I could my own and I turned the TV off.

My parents and Edgar are confused by the media circus outside. They have not asked me any questions and I have made up my mind not to tell.

Edgar made only one statement. On the first day of this new horror, as he fought his way up the garden path, someone asked a question about Molly.

'There's no mystery about the baby,' he said, with one of his most charming smiles, 'Molly is my child.'

The cries went up.

'Is it true that your wife was your sister's lesbian lover?'

'Is it true that she took part in the agents' kinky orgies?'

'Is it true that she was on the game in Glasgow?'

'Why did she kill herself, Mr Porteus?'

I am waiting for Inspector Godfrey but I shall tell him nothing. If he wants to posthumously declare Kerry and Petruchio guilty, he can, but he'll get nothing from me.

Edgar came to me today and asked whether we should put Molly up for adoption, to protect her from all this, so that she could grow up in an anonymous and scandal-free home. It won't do any good, I said. Adopted children generally want to find out who their real parents are. She would only trace us once she had grown up. It would be much worse then.

But actually, I can't imagine much worse than what we are living through now. Molly is crying still, poor little thing. I will go to her in a minute. Perhaps she needs some gripe water.

All I know is that I cannot protect her from what is outside. I cannot protect her from the questions, the dirty speculations. She is sure to find out about it. One day she will ask me and I will be faced with a monstrous choice: Do I tell the truth or do I lie? Do I open the box or keep it shut?

WOLVERHAMPTON
PUBLIC LIBRARIES